JUSTINIAN

JUSTINIAN
THE SLEEPLESS ONE

The story of Uprauda Ystock,
the peasant boy of slave/barbarian origins,
who became one of the greatest of all the
Roman emperors

Ross Laidlaw

First published in 2010 by Polygon,
an imprint of Birlinn Ltd
West Newington House
10 Newington Road
Edinburgh
EH9 1QS

www.birlinn.co.uk

9 8 7 6 5 4 3 2 1

ISBN 978 1 84697 158 7

British Library Cataloguing-in-Publication Data
A catalogue record for this book is available on request from the
British Library.

The publishers acknowledge subsidy from the Scottish Arts
Council towards the publication of this volume

Typeset by SJC

Printed and bound by ScandBook, Sweden

To the memory of Bert Fortune –
big man, big personality, big friend

CONTENTS

ACKNOWLEDGEMENTS

My warmest appreciation to Barbara Halley, also to my son Kenneth for unearthing many useful facts online, to Dr Alberto Massimo for supplying me with topographical information about Lake Bolsena and its environs, to James Rafferty of the Portobello Swim Centre, Edinburgh, for providing copious information about Turkish/Roman baths, to Seán Costello for his superb editing, and to my wife Margaret for freeing me from various domestic duties to give me more time for writing. A special word of thanks to Alison Rae, Managing Editor (Polygon), and to my publishers, Hugh Andrew and Neville Moir, for their steadfast support and encouragement.

MAPS AND PLANS

HISTORICAL NOTE

In AD 468, organized by both the Eastern and the Western Roman Empires, a mighty seaborne expedition – the largest the Ancient World had ever seen, set sail from Constantinople. Its aim: to expel from Africa the Vandals, a ferocious and destructive German tribe who had occupied the Western diocese some forty years before. If successful, the enterprise had the potential to save the Western Empire, crumbling under the onslaught of other German peoples – Franks, Visigoths, Suevi, Alamanni, et al. Prior to the Vandal invasion, Africa had been the West's richest and most productive possession. Liberated, she would have the potential again to provide revenue sufficient to revive the West's economy and to replenish her decimated armies, enabling them to drive out, or at least contain, the barbarian invaders.

In the event however, the expedition was a total disaster. Pinned by contrary winds against a lee shore, the Roman fleet was scattered by Vandal fireships, its vessels doomed to burn, founder on rocks, or be picked off by Vandal boarding parties who had the wind in their favour. With the funds of both empires now exhausted, no further rescue attempts could be forthcoming. Immediately grasping this fact, the barbarians proceeded swiftly to overrun the remaining Western enclaves. In only eight short years the West went from something to nothing; in 476 the last Western emperor was deposed, and the empire he nominally ruled came to an end. In contrast, the Eastern Empire – wealthy, stable, comparatively untroubled by barbarians (it was only threatened by them on its Lower Danube frontier, and had moreover become rather adept at passing on to the West any who invaded; whereas the West had the whole of the Rhine/Upper and Middle Danube border to defend), was destined to continue for many more centuries to come. At the time of West Rome's fall, the only serious threat to East Rome was Persia, with whom the Romans had been at war off and on – forever, it must have sometimes seemed. Persia however – potentially a far more dangerous enemy than any German confederation, was a civilized power that on the whole kept its treaties.

In or about the year the doomed armada sailed, a young Goth – let's call him Roderic (for his true given name has not come down to us), a peasant from the East Roman province of Dardania,* set out with two companions on the high road for Constantinople, capital of the East Roman Empire. In the words of Gibbon, 'the three youths . . . were soon enrolled, for their strength and stature, among the guards of the emperor Leo. Under the two succeeding reigns [of the emperors Zeno and Anastasius], the fortunate peasant emerged to wealth and honours; and his . . . long and laudable service in the Isaurian and Persian wars . . . might warrant the military promotion which . . . he gradually obtained'. All this despite being German – a race both feared and hated by the Romans.

In 496, when our story begins, Roderic is forty-six years of age, a middle-ranking general serving under the *Magister Militum per Orientem* – the Commander-in-Chief of the Army of the East. He is adored by his troops for his generosity, fairness, genuine concern for their welfare, and success against the enemy. He remains however at base a simple peasant (though he has learned to read, literacy being a prerequisite for any officer in the East Roman army), unfitted for any role outside a military command. In that year of 496, the Western Empire has been defunct these twenty years, its former territories now ruled by barbarian kings: Gaul and Spain have been taken over by Franks, Visigoths, Suevi, Burgundians, and Alamanni; Africa has long been under Vandal sway; Italy is in the hands of the Ostrogoths under their powerful and charismatic king, Theoderic – nominally the vicegerent of Anastasius, the aged Eastern emperor, between whose realm and Persia an uneasy truce prevails.

Meanwhile, back in Roderic's homeland of Dardania, his sister Bigleniza cherishes hopes that her brother will be able to advance her gifted and ambitious son, Uprauda . . .

---

*Roughly equivalent to present day Bulgaria. See Appendix I.

PART I

THE DARDANIAN
AD 482–500

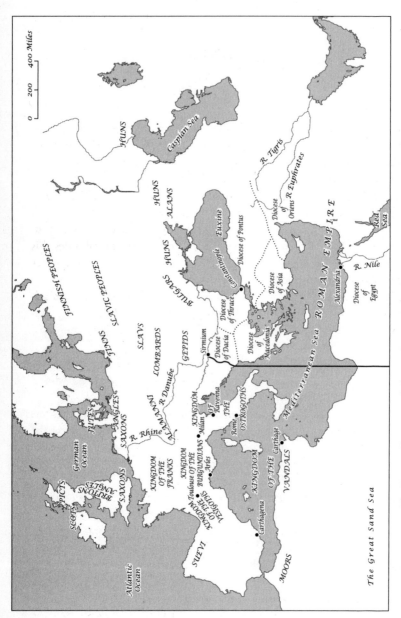

The Roman Empire and the Barbarian kingdoms at Justinian's accession, AD 527

PROLOGUE

'Elephants, sir!' gasped the scout, reining in his lathered mount before the general. 'Scores of the brutes. And they've got cataphracts as well – hundreds of them, in addition to vast contingents of infantry.'

'Calm down, lad,' said Roderic gently. 'Nothing to panic about; Romans'll see off elephants and armoured cavalry every time. Now – just the facts please. Location? Line of march? Numbers?'

Looking slightly shamefaced, the scout dismounted and stood to attention, helmet tucked under arm. 'The Persians are several miles this side of the Euphrates, sir, heading our way,' he reported in more sober tones. 'About twenty thousand altogether, I'd say.'

'Thank you, soldier; you did well. Report to the cook-house and ask for a hot meal – my orders.' Roderic grinned and clapped the young man on the shoulder. 'But first see that your horse gets a rub-down and feed. Dismiss.'

'Of course, sir. Thank you, sir.' Saluting smartly, the scout turned and walked away, leading his horse; he now looked and sounded relaxed and reassured, in contrast to his earlier state of excited apprehension.

Leaving the agora – the town square – Roderic returned to his quarters in the citadel of Palmyra, the strategically important frontier city on the interface between the empires of East Rome and Persia. He'd done his best, he reflected, to prevent that young scout from spreading alarm and despondency among his fellow soldiers. But in truth, he acknowledged to himself, the situation looked bad. At present, all the imperial field armies had been moved north, engaged in suppressing yet another insurrection by the Isaurians – a wild tribal people inhabiting a mountainous region of Anatolia. Roderic had been left with a scratch force of *limitanei* – second-rate frontier troops, to guard the eastern border, pending the absence in the north of his superior, the *Magister Militum per Orientem*. In normal circumstances, this role would have amounted to no more than a routine policing assignment; officially, Rome and Persia were at peace. But the reigning King of Kings, Kavad, was known to be under the influence of his top general, Tamshapur, a maverick commander with dangerously expansionist ideas. Tamshapur was suspected of harbouring dreams of seizing East Rome's Diocese of Oriens, whose territory, back in the days before Alexander, had once formed part of the empire of the Peacock Throne. The scout's report suggested that these suspicions were well founded: that Tamshapur, taking advantage of the fact that Rome's eastern frontier was for the time being virtually undefended, had decided that here was a golden opportunity to launch an attack and make his dreams reality.

Pacing the floor of his spartanly furnished *tablinum* or study, now converted to a command centre, Roderic tried to formulate a plan to counter this appalling threat. He had two choices: to remain inside Palmyra, or engage the enemy. Should he decide on the former, he could probably hold out, for a time anyway, against any siege that Tamshapur (for it was almost certainly he who commanded the approaching army) might decide to mount. Palmyra's walls were strong; but even if they fell, the garrison could then retreat to the virtually impregnable citadel to await eventual relief by a Roman field army. The trouble with that choice was that it would allow Tamshapur to take over the diocese unchallenged, leaving Palmyra isolated within enemy-occupied territory – territory which Rome might, quite conceivably, find itself unable to recover. The other alternative was to take on the Persians – a David and Goliath stance if ever there was, and one that must surely end in annihilation for his tiny force, Roderic reflected gloomily. Clearly, in this situation two heads would be better than one. He would pick the brains of Victor, his trusty *vicarius* or second-in-command; his opinions were always worth listening to.

Victor Marcellinus – great-grandson of the famous soldier-turned-historian, Ammianus Marcellinus, and *vicarius* of the *Numerus Euphratensis*, strode along Palmyra's Great Colonnade – the magnificent mile-long avenue flanked by Corinthian columns which connected the former Royal Palace (now pressed into service as barracks) with the agora and the citadel. As, responding to a summons from his commanding officer, Victor made his way towards the citadel, he reflected on Palmyra's chequered history. In past centuries the place had been the capital of an independent city-state, handling most of the trade between the Roman Empire in the west, and Persia, India, and China, in the east – successfully playing off Rome against Persia, while somehow managing to remain friends with both. Then, a little over two hundred years ago, Palmyra's queen – a formidable lady called Zenobia, taking advantage of a succession crisis in Rome, had invaded

Syria and Egypt, both Roman possessions. This proved to be a serious mistake. A strong Roman emperor, Aurelian, arose, who, after restoring stability at home, descended on Palmyra with several legions, crushed the forces of the upstart queen, and integrated the place fully into the Roman Empire. However, though no longer independent, Palmyra – thanks to its being the focal point of key trade routes and its proximity to the Persian border – remained of vital economic and strategic importance. Whoever controlled Palmyra held the balance of power between Persia and Rome.

Returning the salutes of soldiers that he passed, Victor sensed from their demeanour that a mood of excitement mingled with foreboding was spreading throughout the *Numerus Euphratensis*. The frontier unit was largely made up of raw recruits, its seasoned veterans having been drafted into the field army of the Diocese of Oriens, posted north as a result of the Isaurian crisis. Wryly acknowledging to himself that officers were usually the last to know about the origins of army rumours, Victor wondered what could be the cause of the strange mood.

'Seems we're between Scylla and Charybdis, sir,' commented Victor, when Roderic had apprised him of the situation.

'Silla and Caribs?' The general stared at his *vicarius* with a puzzled frown.

'Sorry, sir,' apologized Victor, mentally kicking himself for his lapse. It was easy to forget that, unlike the vast majority of East Romans – heirs to a culture rooted in Homer and Greek mythology – classical allusions would be lost on Roderic, a Goth from the remote backwoods province of Dardania. He reminded himself of Roderic's background.

Despite the migration to the West of the two great branches of the Gothic people – the Visigoths and the Ostrogoths – pockets of the tribe remained inside the Roman Empire (now consisting only of its surviving Eastern half): a tolerated minority, technically Roman citizens, but both resented and despised by the host nation. Following his arrival in Constantinople, the young barbarian had climbed the slippery pole of military promotion, ignoring racial slurs and put-downs by 'proper Romans', to rise, through sheer courage, perseverance, and aptitude, to the position of a respected general in the finest army in the world.

Victor regarded his commander's homely face, fringed by a stubbly beard (very un-Roman) and topped by a thatch of straw-coloured hair, with mingled affection and concern. Unless Roderic could come up with a miraculous plan to counter Tamshapur's move, then this year of the consul

Paulus* (no Western candidate this year) could well see the end, not only of the general's career, but in all likelihood of his life as well – consequences that applied in equal measure to both of them, Victor suddenly realized with a sense of chill foreboding.

'In legend, sir,' explained Victor, in response to the general's query, 'Scylla and Charybdis were sea-monsters, waiting either side of the Straits of Messina to drown unwary sailors. So the expression, "between Scylla and Charybdis" means –'

'– between a rock and a hard place,' sighed Roderic. 'Well, why the hell didn't you say so?' He shook his shaggy head and grinned ruefully. 'You Romans – honestly. Now, about our Persian friend; any ideas? In plain Greek, if you don't mind.'

'He must be stopped, sir – if that's at all possible. If we just sit tight in Palmyra, he'll overrun the whole diocese. Our field armies in the north couldn't possibly get here in time to intervene.'

'My own thoughts precisely. Dispatch riders are already on their way to Constantinople and Isauria: a futile gesture, I fear. Any relieving force would arrive to find a Persian fait accompli.' The general rose and began to pace the chamber, his brows furrowed in concentration. 'On the face of it, Victor, for the *Numerus Euphratensis* to square up to Tamshapur seems like a recipe for suicide.' He shrugged helplessly. 'But we have to try.'

'Things *may* not be quite as bad as they look, sir,' said Victor. 'Elephants and cataphracts apart, Tamshapur's obvious apparent advantage is enormous superiority in numbers. Now, if that could somehow be made to work against him . . . It's been done before: Alexander against Darius at Issus, Hannibal against Varro at Cannae, and, in more recent times, Fritigern's Goths against our own troops at Adrianople. They all faced overwhelming odds, in situations which they managed to turn to their own advantage.'

'We'd have to force them to fight on a narrow front,' mused Roderic. 'That way, they could only use a fraction of their strength at one time. It's those elephants and cataphracts I'm most worried about. Especially elephants. Roman soldiers have always been terrified by the things, apparently. I've never encountered them myself, however; the Persians seem largely to have abandoned their use as being old-fashioned. Until now, that is. Help me out here, Victor; I'm sure your eminent ancestor, the great Ammianus, has something to say on the subject.'

---

* AD 496 (See Notes.)

'Plenty, sir; unfortunately none of it of much use to us. In his account of Emperor Julian's Persian campaign, he describes their war-elephants in, frankly, tedious detail. He appears to have been both fascinated and appalled by them. Horses don't like their smell; as a cavalry officer, that would have bothered him. Maddeningly, he doesn't explain how our troops dealt with them. Like a lot of historians, he skimps on tactical details as being somehow unworthy in the context of serious literary composition. Arrian, however, has a tip that could be useful; he tells how Alexander had spiked boards laid in the path of elephants. Their weak point is their feet – tender soles, you see.'

Noting the sudden look of distaste on the other's face, Victor pressed on hurriedly. 'But that could backfire. Scipio's tactics against Hannibal at Zama are probably more helpful.' (Despite Roderic's carefully cultivated image of the hard, unsentimental soldier, Victor had long suspected that his commander had a softer side. Witness the general's reluctance to expose the men under his command to unnecessary suffering or danger – a consideration that extended also to cavalry mounts and beasts of burden. Misinterpreted, such an attitude could incur a risk; an officer suspected of *fastidium* – squeamishness, could suddenly find his career going nowhere. Hence Roderic's concern to maintain a persona of iron toughness.) 'According to Polybius, sir,' Victor continued, 'when Hannibal gave the order for his elephants to charge . . .

'Eminence – the Romans have come out of Palmyra,' announced the scout, kneeling before Tamshapur. 'Two thousand at the most, drawn up in battle array not five miles distant. We caught one of their outriders.' And he pointed to a captive Roman pinioned between two Persian soldiers.

This was the best possible news, gloated Tamshapur, dismissing the man. After dealing with the Romans' puny force (the prisoner could prove useful here), he would occupy Palmyra, whose citizens, learning of the garrison's fate, would scarcely dare to close the gates against the Persian host. With Palmyra secure and no one to oppose him, the whole Diocese of Oriens from the Euphrates to the Red Sea would fall into his hands like a ripe plum. And after Oriens – Egypt? The name of Tamshapur would then be forever remembered in the annals, as the commander who restored to Persia the lands filched centuries before by Alexander and since annexed by Rome. Filled with a sense of euphoric anticipation, Tamshapur gave the order for the army to advance.

When a distant line of dust-clouds signalled the Persian approach, the *Numerus Euphratensis* withdrew to the position which Roderic and Victor had reconnoitred a few days earlier. This was a long defile, with towering walls of red sandstone – open-ended, wide at the mouth, narrowing in the centre to a neck just broad enough to be spanned by three ranks of soldiers – a disposition which accounted for the unit's entire strength, barring archers and a small force of cavalry, both stationed elsewhere.

Carrying oval shields of laminated wood and wearing scale-armour hauberks and traditional Attic helmets, the *pedites* or foot-soldiers waited, stiff with apprehension, their young faces pale and set with the effort of concealing their fear. In an elaborate show of nonchalance, their officers, resplendent in muscle cuirasses, lounged atop their horses or strolled among the men, smiling and murmuring encouragement. A little to the fore, the commander and his *vicarius* sat astride their mounts. The *pedites'* equipment was standard regulation issue – with one startling exception. Instead of the normal seven-foot spear, each infantryman held an immensely long pike measuring fully twenty feet.

'Remind you of anything, sir?' Victor asked the general in breezy tones, in an attempt to break the tension, building as the minutes bled away. He waved towards the silent ranks behind them.

'Should it?'

'The three hundred Spartans at Thermopylae, sir – surely you've heard of them?'

'You're forgetting, Victor – your commanding officer is just an ignorant barbarian. Enlighten me.'

'Well, sir, in order to buy time for the main Greek army to come up, an advance force of three hundred Spartans under their king, Leonidas, volunteered to block a narrow pass against an invading Persian army, numbering three hundred thousand. Odds of a thousand to one.' He grinned. 'With us, they're only ten to one; should be a walkover.'

'What happened to those Spartans?'

'Another time, sir – listen!'

A faint susurration, like wind in a cornfield, could just be heard in the distance. This grew steadily to a pattering, then to a muted, rumbling roar. While the van of their army was yet invisible, a small advance party of Persian infantry preceded by a mounted herald came into sight round a bend in the canyon, some five hundred yards ahead. The foremost soldiers held aloft the *Drafsh-i-Kavyan* – the huge gold and silver Sassanian royal flag, stretched on crossed timbers. The herald cantered up, drawing rein before Roderic and Victor. Unfurling a scroll, he proceeded to read (in passable Greek) its contents in loud and contemptuous tones: 'Tamshapur – most noble and illustrious of all the servants of the King of Kings, Protector of the Sacred Flame, and terror to all enemies of the Empire of Iran, out of the great goodness of his heart deigns to show mercy to the Romans who, in their deluded obduracy, have dared to come out in arms against him. Lay down your weapons as a token of surrender, and your lives will be spared. What answer shall I take back to the all-merciful, the ever-victorious Tamshapur?'

'You may tell your master this,' responded Roderic in mild tones. 'Provided he undertakes to remove himself and his troops from the Diocese of Oriens and return forthwith beyond the Euphrates, then Rome is prepared, this once, to overlook such unwarranted and unprovoked invasion of her territory. If not, we will find ourselves compelled to deal with him severely.'

For a few moments, the herald stared at Roderic. Then, finding his voice, he snarled, 'On your head be it, Roman. Learn then, the fate of any of your men unlucky enough to survive the coming battle – a reckoning you will have brought upon yourselves.' And, wheeling his mount, he spurred back to his party.

Carried by several soldiers, a large wooden cross, to which was bound the Roman prisoner taken earlier, was swiftly erected before the Persian group, its base slotting into a massive timber support. Bundless of brushwood were piled around the shaft, and – before any of the horrified Romans could intervene, ignited. Laughing, the Persians withdrew, while Roderic, Victor, and a detachment of his comrades raced to rescue the victim. Too late. A roaring column of fire shot upwards, enveloping the prisoner, who shrieked and writhed against his bonds – before a well-aimed arrow mercifully cut short his agony. As the Romans returned to their position, Victor noted that fury and grim determination had replaced earlier expressions of apprehension on the men's faces. 'If that was supposed to be an object lesson intended to intimidate us,' he observed to Roderic, 'I rather think it may have backfired.'

The ground began to tremble as, round the bend in the defile, the Persian van appeared, fronted by a dense mass of elephants – enormous beasts, with wrinkled grey hides and formidable-looking tusks.

'Africans, I'm afraid, sir,' said the *vicarius* to his commander. 'Note the huge ears and saddle backs; Indian elephants have smaller ears and are round-backed. They're also more docile than their African cousins, who tend to be exceedingly ferocious in attack.'

'Thank you, Victor; just what I wanted to hear. Well, we can only hope that our men keep their nerve and remember the drill we've tried to teach them.' Aware that horses were panicked by the smell of elephants, the two men dismounted and had their steeds taken behind the lines.

A brazen clang of trumpets rang out and the elephants advanced, gradually picking up speed. Faster and faster they moved, trumpeting wildly, huge ears spread like sails, as they rolled towards the Romans like a vast grey billow. Surmounting each animal, and secured by chains, was a squat crenellated turret in which stood two mahouts. 'That Polybius fellow had better be right,' muttered Roderic grimly, then gave a sharp nod to Victor. The *vicarius* raised a whistle to a mouth gone suddenly dry, and blew a loud blast. (He had found that, in the din and confusion of battle, a whistle's shrill note was more easily distinguished than a trumpet call.)

Striding among the men, the *campidoctores* or drill-sergeants shouted orders, and – just when it seemed that nothing could prevent the *Numerus Euphratensis* from being overwhelmed and smashed to bloody pulp – in a twinkling blur of movement the three ranks of Romans suddenly transformed themselves into several long files with wide avenues between. Each column bristled with outward-pointing pikes.

Elephants, like horses, are motivated by self-preservation. Unwilling to face those screens of wicked blades, they thundered down the escape routes provided by the corridors between the files, and out into the empty gorge beyond. Archers, positioned on the canyon's lips or on ledges in its walls, now loosed off a deadly sleet of shafts – skewering the mahouts in their turrets, thus annulling any attempt to reverse the elephants' headlong charge. To make sure they kept moving, groups of soldiers followed, shouting and banging pots and pans from the field kitchen. Returning, as an extra precaution they sowed the ground with caltrops* in accordance with orders from the *vicarius* (orders which the *vicarius* had, however, refrained from divulging to his commanding officer).

Once more the Persian trumpets sounded. The *cataphractarii* formed up and began to trot forward – a glittering wall of iron, the bodies of both men and horses invisible beneath carapaces of armour. The huge steeds were

---

* Three-pronged spikes, one of which would always point upwards.

covered in trappers of scale or chain mail, their chests and faces further protected by moulded plates. Their riders' limbs were encased in laminated bands, their bodies by articulated plates, while their globular or cylindrical helmets – stippled with holes to permit breathing and vision – gave them an unhuman appearance. The trot changed to a canter, the canter to a gallop, and down swung a row of lances, presenting a terrifying sight to the waiting Romans. For a second time that day, it seemed impossible that they could avoid being swept to destruction.

Then, at a signal from Roderic, Victor again blew his whistle; the *campidoctores* bellowed orders and the Romans thrust forward those long, long pikes, butt-spikes firmly anchored in the ground, to form an impenetrable thicket of points.

A charge by massed cataphracts should have proved irresistible. Protected by stout armour, both horses and riders were invulnerable to spears, and the massive weight of a cataphract formation was virtually guaranteed to smash through any line of infantry rash enough to stand against it. However, borrowing a tactic employed with tremendous success by Alexander in his Persian campaigns – the phalanx – the Romans had hit upon the one stratagem that could provide an effective counter.

Like a wave breaking against a cliff face, the cataphracts crashed against the wall of pikes – a wall in which the weapon of every man in the triple line was brought to bear. The Roman infantry, each soldier gripping his pike-shaft several yards behind the point of impact, experienced a collective jarring shock, but to their enormous relief (not unmixed with surprise) their ranks held firm. If presented as separated units, the pikes would have shattered, but opposed to the enemy as a solid mass, their effect was to diffuse the force of impact by spreading it over a wide area. Again and again the cataphracts re-formed, to hurl themselves against the hedge of blades – to no avail. At last a trumpet blew recall and the cataphracts withdrew to make way for the Persian infantry.

Where heavy shock troops had proved unable to break the Roman front, it was hardly likely that foot-soldiers – lightly armed, whose only protection was a wicker shield – would fare better. And so it proved. Constricted by the narrow gorge, they were unable to bring their overwhelming numbers to bear. Pushed forward by the momentum of those behind, the foremost ranks perished on the pikes to form a growing heap of dead, over which the living were forced to clamber. As the Persian advance began to stall, the two Roman leaders sprung the surprise they had prepared in advance.

Concealed till this moment in a side canyon, and now alerted by signals from soldiers posted on the edge of the defile, a detachment of Roman cavalry swept into the ravine and smashed into the Persians' undefended rear. Taken unawares, with no time or opportunity to take up a defensive position, the Persian foot-soldiers fell like corn before the scythe, cut down by lethal swipes from the horsemen's *spathae* – the long, Roman cutting swords, edged with razor-sharp steel. Now, as the Roman phalanx began to advance, morale among the Persian army, its men jammed helplessly together, began to crumble. Their discipline imposed by fear rather than inspired by patriotism, panic began to spread throughout the Persian rank-and-file, resulting in a fatal loss of cohesion. With shocking suddenness, what had been an organized force atomized into a rabble of terrified individuals, each motivated by just one thought – escape.

In disbelief, Tamshapur watched his army disintegrate around him. Screaming imprecations and threats of dire punishment for desertion (the mildest being live burial), he urged his captains to restore order. In vain the officers – from a caste fanatically adherent to a rigid code of loyalty and honour – threatened and pleaded; they were unable to stop the rot. Sensing that the right moment had arrived, Roderic and Victor called off the cavalry, allowing the Persians, now reduced to a huddled, fleeing mob, to escape from the death-trap that the canyon had become. His reputation in tatters, Tamshapur began the withdrawal of his mauled and demoralized force back beyond the Euphrates. East Rome could breathe again; the Diocese of Oriens was safe.

Feeling distinctly awkward and intimidated by the splendour of his surroundings, Roderic entered the vast colonnaded reception hall in Constantinople's Great Palace, and made his way towards the elderly figure swathed in purple, who sat enthroned at the far end of the chamber.

'Majesty – your humble servant is honoured to obey your summons,' mumbled Roderic, clumsily dropping to one knee and bowing his head. Despite his rank, this was the first time that Roderic had been in the imperial presence, and he was uncomfortably aware that his ignorance of court ritual could be causing him to commit gaffes regarding etiquette. Too late, he recalled with a hot flush of shame, that the correct form of address was 'Serenity', not 'Majesty'.

'"Well done, thou good and faithful servant," as Saint Mathew says,' declared Anastasius, a smile lighting up his mild and kindly features. He waved the other to a nearby chair – an unheard-of honour, Roderic sensed, complying. 'We are greatly in your debt,' the emperor went on. 'Thanks to your courage and initiative, a great danger threatening the safety of our realm has been avoided. It is only fitting you should be suitably rewarded. Accordingly, we hereby appoint you *Magister Scholarum*, together with, as a member of our Senate, the rank of *Vir Clarissimus*.'

Commander of the imperial guards and a senator to boot! Roderic's brain whirled. At a stroke his status and circumstances had been transformed. From being a middle-ranking general who had often struggled to make ends meet, he was now holder of the army's most prestigious post, with a seat in the august assembly of those who, in theory at least, made the Empire's laws. And with these honours came wealth. Now, he could at last fulfil the promise he had made his sister in Dardania. He would send for Uprauda – his nephew and her son – and provide the boy with the finest education that Constantinople had to offer.

ONE

The coward calls himself cautious
Publilius Syrus, *Sententiae*, c. 50 BC

'Baptiso te in Nomine Patris, et Filii, et Spiritus Sancti,' quavered the priest – an ancient Goth, dipping the week-old infant in the font then making the sign of the cross upon its forehead. Then, as a special favour granted only to a very few parents (who, through gifts or service to the church given over many years, had earned the privilege), he proceeded to inscribe the child's names and date of birth in the church's Bible – its greatest treasure. This was a precious copy of the Holy Book translated into the Gothic tongue by Ulfilas, the missionary who had brought the Word of God to his own people, the Goths, nearly a century and a half before. Though originally Arians,* those Goths who had settled in the Roman Empire had been compelled by an edict of Emperor Theodosius to adopt the Catholic faith – the Empire's official creed. Hence the Service of Baptism had been carried out according to the rites of Rome.

'Uprauda Ystock,' the cleric wrote in one of the blank vellum pages at the end of the book, his arthritic fingers guiding the pen with difficulty, 'natus pridie Kalendas Septembris Trocundo et Severino consulibus.'**

'At last, Bigleniza, we have a son,' the child's father, Valaris Ystock, declared proudly to his wife when the couple had returned with their baby to their home. This was a thatched hut in the village of Tauresium, a scatter of mean dwellings in a clearing hemmed in by dark woods. 'A son who will work our plot when I grow too old to manage it alone.'

'There will be other sons for that, my dear,' murmured Bigleniza, gazing adoringly at her sleeping infant. 'For this, our firstborn, life holds other ends than tilling the soil.'

Bigleniza, a strong-willed woman of some education, was, so she claimed, partly of ancient Thracian stock, with links to the same family

---

* Arianism: the form of Christianity adopted by Germans; it differed from Orthodox Catholicism in denying the Divinity of Christ.
** Born 31 August in the year of the consuls Trocondus and Severinus. (i.e. 482; see Notes.)

that had produced Spartacus. Valaris – a Goth and former field slave belonging to a wealthy Roman – had been granted his manumission, plus a sum sufficient to buy a peasant holding, after bravely rescuing his master's wife and child from a house fire. An ill-matched couple, many thought, unaware of the strong bond of love and mutual regard that united the pair.

Beyond the confines of Dardania, impinging not at all upon the lives of its inhabitants, the tides of history rolled on: Julius Nepos, the last claimant to the West's imperial throne, died, finally legitimizing the German Odovacar as king of Italy; between East Rome and Persia, a current truce was ratified, and held, precariously; the Visigoths, soon to be challenged by the Franks, secured their hold in Gaul and Spain; within the Empire, a formidable leader, Theoderic, united the two great branches of the Ostrogoths, then, as vicegerent of Emperor Zeno, led them into Italy, there to depose and murder Odovacar; Zeno died (interred alive by accident according to the rumours, his cries within the tomb ignored on account of his being a hated Isaurian), to be succeeded by the elderly Anastasius; in Africa, the harsh barbarity of Vandal rule began to soften, as a hot climate and Roman luxury slowly sapped the original tough fibre of the conquerors.

Meanwhile, Uprauda grew into a tall, strong lad, strikingly good-looking, with large grey eyes and golden curling hair ('my beautiful angel,' Bigleniza never tired of saying), quietly self-contained, but pleasant and polite to all. Though chafing against the grinding monotony of peasant life, Uprauda proved a dutiful son, helping his parents on their little plot, at first minding the livestock, then, as soon as he could manage implements, joining his father in the back-breaking labour of raising crops of wheat and millet. It broke Bigleniza's heart to see her boy trudge back at sunset from the fields, his hands all cracked and blistered from the plough or scythe. True to her original vow, despite the fact that she bore no further sons, she remained unwavering in her resolve that Uprauda's life should follow a more fulfilling path. 'If nurtured, upright stock* will make its way,' she affirmed. To this end, she maintained contact (via letters carried by obliging travellers or traders en route to Constantinople) with her brother Roderic, a rising soldier based frequently in the imperial capital, entreating

* A play on the names *Uprauda Ystock*. As Gibbon shrewdly observed, 'The names. . .are Gothic and *almost English*' (my italics) – evidence that Germanic tongues have a common root.

him to help provide the boy with a sound education, with a view to entering a career – in the civil service or perhaps the army.

'Flamin' heat,' grumbled Crispus, as the squad marched in open order along the narrow roadway, hewn out of the mountainside by Trajan's engineers four centuries before. Crispus was one of the *pedites* in a detachment from the *Legio Quinta Macedonica* – the Fifth Macedonians – sent to investigate a remote region of northern Dardania, following complaints by local villagers of raids by Sarmatian brigands. Untying the laces securing the cheek-pieces of his helmet beneath his chin, Crispus removed the headpiece and tied it to his belt. 'That feels better,' he sighed, as his sweat-soaked scalp began to cool – 'a whole lot better.'

'Put it on, you idiot,' cautioned the man next to him. 'We're supposed to be in a combat zone, remember? The *biarchus*'ll have your guts for garters if he finds out.'

'And how'll he do that?' sneered the other. 'You gonna report me? Oh Christ!' he exclaimed suddenly, as his helmet – carelessly secured, detached itself from his belt and tumbled free. Dropping his spear, Crispus made a frantic grab for the helmet as it rolled to the side of the road. Too late; it toppled over the edge and bounced a hundred feet, before coming to rest in the branches of a shrub sprouting from a crevice in the near-vertical slope.

Delighted by the unscheduled break, the column halted, while the *biarchus* or corporal strode up the line from the rear to find out what was causing the hiatus.

'Well, well – *Pedes* Crispus; who'd have thought it?' murmured the *biarchus* silkily, shaking his head in mock surprise. He peered over the edge. 'Oh dear – lost your helmet, I see. Well now, *Pedes*,' he continued, looking round at the ring of grinning faces which had formed at the scene, 'we'd all be interested to learn what you propose to do about it. Suggestions?'

'Well, we could form a human chain I suppose, *Biarchus*,' mumbled Crispus.

'A human chain,' repeated the *biarchus*, nodding sagaciously. 'Congratulations, *Pedes*. But if you think,' he added, his voice changing to a sarcastic snarl, 'that I'd risk the necks of any of your mates to save your worthless skin, you must be even stupider than I thought. If you get your brains knocked out by a Sarmatian sling-shot because you've got no helmet, it'll serve you damn well right.' He thrust his face to within an inch of the other's. 'You horrible little man!' he shouted. 'What are you?'

'A horrible little man, *Biarchus*,' growled Crispus, fully aware that any other response would land him in even greater trouble than he was in already. This would almost certainly include being on a charge for disobeying the order to wear helmets.

'Listen up, *Pedes*; here's what we do. Once back at base, you will put in a requisition for *two* helmets, chargeable against your pay.'

'But – that's not fair, Biarchus! I only lost one.'

'So you did, soldier. So you did,' purred the other. He went on, with irrefutable military logic, 'You draw a helmet from the stores to replace the one you lost, see. Then you pay for another to replace the one from the stores. Got it?' He turned to the others. 'Right lads, show's over. Let's be having you. Into line. Forward, march!'

One summer Sunday, when Uprauda was approaching his fourteenth birthday, two of his companions – named Atawulf and Wamba – sought him out; both were bursting with excitement, clearly over some news or secret they couldn't wait to divulge. (Despite never putting himself forward, Uprauda's imposing physique and something about his air of calm self-possession, had led him to be chosen as their leader by boys his own age in Tauresium. Though invariably the planner and organizer of youthful escapades, strangely, Uprauda was never the one to be caught or to incur the blame whenever such activities miscarried.)

'Hey Raudie, you won't believe what we've found!' exclaimed Atawulf, the bigger of the tow-headed pair. 'It's a helmet – a real soldier's helmet. Only trouble is, it's stuck halfway up a cliff.'

Uprauda smiled. 'Lead on, then,' he invited, sparing the two from having to plead with him to accompany them.

It being a Sunday, when only essential tasks such as milking (which anyway was girls' and women's work) were carried out, the boys were free until supper-time. Keeping a lookout for wild animals, and also Sarmatian bandits, bands of whom had recently been sighted in the vicinity, the trio set out along woodland trails. There was in fact little risk. Hunted for centuries by gangs of professional *venatores* to supply the Roman Games, large animals such as bear, lynx, elk, and bison had been driven to the verge of extinction, and had only recently begun to make a comeback following the collapse of the Western Empire twenty years before. As for Sarmatians, they were after cattle, goods, and specie, not half-grown youngsters. And even if they were attacked, like all Dardanian boys who had grown up minding livestock, the three were expert slingers, able to give a good account of themselves. A blow on the snout from a round river-pebble delivered with terrific force was usually enough to deter even the most aggressive assailant.

The boys pushed on through dense stands of spruce, oak, and beech, some of the trees rising to a prodigious height. After a mile or so, they emerged onto a flower-stippled meadow fringing a wide but shallow stream. Beyond the far bank towered a cliff of whitish rock, mottled with dark green where vegetation had taken root in cracks and ledges.

'There she is, Raudie,' proudly announced Atawulf, pointing to a winking point of light high up on the cliff-face.

After wading through the stream, they approached the base of the cliff from where they were afforded a clearer view of the object in question, which was wedged in the upper branches of a bush. Surmounted by a scarlet horsehair crest, and complete with brow reinforcement, cheek-pieces, and neck-guard, the helmet – fashioned of bronze – glittered like gold in the strong noonday sunshine. (Presumably it had been dropped by a careless soldier from the roadway far above, Uprauda thought.) A rare prize indeed, one that would make them the envy of all the other boys in Tauresium – if it could be recovered. And that would not be easy, realized Uprauda, staring at that beetling precipice, the ascent of which must surely call for nerves of steel and practised skill.

'Let me try, Raudie,' entreated Atawulf. 'I'm a good climber.'

Uprauda hesitated. Atawulf indeed had an unrivalled reputation for scaling heights. Scarcely a tree of any size around Tauresium had not been climbed by 'Spiderboy', as had (inevitably) the baptistery of the local church, and the ramparts of a nearby abandoned Roman fortress. Nevertheless, any attempt to scale the cliff could prove suicidally risky, Uprauda felt: definitely not something he himself would care to try.

But still . . . In his imagination, Uprauda saw himself (along with Atawulf and Wamba) returning to the village in triumph with the trophy, the focus of excited admiration on the part of his peers. To be the owner of such a glorious find (for his two fellow adventurers would, he knew, insist on presenting the helmet to him) would confer enormous status. Such a helmet Perseus might have worn when he slew the Gorgon, he fantasized, or Alexander when he set out to conquer Asia. (From his earliest years, an ancient local of Hellenic descent had told him stirring tales from Greek and Roman legend and history: of Jason and the Argonauts, the ten-year war of Troy, Horatius who held the bridge against an army, Leonidas and his valiant Three Hundred, of Alexander, of Caesar and of Spartacus' doomed heroic struggle against the might of Rome. Such stories had aroused in him a vague but powerful longing to achieve great things, beyond the stifling restrictions of a backwoods village life.)

'All right, Wulfie,' he heard himself say, 'give it a go. But come back down if it gets too dangerous.'

'Thanks, Raudie – I'll get that helmet; you'll see.' Atawulf cast Uprauda a grateful look. Far more important than retrieving the thing itself was the fact that in doing so he would earn Raudie's approval. He scanned the cliff, looking for possible routes to his objective. What at first glance seemed a sheer rock face, so smooth as to be unclimbable, on closer inspection revealed that it was textured by tiny cracks and wrinkles – just sufficient to afford purchase. Higher up, a long fissure or 'chimney' led up to a pitch not far below the ledge where grew the bush in which the helmet was lodged. '*Es geht*,' he told himself – it could be done.

Combining caution with speed, for he dared not trust any of those minute finger- and toe-holds to support his weight for long, Atawulf began to climb. Establishing a rhythm, he moved upwards steadily and with in-creasing confidence, seeming almost to flow over the rock as he ascended, displaying all the grace and assurance of the born climber. Arriving at the base of the chimney, he wedged himself in and proceeded to push himself up by alternating thrusts of back and feet against the opposite walls.

All went well until, to his dismay, he encountered an obstacle which he had failed to notice when surveying the route from below. The upper part of the chimney was blocked by a chockstone! Peering upwards, he could see light between the chockstone and the back of the chimney. He tried to squeeze through the gap, but was forced to give up after the third attempt; it was just too narrow. Which left him with but one alternative: he would have to climb up and over the outside of the chockstone – a difficult and probably dangerous challenge. For the huge boulder projected proud of the cliff face, its bulging contours presenting Atawulf with the problem of having to surmount an overhang. Would the chockstone's upper surface, which the bulge prevented him from seeing, provide holds? If it didn't . . .

Well, there was only one way to find out, he thought, grimly. Reaching up, his groping hands encountered cracks and roughnesses – enough to provide a grip. Face against the rock, he began to haul himself up, holding himself to the chockstone partly by hand- and foot-holds, partly by the friction of his tunic against the rough stone. Now his eyes were almost level with the outermost bulge of the boulder. This was the moment when he must commit – or abandon the climb. But to disappoint Raudie, and return to Tauresium empty-handed? That was unthinkable. Firmly, he pushed the temptation to give up to the back of his mind.

His scrabbling left hand found a knob of rock, providing a secure anchor. Letting go his hold with his right hand, Atawulf groped upwards – above the bulge. There was only smooth stone. Desperately, he moved his hand to right and left to the limit of his reach; still no hold. He began to retract his right hand – and made an appalling discovery. He could not bring it down again without losing his balance! Fighting panic, he froze against the boulder.

'Wulfie's stuck!' Wamba cried, pointing to where, high above them, Atawulf's immobile form was spreadeagled against the cliff. He turned a worried face to Uprauda. 'What are we going to do, Raudie?'

Uprauda made to answer, found he could not think; his brain seemed paralyzed. The moments crept past. Faint with distance, a cry for help floated down from above.

'Raudie?' Wamba's voice now held a note of desperation.

Uprauda's mind suddenly seemed to unblock itself. He must form a plan – and quickly. He studied the cliff. Not far above Atawulf's position, a ledge (the same whence sprouted the bush supporting the helmet) ran along the cliff face. If he or Wamba could somehow reach that ledge and lower an improvized line to Atawulf . . . One look at Wamba's ashen face and trembling lip told Uprauda that he, not the other, would have to meet the challenge. The prospect was terrifying. Uprauda was no cragsman. Any attempt to scale the cliff in the stretch that he could see was out of the question; it was far too steep – a recipe for disaster. He would have to move along its base and hope to find a point at which the incline sloped sufficiently for him to climb it – assuming that the ledge above extended that far.

'Give me your belt and sling,' he told Wamba. 'Bring men with ropes from the village. Hurry!'

'Try to hold on,' Uprauda shouted up as Wamba set off at a run. 'Help's on its way; I'll try to reach you from above.' It was unlikely that Atawulf could make out his actual words, but just to be able to hear him call would provide some reassurance. But for how long could Atawulf maintain his precarious hold?

After running at his top speed for perhaps a quarter of a mile, Uprauda noticed that the cliff face was beginning to slope back. Within a further hundred yards, to his huge relief, the angle had lessened to the extent that grass grew on what had now become no more than a steep incline – mercifully looking as though it needed no special mountaineering skills to climb. While regaining his breath, Uprauda tied his own sling to Wamba's then joined them to both their belts secured end to end. Now he had a stout line, hopefully of sufficient length and strength to reach Atawulf from the ledge (which still ran above the point now reached by Uprauda), and help him to safety.

A punishing scramble took Uprauda to the ledge – a wide shelf of rock along which he was able to walk in perfect security. Now, in the distance ahead, he could see the bush with that wretched helmet shining like a beacon in the sun. And there, only yards below it, was Atawulf, clinging to a huge boulder projecting from a fissure in the cliff. A tide of euphoria swept over Uprauda. He shouted, to let the other know he was coming, heard an answering cry – then stopped, his elation draining away.

Directly in front of him, the shelf ended suddenly – continuing a short distance further on. Between the two sections was a gap no more than three feet wide, bridgeable by a single bold stride. Uprauda stared at the yawning drop beneath the breach, and shrank against the cliff in terror. With palms sweating and mouth dry with fear, he approached the Bad Step – only to hesitate, then stop, on the very lip. He told himself that there was no risk, that at ground level he could perform such a trifling feat without a second thought. But it was no good; after making several aborted attempts, he knew he could not do it.

He tried to shut his ears to Atawulf's calls – at first of hope, finally of despair. At last there came the terrible moment when he saw his friend, unable any longer to maintain his hold, begin to slip. Then, with a cry of terror the boy fell, his body twisting and tumbling as it plunged into the void . . .

In grim silence, the little procession carrying Atawulf's broken body on a makeshift litter returned to Tauresium. After the grieving and the funeral would come a reckoning. But no direct blame would be laid upon Uprauda for what, after all, had resulted from a collective enterprise. According to his statement, he had tried to save Atawulf, who had fallen before he could be reached. Which was, insofar as it went, a not untrue account, merely an incomplete one. In Uprauda's dreams however, the helmet often reappeared – both a symbol of ambition, and a reminder of his cowardice.

In the branches of a bush growing from a cliff, a pair of nesting falcons made a fortunate discovery: a round hollow object, ideal for their home. It even sprouted a ridge of hair – perfect material with which, along with moss, to line their new abode. As, over the years, their dwelling changed in colour from gleaming gold to bluish green, it witnessed the fledging of many generations of falcon chicks.

TWO

He who has lost honour, can lose nothing more
Publilius Syrus, *Sententiae*, c. 50 BC

' . . . so in conclusion,' pronounced Olympius, holder of the Chair of Law at Constantinople University, 'our judge, having heard all the evidence for the defence and for the prosecution, must make his judgement. How is he to do this?' Inviting a response, his gaze swept round the crowded tiers.

'The Law of Citations would require him to consult the findings of the *jurisconsults** in similar cases, and follow the verdict of the majority,' eventually suggested an intense-looking youth.

Olympius nodded approvingly. 'Correct – as far as it goes. But let us speculate the following: Gaius and Papinian pronounce a guilty verdict, Ulpian and Paulus one of innocence, with Modestinus abstaining. A tie, in other words. What then?'

The low buzz of speculation that followed, accompanied by shrugs and head-shaking as students conferred, gradually petered out. Then the silence was broken by a tall young man with calm grey eyes. 'Papinian would have the casting vote, *Magister*. The judge would be compelled to give a guilty verdict.'

'Well done, young Petrus!' enthused the other. 'You've been reading up your *Responses*, I see.' Once again, his eyes swivelled round the benches. 'As should the rest of you,' he added, with mock severity. The doctor swept up his scrolls and codices. 'Next time, we shall examine what Trebatius terms the Equality of Crime. For example: he who takes a handful of grain from a sack of corn is just as guilty as he who steals the entire contents.' This last statement was delivered in a spray of spittle, a peculiarity which had earned Olympius the soubriquet, *Aspergillum* – the Holy Water-Sprinkler – and was the reason why the two front rows of the lecture hall were always empty for his sessions.

Chatting noisily, the class dispersed via the main entrance, Olympius departing through a small door behind the rostrum.

* The five leading Roman jurors in the past, whose verdicts were accepted as deciding precedent.

'Any budding Ciceros in this year's class?' enquired Demetrius of Olympius. The two old friends were strolling in one of the shady colonnades in the university precincts. Demetrius – once a humble *grammaticus* teaching sons of the aristocracy in the Palace School – had risen, through sheer drive and talent, to occupy the university's Chair of Rhetoric.

Olympius shook his head. 'No such luck, I fear. You know how it is with younger sons – the Army, the Law, the Civil Service; at a pinch, the Church. Hardly calculated to inspire a sense of vocation.' He paused, then added thoughtfully. 'But I'm forgetting; there *is* a student who shows exceptional promise. One Petrus Sabbatius, a truly remarkable young man. Arrived in the capital from some God-forsaken provincial backwater, speaking hardly any Greek. Then, three years later, on leaving the Palace School as its top scholar, enrolls at university. Quite the most ambitious student I've ever had to deal with. Hungry for success – to a degree that's almost frightening. Not in the least pushy or arrogant, though. Just quietly single-minded.'

'Sounds too good to be true. I can't imagine that being so brilliant makes him liked, though.'

'There you'd be wrong. He *is* popular with most of his fellow students; he's gathered quite a following, in fact, who seem to hang on his every word. Plenty of female admirers too. Hardly surprising; he's looks to die for – like an Apollo by Praxiteles. But they're wasting their time where he's concerned.'

'You're suggesting he may have the Greek vice – as in Plato's *Symposium*?'

Olympius laughed. 'Nothing like that. It's just that he's too focussed and driven to have any time for romantic distractions. Now, keep this to yourself; despite resembling your archetypal Greek god, young Petrus doesn't have a drop of Hellenic blood in his veins. I have it from a friend at court that he's a Goth. Nephew of General Rodericus, Commander of the Imperial Guard.'

'Well, if he hopes to make his mark, he's going to need all that determination you say he possesses. As we know, being German is a massive handicap to a career inside the Empire.' Demetrius' expression softened. 'I taught Theoderic, you know. My star pupil at the Palace School when, as Crown Prince of the Ostrogoths, he was a hostage here in the capital. He's doing well for himself – now. King of Italy and vicegerent of Emperor Anastasius. But getting where he is today – that was a titanic struggle that would have crushed a lesser man. It's a fact of life: to get anywhere, a German has to show he's at least twice as good as a Roman. We don't discriminate against other races. Why, we've had emperors who were Spaniards, Gauls, Africans, Illyrians, even an Arab. But never a German. "Discuss" – as one might say to one's students.'

'Not so surprising when you think about it,' observed Olympius. 'Caledonians apart, the Germans were the only people in Europe that Rome never succeeded in conquering. And in the end, it was those same Germans who defeated Rome. West Rome, that is. Romans – West *and* East, find that hard to forgive. However, despite inheriting his people's legacy of fear and hate, I'd be surprised if our young friend Petrus doesn't go on to distinguish himself. And sooner rather than later, would be my guess.'

In the gymnasium of the university's baths, a vigorous bout of *harpastum* – a ball-game between two rival teams, was in progress.

'Catch!' Valerian sent the ball spinning in a low curve above the heads of the opposing team, towards his team captain and friend, Petrus, who had craftily managed to position himself near their opponents' goal area. Reaching up, Petrus grabbed the ball before other grasping hands could close on it, weaved between two hefty opponents converging on him, and planted the ball securely in the scoring circle. Before the two teams could take up their positions for the next round, the *arbiter* called time, declaring Petrus' team to be the winner. A triumphant cheer burst from the throats of the victors.

As the players headed towards the bathing suite to cleanse themselves before reclaiming their shoes and clothes from the receptacles where they had been stored prior to the game, Petrus – the congratulations of his team-mates ringing in his ears – had never felt happier. His mind flashed back three years, to the day when the news arrived that was to change his life . . .

Soon after the incident which had ended tragically in the death of Atawulf, a squadron of cavalry from Constantinople had arrived at the family home, bearing, besides a letter from Roderic – Uprauda's uncle and his mother's brother – an iron strong-box. Bigleniza's hopes had at last come true. Thanks to recent promotion, Roderic was able to offer his nephew an education at the Palace School, the finest scholastic establishment in the capital. The strong-box contained a generous lump sum in golden *solidi*, sufficient to enable his parents to see out their declining years in comfort, when they became too old to work the land.

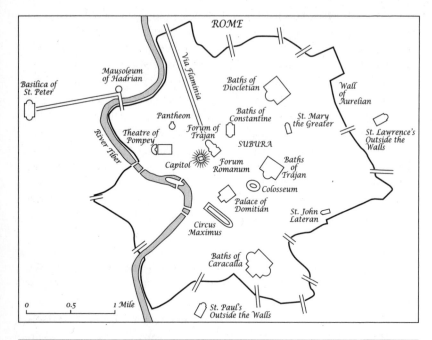

ROME

Basilica of St. Peter

Mausoleum of Hadrian

Via Flaminia

Baths of Diocletian

Wall of Aurelian

Pantheon

Baths of Constantine

St. Mary the Greater

St. Lawrence's Outside the Walls

River Tiber

Theatre of Pompey

Forum of Trajan

SUBURA

Capitol

Forum Romanum

Baths of Trajan

Colosseum

Palace of Domitian

St. John Lateran

Circus Maximus

Baths of Caracalla

| 0 | 0.5 | 1 Mile |

St. Paul's Outside the Walls

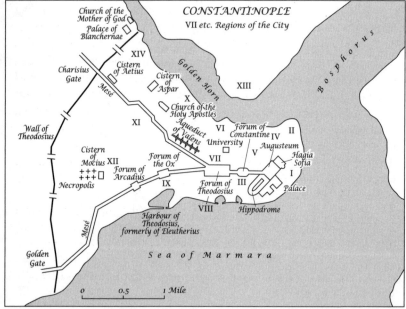

CONSTANTINOPLE

VII etc. Regions of the City

Church of the Mother of God

Palace of Blanchernae

Golden Horn

Bosphorus

XIV

Charisius Gate

Cistern of Aetius

Cistern of Aspar

XIII

Mesé

X

Church of the Holy Apostles

Wall of Theodosius

XI

Aqueduct of Valens

VI

Forum of Constantine

II

University

IV

Cistern of Mocius

XII

VII

V

Augusteum

Hagia Sofia

Forum of the Ox

Forum of Arcadius

III

I

Palace

Necropolis

IX

Forum of Theodosius

Hippodrome

Mesé

VIII

Harbour of Theodosius, formerly of Eleutherius

Golden Gate

Sea of Marmara

| 0 | 0.5 | 1 Mile |

Rome and Constantinople in the sixth century

Uprauda's sorrow on parting from his parents – especially Bigleniza to whom above all he owed this change in his fortune – was offset by excitement at the prospect of the glittering new life he was about to embark on, and which seemed to embody the promise of all his secret aspirations.

'Make us proud of you, Uprauda,' were Bigleniza's parting words, as he prepared to depart with the soldiers on the long journey to Constantinople.

Never would he forget that first sight of the city that was to become his new home: the colossal triple walls of the second Theodosius, studded with massive towers, striped with reinforcing bands of brick; beyond lay columns, domes, cupolas, without number, and, rising above all, the topmost arches of a mighty aqueduct. Entering the city from the south-west via the Golden Gate, they proceeded along the principal thoroughfare, the Mesé, through the four great fora of Arcadius, the Ox, Theodosius, and Constantine, past the Hippodrome and so to the Palace – a collection of magnificent but ill-assorted buildings sprawling downhill to the Propontis.* Here he was introduced to his uncle and benefactor, Roderic, a kindly bear of a man, gruff and unpolished, but in his manner showing a hint of underlying warmth.

In the course of the journey to the capital, by talking with his escort, Uprauda had gained a smattering of Greek – enough foundation for him, as a pupil in the Palace School, to acquire a rapid mastery of the first language of the Empire. Furnished with a new Roman name – Petrus Sabbatius – he underwent a remarkable metamorphosis. A poised and confident young Roman gentleman quickly displaced the Gothic peasant lad. Popular, charismatic and ambitious, a promising future seemed assured for the young man when he entered Constantinople University. The venerable but creaking edifice of Roman Law was ripe for reform; here, surely, was a worthy challenge, to which he could profitably devote his energies, justifying his uncle's generosity, and fulfilling his mother's parting wish. A project which Petrus Sabbatius, but not Uprauda, was capable of tackling . . .

'Catch!' In a savage parody of the pass which had secured Petrus' team's victory at *harpastum*, the captain of the opposing team, Nearchus, sent something skimming through the air at Petrus. Startled out of his reverie, Petrus failed to react in time, and cried out in shock and pain as the object struck him on the temple. The missile dropped to the bath-house floor – it was Petrus' own shoe.

* The Sea of Marmara.

'Butterfingers!' sneered Nearchus, in tones of unmistakeable hostility. A tense silence spread throughout the bath-house, as the teams realized that Nearchus' action was no mere expression of innocent horseplay, but stemmed from some deep, and hitherto latent, feeling of malice towards his fellow student.

Having attracted an attentive audience, Nearchus, his heavy features clouded with dislike, went on to address it. 'See Golden Boy here,' he jerked his chin at Petrus. 'Top of the class, ace games player, the lecturers' favourite student. Well, don't be fooled. Petrus Sabbatius is a fraud. I've been doing some digging and it turns out that that's not his real name – it's Uprauda Ystock. He's a Goth. From the same race of yellow-haired brutes we chased out of the city a hundred years ago, and who've been a thorn in the flesh of the Empire ever since. Want to know more? This paragon, who thinks he's so much better than the rest of us, turns out to be a nobody from a hick village in Dardania. Worse than that: our imposter friend here is the son of a slave.' Nearchus looked round at the ring of thunder-struck young faces and grinned triumphantly. He turned to stare at Petrus. 'Come on then, Golden Boy,' he taunted. 'I dare you to deny that anything I've said is true.'

Dumbfounded and dismayed by this unprovoked onslaught, Petrus crumbled. Where had this flood of vicious bile, like water cascading from a breached dam, come from? He looked round at the faces of those whom, up to this moment, he had imagined to be his friends. Where before he had seen – or thought he had seen, only expressions of warmth and camaraderie, now he seemed to detect doubt, and perhaps the stirrings of contempt. Perhaps, after all, he had been living a lie, his hopes and aspirations built on sand. Could a Goth – *id est* a despised barbarian, one moreover of slave origin – ever hope to be accepted into the magic circle of Roman society? A wave of disillusion and despair suddenly washed over the young man. Retrieving the fallen shoe, he grabbed its partner together with his clothing from a wall-niche, and hurried from the bath-house.

As if drawn by some force he was not consciously aware of, Petrus found himself heading blindly westward through the crowded streets. All around, the sights and sounds of the great metropolis assailed his senses: street-traders calling their wares, native Greeks, Jews, Syrians, hawk-nosed Arabs, Indians, black men from Axum* in the farthest south, mendicants rattling begging-cups, wealthy ladies borne in palanquins by sweating

* Ethiopia.

slaves, senators and civil servants riding mules or horses, off-duty soldiers in pillbox caps and undyed linen tunics with indigo government roundels at hip and shoulder, swaggering supporters of the Blues circus faction* looking vaguely menacing in their adopted Hunnish guise of caftans and long hair. Somehow, all this pulsing life, which only yesterday had seemed familiar and reassuring, now seemed alien – all part of a world to which he no longer truly belonged. He passed beneath the towering arches of the Aqueduct of Valens, traversed the great artery of the northern Mesé, and found himself at last in the Forum of Arcadius, confronting the tall column that rose in the middle of the square.

The monument showed, in an ascending spiral, a frieze of figures in violent motion. The subject seemed innocuous enough, until closer inspection revealed a chilling scene: fleeing Goths, identifiable by their long hair, being attacked by short-haired Romans wielding staves and cudgels. The work represented the violent expulsion from the city of its Gothic population a century before, an event in which several thousand Goths were massacred. Nothing could be plainer, thought Petrus: here, carved in enduring stone, was an official statement of the Roman attitude towards his people – as Germans, the Goths were the age-old enemies of Rome, with whom no accommodation could ever be permitted.

Despite his adopted Roman name, and his complete absorption into Roman culture, he would always be an outsider, Petrus told himself. His mother's hopes, his uncle's kindness, his own ambitions – all these had been for nothing. Better never to have left Tauresium, the home to which he must now return – a presumptuous barbarian who had got above himself, and been found out.

'Thought I might find you here.' Harsh and accusing, Valerian's voice broke in upon Petrus' reflections. 'Wallowing in self-pity isn't going to help, you know. By caving in to Nearchus like that, you're admitting that he's right about you.'

'Well, isn't he?' cried Petrus bitterly. 'I've been shown up for who I really am, that's all. Let's face it, Valerian – as a Goth, especially one tainted by slave parentage, I can never hope to fit in here.'

'Listen to yourself!' snapped Valerian. 'Good God, man, where's your self-belief? A man can be anything he wants to be, provided he has faith in himself. Paul was a Jew, but also proud to be a Roman. Emperor Vespasian

---

* Their rival faction was the Greens. See Notes for Chapter 3.

was a mule-breeder before he joined the legions. Diocletian was of bar-barian *and* slave stock, but that didn't stop him becoming one of Rome's greatest emperors. I could go on . . .'

'Then you, at least, are still my friend?'

'I shan't bother to answer that!' Valerian's voice was thick with scorn. 'The others, too, will still be your friends – but only if you stand up for yourself. By running away, you're simply reinforcing in their minds every-thing Nearchus has accused you of, letting him occupy the moral high ground. Square up to him, and all he's said will cease to seem important. What it boils down to is this: your honour's been challenged; what matters now is that you're seen to defend it.'

'But how? I'm hardly in a position to sue him for defamation; I'm still *in statu pupillari* as far as my uncle Roderic's concerned, and anyway I wouldn't want to drag him into this. Besides, what Nearchus says about me *is* factually correct.'

'Come on, Petrus – you're thinking like a Roman. This is your *personal* reputation we're talking about. What would a Goth do?'

Petrus cast his mind back to the village community in which he had grown up. Though strictly speaking governed by Roman Law, the independent-minded Tauresians had tended to settle disputes in the time-honoured manner of their Gothic ancestors. There, a man showing weakness by allowing a challenge to go unanswered counted for nothing and soon became a social outcast. 'Well, a man could always defend his honour,' he suggested dubiously, 'by arranging for a formal contest with his challenger to be held. It's called Trial by Combat – God being the *arbiter*.'

'In other words, a *duellum* – which, interestingly, is the archaic form of *bellum*. I like it – shades of Achilles versus Hector in the Trojan War! Hard-ly the Roman way of settling scores, but it'll put that blowhard Nearchus on the back foot. Now you're sounding like the old Petrus I was beginning to think I'd lost.' Valerian grinned and clapped his friend on the shoulder. 'I know a little wine shop down by the Theodosius Harbour which sells some half-decent stuff. *And* it's not mixed with resin. A cup or three of Nomentan will help us plan how we go about things.'

Something seemed to click in Petrus' mind, resolving his sudden and most disturbing crisis of identity. For good or ill, he *was* now Petrus Sab-batius, a young Roman with a glittering future in the law – that was the path destiny had chosen for him. As for Uprauda, the Goth – he belonged firmly in the past, and there he must remain. 'Thanks, Valerian,' he said, feeling a surge of gratitude towards the friend who had enabled him to see things in perspective. 'One thing that puzzles me – what has Nearchus got against me? And how did he come by his information? I've never, to my knowledge, done anything to harm him.'

Valerian laughed. 'That's irrelevant. You're so green in some ways, Petrus. You're popular, good-looking, and successful – everything that Nearchus isn't. More than enough reason to make a second-rater with a chip on his shoulder like Nearchus green with jealousy. He's got family connections with the present Master of Offices; hence access to confidential files as a result of a few palms being greased. His sort can only assuage their own pathetic little egos by bringing others down to their own level. Human nature is frail, my friend. For every Marcus Aurelius you get to meet in life, there's likely to be a Caligula lurking in the background.'

'As I was beginning to find out,' concurred Petrus wryly. He smiled, and went on in lighter tones, 'Right; let us sample the delights of this drinking-den of yours.'

Between the Walls of Theodosius and the original (and now partly disman-tled) Walls of Constantine, stretched Constantinople's western suburbs, a strange area whose vast spaces were patchily tenanted by monasteries, churches, market-gardens, and villas. Here were the city's great cisterns – reservoirs, some open, some underground – dedicated to generals and eminent citizens (Aetius, Aspar, Mocius, et al.). One of these huge tanks, a subterranean one, the Cistern of Nomus (a brilliant Master of Offices at the time of the wars with Attila), had been chosen as the venue for the contest between Petrus and Nearchus. Regarding security and secrecy (the university authorities would certainly have intervened to prevent any public settling of scores) the choice of site was ideal. Access to the cistern was made available after receipt of *suffragia* or 'sweetners' by certain staff in the employ of the Department of Aqueducts and Sewers, controlled by the city prefect.

The announcement of the match – a wrestling competition – was intended, by throwing down a challenge to Nearchus, to vindicate Petrus in the eyes of his peers. In this it was totally successful. Greeted with huge enthusiasm by all who had witnessed the scene in the bath-house, the disclosure of the plan neatly turned the tables on Nearchus, who, wrong-footed and furious, had little choice but to accept the challenge. Petrus was accorded something like heroic status for showing great spirit and initiative in responding to intolerable provocation – a perception that was unlikely to change, whatever the outcome of the contest.

However, as the appointed time drew near, Petrus began to entertain serious doubts and fears about the whole scheme. Wrestling matches were no-holds-barred, often brutal affairs, with kicking, punching, biting, and even gouging all legitimate under the prevailing rules. Nearchus was not the sort of opponent to hold back from 'playing dirty' to gain an advantage. He, Petrus, could well end up permanently damaged or disfigured; the thought filled him with horror. More than once, the thought of calling the whole thing off crossed his mind, only to be rejected immediately; the resulting loss of face would cause irreparable damage to his reputation. Then, out of nowhere it seemed, a possible way out, shameful but irresistibly tempting, came to him . . .

Petrus' heart began to thump painfully as, accompanied by Valerian, he descended the steps leading down into the bowels of the cistern. Illuminated by torches in sconces, a scene of bizarre and gloomy grandeur revealed itself. Like a stone forest, hundreds of pillars topped by Corinthian capitals rose from the surface of what appeared an underground lake, to support the roof. Stepping into a punt moored at the bottom of the stairs, Petrus tightened his grip on the hard, round object in his right hand, fearful lest his sweat-slicked palm should allow it to slip. Poled by Valerian, the craft moved off between the pillars towards an 'island' composed of massive ashlar blocks, rising in the middle of the cistern. Petrus started at the sight of two vast, half-submerged Medusa heads, glaring balefully at him from the side of the landing-stage, their serpent-locks appearing to stir in the gently agitated water.

A short flight of steps took Petrus and Valerian to the top of the great platform which served as an anchorage for the boats of the inspection and maintenance workers, and a repository for their equipment. Today, it was ringed by those who had witnessed the scene in the bath-house, enclosing a space about thirty feet across. Clad only in his underwear, his second beside him, Nearchus was already waiting in the centre.

Stripping, Petrus advanced towards his opponent, his height and graceful build contrasting with the other's squat, heavily muscled frame. Dismissing the seconds to the perimeter, the *arbiter* now stepped forward, positioning himself between the contestants. 'No artificial aids permitted,' he declared. 'The first to force the other onto his back, wins.' Moving aside, he called, 'Begin.'

The two young men circled each other warily; then, with a speed and agility that belied his bulk, Nearchus, arms whirling, closed with his adversary in a weaving rush. Clapping a hand to his head, Petrus uttered a sudden, loud cry – and collapsed. Seconds and *arbiter* sprinted forward and bent over Petrus' barely conscious form. 'Foul play!' declared Valerian, pointing to a discoloured lump visibly swelling on his friend's forehead. Picking up a round stone that lay beside the prostrate Petrus, the *arbiter* concurred. Holding aloft the offending object for general inspection, he announced, 'By employing a concealed weapon, Nearchus has flagrantly breached the rules of the contest. I therefore declare Petrus the winner by default.'

In vain, Nearchus angrily protested his innocence. If he'd really hit Petrus with a stone, he shouted, he'd hardly leave the evidence lying around. But it was no good; having already forfeited general sympathy, no one, it seemed, was now prepared to accord him credence. Shunned by his fellow students, he became an increasingly lonely and embittered figure at the university. Meanwhile, his victorious rival's star continued to rise, Petrus' popularity boosted by the face-off with Nearchus.

At night however, Petrus was increasingly troubled by a recurring dream from the past. It would start with the first sighting of that helmet, caught in a bush halfway up the cliff. Then, although knowing what was coming, he would struggle to regain consciousness, but the dream would progress with an awful inevitability: his agony of hesitation at the Bad Step; then Atawulf clinging desperately to the boulder; finally, his friend's cry of terror as he lost his grip and went spinning into space . . . Sweating and terrified, only then would Petrus awake. As if drawn by some strange compulsion, he would study his face in a looking-glass, and note, reflected back at him accusingly, a faint, star-shaped scar on his forehead – the brand of the coward. At such moments his confidence would drain away as he found himself wondering if, after all, Nearchus had been right: could a barbarian and the son of an ex-slave ever hope for real and lasting acceptance by the Roman world?

PART II

EMPEROR-IN-WAITING
AD 500–527

THREE

*The Emperor Caesar Justin . . . assuming empire by universal choice. . .it is
our care . . . to keep you in all prosperity*
Constantine VII Porphyrogenitus, *On the Ceremonies of the Court*, c. 950

'Petrus!'

'Valerianus!'

The two friends (whose diverging paths after their student days ended
fifteen years before, had prevented their meeting save on rare occasions)
embraced warmly, at the Column of Marcian in the capital's prestigious
Eleventh Region – 'Ta Ioulianes'. Valerian, now a junior general serving
under the *Magister Militum per Armenias* (after having flirted briefly with
a legal career), had suggested the rendezvous in a letter written from the
front during the latest insurgency to break out in the Taurus Mountains.

'First grey hairs,' observed Petrus, as the pair took stock of each other.

The other grinned ruefully. 'Those Isaurians could turn your whole
head white. Persistent little buggers. We keep on beating them; trouble is,
no one seems to have told them that.' He studied Petrus with undisguised
curiosity. 'What's with this fancy army uniform? I always thought you were
a confirmed civilian, nose always stuck in a law book.'

Petrus gave a slightly embarrassed smile. 'I'm a *candidatus* – an officer
in the Scholae regiment. Strictly a parade soldier, I'm afraid. These days,
I'm working more and more for my uncle Roderic, who's Count of the
Excubitors – which *is* a fighting unit. As he's also a senator, I write his
speeches for him and help him chair committees and dispense patronage
– all of which he hates doing. He seems to think that a military uniform
gives me a bit more clout. But I haven't deserted the law; I've been working
on a draft for a radical revision of our legal code – in fact, ever since 'the
Holy Water Sprinkler' lectured us on Citations and *Ius Respondendi*.'

Valerian chuckled. 'Dear old Olympius; he never did work out why
those two front rows were always empty for his lectures.' He paused and
gave his friend a sly wink. 'And how many female conquests has "the
Adonis of Byzantium", as the girls used to call you, notched up since we
last met?'

'Well – none, actually,' admitted Petrus with a sheepish grin. Sex, in his opinion, was a vastly overrated pastime, involving an inordinate amount of time and energy which could more profitably be directed towards absorbing and worthwhile pursuits, such as the study of law and theology. He shrugged and spread his hands. 'I never seem to find the time,' he added feebly.

Valerian sighed and shook his head in mock despair. 'Perhaps you've missed your vocation, Petrus, and should have trained to be a priest.' He eyed the other speculatively and chuckled. 'Somehow though, I can't imagine you with a beard. But why, I ask myself, are we standing here wasting valuable drinking time? Diogenes' tavern awaits our patronage, my friend.'

That same morning – the fourth before the Ides of Julius in the year of the consuls Magnus and Anastasius Augustus,* an atmosphere of crisis, approaching one of panic, gripped the Palace. Grim-faced *silentiarii* – gentlemen-ushers, prowled the corridors in an attempt to prevent any leakage of security, while Celer, the Master of Offices, and Roderic, Count of the Excubitors, alerted the troops under their separate commands, swearing them to silence. For during the night, in the middle of a violent thunderstorm, Emperor Anastasius had died at the age of eighty-seven, designating no successor.

Which created a power-vacuum – an especially dangerous one. Ten days' march to the north of the capital was an ambitious general, Vitalian, at the head of a powerful army of Goths and Bulgarians. Twice in the past five years he had tried unsuccessfully to topple Anastasius. At this present juncture, any delay in choosing a new emperor would hand Vitalian an opportunity to attempt a coup. Another potential rival for the purple was Hypatius, nephew of Anastasius and Master of Soldiers in the east. Based as he was at Antioch, it would take many days before news of his uncle's death reached him, and at least an equal amount of time for him to march on the capital. However, as a potential player in the succession game, he most certainly could not be ruled out. Thus, the perfect ingredients for a bloody civil war had all come together at the worst possible conjunction.

It was therefore incumbent on Celer and Roderic, as the two 'strong men' in the capital, to take swift, decisive action to install a new emperor

---

* 10 July 518. The entry in the *Fasti* was later modified to show that Anastasius had died that same year – which began on 1 January with the naming of the consuls.

before Vitalian or Hypatius could enter the arena. Though speed was of paramount importance, the candidate for the purple must yet be chosen with the utmost care. He would have to be acceptable not only to the Senate and the Army, but most of all to the people – the volatile, strong-willed, and passionate citizens of Constantinople (whose views could be said to reflect in microcosm the opinion of the Empire as a whole), without whose approval no emperor could hope to keep his throne.

Eagerly exchanging reminiscences, the two men headed south into the Twelfth Region (less distinguished than the Eleventh, but still respectable), bound for the Harbour of Theodosius.

'Phew! After campaigning in the highlands of Isauria, I'd forgotten just how hot the city gets in July,' murmured Valerian, mopping his brow as they crossed the wide and crowded Mesé, its arcaded sides filled with shops selling silks, jewellery, scent, and a hundred other luxuries. All around them swirled a dense mass of humanity, colourful, cosmopolitan: wealthy citizens bejewelled and dressed in the height of fashion, attended by a train of servants and hangers-on; members of the new order of patricians, distinguished in their white robes edged with purple; monks and bearded priests; off-duty soldiers; blue-eyed Germans, conspicuous by their fair hair and pink skins; peasants from the country, driving carts full of vegetables; Egyptian sailors on leave from the grainships of Alexandria; soberly clad merchants . . .

A group of Blues supporters approached, everyone in their vicinity giving them a wide berth. On passing Petrus and Valerian however, they greeted the former with respectful salutations.

'You're not involved with that bunch of thugs, surely!' exclaimed Valerian.

'Purely on a business basis. Call it mutual back-scratching: I keep the city prefect's police off their backs, in return, they employ, ah – "persuasion", to expedite certain contracts for my uncle. You've no idea the amount of tedious bureaucracy you have to cope with if you go through the normal channels.'

'You dark horse, you.' Valerian shook his head, half in disapproval, half in admiration.

As the two threaded the narrow lanes of wooden houses leading to the harbour area, they became aware of a distant shouting coming from an eastern direction. It grew steadily in volume as it swept westwards through the city like an advancing wave. At last, what had at first been a confused babel of sound, resolved itself into intelligible phrases: 'Anastasius is dead . . . the emperor is no more . . . our "little father" has been taken from us . . .' The efforts of the imperial staff to stop the news from getting out had failed – little wonder, considering that the Palace was not a single edifice but consisted of two dozen separate buildings: pavilions, banqueting halls, state rooms, offices, chapels, barracks . . . Given such a scenario, total security was virtually impossible.

'I must get back to the Palace!' exclaimed Petrus, immediately aware of the potential crisis that the news would have precipitated. 'As a member of the Scholae I'll be expected; I'd have been there already but for the fact that, thanks to my uncle, I'm excused living in barracks. I just hope to God that Celer and uncle Roderic can keep a lid on things and instal a new emperor before Vitalian or Hypatius can stir things up.' He smiled apologetically at his companion. 'Sorry, old friend, our session at Diogenes' will have to –' He broke off suddenly, his face turning ashen. 'Listen!'

The rapidly approaching roar of the crowd had changed from a confused tumult expressing sorrow and consternation over the death of Anastasius to a rhythmic chant demanding its choice for a new emperor: 'Rodericus Augustus! Rodericus Augustus!'

'The fools!' gasped Petrus, turning an anguished face to his friend. 'My uncle can't be emperor – he'd be totally out of his depth and never be able to cope.'

'Too late – he's been named. That means he'll be seen as a rival for the purple by whoever else decides to throw his hat into the ring. And if he's defeated . . .' Valerian gripped the other by the arm and stared bleakly into his face. 'Well, we both know what that could mean.'

'Blinding or death,' whispered Petrus. 'Oh God, Valerian, what a mess.' He tried to think constructively but his brain refused to respond, his mind seemingly paralyzed.

'Petrus – get a grip!' shouted Valerian. 'We can save your uncle, but only by making sure he becomes emperor. And that means acting, *now*!'

'What, what must we do?' Petrus' mind cleared, but a sick, hollow feeling of dread began to grow inside him.

'Go immediately to the Senate House, persuade the Senate that your uncle's the best man to wear the purple. You know the sort of things you have to say; you've done the course in Rhetoric as part of your legal training. Meanwhile, I'll go to the Hippodrome where the crowds'll be gathering, try to whip up support for your uncle. If we can get the backing of the House and the people, the soldiers will likely follow suit. Right, let's go.' And the pair set off eastwards at a fast pace towards the huge complex comprising the Hippodrome, the Imperial Palace, the great church of the Holy Wisdom* – Hagia Sophia – and the Senate House.

Recognizing the nephew of the Count of the Excubitors, the porters on duty outside the great ivory-panelled doors of the Senate House admitted Petrus into the building. Inside, all seemed confusion, with anxious-faced senators in their archaic togas milling about, and talking in low, excited tones. Not having been primed to announce any bills or official business, Methodius, the *Caput Senatus***, a stooped and venerable figure, hovered irresolutely before the rostrum. Only the Patriarch, Epiphanius, seated in his *cathedra*, aloof and splendidly garbed in his ecclesiastical robes, seemed unmoved by the occasion.

'Ah, there you are Sabbatius,' snapped Celer, the Master of Offices. Burly and bald, imposing in muscle cuirass of gilded bronze, the commander of the Scholae exuded authority and confidence. 'Better late than never, I suppose. I was about to put my name forward as the most suitable replacement for our newly deceased emperor. As the nephew of General Rodericus – who is not without influence in the places where it counts – your support could be useful to me.'

Events had moved beyond his ability to influence them, Petrus told himself, mortified to realize that his chief reaction was a feeling of relief. With Celer about to enter the race, and no sign of Roderic in the chamber to contest him, the result was virtually a foregone conclusion. The nerve-racking prospect of having to address the Senate had evaporated. Then a hot flush of shame swept over Petrus. Even if it now came too late to achieve anything, it would be unforgiveable cowardice not to speak up for the man to whom he owed everything. Twice before, in circumstances forever branded into his memory, he had let cowardly self-interest dictate his actions. But not this time.

'I'm sorry, sir,' he heard himself say, 'but I can't support you. The people have started calling for my uncle. It's him that I must help.' He went on, a note almost of pleading entering his voice, 'Surely you can see that, sir.'

'I can see nothing of the sort,' snorted Celer. 'General Rodericus as emperor? The idea's preposterous; he wouldn't last a week. As for you, Sabbatius

---

* Not the present Hagia Sophia which was consecrated in 537, but a rebuilding of 404 of Constantine's fourth-century church. It was in this building that the marriage of Justinian and Theodora took place in 525
** The Head of the Senate: in Westminster terms, something between the Speaker and the Father of the House.

– may I remind you that as a serving officer under my command, it is nothing less than your plain duty to give me your backing. Refuse, and the consequences for your career will be extremely serious.' And he strode off towards the *Caput Senatus*, with whom he was soon deep in conversation.

By the time Valerian reached it, half Constantinople seemed to have swarmed into the Hippodrome. Already, the crowds had split into two rival camps: one, egged on by the Greens, shouting for Celer to be emperor, the other, supported by the Blues, demanding that Roderic be chosen. Armed and armoured, the Excubitors and units from the Scholae regiments patrolled the expanses of the vast racetrack, modelled on the Circus Maximus in Rome.

Spotting Valerian, a harassed-looking Roderic, still upright and vigorous despite his sixty-eight years, marched up to him. 'Thank God for a friendly face,' declared the general. 'I could use some help if things turn ugly. Those toy soldiers from the Scholae are deliberately siding with the Greens – turning a blind eye when Blues get roughed up, joining in when it's the other way. And the Blues aren't helping: whipping up support for me to be emperor. They must be mad. I'm the last person who should don the purple; I'll have nothing to do with it.'

'You may have to, sir,' urged Valerian, who knew and liked the other, having once briefly served with him in Armenia in a border dispute concerning Roman and Persian zones of influence. 'If Celer wins, to say nothing of Vitalian or Hypatius, you'll be a marked man.'

'You really think so? But the last thing I'd want to do is contest their claims. None of them has anything to fear from me.'

'*I* know that, sir. And so do most informed people at the top.' Valerian found himself having to shout above a rising clamour, as more and more people streamed into the Hippodrome. 'But we're talking here about ruthless, scheming men. In the event of any of them becoming emperor, their first priority would be to liquidate anyone who seemed to offer even the remotest threat to their position.'

'I hear what you say,' said Roderic, a hint of desperation creeping into his voice. 'But I'd be hopeless as emperor. Diplomacy, administration, legal problems, religious disputes – all that stuff's completely beyond me.'

'You'd have advisors, sir. Your nephew Petrus would steady the ship while you learned the ropes – forgive the nautical metaphors. He's in the Senate House at this very moment, arguing your case. Anyway, you'd make a damned sight better emperor than any of those others, who'd only be in it for personal gain and power.'

'Oh very well then,' sighed Roderic resignedly. 'Let's go for it. Tell the Excubitors and their following that I accept.'

Minutes later, the triumphant Excubitors, in a gesture the Romans had adopted from the Germans, raised their commander on a shield for all to see. Such a powerful symbol had an immediate effect. Calls for Celer to be emperor began to falter then to die away, while shouts of 'Rodericus Augustus!' rose to a rhythmic, deafening din. Followed by an excited crowd, the jubilant Excubitors carried their leader out of the Hippodrome, and headed for the Senate House.

Banging his staff on the marble floor, the *Caput Senatus* called the House to order. Sensing that at last a significant development was in the offing, the senators fell quiet and took their seats.

'Seeing that this is an emergency session of the House,' quavered old Methodius, 'the Patriarch and I have agreed to dispense with the customary prayers and preamble, and proceed straight away to attend to the urgent matter which has brought us all together: namely, the nomination of a successor to Anastasius of blessed memory, who sadly departed from us in the night. I now call upon Celer, Master of Offices and Commander of the Scholae Palatinae, to address the House.'

Celer stepped up to the rostrum and, head thrown back, seized the lectern with both hands – a gesture somehow conveying the image that here was a strong, capable man able to take charge, a safe pair of hands who could be trusted with the running of the Empire.

'Romans, fellow citizens,' Celer declared in ringing tones, 'as a humble servant of our glorious republic, I would be found wanting in my duty if I were to stand aside at this most critical and dangerous of times, and fail to offer myself as choice of emperor. For that would be to leave the vacant throne to be contested by men who are unworthy to wear the purple. A would-be usurper, a weakling, and an incompetent – any one of whom would destroy our prosperity and sap our strength, undermining our ability to resist those enemies who threaten us on every side, just waiting to exploit the slightest signs of Roman weakness: Bulgars, Slavs, and Lombards to the north and west, Persians to the east, and, to the south, the savages of Aethiopia and Nubia.*

'Let us look closely at these men who threaten to besmirch that most ancient and honourable title – *Augustus Romanorum*. First, Vitalian – a power-hungry opportunist who, on two occasions, sought to oust our

* Northern Sudan.

beloved Anastasius, now sadly taken from us. Nor should we forget that Vitalian is a member of that ferocious and fickle race – the Germans. For more than five hundred years, the legacy of these barbarians for Rome has been aggression and bad faith. Arminius, Alaric, Stilicho, Gainas – all Germans who fought for Rome, all ending up betraying her. Can we expect different from Vitalian?' Celer looked round the rapt faces of his audience. 'I think we know the answer to *that*,' he chuckled.

'Hypatius? A career soldier, who only rose to his present position of *Magister Militum per Orientem* through the patronage of his uncle, the late emperor. His military record is hardly an impressive one – thrashed by Vitalian when, reluctantly, he was forced to take the field against him. So, if you want a broken reed for emperor, Hypatius is your man.

'Finally, Rodericus.' Celer paused and shook his head, his expression one of amused disbelief. 'The man's a joke, a semi-literate peasant who couldn't even sign his name when first he arrived in the capital. As emperor, this doddering geriatric who should have been pensioned off years ago would have to deal on a daily basis with the complex departments of ministers and officials: the Count of the Domestics, the Master of Audiences, the senior clerks and their staff, the Counts of the Privy and Public Purses, diocesan and provincial governors . . . to name but a small selection. As well expect an ape to understand a water-clock. I would also mention, should you need reminding, that Rodericus, like Vitalian, is German – a Goth and a barbarian. Enough said.' Smiling, Celer bowed his head and, amid enthusiastic applause, returned to his place on the marble benches.

Taking Celer's place on the rostrum, Methodius, the *Caput Senatus*, announced, 'Unless anyone here present has anything further of substance to say, I suggest we proceed to nominate Celer as our choice of emperor, subject to ratification by the soldiers and the people. Accordingly –'

Petrus, who, not being a senator had been forced to stand in a side aisle, raised his hand. In a voice he barely recognized as his own, he found himself saying, 'As his nephew, I would like to speak on behalf of General Rodericus.'

A buzz of astonishment tinged with irritation swept round the chamber. Methodius regarded Petrus sternly. 'A stranger in the House can have no leave to address this assembly,' he declared in disapproving tones.

'That depends,' broke in a white-haired senator, rising. 'If one of us is unable to attend a session of the House, he may, according to the Senate's rules, delegate another to speak on his behalf.' A murmur of agreement from the benches followed his remark.

'Well, young man,' snapped Methodius, addressing Petrus, 'has the commander of the Excubitors appointed you his representative?'

'Not exactly,' faltered Petrus, beginning to sweat with embarrassment. 'But only because he has not had any opportunity to contact me. As with all of you, this crisis has caught him unawares. I expect he felt he had to give priority to keeping order in the Hippodrome over coming to the Senate House.'

'That's as may be,' replied Methodius testily. 'But we cannot start bending the rules just to accommodate every change of circumstance. Permission to speak denied.'

'Oh, come now – isn't that a bit unreasonable?' put in the senator who had spoken earlier. 'It would appear that General Rodericus is unselfishly putting the public good above his own interests, thus preventing him from attending this unscheduled meeting in his role of senator. Must he be penalized for that, through slavish observance of a procedural nicety?'

A growing groundswell of assent arose: 'A fair point . . . Let the nephew have his say . . . What difference can it make?'

Methodius banged his staff for silence. 'Oh, very well,' he declared with a hint of exasperation. He called to Petrus, 'The floor is yours, young man.'

Feeling like a condemned prisoner walking to the place of execution, Petrus advanced to the rostrum. Self-conscious in his drab undress uniform, and aware that he must be the youngest person in the chamber, he faced the rows of white-clad senators, their faces etched with experience, expectant, critical. A sudden wave of panic swept over him; he felt his mouth dry out and his palms begin to sweat. For a terrible moment his mind went blank and he felt unable to speak. Then the words of Celer's sneering denigration of his uncle – the man whom he loved and respected above all others – seemed to sound in his brain, dissolving his mental paralysis and replacing it with indignation.

'What the *Magister Officiorum* has told you concerning Vitalian and Hypatius may well be true,' Petrus began, speaking slowly in order to gain time to marshall some sort of argument. 'I myself am not sufficiently informed to judge. But in seeking to cast a slur on the name of my uncle, General Rodericus, he not only dishonours the traditions of his office, which have always stood for probity and fairness, but slanders a good and loyal servant of the Empire.' Growing anger over the injustice of Celer's attack on Roderic welled up inside him. His training in rhetoric warned him to be careful; properly harnessed, anger could lend force and conviction to a speech; unrestrained, it was likely to destroy it, by causing incoherence and diffusion of focus.

'Cast your minds back, if you will,' Petrus continued, choosing his words with care, 'to the year of the consul Paulus,* when East Rome faced perhaps the most terrible threat in her history, a danger greater even than that posed by Attila – the conquest of the Diocese of Oriens and that of Egypt, by the Persians: half the Empire's territory. With the imperial armies tied down in Isauria, all that stood against a vast Persian host was a tiny force of *limitanei* under my uncle's command. Faced with such overwhelming odds, most generals would, without dishonour, have opted for a tactical withdrawal. Not Rodericus. Knowing the tremendous issues that were at stake, he took on the Persians, and – through a combination of coolness, courage, and inspired leadership – inflicted on them a crushing defeat.'

Suddenly, out of nowhere it seemed, a daring thought occurred to Petrus. He had done his best to rehabilitate his uncle in the minds of his audience. What if, at the same time, he were able to inflict a telling blow against Celer – one that would damage his credibility? It would mean taking a colossal risk, and, however it turned out, making of Celer an enemy for life – a powerful, dangerous, and unforgiving one. Petrus hesitated, aware that he had arrived at a personal Rubicon . . .

One of the strengths of the imperial bureaucracy was its openness and comparative accessibility. Armed with a permit from the appropriate official, Petrus had often had occasion to search state records on behalf of his uncle, in the latter's capacity of senator. The year of the consul Paulus had been memorable, not only for Roderic's defeat of Tamshapur, but for an exceptionally poor harvest, leading to bread rationing in the capital. Significantly, it was from this time that Celer's name had begun to appear in the records of various *scrinia* or state departments, especially those of the *Comites Sacrarum Largitionum* and *Rei Privatae*: the Counts of the Public and Privy Purses, respectively. Over the years, Celer's promotion in these two departments had been steady if hardly rapid, progressing from *palatinus* or clerk, to committee secretary, to *comes commerciorum* or customs officer, to *curiosus* of the *cursus publicus* – inspector of the public post. Transfer to the *Scrinium Officiorum*, had seen his rise from *agens in rebus*,**

---

* AD 496. See Prologue.
** *Agentes in rebus* (a catch-all title) were imperial agents with wide-ranging executive or inspectorial powers, covering anything from diplomacy to spying.

via *Magister Admissionum* or Master of Audiences, to his present position of *Magister Officiorum* – the most powerful post in the Empire, barring that of the emperor himself.

In the course of his researches, Petrus had taken no particular note of Celer's name – just one among many others. But his legal training and search work had developed to an extraordinary degree Petrus' powers of selective recall, so that at any given moment he could summon in his mind sections of documents he had studied in the past, and visualize particular names included therein. Before Paulus' consular year, the name of Celer had nowhere appeared in the records; after it, hardly a year had gone by but Celer's name had featured. Something, Petrus reasoned, must have happened in that particular year to cause a dramatic improvement in Celer's fortunes. To obtain a post in the civil service, money, influence, or exceptional talent were necessary to obtain a foothold on the ladder. Celer's family was neither wealthy nor distinguished, and Celer himself, while competent enough, was of no more than run-of-the-mill material. Payment of *suffragium* – a 'sweetener' to cover the going rate for purchase of a post – was virtually standard practice; though strictly speaking illegal, it was widely connived at. However, to ensure that the administration maintained its efficiency, a formal examination ensured that only candidates of sound ability were accepted. All of which suggested to Petrus that Celer had suddenly come into funds in that particular year – enough to enable him to secure a post in the administration. With the sort of instinct that had often enabled him to surmise a defendant's guilt or innocence in advance of the verdict, Petrus *knew* where those funds must have come from – speculation in grain!

Petrus could imagine a grubby little scene: an ambitious young Celer (penniless but with a network of shady contacts) arranging a deal with the skipper of one of the grain ships from Alexandria – a scheme that would make them both rich. A consignment of 'spoiled' grain would be transferred to one of the state warehouses (whose supervisor would naturally receive a generous *sportula* or tip), then sold on to a starving populace at inflated prices . . .

All these reflections raced through Petrus' mind in seconds. His heart thumping painfully, he wet lips that had suddenly gone dry.

'Honourable members of this great Assembly,' he declared, 'I have but one more point to make. Ask yourselves this: when my uncle was risking his life to save the Empire from the Persian threat, and the poor of Constantinople were clamouring for bread, what was Celer doing that enabled him suddenly to acquire great wealth?' His tunic drenched with sweat, walking stiffly to conceal the trembling in his legs, Petrus left the rostrum and returned to his position in the aisle.

A thunderous silence filled the Senate House. In an agony of suspense, Petrus waited for the angry denunciations that Celer would be bound to utter, if his, Petrus', implied indictment should be false.

At last, the charged hush was broken by Celer. 'If the best that this young man can do to vindicate his uncle is to bandy about wild accusations aimed at myself,' he blustered, with a nervous laugh, 'I suggest that we ignore him.' As a riposte, it lacked force and all conviction. Petrus sagged with relief as he realized his gamble had paid off. Celer dare not take him to task for fear that Petrus was in possession of knowledge which would enable him to make damaging disclosures. The fact that Petrus had no *proof* of any wrongdoing on Celer's part, was obviously something that the Master of Offices could not risk assuming. His failure to challenge Petrus amounted to an admission, in effect, that he had something to hide.

The atmosphere in the Senate House had subtly changed, the altered mood manifesting itself in a ripple of claps, which – mingled with cheers, gradually swelled to a sustained ovation. He had won, Petrus realized with a sense of wonder. There had been great gaps in his speech, he reflected: for example, he hadn't actually proposed that Roderic should be emperor; nor had he replied to Celer's charge that Roderic, as emperor, would have been unable to cope. (With hindsight, he told himself that he could have countered this charge by pointing out that he, Petrus, with his familiarity with the workings of the imperial bureaucracy, could have managed the administration while his uncle grew into the job.) But none of these omissions seemed to matter now.

As the cheering gradually subsided, a distant clamour could be heard that, gradually approaching, resolved itself into a rhythmic shouting: 'Rodericus Augustus! Rodericus Augustus!' Methodius signalled that the doors of the chamber be opened, whereupon, borne by his Excubitors upon a shield, General Roderic entered the Senate House, to be greeted by acclamations from the senators.

The Excubitors formed a protective screen around their commander who, when they stepped aside, was revealed clad in a purple robe – an impressive figure with his height, breadth of shoulder, and mane of grizzled hair. The Patriarch now stepped forward and, placing the imperial diadem on the general's brow, announced in ringing tones, 'Behold your new Augustus, henceforth to be known as "Justinus", signifying "most suitable" – a fitting appellation for one who has served his Empire so honourably and so well.'

Looking happy and at the same time slightly bewildered, the new emperor held up his hand to stem the storm of applause that followed the Patriarch's address. 'Noble senators of New Rome,' he declared, in a voice hoarse with emotion, 'my given name is Roderic which, in my own tongue means "of good report" – a designation I have always tried, though doubtless often in vain, to live up to. But I gladly now surrender it for the one you have honoured me with, since, by the choice of the soldiers, the people, and now the Senate, it would appear that you have chosen me "most suitable" to wear the purple. Accordingly, I pledge that I will always strive my utmost to justify your trust, and to keep you in all prosperity.'

Somewhere, he had heard that a man had only so much courage, Petrus (ensconced in a quiet corner of the Palace gardens to collect his thoughts) reflected later. Like a sum of money placed for safe keeping in a goldsmith's vaults, you could draw upon it only so many times before it was exhausted. How much of that deposit had he used up in the Senate House today? he wondered. And how much of it was left? Enough to enable him to cope with the tremendous demands that would, from this time on, be made of him? For it was beginning to dawn on Petrus just how momentous was the change that, thanks to the events of the past few hours, had been wrought in the circumstances of his uncle and himself. Suddenly and without warning, Roderic (whom he must now start thinking of as 'Justin'), a tough and experienced old soldier but a child in the sphere of high politics, had become the most important person in the Roman world. Which meant that he, Petrus, by virtue of his being his uncle's right-hand man, was now the second most important! But was he equipped to rise to this stupendous and quite terrifying challenge? Petrus cast his mind back a decade and a half, to when he had completed his studies at the university . . .

Somewhere along the way, his career had stalled. The brilliant and ambitious young embryo lawyer with bold plans to reform the whole vast structure of the Roman legal system, had somehow drifted into becoming a dilettante-scholar who had allowed his interest in theological studies to take precedence over his legal goals. A desire to help his uncle cope with his senatorial duties had enabled him to follow up an academic interest in archives* and the machinery of state administration, without the inconvenience of actually having to work for any department. Happily absorbed in these researches, he had hardly noticed as his twenties slipped into his thirties; then suddenly early middle age loomed just ahead, causing Petrus to sit up and take stock. A frank session of self-analysis and self-assessment had left Petrus with a vague feeling of failure and frustration. His life (its material wants looked after by his uncle) was comfortable and pleasant, and not without a certain modest standing, which was boosted by the cachet of his (albeit virtually honorary) military rank. But what had he actually *achieved* in life? 'Make us proud of you,' had been his mother's parting words. But could he, in all honesty, say that he had done so?

Now however, through a turn of Fortune's Wheel, all aspects of his curriculum vitae to date, Petrus realized, constituted the perfect set of qualifications for him to become plenipotentiary for his uncle, in his capacity of emperor. Petrus' intimate knowledge of the workings of state departments put him in an ideal position to check the pulse of the administration and, where necessary, apply corrective measures. And now that, through his uncle, he had access to the levers of executive power, he could at last entertain realistic hopes of being able to implement his cherished schemes of law reform. Also, his interest in theology would help him to take up the vitally important role of mediator in the conflict between the two opposing Christian creeds within the Empire. These were: the Chalcedonian, which held that Christ had two natures, both human *and* divine; and the Monophysite, which believed that Christ had but one, divine, nature. Unresolved, these differences (such was the central importance they assumed in people's minds) had the power to bring about a damaging schism, which could split the Empire into two mutually antagonistic camps.

A sobering consideration now occurred to Petrus. Roderic (no – *Justin*, he corrected himself) was sixty-eight. His successor, therefore, could reasonably be expected to ascend the throne in the not too distant future. And, Justin being childless, that successor (barring some unforeseen accident) would, Petrus realized with a shock, be him! Though no longer

---

* The state records were housed in an extraordinary complex – beneath the arches supporting the stands of the Hippodrome! In Rome, a similar 'World-below-the-Arches' was the milieu of a colourful under-class: entertainers, snack-vendors, jugglers, prostitutes, pimps et al.

a prerequisite, military experience was always a distinct advantage for anyone aspiring to the purple. So, even though in Petrus' case this was limited to largely ceremonial duties, the fact that he had held an army rank would count in his favour regarding his acceptability as Justin's heir.

Bent on some official errand, a *silentiarius* came by. Noticing Petrus, he paused and bowed, murmuring a deferential, '*Illuster*,' as he passed. Yesterday, he had been just a plain Roman citizen, Petrus reflected. Today, through some strange constitutional alchemy, he had become one of the *Illustres* – the highest grade of Roman society! Feeling oddly disorientated, Petrus told himself that he was still the same person. Yet he knew that in some indefinable way this was no longer quite the case, and that his world would never be the same again.

FOUR

*She was extremely clever, and had a biting wit, and she soon became popular
as a result*

Procopius, *Secret History*, c. 560

Seated in Cyrene's theatre beside her 'patron' – Hecebolus, governor of
Libya Pentapolis – Theodora was hot, bored, and uncomfortable. The par-
asol held above her head by a slave was scant protection against the fierce
African sun, as was the silk cushion against the hardness of the marble
tier. And the play – *Antony and Cleopatra*, penned by an influential friend
of Hecebolus with literary ambitions, which the governor was paying to
produce, was unbelievably tedious, portraying Antony (who in real life, as
everyone knew, was a loveable hedonist) as a stage villain of the deepest
dye, who must be brought low for the crime of heaping disgrace upon the
name of Rome.

As Cleopatra opened the basket containing the asp (actually a harmless
tree-snake) preparatory to holding it to her bosom, the creature escaped.
In the ensuing hiatus, while stage menials rushed around the orchestra in
a futile search for the offending reptile, Theodora let her mind drift back
fifteen years to when she was a child of five, the daughter of Akakios, a
bear-keeper in Constantinople's Hippodrome . . .

The world of the Hippodrome into which she was born was unbelievably tough, where survival depended on courage, adaptability, quick wits,
and shrewd judgement. Yet, though hard, it was an exciting and colourful
world, populated by barkers, hawkers, dancers, strolling players, acrobats,
sneak-thieves, clowns, pimps, and prostitutes – all operating under licence
from the minions of the two circus factions, the Blues and the Greens,
who managed the day-to-day business of the place. At least her father's job
as animal-trainer gave his family security, until, in Theodora's sixth year,
Akakios' sudden death plunged them into destitution. Rapidly re-marrying
(or at least securing a live-in partner to provide a bread-winner for her
family), the mother pleaded with Asterius, the manager of the Greens,
to give her late husband's job to her (unfortunately unemployed) new

partner. But she was too late; Asterius, on payment of a bribe, had already given the job to another.

With an initiative born of desperation, the mother, in a direct appeal to the ordinary members of the Greens for help in their extremity, appeared on a race day before a packed crowd in the Hippodrome, driving her three small daughters before her, their little heads crowned with chaplets of flowers, their hands held up in supplication. Never would Theodora forget her feelings of desperation and bewilderment when the Greens reacted to their appeal by bursting into roars of derisive laughter. Then, as in a state of utter humiliation and distress, mother and daughters were hurrying towards the exit, the Blues called for them to stop. The Blues' manager then assured them he would find a job for the girls' stepfather. No doubt the gesture was made as much from a desire to score points against their rivals, the Greens, as from compassion. But Theodora never forgot that act of spontaneous generosity, and thereafter was the Blues' most ardent supporter, and the Greens' bitterest enemy.

The family's security once more established, Theodora's elder sister, Comito, began from the age of fifteen to make a contribution to its income, by appearing as an actress on the stage, accompanied by the twelve-year-old Theodora as her dresser. In no time, Theodora's impish humour and gift for mimicry was convulsing audiences, and providing serious competition for the older sister. Soon, Theodora was given minor parts of her own; by sixteen, she had left Comito behind and was fast becoming the star of the theatre in her own right.

The downside of success on the stage was that actresses were equated with prostitutes, thereby consigned to the lowest rung of the social ladder and legally forbidden to marry anyone of high rank. Indeed, at times when acting parts were hard to come by, Theodora was forced to sell her body – never a problem, as she had developed into a ravishingly beautiful, petite young woman, with huge dark eyes in an oval face, and possessed of a vivacious charm. She regarded such liaisons as purely business transactions, undertaken from necessity and performed without emotion.

One day, a celebrated troupe of female dancers from Antioch arrived in the capital. Booked for one night only at the same theatre where Theodora was playing, their sensuous, exotic performance received tumultuous applause. As the troupe was exiting, one of the girls – a handsome brunette a few years older than Theodora – noticing the latter waiting in the wings prior to her act, signalled Theodora to join her on the stage. Puzzled yet intrigued, Theodora complied, whereupon the other, taking her by the hand, began to lead her in a dance. Theodora, who, apart from that one occasion when her mother had pleaded with the Greens in the Hippodrome, had never been embarrassed in her life, reacted with unwonted shyness. No dancer, she responded stiffly at first to the other's guiding steps. Then, some quality of warmth or empathy – and something else she was unable to define – communicated itself. Suddenly she seemed to lose her inhibitions, and found herself moving with her partner in perfect synchrony. Faster and more abandoned grew the evolutions of the dance; Theodora began to experience a strange sense of arousal, something she had never felt before, accompanied by a warmth spreading through her loins. As the dance reached its climax, her eyes met the other girl's. Mutual desire flashed suddenly between them, and Theodora found herself reciprocating as her partner's eager face bent forward to approach her own. Next moment, their mouths were locking in a passionate kiss. Shaken to the core, her heart pounding madly, Theodora fled the stage, her mind in turmoil, while the theatre erupted in wild applause, mingled with ribald cheers and laughter . . .

The memory of that strange happening was slow to fade, causing Theodora at times to feel restless and filled with vague longings. Reluctantly, she put the incident to the back of her mind. It was the male sex who ran the world, she told herself; only through relationships with men could she hope to make her way in that world. A bleakly cynical philosophy? Perhaps, but one that seemed to have paid off handsomely when, one night after her turn in the theatre, she received a message in her dressing-room. If she could spare the time, a gentleman would like to meet her.

This turned out to be one Gaius Sempronius Hecebolus, newly appointed governor of the Pentapolis. Bombastic, middle-aged, and paunchy, Hecebolus professed to be greatly impressed by Theodora's talents. He would be honoured if she were prepared to accompany him to Cyrene, to act as hostess for the social events over which he would be expected to preside. Cyrene, home of Eratosthenes, the great mathematician who had measured the earth's circumference, had a theatre, one of the oldest and finest in the Empire. If she wished, an opening for her to display her gifts, could be found on its stage.

Theodora had no illusions as to the bargain being proposed. In return for a life of ease and status as a 'governor's lady', she would become a courtesan. As for a role in the theatre, that was never going to happen; the social code would not permit a high-ranking official to be openly associated with an actress.

Thus far however, Theodora had, she allowed, little cause for complaint. She had fine clothes, jewels, slaves to attend her, a beautiful home, delicious food and plenty of it (and she did love her food). All that was expected of her was to entertain guests (for which she discovered she had a natural talent), and endure the occasional sexual encounter with the governor – mostly a drunken fumble ending, as often as not, with him falling asleep before achieving penetration. So it was perhaps perverse of her, Theodora admitted to herself, that she found she missed Constantinople with all its colour, excitement, and vulgarity, despite the insecurity and privation that a life on the stage entailed. Compared to the capital, Cyrene was inexpressibly dreary – respectable, provincial, uneventful. As for Hecebolus, he was pompous and dull beyond words; having to pretend to be interested while he rambled on about tax returns or the cost of repairing the city drains, was, to her, sheer torture.

Interminably, it seemed, the play dragged on throughout the long, hot afternoon, with the audience growing increasingly bored and restless. At last the curtain descended* for the final scene, with Antony, ridiculous in buskins and enormous helmet-plume, confronting (with scant regard for history) the freshly expired form of Cleopatra. Hand upon heart, and casting his eyes imploringly around the audience, he exclaimed, 'Alas, what shall I do?'

Theodora just couldn't help herself. Displaying to the full the gift of bawdy repartee for which she had been famous in the capital, she called back, 'Have her, while she's warm!'

Uttered in the tones of someone offering helpful advice, the obscenity floated into the auditorium, creating a charged and spreading silence, like concentric ripples from a stone dropped in a pool.

Then, like a pricked bubble, all the pent-up boredom of the audience released itself in an explosive gale of laughter. Even the *principales* – Cyrene's leading citizens, struggling to maintain expressions of shocked disapproval, cracked at last. Tears streaming down their cheeks, they held their sides and howled with helpless mirth.

Hecebolus alone, it seemed, was not amused. With a look of outraged fury, he grabbed Theodora by the wrist and hustled her from the theatre.

'You foul-mouthed little guttersnipe!' he roared, sending her reeling with a hefty slap across the face. 'I should have known better than to take

---

* In the Greek and Roman theatre the curtain rose from below, instead of falling from above, as in modern times.

you on. Not only have you ruined the first performance of a potential literary masterpiece, you've made me – the governor – look a fool.'

'Oh please, Gaius, don't be angry,' pleaded Theodora, her face stinging from the blow. The enormity of her gaffe began to register. 'I'm sorry, truly sorry; it was thoughtless of me – unforgiveable. I swear I'll never let you down again.'

'You needn't think you'll get the chance! Go – I never want to see your face again!'

'But you can't just send me away, Gaius,' protested Theodora, appalled by the prospect of sudden destitution. 'Where will I go?'

'Not my concern. Perhaps you should have thought of that.'

'My clothes, my jewels –'

'*I* bought them – same as *I* paid for everything you've had since you became my mistress. You've no claim on me. Now get out of my sight, whore, before I call the magistrates.'

Alone, without friends, a thousand miles from the only place she knew as home, with employment on the local stage barred to her (Hecebolus would see to that), Theodora, in the only other way she knew, earned enough to keep body and soul together, plus the fare for a voyage to Alexandria. In that great metropolis she would surely find employment for her theatrical talents, and be able to save enough to return to Constantinople. Meanwhile, she swore that never again would she depend upon a man for her livelihood. In fact, from this time on, the less she had to do with men, the better.

FIVE

Though separate by nature, fire and iron come together in the one entity that
is a red-hot ingot
Leontius of Jerusalem, *Against the Monophysites*, 532

'To insist that Christ has two natures – human *and* divine, is to deny that
the Virgin Mary was the *Theotokos*, the Bearer of God, as Cyril, Patriarch
of Alexandria, made clear at the Council of Ephesus ninety years ago.'
Irene, abbess of a remote religious community in Egypt, smiled at Theodora and sighed apologetically. 'Forgive me, my dear; why should I assume
that a lay person such as yourself should share my concerns about the true
nature of Christ?' The two women were standing at the rail of *Argo* – a
small merchant vessel two days out from Apollonia, the port of Cyrene,
and bound for Alexandria. Like other passengers, they had had to bring
their own food and bedding, sleeping at night in a deck-house. This was
divided down the middle by a thick canvas sheet, separating the men from
the women.

'But I find it all fascinating,' insisted Theodora, who had found, rather
to her surprise considering her lack of formal education, that conversations
with the abbess concerning religious topics had proved intellectually stimulating. She wondered briefly if this perhaps owed something to her Hellenic
heritage (both her parents were of pure Greek stock from Cyprus), which
had given the world some of its greatest thinkers and mathematicians.
Although the victim of a sudden and traumatic reversal of fortune, Theodora
felt strangely calm, almost happy in fact, as she contemplated an uncertain
future. Her decision that, following her dismissal by Hecebolus she would
henceforth lead an independent life, had left her feeling somehow stronger
and with her self-belief enhanced. Simultaneously, her intention to recoup
her fortunes by exploiting her talents as an actress seemed to have lost much
of its original appeal.

'If, as you say,' Theodora continued, 'Mary gave birth to God, then
Christ, her son, must surely be divine? Which is what I'm told the Monophysites of Syria and Egypt believe. Yet our new emperor, Justin, backed
by the Patriarch of Constantinople, tells us that this view's now heretical. It

seems we must now accept the decree of the Council of Chalcedon – that Christ has *two* natures: a human as well as a divine one.' Theodora gave a wry smile. 'Confusing, to say the least.'

'It's all totally unsatisfactory,' declared Irene, shaking her head. 'By reviving Chalcedon – held seventy years ago under Emperor Marcian – Justin has split the Empire: north and west for Chalcedon, south and east Monophysite. Fortunately, Justin seems to have had the good sense not to push things too far. Monophysite Egypt, which, significantly, supplies the Empire with its corn, has not been targeted for persecution; and anti-Chalcedon so-called heretics have been permitted to seek refuge there.'

'What an incredibly bright star,' observed Theodora, indicating a brilliant, steady point of light on the southern horizon.

'That's no star,' laughed Irene, standing beside the other on the *Argo*. 'It's the *Pharos* – the lighthouse of Alexandria; they say it has the brightest flame ever produced, on top of the tallest tower ever built.'

The flame's light quickly faded in the brief sub-tropical dawn, then the sun rose on a stupendous vista of turreted walls, beyond which rose a glittering frieze of domes and columns, obelisks, temples, and palaces; and in the foreground, towering impossibly high above the city's Great Harbour, rose the fluted column of the ancient lighthouse.

During the week-long voyage, Theodora had become firm friends with Irene, to whom she had confided her predicament. Sympathetic and non-judgemental, and also impressed by Theodora's keen if untutored intellect, the abbess before parting furnished the girl with a letter of introduction to Timothy, the Patriarch of Alexandria – a Monophysite sympathiser, and a wise and great-hearted man, she affirmed. The archbishop, she assured Theodora, would help her in her quest for a new direction in her life.

After disembarking from the Eunostos Harbour, separated from the Great Harbour by the *Heptastadion* – an immense mole nearly two miles long, the two women exchanged fond farewells and went their separate ways: Irene to the principal post station* for the next stage of her journey, Theodora to the palace of the Patriarch.

Theodora was thrilled and fascinated by the great metropolis, founded eight and a half centuries before, by the young Macedonian conqueror. In contrast to Constantinople, with its hills and jumble of narrow lanes, Alexandria was flat, laid out on a grid system with wide avenues and

---

* The Alexandrian terminus of the *cursus publicus* – the imperial post. See Notes.

grand squares, and bisected by the *Canopic Way* – a magnificent hundred-foot wide promenade, reputedly the longest street in the world. This was crossed by the equally broad *Argeus* running north and south, the inter-section of the two forming the hub of the municipal and administrative district. Everywhere among the crowds were clerics – monks, nuns, priests, ragged anchorites – many of them, Theodora suspected (remembering the words of Irene), Monophysite refugees fleeing persecution. From one, she obtained directions to the dwelling of the Patriarch, a modest villa adjoin-ing the cathedral of St Mark.

After waiting for an hour with others in an outer chamber, Theodora's turn came to be admitted to the bishop's presence. She entered a sparsely furnished *tablinum* or study, its lack of chairs and tables compensated for by open cupboards crammed with scrolls and codices. Timothy, a full-bearded giant exuding energy and confidence, waved her to a chair, the room's only seat barring that occupied by the bishop himself. To Theodora's surprise, he wore a simple priest's robe instead of the richly embroidered vestments proper to the office of a Patriarch.

'Well, it would seem my good friend Abbess Irene, our sister in Christ, has formed a high opinion of you,' boomed Timothy, after perusing the abbess' letter of introduction. 'She hints that you have had a chequered past not without its share of troubles, but that now you wish to follow a fresh path in life. She maintains that despite lacking any advantages of wealth or education, you possess in your favour youth, courage, a gener-ous heart, and an excellent mind.' Looking up from the missive, Timothy barked, 'None of which, of course, will be the slightest use to you, unless you also have that most essential of ingredients – luck.'

'Was it not luck, Your Holiness, that directed I should meet Irene, and thus yourself?'

The bishop stared at Theodora, then shook his head and chuckled. 'You may have a point. At least you've got a ready tongue, which counts for something, I suppose. I'm wondering how I can be of service to you.' Shooting her a keen glance, he went on, 'I could always recommend you to a nunnery as a postulant. Perhaps not,' he continued hurriedly, as Theodora gave a slight shake of her head. 'Well then – how about working as an almoner until you find your bearings? Free bed and board, plus allowance – only a tiny one, I fear.'

'Yes, I'd like that,' replied Theodora, immediately attracted by the idea of working with deprived people, helping lives less fortunate than hers.

And so began the happiest period Theodora had thus far known in her short life – a strange, fulfilling interlude in which she discovered, through her work with the poor, a natural empathy and ability to communicate with others. Her peregrinations sometimes took her past the theatre, situated near the waterfront; somewhat to her surprise, she felt not the slightest twinge of regret or nostalgia on these occasions. From her base in the Convent of St Catherine situated in Rhakotis, a poor quarter in the west of the city, she made periodic reports to Timothy, who seemed to take a personal interest in her welfare as well as in the progress of her work. Noticing the curiosity she displayed towards his impressive collection of volumes, he gave her the freedom of his library, a privilege which afforded Theodora enormous satisfaction. She simply could not get enough of books; her keen and active mind, so long starved of knowledge, hungrily absorbed their contents as fast as she was able to unroll papyrus scrolls or turn the pages of parchment codices. Plato, Aristotle, Isocrates, Aeschylus, Sophocles, Polybius, Caesar, Tacitus, Dio Cassius, Ammianus: all were greedily devoured (Latin authors in Greek translations, for although Constantinople was a bilingual city, Theodora had but a smattering of the tongue of Cicero and Virgil). The subtle metaphysics of Christian theologians such as Athanasius or Augustine proved a tough challenge, but also a source of gratification when she found she could (mostly) unravel their complexities.

'A pity you can't supplement my poor collection from the richest store of knowledge known to man,' sighed Timothy one day when she showed up to present her report, ' – the great library of Alexandria, burned down by a Christian mob over a century ago in the time of the first Theodosius.' He shook his great head sadly. 'Misguided bigots. Fanaticism – the curse of the Eastern mind, I fear. Hence the present unhappy state of near-schism between the Monophysites – Easterners of Syria and Egypt, unbending in devotion to their creed – and the Chalcedonians of the West.'

'But Irene said you favoured the Monophysites.'

'True. But not too openly, I fear.' Timothy grinned ruefully and spread his hands, as if to disown what he was about to say. 'As Patriarch, officially I represent the emperor in a spiritual sense, so can't afford to wear my heart upon my sleeve. Monophysites, you see, can tolerate a bit of mystery in their creed. Christ, to us, though born of woman is still entirely God, and so can have but one, divine, nature. Egyptians like myself, and Syrians – a Semitic people – have no problem accepting that apparent contradiction. Try to force us to abandon our belief and you risk provoking insurrection on a massive scale. Of the multitude of monks and nuns on the streets out there, scarcely one but would gladly give their life to defend a view we hold so passionately – fanatically, if you like. Although, speaking for myself, I can understand the Chalcedonian point of view, and – tell it not in Gath – even sympathize with it to some extent. Luckily, the present imperial regime has the good sense to turn a partial blind eye to what it regards as Monophysite heresy – at least in Egypt. Four centuries ago, Titus and Hadrian faced the same sort of problem when they stirred up a hornet's nest by tampering with the religion of the Jews – another race of Semites.'

'Then why on earth does the government insist on uniformity, when that risks turning half the Empire into heretics?'

Timothy rose, and began to pace the *tablinum*. 'Ah – there you have the Graeco-Roman mind,' he boomed, wheeling to begin another circuit of the chamber, 'whose legacy is Greek philosophy and Roman law. You Westerners, with your restless probing intellects, never satisfied until you have defined a thing precisely, or worked out a rational solution to a problem. To you, Christ, because He walked the earth as man, yet also was the Son of God, logically *must* have two natures: human and divine. Q.E.D., as Euclid would have said. Anyone who can't see that is just being obstinately unreasonable. And as one true belief is as important for personal salvation as it is for promoting political unity within the Empire, orthodoxy must be made to prevail. Anyway, that's how the Chalcedonians would see it.'

'Then the Chalcedonians are stupid as well as narrow-minded!'

'Really, my dear,' declared Timothy, holding up his hands in mock horror, 'such views – while refreshingly forthright – are also hopelessly naive.' He halted his perambulations to stab an accusing finger at Theodora. 'Heaven help you if you were ever called upon to defend them in argument. You would be utterly demolished, and deservedly so. I have a suggestion: tomorrow, I visit an old friend, one Severus, Patriarch of Antioch and an ardent Monophysite, so presently in Alexandria as a refugee from persecution. He's renowned throughout the Roman world for his skill in disputation, and as a teacher. Were I to ask him, I'm sure he would be willing to accept you as his pupil. What do you say?

Under Severus' benignly merciless tuition, Theodora learned to hold her own in theological argument and debate. By the end of three months in the Egyptian capital, Theodora's metamorphosis was almost complete. Like a butterfly emerging from its chrysalis, she had become transformed from the frightened lonely derelict who had fled from Apollonia. In a world which had shown her little kindness, she had at last encountered others who had given her true and disinterested affection. (That two of these were male had shown her that there were at least some men prepared to value her for herself alone, and not just for the pleasure her body could provide.) Buoyed up by the friendship of two eminent and respected figures who had helped her to regain her self-respect and cultivate her mind (as well as imbuing her with sympathy and admiration for the Monophysites), she was ready to embark on the next stage of her voyage of self-discovery. For Alexandria, she knew, could only be a staging-post. She must find her destiny, whatever that should prove to be, in her home city, Constantinople, with its strong pull of family and *genius loci* – the place's soul.

'I understand, my dear,' said Timothy sadly, when she told him the time had come to move on. 'In my Father's house are many mansions,* and you must seek your fortune wherever it may call you. I can't pretend you won't be greatly missed; the poor whom you served so well have come to love you – as have I, as a father loves a daughter. May I suggest you break your journey in Antioch, where an old friend of mine lives – a wealthy widow with many contacts in the world of trade and business. I'd be surprised if Macedonia were unable to help you find an opening in work you'd find congenial. I'll give you a letter of introduction.'

Timothy did more than that. Although Theodora had saved enough (just) from her stipend to cover the cost of the voyage home, the bishop pressed on her a bag of *solidi*, 'for unforeseen emergencies' (a kindness Theodora would one day repay a thousand-fold**).

Disembarking at Seleucia – Antioch's harbour, fourteen miles from the sea on the River Orontes – Theodora entered 'The Crown of the East' via the great city's Watergate. Before her stretched a vast townscape, its suburbs chequered with orchards, olive groves, and vineyards, extending to the lower slopes of Mount Casius three miles distant. A few enquiries enabled her to track down Macedonia's home, its entrance opening onto the street in the wealthy suburb of Daphne. On producing Timothy's letter of introduction, she was conducted by a porter to the *atrium* – a courtyard floored with magnificent mosaics and surrounded by colonnaded walkways. 'The

---

* In this quotation from the Bible, 'mansion' doesn't mean a large house. The English meaning of the Latin *mansio* is 'station, stage' (Cassell's *New Compact Latin Dictionary*) – i.e. a staging-post on the *cursus publicus*.
** See Notes.

Domina will be with you presently,' the man murmured respectfully and withdrew. A little later, an attractive and elegantly clad lady entered the *atrium* and approached Theodora. While still some yards away, she halted, and exclaimed, 'The actress from Constantinople!'

'The dancer from Antioch!' gasped Theodora in sudden recognition, as a tide of feelings, long suppressed, surged up inside her.

SIX

And on soft beds . . . tenderly . . . we would satisfy desire
Sappho of Lesbos, *Fragment 94*, c. 600 BC

Macedonia was the first to recover. Taking the letter from the other's unresisting hand, she perused its contents then looked up with a smile, in which there lurked a hint of mischief.

'Well, Theodora, who'd have thought we'd meet up again like this? I'll be delighted to help you – if I can. Archbishop Timothy speaks highly of you; I'm sure we can find something that will suit. But before discussing your situation, we must catch up with each other's news over *cena*;* I'm all agog.'

Extended on a couch in the *triclinium* or dining-room beside her hostess, Theodora – to cover the embarrassment that had suddenly engulfed her – prattled on inconsequentially about life in Alexandria, scarcely tasting the delicious dishes from the table beside her. At last, aware that a mounting flush was colouring her neck and cheeks, she floundered to a stop.

'It's all right, my dear,' murmured Macedonia, in tones of understanding mingled with amusement. 'We don't need to be shy with each other.' Moving from her couch, she stretched out beside Theodora, and putting her arms around her, kissed her gently on the mouth.

Immediately, Theodora felt herself responding, and returned the kiss with ardour. Unbelievingly, she became aware of the other beginning to undress her; arousal coursing through her veins, she helped Macedonia complete the process then returned the service, till soon both women were lying naked, side by side.

'Are you ready for this?' asked Macedonia softly, beginning to stroke the other's breasts.

For a brief moment, Theodora felt herself stiffen. Never before had she been touched by a woman; thus far, her only experience of sex had consisted of fleeting intercourse with male clients, coldly commercial acts, undertaken not from choice but simply to keep the wolf from the door.

* Dinner.

Barring a mild disgust both for herself and for the man who had purchased the temporary use of her body, she had felt nothing on these occasions. But this was different. As delicious sensations from the other's cunning fingertips began to spread throughout her bosom, all resistance melted and she whispered in a voice husky with excitement, 'Yes, I'm ready.'

Theodora gasped as Macedonia caressed her nipples, causing them to swell erect, her pleasure mounting in intensity as lips and tongue replaced the work of fingers. She felt Macedonia's hand slide down her body, explore those other lips now slippery with expectation, fondle the swelling bud until she cried aloud in ecstasy, as the sensations climbed to a pinnacle of exquisite delight. Then suddenly she was convulsing in a violent orgasm, which gradually subsided to a glow of blissful satisfaction, leaving her shaken but at peace.

'I didn't know anything could be so beautiful,' she whispered to Macedonia, gazing adoringly at her lover's face. 'Now, I must try to do the same for you. Be warned though – I don't know if I'll be any good. All this is new to me, you see.'

'Provided a willing pupil has a good teacher, what's there to worry about?' murmured Macedonia. Smiling, she lay back languorously, and closed her eyes in sensuous anticipation.

To the short list of the only true friends she had ever known – Irene, Timothy, and Severus – Theodora was now able to add another name, Macedonia, one associated with a new dimension in her life – passion. The next few weeks passed in a delectable blur – long, intimate talks sometimes lasting far into the night; delicious meals complemented by the finest of wines; excursions around the splendours of Antioch, its colonnaded streets, magnificent circus, theatres, baths, and great churches;* bouts of tender lovemaking.

In the course of sharing confidences about their past lives, Macedonia revealed to Theodora that she had been briefly married to a successful merchant, before his untimely death from ague. 'Mathias was a sweet, kind man,' she recounted, 'who fell in love with me after seeing me perform with my troupe of dancers. It was hard to refuse his proposal of marriage; he offered me security, genuine affection, a life of luxury beyond the wildest dreams of a mere dancing-girl from a poor background. And I was truly fond of him. Not, of course, in the way I feel about yourself, my love, but

* All to be laid low seven years later, in the catastrophic earthquake of 29 November 528.

as a dear friend, whose death left me with a devastating sense of loss and sadness. He willed me his trading empire which, though I say it myself, I manage pretty well; if there's one thing my sort of upbringing has taught me, it's how many *nummi* make a *solidus*.'

'You were lucky; my own seeming passport to a better life came about in circumstances not dissimilar to yours,' remarked Theodora, adding with a rueful laugh, 'but instead of a Mathias, I ended up with an absolute bastard.' And she related the story of her sojourn with Hecebolus.

But nothing lasts forever; as the days grew shorter, warning of the autumn gales to come which would make voyages by sea impossible, Theodora knew that the time had come when the idyll had to end.

'You don't have to go,' entreated Macedonia. 'We could be partners in business, as in love.'

'Darling, I have my path to find,' Theodora responded gently. 'We'll meet again, I promise. But first, I have to make a new life for myself.'

And so, with many tears and kisses, they parted, Theodora embarking from Seleucia on a vessel bound for the Golden Horn. Packed with her belongings was a business plan for a wool-spinning enterprise, drawn up by Macedonia; also a sheaf of letters of introduction.* Among the latter was one addressed to a certain 'Petrus Sabbatius, *Comes, Vir Illuster, Consul et Patricius*' (Count, the Illustrious, Consul and Patrician).

* See Notes.

SEVEN

Barbarian nations . . . know the scale of our exertions in war
Justinian, *Institutes*, 533

Looking across the camp fire at his friend Petrus ('*Justinian*', he corrected himself – the official name bestowed on Petrus in January as one of last year's* consuls), Valerian felt a twinge of concern. Here they were, deep in the wilds of Aethiopia two thousand miles from Constantinople, heading a probably dangerous mission the success of which could not be guaranteed . . . Yet, from his relaxed, almost carefree demeanour, you would think Petrus ('*Justinian*', he reminded himself again) didn't have a care in the world.

Beyond the glowing circle of light from their own camp fire, hundreds of flickering dots, extending to a radius of several hundred yards, indicated the presence of the Roman expeditionary force supplemented by its Aethiopian guides. Perhaps he was being unduly apprehensive, Valerian conceded to himself. Thus far, he had to admit, the expedition had proceeded without a hitch. Sailing from the Golden Horn three months ago, the force (comprising a large contingent, mainly cavalry, from the Army of the East) had disembarked at Pelusium on the Nile Delta, marched the short distance overland to Arsinoe at the head of the Sinus Arabicus,** whence a fleet of transports (making excellent progress with a steady wind on the beam) had conveyed them to the port of Adulis on the coast of Aethiopia, a thousand miles further to the south-east at the other end of the Sinus.

Led by native guides sent to meet them at the port, the expedition had then struck inland across a rising tract of barren scrub-land to a high pla-teau – blessedly cool, Valerian found, after the energy-sapping heat of the coastal strip. Ahead towered a vast rampart of cliffs split by a mighty defile, before whose entrance the expedition made camp for the night. Next day, the force threaded the Great Pass, as the defile was known, through a series of striking and ever-changing scenes: groves of mimosa and laurel, flower-starred meadows, stands of pine and fir on the lower slopes and (just to remind you that this was Africa and not, say, Isauria or the Caucusus,

* 521.
** The Red Sea.

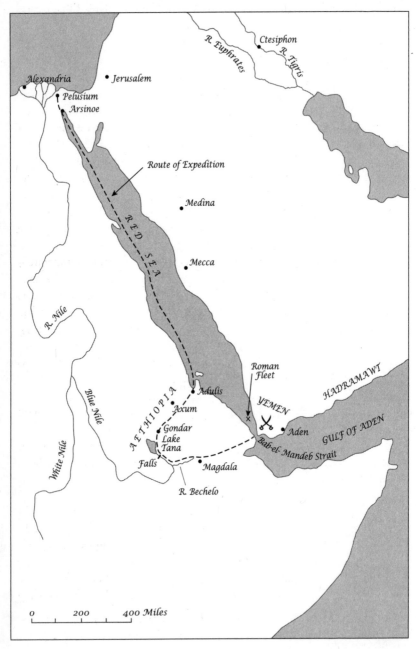

The Dhu-Nuwas Expedition, AD 522–3

thought Valerian) higher up, clumps of strange cactus shaped like many-branched candelabra.

Beyond the Great Pass the scenery changed abruptly, the way climbing up into range upon range of stark mountains – a nightmare vision of fantastically shaped peaks, some like fangs, others like flat-topped pillars, riven by boulder-filled gullies or dizzying precipices. For weeks the column inched its way south-westwards through that fissured wilderness, whose only sign of human habitation was an occasional stone fortress impossibly perched atop sheer cliffs. At last, to everyone's huge relief, the terrain began to descend, barren mountains giving place to rolling veldt – a sea of waving grass, relieved by crystal streams fringed by stands of sycamore fig, and stippled by herds of antelope, also a curious species of black-and-white striped horse. Although (assuming the great geographer Ptolemy was correct) Valerian reckoned they must now be midway between the line of the Tropic in the northern hemisphere and that of the Aequator, the climate, on account of the elevation of the country, was delightfully temperate – warm rather than hot by day, and cool at night. They passed many villages, each a cluster of cone-shaped thatched huts surrounded by a stockade. The inhabitants (tall, slim, brown-skinned people with, rather to Valerian's surprise, an Arabic rather than a negro cast of countenance), negotiating with the expedition's guides, were happy to exchange, for sticks of salt, fresh milk, bread, and meat – all much appreciated by the troops who had survived up to this point on hard tack and dried beef. In the midst of this Elysium, they came at last to Gondar* – an imposing hill-top city of stone-built houses, shops, and churches, and the agreed rendezvous with the King of Axum.

As the soldiers set up camp outside the town, Valerian recalled that fateful briefing in the Empire's capital, when the expedition had been planned . . .

Early in Justin's reign, in the year that his friend Petrus was made consul (his name on the occasion being changed to Justinianus, as being thought more fitting for the nephew of an emperor), Valerian, along with Justinian, received a summons to attend a meeting at the palace.

A *silentiarius* conducted the pair to an audience chamber in which were seated Justin, wearing plain undress military uniform (he hated wearing

---

* In the next century, Gondar would replace Axum as the country's capital. Ethiopia had been Christian since the 320s – nearly three centuries before St Augustine's mission to England!

the imperial regalia of diadem and purple robe, and avoided doing so whenever possible), and a large, red-faced, coarse-looking man, whom Valerian recognized as John the Cappadocian* – a clerk in the *scrinium* for military billeting. Justin waved the friends to a bench.

'Dhu-Nuwas has invaded Arabia Felix,'** announced John, speaking in a pronounced mid-Anatolian accent. 'What does that tell you?' He stared expectantly at Justinian and Valerian.

When, after a lengthy pause no answer had been forthcoming, John sighed ostentatiously and continued, 'A crisis, gentlemen, that's what it means – a crisis linked to spices, silk, and Christianity.' Raising his considerable bulk from his seat, he moved to an easel supporting a large wall-map showing the Arabian peninsula, the Sinus Arabicus, and the adjoining coast of Africa. With a pointer, he rapped the south-west tip of Arabia. 'Arabia Felix – the home of an ancient race, the Sabaeans. It comes within the sphere of influence of Aethiopia, which has extended its power across the straits which the Arabs call Bab-el-Mandeb – the Gate of Tears, from shipwrecks caused by the strong currents there. Arabia Felix is now virtually an Aethiopian colony. Aethiopia, as I'm sure I don't need to remind you, has been Christian for the past two hundred years; the Sabaeans were quite happy, it appears, to give up their primitive sun and moon worship in favour of the faith of their new masters.'

'I don't quite see what all this has to do with Constantinople,' put in Justinian.

John rolled his eyes impatiently. 'Give me strength. Aethiopia is Christian, thus entitled to the protection and support of the Christian Roman emperor. So Aethiopian control of Arabia Felix effectively means Roman control of the straits.'

'Forgive my obtuseness,' objected Valerian, clearly nettled by the other's abrasive manner. 'The Aethiopians are Coptic Christians, I believe – Monophysites, in other words. Which makes them heretics. So why should Rome support them? Also, you mentioned "Roman control of the straits". Just why is that so important?'

'*Within* the empire, Monophysites may be heretics; but *outside* it – well, we can't afford to be too nice in our discriminations.' John spoke slowly, in the tones of a schoolmaster explaining a point to a not-very-bright pupil.

---

* Famous both for bluntness and efficiency, within ten years John the Cappadocian would rise from humble clerk to praetorian prefect – in effect Justinian's chief minister. (See Notes.)
** The Yemen.

'Not if we hope to extend Rome's influence, and build alliances beyond her frontiers. As for the importance of Roman control of the straits – I'd have thought that was blindingly obvious. But as that doesn't appear to be the case, I suppose I must endeavour to –'

'Uncle,' interrupted Justinian, with uncharacteristic heat, 'Do we have to put up with this fellow's rudeness? I wouldn't have thought a little basic courtesy was too much to expect.'

Justin shifted in his chair and smiled uncomfortably. 'It's just his manner, nephew, nothing personal; he even speaks to me like that. Try to overlook his bluntness, if you can. I tolerate him because his advice is invariably excellent, and given without fear or favour.' He turned to the other. 'John,' he went on, in conciliatory tones, 'try to remember that Flavius Justinianus is a favoured member of my household, and that Valerianus Comes is a serving Roman officer with a distinguished record. A little tact wouldn't come amiss.'

'I'll try to remember that, Serenity,' responded John, inclining his head in mock humility. 'To continue, gentlemen,' he went on in tones of exaggerated politeness, 'Roman control of the straits is important to us for two reasons. Strategically, a Roman foothold in Arabia could enable us to counter Persian influence there, while a friendly Aethiopia could in time perhaps become what used to be called a "client kingdom", paving the way for imperial expansion in eastern Africa. Rome may have lost her Western provinces, but who's to say she can't extend her power to the south and east – the realms of Prester John and Alexander? Just a thought.

'Commercially, the straits are also of enormous significance, command-ing as they do the sea-routes both for spices from the Indies and silk from Serica.* Spices – essential for preserving autumn-killed meat throughout the winter. Silk, though not an article of general consumption, is of considerable importance in Roman society as a prestige possession – a badge of rank, a reward for merit. We mustn't forget that silk and spices are important not just to Rome, but to Rome's Eternal Enemy, Persia. Technically, we may be at peace just now. But there exists between the two powers a state of what I think we can fairly describe as "cold war" – especially on the trading front. As Persia commands the land routes, it can, at will, block supplies of silk and spices from reaching the Roman Empire. Which is why maintaining Roman control of the sea-routes is vital.'

'And that control has now been threatened,' put in Justin. 'This Dhu-Nuwas that John mentioned is a prince of the Himyarites – a Jewish

* China.

community in southern Arabia. Like the many other Jewish groups throughout the peninsula, it enjoys special Persian protection. In this "cold war" that John speaks of, a Jewish bloc in Arabia is useful to Persia, because it will naturally oppose the formation of any Christian – i.e. Roman-backed, regime. Hence Dhu-Nuwas' invasion of Arabia Felix, and expulsion of its Aethiopian garrison.' He turned to John. 'I think that's more or less the picture?'

The latter nodding his agreement, the emperor continued, 'I've had a direct appeal, via Timothy the Patriarch of Alexandria, from Ella Atsbeha, the king of Aethiopia – or Negus of Axum, as he styles himself – for help in restoring the status quo ante.' The briefing having now shifted from the sphere of high politics to a straightforward military one, Justin sounded briskly confident. 'What I propose is this: that a Roman army be sent to Aethiopia, there to join forces with the Negus' troops in a great expedition to recover Arabia Felix.' The emperor turned to Justinian and smiled. 'The post of *Magister Militum per Orientem* – Commander of the Army of the East – can become vacant, if you wish to fill it.* How does the idea of taking over, with a view to spearheading the Roman side of the expedition, appeal to you? Your friend Valerianus here, could be your second-in-command.'

Striving to conceal his alarm, Valerian tried to read his friend's reaction: suprise, then gratification chased each other across Justinian's features. Valerian's heart sank as, after a longish pause, Justinian replied in a slightly awed tone, 'I – I'd be honoured to accept, uncle. What can I say? – except to express my humble gratitude.'

'You've earned it, nephew,' said Justin warmly. 'Without your help, and that of John here, I'd never have managed to run the Roman Empire.'

Undeniably true though Justin's tribute to his nephew was, Valerian reflected, he felt that in accepting command of the eastern army his friend was making a profound mistake. Insofar as he possessed a gift of inspiring devoted loyalty in others, Justinian displayed undoubted leadership. But while he might be a superb administrator, he was, in Valerian's opinion, no man of action – although clearly, from what had just transpired, he saw himself fulfilling such a role. That, Valerian was convinced, was self-deception – a state of mind usually attended by hubris. His friend's experience of soldiering had been purely ceremonial; how would he rise to the challenge of leading an army in remote and no doubt difficult terrain, in

* It was occupied at the time by Hypatius, nephew of Anastasius.

conjunction with semi-savage tribesmen, against an enemy whose power and resources could only be guessed at? During their long friendship, Valerian recalled, there had been pointers indicating a potentially dangerous failure of nerve in moments of crisis on Justinian's part: the incident with Nearchus from their student days, and his reaction, now three years ago, when first he learned that his uncle had been named for emperor. Well, provided not too many unforeseen complications developed, Justinian *might* just carry things off without mishap, Valerian supposed. And besides, he himself would be there at his friend's side, to advise and assist.

Or, it could all go horribly wrong – like Crassus' disastrous Parthian adventure centuries ago. The Roman financier and politician had fancied himself in the role of general, with fatal consequences for himself and for the men he led. However, no purpose would be served, Valerian decided, in telling his friend he should never have accepted the command. That would only be to sow a seed of doubt which could erode his confidence, in circumstances which called for steadfastness of purpose above all else.

Two days after the Roman force reached Gondar, the Negus (*Negusa Nagast za-Ityopya*, King of Kings of Aethiopia, to give him his full title) arrived at the city with part of his army – ten thousand lean, hawk-nosed warriors, armed with spears and swords, and carrying rawhide shields. A formal meeting then took place between the Roman leaders and the Negus and his entourage. The Negus, Ella Atsbeha, was, thought Valerian, an impressive figure – a tall young man with aquiline features and an air of natural dignity, which alone marked him out from his retinue. His clothing, a robe not unlike an old-fashioned Roman toga (a garment now only worn by senators), was, save for a broad red stripe along the border, identical to theirs. Justinian, arrayed in the full panoply of a Roman general with muscle cuirass and bronze-studded *pteruges*,* greeted the king graciously, assuring him (through interpreters) that, as a Friend of Rome, he could count on the Empire's help in restoring Arabia Felix to Aethiopian rule. His friend seemed in his element, Valerian noted approvingly: gracious, cordial, almost regal in deportment, he was clearly creating a most favourable impression on the king and his followers. Perhaps, after all, he had misjudged Justinian and all would be well. So far, his friend's behaviour couldn't be faulted; on the march Justinian

---

* Part of a Roman officer's military outfit, *pteruges* were leather strips protecting the thighs and upper arms. They are clearly depicted in statues and carvings of Roman emperors from Augustus to Justinian.

had projected a persona of calm composure, being invariably friendly, cheerful, and considerate towards the troops, who clearly adored him – a seeming second Caesar, another Alexander. But then, Valerian reflected, he hadn't yet been tested.

That, however, was something that was set to change. For that very evening, news arrived that would put in jeopardy the whole expedition.

EIGHT

He [Justin] purported that the Ethiopians by purchasing [Chinese] silk
from India and selling it among the Romans, might themselves gain . . .
while causing the Romans no longer [to] be compelled to pay over their
money to their [Persian] enemy
Procopius, *History of the Wars of Justinian*, after 552

On the night of his arrival in Gondar, the Negus – Ella Atsbeha – gave
orders for a great feast to be prepared to welcome his Roman allies. Justinian and Valerian, together with a dozen of their senior officers (*tribuni* and
their seconds-in-command, *vicarii*) were ushered into a great hall, part
of the governor's palace, down the centre of which was a long, low table,
flanked by cushioned stools. When all the guests were seated (Romans
paired with Aethiopian commanders clad in their toga-like *shambas*), the
Negus rose and raised a goblet of *tej* – fermented honey and barley – and
(via an interpreter, one of which stood behind each pair of guests) proposed
a toast, 'to Rome and Aethiopia – brothers-in-arms in Christ'. When all
had resumed their seats after downing the sweet, fiery liquor, appetisers
were served: curries from India, and delicious savoury balls (powdered locusts bound with fat, Valerian discovered after making enquiry), washed
down with more *tej*.

An atmosphere of noisy cordiality soon prevailed, Valerian discovering
that his hosts were surprisingly well-informed as to world affairs: relations
between Rome and Persia; the German kingdoms which had taken over
the lands of the old West Roman Empire; the religious divide between
the Chalcedonians and the Monophysites; trade with China and the Indies. Then, to the accompaniment of agonized bellowing from outside, the
speciality of the meal arrived: platefuls of raw red beef. His gorge rising,
Valerian gazed in horror at the bleeding chunk of flesh before him, realizing that it had just been cut from a *living* animal! '*Brundo* – it's delicious,'
the Aethiopian to Valerian's right informed him. 'A special treat, in honour
of our Roman guests.' With a forced smile, Valerian hacked off a sliver of
the steaming meat and began manfully to chew it. Noticing that, in the
next but one place, Justinian, white-faced and immobile, was staring at

his plate, Valerian hissed, 'For God's sake try to eat it – some, at least. Otherwise, you'll give offence.'

Justinian turned an anguished face to his friend. 'I can't, Valerian,' he whispered. 'It's just not possible; I'll be sick.'

Banishing the atmosphere of friendly jollity, a stony silence was spreading down the table as Justinian's reluctance began to be observed. Cursing the other's *fastidium*, Valerian tried to make excuses on his friend's behalf, uttering some impromptu nonsense about uncooked meat being against Justinian's strict religious observance. A small roast guinea-fowl was exchanged for the offending plate of *brundo*, and the feast continued – but in an ambience of cool and stiff politeness.

Then all tension was overshadowed by an event of greater consequence. A travel-stained messenger suddenly burst into the chamber and, hurrying over to the Negus, whispered in his ear. The young king rose, his expression grave. 'Roman friends, fellow Aethiopians – the news is bad. One of Dhu-Nuwas' generals has crossed the straits and, backed by our traditional enemies the Galla, has seized our great fortress of Magdala. Our route to the coast is therefore blocked.'

Whether resulting from his shortcoming at the feast, or apprehension regarding the news concerning Magdala, Justinian's facade was beginning to crack, Valerian opined. Before Gondar, his friend's mood had been positive and optimistic (sometimes verging on the manic). After leaving the city, he became silent and withdrawn, his contact with the troops now limited to necessary orders relayed through subordinates. It was as though he had awakened from a dream into a reality both alien and frightening. More and more the burden of everyday supervision of the Roman column fell on Valerian's shoulders, to the latter's disquiet and increasing irritation.

Swelling by the day as more and more warriors streamed in from outlying settlements, the united force pushed on to Lake Tana – a beautiful sheet of shimmering blue pocked by surfacing hippopotami, and fringed by stands of noble trees and flower-studded meadows filled with grazing herds of antelope and buffalo. Here, the expedition turned east, following the river Abai* past a stupendous arc of falls called Tisisat, to its junction with the river Bechelo. Following the latter, the force wound upwards through high wooded hills to a bare plateau broken by cliffs and ravines, the Bechelo here running through a rocky gorge. In this stony

* The Blue Nile.

wilderness, the only sign of life consisted of large, aggressive monkeys with dog-like snouts,* which chattered angrily at the human intruders, their 'sentries' flashing up top lips to reveal rows of vicious fangs. Storm clouds now rolled up from the south, and the expedition found itself pushing on through squalls of hail and icy rain. Then, as suddenly as they had darkened, the skies cleared, revealing to the cold and sodden troops an arresting prospect: rising steeply from the tableland ahead, a series of dramatic, flat-topped heights, and beyond them in the distance a monstrous, towering cylinder of naked rock, crowned by the ramparts of a mighty fortress.

'Magdala,' declared the Negus to Valerian. The pair, who had ridden out ahead of the army, had formed a close bond in the course of the march. Intelligent and well-informed, Ella Atsbeha, in addition to his native Amharic, spoke several languages: Gez, the ancient aboriginal tongue with links to Arabic, now virtually a literary language used mainly by the clergy; Arabic itself; even a little Greek. Daily conversation with Valerian had improved his fluency in the last-named, to the extent that he could now dispense with an interpreter.

'Impossible!' breathed Justinian, riding up to join the pair. 'That place has to be impregnable. Only a lengthy siege could hope to bring about its capture.'

'It can and must be taken, sir,' rapped back Ella Atsbeha, whose relationship with Justinian, in contrast to his friendliness towards Valerian, had become notably cool since leaving Gondar. (The cause, thought Valerian, had more to do with impatience on the Negus' part towards Justinian's mood of passive introspection, than over any slight he may have felt regarding the latter's conduct at the feast.) 'Magdala has enough reserves of food and water to last for many months. Were we to spend time investing it, Dhu-Nuwas, with Persian backing no doubt, would secure his grip on Arabia Felix. Permanently.'

'I don't suppose we could just bypass the place for the nonce,' suggested Valerian tentatively. 'Sort out Dhu-Nuwas first, then deal with Magdala later?'

The Negus shook his head. 'That would be to invite disaster. You don't know the Galla, my friend.' He gave a rueful smile. 'A southern tribe of unreconstructed savages, they're my subjects – officially. But they've never wholly accepted Aethiopian rule, or for that matter, Christianity. With

---

* Could these Gelada baboons be the origin of the legend of the 'dog-faced men' – a belief that stubbornly persisted throughout the Middle Ages?

our army absent in Arabia, the Galla, like angry locusts, would swarm out from Magdala, also from their homeland in the south, and devastate the land with fire and slaughter.'

'I see,' rejoined Valerian. 'Then our only option is to take the place by assault.'

'But even if that were to succeed,' put in Justinian, 'and it seems to me a very big "if", the casualties would surely be horrendous.'

'Not necessarily,' objected Ella Atsbeha. 'You Romans have brought engines with you – capable, you say, of breaching the most powerful defences. Below the rock on which the fortress stands is a plain called Islamgee. If you could site your engines there . . .?' He looked enquiringly at the two Romans.

'A good point, Your Majesty,' Valerian responded. 'I was wondering myself how best to deploy our catapults. All right, suppose we manage to batter down the gates, or knock a hole in the curtain wall; what then? From here, the rock looks unclimbable.'

'Not so. There *is* a path, steep and narrow certainly, but not an impossible approach for an attacking force, provided it is well-armed and determined. That said, getting in is bound to be a costly business. Something we just have to accept, I'm afraid.'

'The loss of life will be appalling, if we go ahead with this crazy plan of storming Magdala!' Justinian protested to Valerian over dinner in their tent that night. 'Anyway, it's almost bound to fail. We ought to call the whole thing off, and besiege the place instead.'

Something seemed to snap inside Valerian. 'For God's sake, Petrus, stop being so negative!' he heard himself shout, unconsciously reverting to his friend's old name. 'If you'd been listening to what the Negus said, you'd know a siege was off. *You're* supposed to be in charge, not me,' he went on, weeks of pent-up resentment at the other's inaction spilling out like a lanced boil. 'I'm tired of taking responsibility for everything, of carrying you, in fact. Call yourself a Roman! Since Gondar, you've been worse than useless. It's high time you started pulling your weight.'

Justinian stared at Valerian, taken aback by his outburst. Then, as the significance of the latter's words registered, loosing the cords of inhibition that had been holding him in thrall, he shook his head as if to clear it. As with Paul on the road to Damascus, the scales seemed to drop from his eyes, enabling him suddenly to see his recent behaviour objectively. 'You're right, old friend,' he acknowledged quietly. 'Thanks for that – I needed putting straight.' He grinned sheepishly. 'Tomorrow, what say we recce Islamgee and decide where to site those catapults. All right?'

'All right,' replied Valerian with a smile, gripping the other's proferred hand. 'And – welcome back.'

The great machines – till this moment mere strangely shaped and innocent-looking pieces of timber and metal transported in sections by muleback or on carts – were duly being assembled on the plain of Islamagee, facing that titanic pillar, the rock of Magdala. Carrying out the task under Valerian's supervision was a team of engineers, who had, despite frequent squalls of driving rain, been working steadily since dawn. Behind the engineers and to one side stood a small force of Roman cavalry and native spearmen, commanded by Justinian with an Aethiopian officer as his second. This was more of a routine precaution than anything else; vastly outnumbered by the expedition's strength, Magdala's garrison was hardly in a position to sally forth and offer battle.

Justinian was almost happy. On coming to himself following the exchange with Valerian, he had experienced a hot flush of salutary shame which had left him feeling purged, his outlook once more positive. An image of himself, long-cherished, as a *real* soldier in charge of men in a combat situation, was now being realized, he told himself with quiet satisfaction. Even the weather, gusty with icy showers, was something to be relished; indifference to physical discomfort was the mark of a true soldier.

The task of creating a breach fell to the aptly named *onagri* – 'kicking asses'. Each *onager* consisted of a long beam powered by the torsion of twisted sinews in a frame, and faced by a padded retaining bar to absorb the shock when the arm was released by a trigger mechanism. Attached to the end of the arm was a sling to carry the missile – a large ball of stone or iron. Delivered with terrific force, these projectiles were capable, by a series of repeated hits, of smashing through stout wooden gates, or, given time, reducing stone walls to rubble. The other type of artillery was the *ballista* – for killing men. A cord connecting two torsion-powered arms mounted in a frame was cranked back by a ratchet device. When released by a catch, it would hurl a bolt (resting in a wooden trough) whose impact could skewer several bodies at the same time, or punch through shields or armour like a nail through putty.

Though no doubt warned by their Jewish allies (to those below, dis-tinguishable from the tribesmen by their helmets and pale faces) of the destructive potential of the Roman catapults, the Galla – jeering and catcalling from the ramparts, seemed more amused than intimidated by the operations of the engineers, as they slowly pieced the great machines together.

'When you're ready, *ducenarius*.' Valerian nodded to the sergeant in charge of *Onager Primus*.

With six artillerymen bending to the winding levers, the ratchet clanked, bringing *Onager* Number One's throwing arm back to its loading cradle, when a heavy iron ball was placed in the sling.

'*Jacite!*'* ordered the *ducenarius*. The release catch was thrown and the arm flew forward, slamming against the retaining bar and sending the missile whirring through the air in an arcing trajectory. The ball struck the breastwork above the gatehouse tower, sending up a spray of stone chips. A cheer arose from the catapult crew.

'Good shooting,' called Valerian. 'Fire at will.'

'Down one,' ordered the *ducenarius*; this time the crew counted one less click of the ratchet before loading. The missile smashed against the wood-work of the gate itself. As if suddenly realizing the very real threat posed by the catapults, the Galla on the battlements fell silent. Soon, all four *onagri* were in action, inflicting visible damage on the gate and its flanking towers, while volleys of bolts from the *ballistae* forced the enemy to keep their heads below the ramparts. Watching from his station, Justinian wondered just how long the entry to the fortress could sustain such unrelenting punishment.

Without warning, a sudden burst of heavy rain swept across Islamgee, instantly blotting out all vision beyond a few yards. Having found the range, however, the engineers continued their bombardment uninterrupted.

Then, as quickly as it had commenced, the rain cleared – revealing to Justinian an appalling sight. A large party of Galla (who must have descended the path from the fortress to the base of Magdala, under cover of the squall) was charging towards the catapults! Justinian stared in horror at the rapidly advancing mass of warriors – immensely tall men with pitch-black skins, and beardless faces surmounted by monstrous globes of fuzzy hair, their delicate, almost effeminate features contorted with battle frenzy, vicious-looking spears poised to strike. He opened his mouth to give the order to charge – but no sound came. He was aware that instant action was imperative, but seemed frozen in the saddle.

* Shoot. Orders in the East Roman army were still being given in Latin.

'*Ras!*'* exclaimed his second-in-command, turning to him with a desperate expression. The urgency in the man's cry jolted Justinian out of his immobility; turning to his men, he shouted, 'Charge!'

The Roman cavalry, the Aethiopians racing at their side, swept down on the Galla; but too late – just – to save the engineers, who perished to a man, skewered by those terrible spears. Justinian saw Valerian go down, a reddened blade projecting a hand's-breadth from his back. Then the horsemen were among the Galla, cutting them down with lethal swipes of their long *spathae*. The encounter was brief and bloody. Despite displaying ferocious courage, the Galla – incapable through temperament and tradition of presenting a defensive ring of spears against the cavalry, the only tactic that might have proved effective – fell by scores, before suddenly turning and retreating pell-mell back to the citadel.

In an agony of grief and self-recrimination, Justinian, in conjunction with the Negus and both their senior officers, now threw himself into organizing the assault. The Galla in their sortie had not had time to damage or destroy the catapults; fresh teams of engineers resumed the bombardment, and by noon the main gate had been battered down. After bitter hand-to-hand fighting, a storming-party then managed to clear the entrance long enough for a large contingent from the expedition to gain access to the fortress. As was usual in such circumstances, no quarter was shown to the defenders, who were hunted down and killed like rats.

After the fall of Magdala, the remainder of the campaign came almost as an anti-climax. Without further incident, the expedition proceeded to the coast, where waiting Roman transports conveyed it across the straits to Arabia Felix. Dhu-Nuwas and his army were duly brought to battle and decisively routed, the Himyarite leader being killed in the fighting. With Aethiopian rule and Christianity restored to the Sabaeans, the Negus and his warriors returned to Africa, and Justinian – victorious but sick in soul – sailed back with the Romans to Constantinople.

* Lord.

NINE

They [Theodora and Justimian] set free from a licentiousness fit only for slaves
the women who were struggling with extreme poverty, providing them with
*independent maintenance and setting virtue free**

Procopius, *On Buildings*, c. 550

'Benedico vos in nomine Patris et Filii et Spiritus Sancti,' intoned Epiphanius, Patriarch of Constantinople, at the conclusion of the marriage service in the great Church of the Holy Wisdom, adorned by splendid mosaics and myriad statues of emperors and saints, with windows glazed by plates of translucent marble. Justinian and Theodora were then given the sacrament of Christ's body, followed by that of His blood in a silver spoon. The veil held over the pair was now exchanged for nuptial crowns, and hand in hand, they walked slowly down the thronged nave, past courtiers, senators, patricians, officers of the Excubitors and Scholae, ministers and civil servants – all splendidly arrayed in parade uniforms or long silk robes. Peering down excitedly from the gallery, among the assembled ladies-in-waiting, maids of honour, and wives and daughters of the dignitaries in the nave below, were Theodora's mother, and her sisters Comito and Anastasia.

Emerging from the church into the Augusteum, Justinian and Theodora showed themselves to the vast and enthusiastic crowd waiting in the great square. Only among the upper classes, following the wedded pair in procession, were murmurings of disapproval heard: '. . . He's not one of us, that's for sure . . . a pair of upstarts . . . He's got barbarian ancestors, I've heard, and she used to be an actress – an *actress*! Justin had to change the law forbidding stage performers from marrying people of higher rank . . . the wedding had to be postponed, you know, until the old Empress Euphemia died; *she* wasn't going to countenance that common little tart succeeding to the throne . . . and did you see her mother and sisters in the gallery, dressed up to the nines in those *ghastly* outfits, fancying themselves as good as senators' wives? I hear that Comito, the eldest daughter is to marry a *general*; whatever next – patricians' daughters marrying charioteers . . . ?'

* Procopius is here referring to ex-prostitutes rehabilitated in the Convent of Repentance, following the ban against brothel-keepers..

Theodora's heart swelled with pride as the crowd began to cheer. Eat your heart out, Hecebolus, she thought, and you Greens who taunted my family and me when we appealed to you for help in the Hippodrome all those years ago, and you narrow-minded snobs among the aristocracy and, worst of all, among the nouveaux riches, who'd looked down on me because I trod the boards. From being regarded as the lowest of the low I'm now above the lot of you, married to one destined to become the ruler of New Rome, the most powerful man in the world. Fondly, she glanced at the tall, handsome figure to her right: this kind, brilliant, sensitive, ambitious, *vulnerable* man – whom she'd mended and made whole, and who would never come to harm as long as she was by his side. She remembered their first meeting, a year ago . . .

Following her return to the capital from Antioch, Theodora invested some of the money Timothy had given her into renting a property in Region VIII near the Julian Harbour – an area populated by small craftsmen, where in consequence the rents were not too high. Above the living quarters of the house was a large, well-lit garret, which (consulting Macedonia's business plan) she set about converting into a workshop for spinning wool. Bypassing middlemen, she contacted (from a list again supplied by Macedonia) various suppliers from whom she obtained stocks of fine quality wool grown by sheep-farmers in the high central plateaux of Anatolia. Next, following a cause close to her heart, she recruited out-of-work actresses as workers in her business. As she knew from bitter personal experience, they might otherwise be tempted into prostitution to make ends meet. With experienced spinners hired to train her workers, Theodora's business flourished, as clothiers, soon recognizing the quality of her product, competed to buy her yarns.

She longed to offer employment to girls forced to work in brothels, but accepted, sadly, that this was something beyond her present power to achieve. The plight of such females was wretched, amounting to virtual slavery. With the hope of enlisting a powerful ally in tackling this evil, she decided to approach Petrus Sabbatius (renamed Justinian on his becoming consul, she discovered), to whom she had a letter of introduction provided by Macedonia. His impressive list of titles suggested a man of standing and importance who might, she thought, be able to help provided she could win him round. Her hopes were further raised when she learned that this Justinian was none other than the nephew of the emperor.

Presenting herself at the Chalke or 'Brazen House' from its great bronze doors – the grand entrance vestibule of the imperial palace – she produced her letter of introduction. 'You'll be lucky,' grunted the porter after briefly scanning the document. 'His *Nobilissimus* ain't receiving visitors these days – not since he got back from Arabia. Suppose there's no harm in trying, though. Ask at the *Magnaura* – that's the main audience hall.'

Entering the sprawling collection of buildings and gardens connected by porticoed walkways, Theodora, with some difficulty, eventually tracked down the *Magnaura*. The *silentiarius* on duty in the corridor outside, studied the letter then shook his head. 'I'm afraid you've had a journey for nothing,' he declared in tones of polite regret. 'The Count of the Domestics – His Most Noble, the Patrician – is unable to see anyone at present.'

'Oh, please,' Theodora entreated, assuming her most winning smile, 'it's about something that's very important to me. He may be the only person who can help, I think.' Feeling in her purse for an obol piece with which to tip the man, she remembered, just in time, that these were *gentlemen* ushers, who would be greatly offended if offered a gratuity. Something of the charm and force of personality that had so affected Timothy seemed to penetrate the armour of the usher – member of a tribe of past masters in the art of administering courteous rebuffs.

'Wait here,' he said with a wry grin, shaking his head. 'God knows why I'm doing this.' And he set off down the corridor. Returning after a few minutes he declared, 'The Patrician will see you now,' and conducted her along a maze of passages to a porchway opening onto a small colonnaded garden. Chin resting on his hands, a solitary figure sat beside a fountain.

'Theodora – the protégée of Macedonia of Antioch, Patricius,' announced the usher, and withdrew.

The seated figure rose and smiled at Theodora, who was immediately struck by several things about him: tall and good-looking, the man had a quiet presence; his affable expression suggested a kind and gracious personality; but dark shadows beneath the eyes, and lines around the mouth, hinted at some secret and deeply troubling worry.

'Macedonia – a charming lady, as I recall,' the man said, his voice low and pleasant, yet with a note of underlying sadness. 'One of our chief suppliers of olive oil and wines. I would gladly be of service to one who is her friend.'

Theodora explained how, with help from Macedonia's business plan, she had started her wool-spinning project and staffed it with unemployed actresses, thus saving them from having to sell their bodies to make ends meet. 'But what I have really set my heart on, Patricius,' she went on (copying the form of address the *silentiarius* had used), 'is to do something to help those whose only livelihood is prostitution.'

'I don't wish to appear hard-hearted,' said the other gently, 'but if that is what they choose to do, why should they be helped? Though Augustine might disagree, God, as Pelagius points out, has given us all free will to make our own decisions.'

'But Patricius,' declared Theodora passionately, 'the girls who work in brothels are *not* there from choice! Let me explain. Prostitution is big business, providing for a certain loathsome type of parasite a chance to make a quick and easy living. These pimps travel round the provinces, persuading poor families to part with their daughters for a few gold coins – a fortune to penurious *coloni*,* often saddled with crippling debt. The inducement offered never varies: a promise of a better life for the girl in Constantinople or some other big city, working as a governess or maid or such like, to some wealthy aristocrat. Once they arrive at their destination however, a cruel surprise awaits the poor, duped girls. Sold on by the pimps to brothel-owners, they are asked to sign a contract; of course they've no idea what they're letting themselves in for, thus legally binding themselves over to a life of prostitution. No fine clothes or rich food, no light domestic work plus a good salary with which to augment their parents' income. Only a wretched and degrading form of slavery, from which the only escape is to become too old or worn-out to be of further use to their master – when they're thrown out onto the street to fend for themselves'

'That's appalling!' the Patricius exclaimed, appearing genuinely shocked. 'I confess I'd no idea such a thing went on. Thank you, Theodora, for bringing it to my attention. Be assured, I'll speak about this to my uncle. Between us, with the help of one Procopius – a brilliant young lawyer who has done good work for us – we will make a beginning: draft measures which, hopefully, will eventually become legislation.'

'That's wonderful!' declared Theodora, hardly able to believe that her appeal had produced such an immediate and positive response. 'Dare I ask, Patricius – how long?'

'Unfortunately, Theodora, such things take time. From what you say, the practice would seem deep-rooted and widespread, involving ruthless men with vested interests. But imperial decrees have cracked tougher nuts before. Have no fear that something will be done – just as soon as we can get the wheels of law to turn. Come to me next week – same day, same time – and I'll tell you what we've managed to do.'

* Tenant farmers/peasants.

Delighted to have made such progress, Theodora left the palace (Region I) and returned to her workshop in Region VIII. In the course of the short journey, she recalled something which caused her heart to lift. On parting from the patrician, she had noted that the signs of worry on his face appeared to have lifted somewhat. Her imagination? Or the result of her having provided him with a positive interest to help take him out of himself? That it was an altruistic cause he had taken up convinced her that she was dealing with a good and conscientious man, who would back his words with action.

During the next few weeks, Theodora had regular meetings with the patrician. At first, their discussions were confined to juridical details regarding the legal status of prostitutes. But over time, discovering a mutual interest in theology and certain aspects of philosophy as they impinged on law, these topics were included in debate. When Theodora (thanks to her voracious reading in Timothy's library in Alexandria) was able to quote Isocrates* in the latter context, Justinian was visibly impressed, and took to consulting her opinion on various matters on a regular basis.

This enabled Theodora to put in a good word for the Monophysites. 'The people of Syria and Egypt are your loyal subjects, Patricius,' she pleaded, 'who wish only to be allowed to worship in their own way. By continuing to persecute them, you run the risk of alienating half the Empire. I ask you – is it worth it? And is it right that brilliant minds like Timothy and Severus, good men and ornaments of Rome, should be made to suffer for their faith?'

'You're fast becoming a Seneca to my Nero,' replied the Patricius with a smile. 'Hopefully the *young* Nero – before power went to his head. As always, Theodora, your words give food for thought. You have a point; I daresay in our concern for uniformity my uncle and I may have erred on the side of being overzealous. I'll mull over what you've said.'

Without either being consciously aware that such a thing was happening, a deep friendship began to form between the two – something at last openly acknowledged when the patrician invited her to call him by his name, Justinianus. So it seemed entirely natural and unobtrusive when, one day (during a bout of the depression which visited him periodically), she found herself asking, as a concerned friend would, if anything was troubling him.

* A brilliant orator and rhetorician, Isocrates, 436–338 BC, devoted his talents to producing written models on how to win legal cases. (See Notes.)

Justinian looked up, his face a mask of misery. 'I'm glad you asked me that,' he said. 'For far too long I've kept my tribulation to myself. But you, I think, alone of everyone I know, will understand – even perhaps be able to offer me advice.' He paused, then went on in a whisper, 'I'm cursed, you see, Theodora. It seems I have the gift of inspiring others to wish to follow me; a fatal gift, I fear, like that vouchsafed to Midas. Only with me, it's not myself I harm, but others.' It all came out then, as though gushing from some deep well of sorrow and regret: the deaths of Atawulf and Valerian, the duel with Nearchus in his student days, his near-fatal hesitation before recommending Roderic for emperor to the Senate. In each case, cowardly irresolution on his part had prevented or nearly prevented him from acting, leaving his conscience permanently scarred.

'In my dreams I still see that helmet on the cliff!' he cried, ' – still hear Atawulf's despairing calls for help, still see my dearest friend Valerian spitted by a Galla spear, still feel the blow I inflicted on myself in the Cistern of Nomus. Look – I yet bear the mark!' And he pointed to a faint, star-shaped scar on his forehead. 'The truth is, Theodora, I'm bad for those I allow to become close to me.' He shot Theodora an anguished glance. 'I'll probably turn out to be bad for you as well – something I would not have happen for the world. Perhaps it's best we don't see each other any more.'

Instinctively, Theodora rushed over to him, took him in her arms. She felt an overwhelming surge of pity and affection. 'Oh, my dear,' she murmured, cradling his head against her breast, 'there's nothing wrong with you that can't be put right. I think I understand what the root of your problem is. In the past, you've seen yourself – as many Romans think they *ought* to see themselves – as a man of Mars: strong, courageous, displaying active leadership. But perhaps you're not a man of action,' she continued gently. 'And there's no shame in admitting that. Inspiring and directing men need not consist in leading from the front. Let others do that for you. Don't you think that that's where your true genius may lie, Justinian – in choosing the right men to carry out your plans?'

'Perhaps you're right,' breathed the other, wonderingly. He paused, then went on, 'Yes – I believe you *are* right. Why could I not have seen that for myself?'

'Sometimes it takes another to see in us what we can't ourselves perceive. Isn't there a verse in Scripture somewhere about motes and beams?'

'"Why beholdest thou the mote that is in thy brother's eye, but perceivest not the beam that is in thine own eye?"' quoted Justinian with a smile. 'Luke 6, verse 41.'

From that moment Justinian's mind began to heal. Freed from the burden of past guilt, he began to form plans – schemes that suddenly now blossomed (from what had previously been vague aspirations) into designs for ambitious projects. As though it were the most natural thing in the world, he found himself eagerly discussing these with Theodora: reform of Roman Law; great buildings which would incorporate exciting new design ideas, enabling, for example, the construction of stupendous domes of a size never before conceived; and – something he had hardly yet dared to think about, so mind-blowing in its boldness was the concept – the recovery of the Western Empire from the barbarians who had over-run it. 'Together, we shall make Rome greater than she's ever been before,' he enthused.

'Together?' Theodora smiled indulgently. 'You flatter me, Justinian. You make us sound like partners.'

A silence followed, a silence in which both came to realize that an invisible boundary had somehow been crossed. 'We *could* be partners, Theodora,' Justinian said at last. 'In every way.' He smiled gravely. 'I'm hopelessly in love with you, you know – something I've never felt before for any woman. Theodora – I'm asking if you'll marry me.'

Theodora's mind reeled as she tried to analyze her reactions. She liked Justinian enormously, and, as a result of helping to restore him to himself, felt (mingled with a Pygmalion-like concern for her 'creation') a fierce protectiveness towards him that was almost maternal in its tenderness. But did this amount to love? She thought perhaps it did – a kind of loving, anyway. But, admittedly, as different from the love she had for Macedonia as a quiet stream is from a raging flood. To become the wife of Justinian! – that opened up unimagined possibilities. After Hecebolus, she had promised herself that never again would she become dependent on a man. But to the spouse of the emperor-designate that condition scarcely applied. She herself would hold patrician rank, and thus be entitled to a palace and income of her own, in perpetuity. However, since Macedonia had shown Theodora her true nature to herself, would she not be living a lie if she married? Whatever she decided, nothing would be gained, she told herself, by being anything but honest with this fine, good man.

And there were considerations beyond the strictly personal to be taken into account – factors which seemed to tilt the scales in favour of accepting Justinian's proposal. Her efforts to alleviate the plight of prostitutes would be immeasurably strengthened. Why limit that to prostitutes? The status of all women throughout the Roman world was circumscribed by laws which favoured men. As Justinian's consort, she would be in a position to change that for the better. Then there was her family – her two sisters and her mother; at a stroke, their lives could be lifted out of poverty into security and comfort. And what about the Monophysites, especially her dear friends Timothy and Severus, at present suffering under unjust persecution? She had made a good beginning there, in getting Justinian to see the benefits of toleration. But think how much more she could achieve, as his wife.

'May I dare to hope?' asked Justinian softly, with a gentle smile.

'I must be frank with you, my dear,' replied Theodora, taking him by the hand and looking fondly into his face. 'I cannot love you in the way that is usual between a woman and a man, for such is not my nature. But I love you, or at least I think I do, in the sense that Plato means when he says, "The true lover loves the beauty of the soul rather than the beauty of the body". If you can accept me on those terms, Justinian, then I will gladly marry you.'

Was it relief that she saw in his eyes – relief that was more than the joy of the accepted suitor, hinting that his love for her was of the same kind that she felt for him? If so, theirs should be a happy union indeed, their kind of love the strongest bond of all – *agapē*, the pure love that blossoms between soul-mates.

During the weeks when she was getting to know Justinian, one incident occurred which marred, momentarily, Theodora's serenity of mood.

Reporting one day for her regular meeting in the palace, she found, instead of Justinian, a smooth and self-possessed young man who introduced himself as, 'Procopius of Caesarea, lawyer, man of letters, and world-citizen.' Today, he explained, Justinian was unable to be present and had asked Procopius to take his place. They were to discuss the business of compensation for brothel-owners, in the event of legislation being passed that would outlaw prostitution.

'I have here a list of samples, taken from every province in the Empire, of the various rates paid for girls by brothel-owners. As you will see when you peruse it, they vary widely. The best solution is to work out a mean rate as the basis for a standard payment, one that will satisfy all brothel-owners.'

At the conclusion of the session (with the task barely half-completed) after tying up his *codices*, Procopius seemed inclined to linger. 'If you're hoping to become his mistress,' he said with a conniving wink, 'then you're in for a long wait. Justinian's a cold fish. He wouldn't be interested, even if you offered it to him on a plate.'

'The thought never occurred to me,' replied Theodora icily. 'You've got a filthy mind, Procopius. I think you'd better go.'

'Come on, don't give me that,' sneered the other. 'I know your sort, Theodora. Proper little prick-teaser, aren't you? Don't imagine I haven't heard that you once trod the boards. Everyone knows that actresses are always ready to turn a trick. Well, let me enlighten you, my dear. You're wasting your time where Justinian's concerned. Instead, why not share my bed? You're quite a looker, I'll give you that. I'd pay good money.'

'You disgust me,' Theodora retorted. 'Just get out.'

'Playing hard to get, are we? Well, I don't mind; it adds a little spice to the proceedings.' And with a lascivious grin, Procopius slid an arm around her waist, and with his free hand gripped her chin.

Reacting instantly, Theodora jerked her head free and bit the offending hand on the fleshy part below the thumb.

'Bitch!' yelled Procopius, whipping his hand away. He stared at a row of tooth-marks in his skin, some already welling blood. 'I'll pay you back for that,'* he snarled, and stormed away.

Following the wedding, the transfer of power from Justin to Justinian – a process whose pace had been steady rather than rapid, began swiftly to accelerate. With the old emperor's health – mental as well as physical – now failing fast, Justinian found himself managing affairs of state virtually alone. Accordingly, eighteen months after his marriage, Justinian was made co-emperor (with Theodora as empress). Then, four months later Justin died,** and was succeeded by his nephew as sole ruler of the Roman world.

Mindful of Theodora's advice, Justinian, having abandoned the idea of leading any project personally, had already (following his instinct, which proved invariably sound) delegated the implementing of his plans to men of his choice. Selected first and foremost for efficiency and loyalty, and (as a matter of priority) *not* from any of the great Roman families who sullenly resented the upstart from Tauresium, they made a formidable team. With a view to consolidating his power, Justinian intended these to be long-term or even permanent appointments (depending of

* Which he duly did – 'in spades', as they say. (See Notes.)
** On 1 August 527.

course on performance), thus breaking with the age-old tradition of very short tenures of office. Among several generals (one of whom, Sittas, was honoured by being allowed to marry Comito, Theodora's elder sister), pre-eminent were two very different men: Belisarius, a dashing young cavalry officer and a veteran (at twenty-one!) of a campaign against the Persians; and a much older man, Narses, a eunuch from Persian Armenia. Slight and frail-looking, a Monophysite – hence attracting Theodora's support, Narses (belying popular beliefs regarding eunuchs) was extremely courageous, honourable, and energetic. With a view to implementing his long-cherished plan of reforming Roman Law, Justinian selected one Tribonian, a lawyer supremely gifted as an organizer and collator. And to carry out his building schemes, he was to choose the brilliant engineer and architect, Anthemius of Tralles. Finally, to streamline and reform the civil service, he appointed one who had already impressed him under Justin – John the Cappadocian.

With the Blues behind him to 'discourage' any who might challenge his authority, Justinian now felt himself the undisputed master of the realm he had inherited. But, unwittingly, in making one of his appointments, he had sown the seed of something that would shake his grip on power and almost bring about his downfall.

PART III

RESTITUTOR ORBIS ROMANI
AD 527–540

TEN

Cappadocians are always bad, worse in office, worst where money is concerned,
and worse than worst when set up in a grand official chariot
Popular saying (quoted against John the Cappadocian),
fifth or sixth century

With confidence renewed, and buoyed up by the support of a loyal and
devoted helpmeet, Justinian contemplated with relish the prospect of
carrying out his Grand Plan – the reconquest of the Western Empire,
and the establishment of religious uniformity throughout his realm.

There were other projects, almost as exciting but perhaps less pressing:
the reform of Roman Law; an accommodation with the Monophysites,
whose erroneous views were based on a simple misunderstanding, which
could surely be resolved in synod by reasoned argument; the amelioration
of women's legal status in general, and that of prostitutes in particular
(both of these causes dear to Theodora's heart); an ambitious building
programme which would truly reflect the glory of what Justinian intended
would prove a glittering new chapter in the history of Rome; diplomatic
missions to the Persians and the barbarians beyond the frontiers, in order
to ensure peace – an essential precondition for the implementing of his
cherished Plan.

For all these projects (especially the reconquest of the West) to become
reality, one thing above all was essential – cash. Unfortunately, the surplus
built up in the Treasury during the reign of the careful Anastasius had become
exhausted under Justin, thanks largely to frequent lapses of the truce with
Persia. This had caused fortifications on a massive scale to be erected along
the eastern frontier – in particular the building of a colossal (and colossally
expensive) fortress at Dara in Mesopotamia. However, Justinian had every
faith that his newly appointed praetorian prefect, John of Cappadocia, could
be depended on to provide a solution . . .

'Never fear, Serenity, I'll get you all the cash you need,' declared the prefect to the emperor, ensconced within the latter's private study in the palace.
'The Empire's wealthy, just needs squeezing in the right places to give you
what you want – like an actress from the Hippodrome.' He chuckled, and

tapped the side of his nose. 'For starters, the civil service is top-heavy with jobsworths holding down sinecures, or operating private rackets and fiddles. Plenty of dead wood there we can clear out, and malpractices we can put a stop to. Then there's the privileged classes – the big landowners, and the wealthy merchants and traders. In the past, they've got away with evading taxes by knowing just how to fiddle the books. Consequently, it's always been the peasants and the urban poor who've had to shoulder an unfair proportion of the tax burden. Time we put an end to that, wouldn't you say, Serenity? Unlike prefects in the past, I'm not afraid to take on the toffs. In fact I'll enjoy it – squeeze 'em till the pips squeak. I'm guessing you won't mind too much either, Serenity.' And he gave a conspiratorial wink.

What the prefect was saying, Justinian knew, was that both of them, as parvenus looked down on by their social superiors, would relish any opportunity to even the score. The man was taking an outrageous liberty, thought the emperor indignantly, but no doubt secure in the knowledge that he was indispensable to Justinian's plans, felt that he could exploit his position with impunity.

'I'll put the points you've raised to the Senate and the Council,' responded Justinian, swallowing his irritation. 'I don't suppose they'll find anything to disagree with.'

'Who the hell cares if they do?' chuckled the other. He belched, eased his gross bulk on its stool, and scratched his bottom. 'That's better,' he went on, with a sigh of satisfaction. 'Wake up, Serenity. The Senate and the Council? – redundant anachronisms, whose only purpose is to allow the aristocracy to hang on to the comforting illusion that they need to be consulted. They've no longer any place in the running of a modern Empire. The only power that matters is held by you, the emperor. Best you tell 'em that and end the current farce of discussions in the House.'

John was right, thought Justinian, as a tremendously exciting and liberating conviction slowly began to form in his mind. Could it be by mere chance that a barbarian lad from the backwoods of Dardania had become emperor of New Rome? Surely something so unprecedented, so astonishing, could only be evidence of divine intention? – as it must also have been God's purpose, to send him Theodora in his hour of need.

Elated and enthused by this sudden revelation, Justinian dismissed the prefect with instructions to implement with all speed the measures he had proposed. Then he sent word, via his Master of Offices, to all senators and councillors presently residing in the capital or its vicinity, to attend him in the *Magnaura* three days hence.

'It's outrageous!' quavered old Methodius, the *Caput Senatus*, as the senators and councillors filed out of the audience chamber. 'He hasn't even the decency to tell us in the Senate House that we're surplus to requirements.'

'Jumped-up nobody,' declared a councillor. 'Anastasius, or even Zeno – that hick from Isauria – would never have behaved like that.'

'Just who does he think he is?' stormed a silver-haired senator. 'Presuming he can run the Empire without consulting us – the people's representatives. So much for S.P.Q.R.* Let's face it, gentlemen – it seems we're now to live under a totalitarian autocracy.'

'Tyranny, more like,' put in another senator, adding darkly, 'A pity those nephews of Anastasius – Hypatius, Probus, and Pompeius – were passed over as possible successors. Any one of them would be ten times better than Justinian. At least he'd have been one of us.'

Another influential faction to be bitterly offended when Justinian ended his association with its members was the Blues. 'Thinks just because he's on the throne, he can chuck us aside like an old shoe,' complained the manager of the Blues to his inner circle of henchmen. 'He's conveniently forgetting it was us who helped to put him there. Well, boys, two can play at that game. We can make it hot for him in the Hippodrome – very hot indeed. Come the racing season, what say we do just that? Agreed?'

'Agreed!' the others roared in unison.

In furtherance of achieving his goal of religious uniformity, Justinian began a dialogue with the Monophysites. True to his promise to Theodora, the persecution of the sect was relaxed, exiles permitted to return, and Monophysite leaders, especially Timothy and Severus, invited to attend a religious conference in the capital, to be chaired by Justinian himself. By the conclusion of the synod, a face-saving formula (carefully avoiding the expression 'two natures', and emphasizing the 'one person' of the Trinity) had been cobbled together, with which Justinian declared himself satisfied. More fudge than solution, its chief effect was to enrage the leaders of Orthodox Catholicism (the Empire's official creed), who saw it as a shameful giving in to heretics.

Also dismayed and outraged as a result of the emperor's religious policy were intellectuals throughout the Empire (collectively, a powerful group capable of influencing public opinion), when (the sale of its assets providing a welcome bonus to the Treasury), the ancient University of

---

* *Senatus Populusque Romanus* – the Senate and People of Rome.

Athens was closed.* Because the institution contained the famous Academy – where Plato and Aristotle had once held court – it was seen by Justinian as a bastion of pagan thought. Its two leading professors, Damascius and Simplicius, along with five of their colleagues, thereupon accepted an invitation from the Peacock Throne to come and teach in Persia. Their acceptance constituted a massive and humiliating snub, not only to Justinian himself, but to the whole Roman Empire whose supposedly enlightened values he was held to represent.

John of Cappadocia, a spiteful man of humble origins, needed no encouragement to set about his task with relish, seeing as a bonus the chance to get even with the upper classes, whose aspersions in the past he had endured with impotent resentment. Arriving one day with his retinue of *compulsores* – thugs whose function was to 'persuade' reluctant citizens to settle their tax dues – at the estate, in the Anatolian province of Galatia, of one Maxentius, a wealthy landowner, John marched into the villa, and confronted the owner partaking of his *prandium* or midday meal.

'What's the meaning of this?' demanded Maxentius, rising, his fine patrician features dark with anger. 'How dare you burst into my house uninvited.'

'Tax defaults sir, I'm afraid,' murmured the prefect in an apologetic-sounding voice. 'You seem to have overlooked declaring some of your assets. An oversight, I'm sure sir. Perhaps you'd care to clear things up?'

'See my steward, if you must,' snapped the other. 'You'll find my tax returns all logged and paid in full.'

'But only for this estate, sir,' persisted John in reasonable tones. He shook his head regretfully. 'You see, we know all about those warehouses in Tarsus, and your . . . "understanding", shall we call it, with the harbourmaster. Very co-operative he proved – after two of his fingers got broken. Nasty accident. All those Chinese silks smuggled in from Persia, those amphorae of olive oil from Crete, wines from Syria . . . Want me to go on, sir?'

'I don't know what you're talking about,' blustered Maxentius, his face suddenly turning pale.

'Tut, tut.' John sucked in his cheeks and wagged an admonitory finger. 'That wasn't very wise, if I may say so, sir.' He nodded to his followers who, removing cudgels from their belts, advanced towards the landowner.

'I'm a *decurion* – a leading citizen!' cried Maxentius. 'You can't touch me – it's against the law.'

* In 529.

'No longer, I'm afraid, sir. Times, they are a-changing. All tax evaders, whatever their rank, are now liable for physical coercion. But only if they prove . . . ah, "unaccommodating", let us say . . .'

Ten minutes later, Maxentius, now with two cracked ribs and bruises purpling his face, signed a list of his undeclared assets with the appropriate amount of tax entered beside each item.

'Collect what's owing from my steward,' mumbled Maxentius between split and swollen lips.

'Thank you, sir. You've really been most helpful.'

In the second year of what could virtually be called their joint reign, Justinian and Theodora received news that Antioch had been devastated by a terrible earthquake. Generous and compassionate by nature, they hastened to disburse from the *Res Privata* and the *Sacrae Largitiones* – the Private and Public Purses – vast amounts of money to rebuild both the stricken city and the lives of its inhabitants. An individual beneficiary from their largesse was Macedonia. 'We must do all we can to help our friend,' Justinian declared to his spouse. 'While her house is being restored and her business rehabilitated, she must come and live in the Imperial Palace.'

Theodora looked forward to the arrival of her former lover with a mixture of delight and trepidation. The deep love she had for Justinian was the steady glow of *agapē* rather than the roaring flames of *eros* which she had experienced with Macedonia. When they met again, would those flames rekindle and consume them both, causing them to consummate a mutual passion? She had never been unfaithful to Justinian, nor had she been tempted in the slightest to form any liaison outwith marriage. So far. But would any resumption of her affair with Macedonia constitute adultery? Probably not – at least in the strict legal sense, she thought.

In Roman Law, the question of adultery only arose when the progeny of a marriage could be shown to be other than the father's by his spouse. So long as legitimate inheritance was not threatened, liaisons outwith marriage, though strongly disapproved of by the Church, could not be held to be adulterous. Even so . . . Theodora made up her mind that she and Macedonia would resume their relationship as dear friends, and nothing more. She would not do anything that might be held to betray Justinian or cause him hurt. Anyway, temptation would be kept at arms's length; the month being July, Theodora was, as usual, residing in her summer palace at Hieron, a small town on the Asiatic side of the Bosphorus.

Assuming that Macedonia would be given the use of a suite in the

Imperial Palace in the capital, Theodora was taken aback when Justinian suggested that Macedonia join Theodora at Hieron. 'You two have years of gossip to catch up on,' he declared with a fond smile. 'Living in the palace on her own, poor Macedonia would soon get bored, despite your no doubt frequent visits.'

Accordingly, after a formal reception for Macedonia followed by a grand dinner at the palace (a tinglingly polite affair), the two women were conveyed by litter and private ferry to Hieron. At last, after Macedonia had been introduced to the household, and the slaves had unpacked her luggage in her suite, she and Theodora found themselves alone – in the luxurious surroundings of the *cubiculum* or bedroom assigned to Macedonia. With the restraints imposed by the presence of others now removed, Theodora suddenly felt at a loss as to how to proceed.

'Is everything to your liking?' she asked her guest hesitantly.

Macedonia did not answer. Instead, she held out her arms and murmured softly, 'Come.'

Her former resolution crumbling in an instant, Theodora flew into Macedonia's embrace. Their mouths locked hungrily; then, with a tender urgency, they removed each other's clothes and gazed in longing at one another's naked bodies.

'It's been a long time, darling,' said Macedonia, her eyes glowing with desire.

'Too long,' whispered Theodora, and traced her fingers across the other's breasts. Shuddering with delight, Macedonia reciprocated the gesture, then, when both were fully aroused, led Theodora to the bed and lay on top of her, reversed, her mouth against her partner's vulva. Theodora gasped in rapture as the other's flickering tongue caressed her clitoris. Engulfed in waves of unimaginable pleasure, she performed the same service on her lover, both climaxing together with cries of ecstasy. Satiated and happy, they lay long in each other's arms exchanging news and kisses, until at last sleep claimed them . . .

Waking before dawn, Theodora slipped out of bed taking care not to wake her sleeping companion. Tormented with guilt, she forewent her usual early morning routine (breakfast in bed, bathing, making up her face and doing her hair with the help of several maids, dressing, choosing jewellery) and, clad in a simple tunic over which she threw a cloak, slipped out of the palace undetected and made her way to Hieron's quayside. Here, she hired a boatman to ferry her across the Bosphorus to the Harbour of Phosphorion on the Golden Horn.

Last night had been a moment of madness, she told herself – wonderful, delicious madness; but it must not be repeated. She could not live with herself, she thought, unless she made a clean breast of her affair with Macedonia to Justinian. A keystone of their marriage had always been complete honesty. Surely he would understand and forgive, especially as sex had never been an important aspect of their relationship. On the other hand it was conceivable he might be outraged, even seek to divorce her. It was a risk she felt she had to take.

Entering the city via St Barbara's Gate just as it was opening, she threaded the narrow lanes of the Fourth Region – already stirring into life as metal-workers, blacksmiths, carpenters and other craftsmen began to ply their trades, everywhere the clink of tools sounding from their workshops. Traversing the wide spaces of Region V with its granaries and oil stores, and the mouth-watering smell of new-baked bread wafting to her nostrils from the public bakeries, she crossed an invisible boundary into Region I – home of the court, the aristocracy, and the great offices of state. Not having risen so early for many years, she had forgotten just how beautiful Constantinople could appear at this hour, before the streets filled up with noisy crowds and vendors. Away to her right, the topmost tier of arches of the Aqueduct of Valens along with the statues atop the columns in the fora of Constantine and Theodosius, flamed in the dawn rays, while before her rose the shining marble walls of the Palace and the Hippodrome, overtopped by the towering elegance of Hagia Sophia.

'Augusta,' murmured the sleepy porter at the Chalke – the grand entrance to the Palace, clearly surprised to see the empress informally dressed and seeking admittance at such an early hour. After passing through the great bronze doors then negotiating the building's labyrinth of corridors and walkways, she found Justinian – 'the Sleepless One', as he was known – at work already in his private study, surrounded by a clutter of *codices* and scrolls. An elegantly dressed and pleasant-faced man was seated at a desk beside the emperor's. Both rose. Theodora's heart began to race at the thought of what she was about to disclose to her husband.

'My dear – what a delightful surprise!' exclaimed Justinian, his expression welcoming. 'This is Tribonian, the Empire's most distinguished jurist.' (The other man bowed, and gave a charming smile.) 'He and I have started a tremendously important task, something that has never before been attempted – nothing less than a complete reform of Roman Law.' Justinian's voice was vibrant with excitement and enthusiasm. '*Our* Code will totally replace that of Theodosius II, now a century old, a mere mechanical compilation of imperial decrees. The new corpus will go far, far beyond that – a complete re-drafting, removing all uncertainties and contradictions in previous enactments, and scrapping irrelevant archaisms.' He clapped Tribonian on the shoulder. 'This paragon assures me that all will be complete in eighteen months.'* He shook his head in uncomprehending admiration. 'Incredible. Now my dear, what was it that you wished to see me about?'

For once, Theodora's courage failed her. Seeing her husband so happy and absorbed over a project that she knew had long been dear to his heart, she could not bear to spoil his mood. What she had to say would keep until a more appropriate occasion. 'Oh, I just came here on a whim,' she said lightly. 'For some reason I couldn't sleep, so I thought to see our city in its morning raiment. A little adventure, if you like.'

'The vagaries of women,' sighed Justinian to Tribonian, with a smile and a shrug of simulated helplessness. 'You must be hungry, my dear,' he said, turning back to Theodora. 'Perhaps you'd like to order breakfast for us both – to be served in the garden where we used to hold our meetings.'

'Oh my dear, I cannot tell you how relieved I am you did not tell him!' Macedonia exclaimed, after Theodora had rejoined her later that day, and confessed what she had planned to do. 'Not so much because it would have jeopardized our own relationship, but that it could have come between yourself and him. Men, far more than women, tend to be sensitive and insecure where their self-image is concerned. Most husbands, learning that their wives had done what we have, would – however irrationally – feel jealous and diminished. From what you tell me of Justinian, he may well be above such sentiments, but I would not like to bank on it.'

Taking Theodora's hand, Macedonia looked imploringly into her eyes. 'Darling, you do not have to choose between us. Your husband and I are not in competition for your love. I think it was a Chinese sage, one Kung Fu-tze,** who said that for a serene and happy life free of inner conflict, the wise person should keep the different aspects of his life in separate compartments. In former times, Greek women were free to love each other outwith marriage. Soon, my dear, I must return to Antioch; we may not meet again for many months. So let us take what joy of each other the Gods allow us, while we may.'

---

* It was in fact completed in just under fourteen months: begun on 13 February 528, and published on 8 April 529 – a staggering achievement!
** Confucius.

'Very well, my love,' said Theodora softly, slipping an arm around the other's waist. 'I'll say nothing to Justinian. You have convinced me – almost – that keeping silence is the best and wisest course. Anyway, I don't think I could bear to give you up.' She laughed tremulously, and went on. 'I shall do as you suggest, and put our love in a box marked 'Macedonia'. It'll be our special secret.'

Aided by unscrupulous subordinates, with names like 'Alexander the Scissors' or 'John the Leaden-Jawed' attesting their unpopularity, John of Cappadocia pressed on apace with his drive to fill the Treasury. Tax defaulters were treated with callous disregard for individual circumstances: one Petronius – a respected citizen of Philadelphia – was chained in a stable and beaten, until he had agreed to hand over the family jewels in lieu of payment of a supposed new tax on inherited wealth; in the same town, an old soldier hanged himself after being tortured to force him to pay up, despite being destitute. Far from being exceptional, such examples were typical of the lengths to which the prefect and his enforcers were prepared to go, in order to keep the revenue from taxes flowing in.

A regimen of swingeing cuts was visited upon the civil service. To squeals of anguished but ineffectual protest, mass sackings with savage pruning of departments became the order of the day. When the administration had been purged of all excessive fat, the prefect directed his economizing zeal towards the *cursus publicus*. The state postal service was not so much trimmed as virtually destroyed, leaving the infrastructure of but one route intact – that of the strategically important highway from Constantinople to the Persian frontier. On all other roads throughout the Empire, the following were totally abandoned: maintenance, relays of horses, postal stations, the hire of vehicles for travel or transport. The effect of this particular cost-cutting measure was immediate and disastrous. Farmers in the inland provinces were suddenly deprived of the means (on which they had relied for centuries) of conveying their goods to the ports, whence they were shipped to Constantinople and other centres. With the cost of private transport beyond the reach of the majority, many were reduced to trying to carry their goods to the ports themselves . . .

Staring at the roadside corpse, a half-spilled sack of corn beside it (the sixth such he had encountered that morning), Basil – a small farmer from the province of Lydia, en route to Ephesus – lowered the heavy bale from his shoulders to the ground. He turned towards his wife, several paces behind and tottering beneath the weight of an enormous sack of grain.

'Enough,' he declared bitterly. 'We will turn back now – unless we wish to end up like one of these.' And he indicated the body on the road.

'But how will we live unless we sell our produce?' cried the woman, and began to weep. 'If we can't get it to market, our corn will just rot in the fields.'

'Hush, my dear,' soothed Basil, putting his arms around her. 'Let it rot. We can harvest enough for ourselves to see us through the winter. Next year perhaps, the emperor will come to his senses and appoint another prefect. We can but hope.'

Basil's plight was shared by countless other *coloni*. Everywhere, farmers went bankrupt and flocked to the cities in search of employment, adding more hungry mouths to a near-starving urban population. For, with food production stalling, a state of famine threatened to develop in many areas. The farmers were not alone in their resentment. At the beginning of a bitterly cold January in Justinian's sixth regnal year – the two hundred and third from the Founding of New Rome* – there converged upon the capital a host of angry citizens: members of the upper classes (senators and councillors making common cause with the great landowners); small farmers, representative of the great mass of the population; supporters of the Blues; Church leaders; intellectuals; those ruined by the tax-collectors, or denied justice because they lacked the cash to bribe Tribonian, Justinian's brilliant but corrupt top jurist. Disparate they might be, but all groups were united by a single purpose – to make the emperor listen to their grievances (above all those to do with John of Cappadocia), when he opened the races in the Hippodrome on the Ides of January.**

Meanwhile, delighted with the spate of revenue pouring into the Treasury (surely a sign of God's approval), and blissfully unaware of the impending storm, Justinian was preoccupied with plans to replace his native village with a splendid new city – to be named Justiniana Prima. In doing this, he would be honouring his promise to fulfil his mother's wish, to 'make us proud of you'.

---

* 532. (See Notes.)
** Tuesday the 13th.

ELEVEN

Nika!*
Cry of the mob rioting in Constantinople, 13 January 532

The ninth day of January of that year, the two hundred and third from the Founding of New Rome, dawned cold and grey. A bitter wind from the Bosphorus gusted through Constantinople's streets, causing beggars and the destitute huddled in doorways to wrap rags and blankets more tightly round their shivering frames. As the city stirred into life, angry restless crowds everywhere materialized, swirling about the squares and thoroughfares in sullen knots and eddies. Above the throngs placards bobbed: 'Give us work' . . . 'Give us food'. . . 'Down with Tribonian' . . . 'Hang the Cappadocian'. As the morning wore on, the mood of the crowds grew steadily more tense and menacing. They began to search for a target on which they could vent their wrath. That target would soon, obligingly, present itself . . .

Eudaemon, the city prefect, was a worried man. A report had just reached him in his headquarters – the Praetorium – by messenger from the *curator* of Region V, informing him that the crowds, now grown noisy and unruly, were massing in the Forum of Constantine.

'Too close to the Palace for comfort, Phocas,' Eudaemon muttered to his second-in-command. 'Time perhaps to show the flag.'

'No "perhaps" about it, sir,' the *optio* retorted. 'We should have cracked down hard hours ago. Arrested the ringleaders. Dispersed the rest by force. Now, we'll be lucky not to have a riot on our hands.'

'You're forgetting, Phocas,' responded the prefect with asperity, 'these people have good reason to be angry.' He regarded his Number Two – a burly six-footer with a nose broken in suppressing some street brawl – disapprovingly. 'They're not your average troublemakers, like the Circus factions, say. Most are ordinary decent citizens – frightened and desperate, thanks largely to the policy of John of Cappadocia. What they need are reassurances, not threats.'

'My heart bleeds, sir. Meanwhile, as we sit here discussing the rights

* Conquer.

105

and wrongs of the situation, things out there are getting out of hand. Permission to call the men to action stations?'

Minutes later, Eudaemon and Phocas, at the head of several hundred *vigiles*, set out from the Praetorium near the Palace towards 'the Forum', as the Forum of Constantine was colloquially known. Each policeman, helmeted and carrying a riot shield, in addition to his nightstick, had been issued a baldric from which was suspended a military *spatha*. As the force entered the vast circular enclosure dominated by a tall column surmounted by a statue of the City's Founder, via the easternmost of its two great gates, Eudaemon's heart sank. The crowds had now morphed into that most dangerous of entities – a mob. Such an assembly was animated by a seemingly collective will, which could, in an instant, turn mindlessly ferocious, however rational its constituent parts might be.

Orchestrated by prominent members of the Greens and Blues, the huge concourse, on spotting the *vigiles*, broke into a baying chorus of boos and jeers, chilling in its menacing hostility. Mounting the tribunal beneath the gate's central arch, Eudaemon tried to reason with the mob, assuring them that if they went home quietly, their grievances would be addressed. His (largely inaudible) words seemed merely to inflame his audience, who responded with a barrage of catcalls and abuse.

Then someone threw a stone, and things turned ugly. The air was suddenly filled with flying missiles, one of which struck the prefect (who, in order to appear less confrontational, had removed his helmet) on the head. Blood pouring from his temple, the prefect staggered, but before he could collapse, was helped down from the platform by two of his men.

'Enough of this,' snarled Phocas, to no one in particular. Without waiting to consult his wounded superior, he turned to the helmeted ranks behind him and shouted, 'Charge!'

Now thirsting for revenge on behalf of their stricken leader, the *vigiles* advanced behind a wall of shields, and commenced laying into the densely packed mass of people with their batons. Beneath a steady rain of blows from the disciplined ranks of police, the crowds began to waver and fall back – until rallied by demagogues of the Blues and Greens, who urged them to fight back with stones and other improvised weapons. Soon, a pitched battle was raging, with individuals falling on both sides. Then, as the *vigiles* lost patience and exchanged their clubs for swords, the mob broke up in panic, leaving the Forum strewn with bloody corpses – but not before several of the ringleaders had been identified and rounded up.

'Bring in the defendants and the witnesses!' shouted the sergeant-at-arms. Accompanied by guards and ushers, the two respective parties filed into the basilica, the expressions on the faces of the accused variously defiant, terrified, or resigned. The witnesses (their role in this case doubling as accusers) took up their positions to the right of the judge. This was Tribonian, – hastily appointed as *quaesitor* to investigate the serious breach of public order that had occurred in the Forum of Constantine the previous day. The accused then lined up to Tribonian's left. A State of Emergency having been proclaimed throughout the city following the riot in the Forum, the prefect, with the emperor's authority, had decreed that this was to be a summary trial. Niceties like the offices of *defensor* (whose function was to weigh up evidence from both Defence and Prosecution) and *adsessor* (a legal expert to advise the *defensor* on finer points of law) would be dispensed with, and the court barred to the public. Other than the abovementioned, the only other persons in the courtroom were, seated on benches, a selection of the *vigiles* present at the scene of the disturbance, and Eudaemon the prefect, his head swathed in bandages.

The first accused being called, the man shuffled forward nervously to face the judge.

'Your name is Peter, a cobbler to trade, of Aphrodisias in Caria?' enquired Tribonian, his expression benevolent, his tone polite, kindly even.

The man nodded.

'The charge against you is most serious, Peter: namely that, maliciously, feloniously, and seditiously, you did throw a stone or some such hard and weighty projectile at the *Praefectus Urbis*, causing it to strike him on the head, to his severe distress and hurt. How plead you to the charge?'

'I wouldn't do a thing like that, Your Most Notable!' cried the man in desperation. 'I've never hurt anyone in my life. I – I just got caught up in the crowd and happened to be there when the prefect got hit.'

'It were him all right, Most Notable,' affirmed the first witness – one of the dreaded crew of *delatores* or informers, whose evidence was much called upon in public order cases. 'I recognize him from that birthmark on his cheek.'

'Then, Peter, I must find you guilty as charged,' pronounced Tribonian in a sad voice. 'As your action seems, on the evidence, to have been contributory to causing a violent affray in which several innocent parties were killed or injured, there can only be one sentence: death by hanging. Remove the prisoner.'

As Peter, white-faced and protesting, was bundled from the court-room, an usher came up to the judge and whispered in his ear, 'Next one's a bigwig in the Blues, *Spectabilis*. Says the management'll stump up five hundred *solidi* on his behalf.'

The next accused was found not guilty, despite two witnesses – one of them a *vigil*, swearing they had seen and heard him urging on the mob . . .

The vast crowd assembled at Blachernae – a suburb of the capital just outside the great Wall of Theodosius where it sloped down towards the Golden Horn – fell silent as the last of those condemned following the riot in the Forum mounted the scaffold. Sweating and nervous, the hangman with trembling fingers tied the nooses round the necks of the ashen-faced *damnati*. He'd be glad when this particular job was over, the man thought fervently. Usually, the spectators were in a holiday mood at hangings. This time however, the crowd was hostile, roaring its sympathy and disapproval as each of the two previous batches was despatched. He modded to his assistant.

The hangman's helper pulled away the bolt securing the platform on which the condemned men stood. The trap swung down on its hinges; the three men dropped. One hung suspended, his neck broken by the jerk, but the other two fell to the ground, the nooses having come untied. As they lay wriggling on the ground, their hands tied behind their backs, the crowd roared once more, surging forward in a menacing wave as the ex-ecutioners, now visibly frightened, made to resume their grim task. Shouts of 'String them up!' – directed at the hangmen not their victims, filled the air. At the same time, a party of monks from the nearby monastery of St Conon ran forward, seized the prostrate pair and, protected by a wildly cheering crowd, rushed them to the Church of St Lawrence in the vicinity, where they were granted sanctuary.

The following day – Monday the twelfth of January – as the news spread that one of the men taken to St Lawrence was a Blue, the other a Green, the two Circus factions abandoned their traditional hostility, and joined forces to become the mouthpiece of the mob. Mass demonstrations organ-ized by the Blues-cum-Greens assembled in front of the Praetorium, the Palace, and the Law Courts, shouting for the dismissal of the prefect, of Tribonian, and of John the Cappadocian, as well as for the pardon of the two in St Lawrence.

'Best they get it out of their systems; by tomorrow they'll have calmed down,' Eudaemon said to his Number Two in the Praetorium, raising his voice in order to be heard above the baying of the mob outside. 'With the opening of the races, they'll be able to put their grievances directly to the emperor. Justinian's basically decent and fair-minded. I'm sure he'll listen to what they have to say, and try to put things right.'

'Listen to yourself,' sighed Phocas, shaking his head. 'There are times, sir, when your faith in human nature is most touching. Unfortunately, things have got beyond the point where appeals to reason will –' He broke off, as the shutters over the windows started juddering as a barrage of missiles from outside thumped against them. 'See what I mean, sir?' he went on with a sardonic grin. He shrugged. 'Still, I suppose I *could* be wrong. Let's hope I am, for all our sakes. Pray for rain, sir. A solid downpour will disperse a crowd far better than a baton charge.'

But the weather held. Tuesday, the thirteenth day of January – the Ides – dawned crisp and clear. From an early hour, the crowds, noticeably much larger than in previous years, poured into the Hippodrome, filling up the tiers in a close-packed mass, with standing-room only in the topmost row. And something else was different compared to previous occasions: instead of the usual background hum of excited chatter, silence, ominous and oppressive, hung over the scene. Justinian however, seated in the *kathisma* or royal box, alongside his spokesman, the *Mandator*, and the city prefect, seemed unaware of any tension in the atmosphere.

'How's the head?' he enquired solicitously of Eudaemon, whose cranium was still swathed in bandages.

'Still throbs a bit, Serenity, but improving by the day. My *medicus* assures me there's no permanent damage.' He went on in anxious tones, 'Serenity – if I may presume to suggest, the sooner we get the races started the better. I don't like the mood of the crowd.'

'Really? The fact that they seem unusually quiet suggests to me they know they've gone too far, and are feeling chastened and contrite.' He smiled at Eudaemon and patted his arm reassuringly. 'I bow, however, to your judgement.' Summoning one of the attendants on duty below the *kathisma*, he told the man, 'Tell the *editor** to hurry things along.'

Shortly afterwards, the man returned with a message: the editor would forego the usual perquisite of staging a procession, and let the races start immediately. A trumpet sounded, and from the open end of the stadium's vast U shot the competing chariots, extremely light affairs with wide tyres

* Organiser of the races.

for extra grip, each drawn by four horses, the inner pair yoked to the pole, the outer held on traces. As the vehicles flashed around the *Spina* – the long central barrier – it became immediately obvious, from their continued silence, that for once, the crowd had not come here for entertainment, but to confront the emperor. At the end of the first race, the two *Demarchs* – the official spokesmen for the Greens and Blues – addressed Justinian.

'Thrice August One, knowing that you are just and merciful, we beg you to pardon the two *damnati* who have sought sanctuary in the Church of St Lawrence.' Their tone, though respectful, held a hint of steel, suggesting they would not be satisfied until they had an answer – one moreover that acceded to their request (or rather, their politely framed demand).

While the *Demarchs* waited for a reply, Justinian whispered to Eudaemon, 'Are the criminals securely held? We wouldn't want a gang of vigilantes springing them from the church.'

'Absolutely, Serenity,' replied the prefect. 'I've posted armed guards around St Lawrence. No one can get in or out. However, I do think it might be wise to do as the *Demarchs* ask. That would defuse the situation, and we'd still be seen to be acting from a position of strength.'

'Certainly not,' declared the emperor, sotto voce. 'I'm surprised at you, Eudaemon. By letting the two men off, we'd appear weak, not strong. If we give in to pressure over this, the plebs will stage a riot every time they imagine they've a grievance.' He turned to the *Mandator*. 'Say nothing,' he instructed.

The racing continued, the *Demarchs*, with mounting insistence, repeating their demand at the end of every race, only to be ignored. The silence of the spectators gradually gave way to an ominous low buzz of anger and frustration. Even a spectacular crash (known as a *naufragia* or 'shipwreck') failed to move the crowd.

Closely followed by a rival chariot, the leading vehicle, a Blue, had just rounded the end of the *Spina* for the seventh and last time, to hurtle down the final straight. But the pursuing Green, coming up on the inside, rapidly eroding the other's lead drew level three hundred paces from the finish. Then the Blue, in a supremely daring move, swerved his chariot in beside the Green, hooked his right-hand wheel inside the other's left then suddenly swung his team out, wrenching the wheel clean off. The Green's axle bit the ground, causing the whole equipage to somersault and smash against the *Spina* in a tangle of flailing hooves, splintering wood, and whipping traces. The wretched driver, unable in time to draw his knife and cut the traces (tied around his waist for extra leverage on the turns), died, mangled in the wreckage. Normally, such an event would have elicited a collective gasp of fascinated horror from the spectators. This time however, preoccupied by the duel between *Demarchs* and *Mandator*, they remained indifferent.

The final race of the day, the twenty-second, ended without the emperor breaking his silence. The *Demarchs*, abandoning their appeals to spare the fugitives, suddenly began to shout, 'Long live the humane Greens and Blues!' – an unprecedented show of co-operation, clearly evidence of a pre-arranged plan. Again and again, the cry was repeated, the Hippodrome erupting into a deafening uproar as the crowd joined in. Suddenly, a new, and chilling, watchword rose above the din: '*Nika*! – Conquer.' This was incitement to revolt; as if animated by a single mind, the crowd, chanting its new-found war cry, '*Nika! Nika! Nika!*', began streaming from the Hippodrome, intent on forcing the authorities to answer its demands.

Bewildered, Justinian turned to the prefect. 'Eudaemon – what's happening?'

'Their patience has finally snapped, Serenity. I did try to warn you. No telling what they'll do in the mood they're in now. You must return at once to the Palace; meanwhile, I'll go to the Praetorium and try to stall things. What shall I say to them?'

Dismayed and alarmed by the course events were taking, Justinian hesitated. Then he remembered: had he not received assurance he was God's Appointed? As his actions were determined by Jehovah's Will, surely then he need not fear their consequences? With confidence flooding back, he answered Eudaemon's query, 'Why – tell them nothing, of course.'

'But Serenity!'

'Courage, friend. We mustn't waver now. If we stand firm, the people will be made to realize there's nothing to be gained by violence or noisy demonstration.'

The pair descended the spiral staircase behind the *kathisma* to the short passage connecting the Palace to the Hippodrome. While Justinian summoned the courtiers and Palace Guard, the prefect, shaking his head in despair, set out for the nearby Praetorium. He was met by a dishevelled Phocas heading towards him from that building.

'Get back, sir!' shouted the *optio*. 'There's nothing you can do. The mob's broken into the Praetorium, freed the prisoners from the cells, and killed any *vigiles* who tried to stop them. I barely escaped with my own life.

Look – they've set fire to the place!' And he pointed back to where lurid flames were shooting up against the evening sky.

The two men retreated to the Palace – not a moment too soon, as it transpired. Hardly had they been admitted via a postern gate than the mob, satisfied that the Praetorium was well ablaze, surged into the Augusteum – the great square before the Palace – shouting for the prefect and the emperor to appear. Their demands being met by silence, the mob – chanting, '*Nika! Nika! Nika!*' – vented its frustration by setting fire to the Chalke.

With the gatehouse an inferno, its great bronze doors reduced to pools of molten metal, the rampaging crowds, intoxicated by their own unpunished daring, moved on to fresh targets. '*Nika! Nika! Nika!*' Soon the huge church of Hagia Sophia was engulfed in flames, followed by the Senate House. '*Nika! Nika! Nika!*' At last, after setting fire to some public buildings on the Mesé, the mob dispersed in the small hours, sated with violence and tired out by the day's excitement.

Meanwhile, the Guards – more decorative than belligerent – instead of confronting the attackers had remained inside the Palace, preferring discretion to valour.

Within their private suite, God's Appointed, his earlier confidence now badly shaken, cried out to the empress, 'God has abandoned me, Theodora! The people turn against me; the Guards' loyalty is suspect; I feel I cannot trust the courtiers and senators within the Palace! If I am still His Chosen One, then why is all this happening?'

'God has *not* abandoned you, my dear,' Theodora said firmly, taking Justinian's hands in hers. 'Merely tested you, as He tested Job, or His own Son when Satan tempted Him upon the mountain. Tomorrow, you must face the people; listen to what they have to say. It would appear they may have suffered grave injustices – carried out in your name by unworthy ministers. Promise to put things right, and all may yet be well.'

Comforted, 'the Sleepless One' retired to bed, to snatch an hour or two of rest against the challenge of the coming day.

That same night, in another part of Region I, in the house of Methodius the *Caput Senatus*, there took place a meeting of senators, councillors, and great landowners. A distinguished-looking aristocrat was addressing the assembly. 'Gentlemen – the Greens and Blues have served us well by stirring up the plebs against Justinian's regime,' declared the speaker, one Gaius Anicius Julianus, a senator who, from the moment of its convening, had stamped his personality on the gathering. (Julianus was a member of the great West Roman family, the Anicii, and a refugee from an Italy under Ostrogothic rule.) 'But what they have created is only a riot, which, by its nature, will soon burn itself out. Before that happens, we must build upon the popular discontent to bring about –'

'A revolution?' interrupted old Methodius. He sounded horrified. 'That's not the way we do things in the East, Anicius.'

'Usurpation by ambitious generals – that was long the curse of the Western Empire,' conceded Julianus. 'The resulting instability undoubtedly weakened the state, helping to pave the way for the barbarian invasions. But sometimes, for the general good, it becomes necessary to remove a bad emperor. Think of Nero, Caligula, or Commodus.'

'But those were monstrous tyrants,' objected a councillor. 'Justinian hardly fits that mould.'

'Agreed. But what perhaps is worse – the man's obsessive. Preoccupied with grandiose building schemes, and plans to re-conquer the West. Which all costs money – vast amounts of it. But as long as he gets it, he seems oblivious to how it's obtained, and all the misery that's causing.'

'You have a plan?' This from Maxentius, a landed magnate who had suffered at the hands of John of Cappadocia's *compulsores*.

'Indeed I have. The time is perfect for a coup. Justinian is hated. And he's weak; all units of the army are absent from the capital, bar a few thousand German mercenaries and the Palace Guard. We can discount the last-mentioned – toy soldiers of dubious loyalty, who'll come over to us if they see we're winning. As will most senators and courtiers within the Palace, fellow aristocrats all. There are excellent candidates to replace Justinian: the three nephews of Anastasius, all here in Constantinople – true Romans like ourselves, and of our class. Hypatius is probably the best choice – popular, and a successful general. We must, however, discount him, also his brother Pompeius, both presently immured within the Palace, where they'll obviously remain until the streets are safe. Which leaves the third nephew – Probus.'

'And is Probus aware of his imminent promotion to the purple?' asked a senator drily.

'Not yet; nor must he become so.' Julianus looked intently round his audience, to emphasize the point. 'Probus is a cautious man, who wouldn't voluntarily seize the throne. He must be elevated to it by a fait accompli. Tomorrow, in the Hippodrome, if we proclaim him emperor and the plebs support us – which they will – he'd hardly then be in a position to refuse.'

'And would you be willing to take on the role of Nymphidius?'* Methodius enquired of Julianus.

'Provided a majority of you being in favour of my plan agree that I should do so,' replied the Anician, with a modest inclination of the head.

'Then I nominate Julianus as our spokesman,' declared Methodius. 'If any disagree, then let him raise his hand.'

No hand was lifted.

---

* The praetorian prefect who proclaimed Nero deposed, in favour of Galba.

TWELVE

Hypatius and Pompeius paid the penalty and lost the empire before they could obtain it
Marcellinus Comes, *Chronicle*, 534

On Wednesday, the fourteenth day of January, the sun rose on a city shrouded in palls of smoke from smouldering ruins. Soon afterwards, word went out from the Palace that the races would begin again, in the presence of the emperor. Apprehensive but hopeful, his resolution stiffened by his wife's advice, Justinian, holding a copy of the Gospels and accompanied by his *Mandator* and the city prefect, ascended the spiral staircase to the *kathisma*. At once, he sensed an atmosphere of almost palpable hostility emanating from the vast and silent crowd. He sent word to the editor to cancel the races; clearly, the people were in no mood to be fobbed off by such diversion.

'I suspect they may ask for your dismissal,' he murmured to Eudaemon. 'If so, I'll have to play along. Don't worry, though; it will only be a temporary suspension. As soon as things blow over, I'll have you reinstated.'

The *Demarchs* approached the royal box. They repeated their request of the previous day, that the two *damnati* in St Lawrence's Church be pardoned, then went on, 'In addition, Serenity, we demand that you dismiss three ministers: first, Tribonian, who sells justice to the highest bidder like a huckster at a market stall; second, Eudaemon, whose answer to the people's legitimate complaints is blows; and last but by no means least, John the Cappadocian – guilty of gratuitous brutality against many Roman citizens, and whose rapacity and cost-cutting have ruined thousands of good men throughout your Empire.'

A roar of approval erupted from the crowd.

Justinian rose to his feet. Holding aloft the Gospels in his left hand, he placed his right upon the Holy Writ and nodded to the *Mandator*. 'Tell them I assent,' he said.

'Our most wise and merciful Augustus,' announced the *Mandator* in stentorian tones, 'hears your petition and agrees to its terms: the two criminals presently in the Church of St Lawrence to be granted full pardons, and the Quaestor of the Sacred Palace,* together with the prefect of the city and the praetorian prefect, to be instantly dismissed.'

The muted sigh – like the sound of distant breakers rushing on a beach – that arose from the crowd suggested to Justinian that the crisis might have passed. His acquiescence would surely guarantee, as on many previous occasions with former emperors, that the people would be appeased and things return to normal. So it was with shock that he heard a voice declaim, 'You lie, you swine!' Addressing the crowd from the foremost tier, the speaker went on, 'Don't let yourselves be taken in; his promises are worthless, made only under duress, from weakness. He'll break every one of them as soon as you go home.'

Instantly, the mood of the crowd seemed to change – from sullen acceptance to angry suspicion. Yesterday's orgy of destruction had by no means assuaged their bitter sense of injustice at their treatment by the agents of the government. The speaker's words reminded them that they had tasted power and were due revenge. A thunderous growl of agreement with his statement swept around the vast assembly.

'Let us choose a new emperor,' went on the speaker – a tall commanding figure, whom Justinian recognized as Anicius Julianus, a leading senator and member of the Roman diaspora from the barbarian-occupied West, 'one who will reign with equity and justice. Justinian has shown he is not worthy to rule the Romans. Let us replace him with one who is – a nephew of the noble Anastasius, and one in whom integrity and strength is wedded to ability. People of New Rome, I give you – Probus Augustus!'

A stunned silence filled the Hippodrome. Then, isolated at first, but swiftly growing to a mighty, swelling chorus, came the shouted response: 'Probus Augustus! Probus Augustus! Probus Augustus!'

His initial disbelief swiftly turning to panic, Justinian allowed himself to be hastily escorted back to the Palace. There, in his private study or *tablinum*, he summoned a council of war. Present, besides himself, were: Marcellus, captain of the Palace Guard, and two of his most trusted generals who, along with their contingents of German mercenaries happened to be in the capital – young Belisarius and Mundus, a doughty veteran of many tough campaigns. To these three, Justinian, close to tears, gabbled an account of the scene in the Hippodrome in which he had just been involved. 'Gentlemen – I confess I'm at a loss as to what should now be done,' he concluded, in tones of desperation. 'I would greatly value your advice.'

* Tribonian's official title.

First to speak was Belisarius. 'Serenity – it seems to me that while we face an admittedly daunting challenge, it's by no means an insurmountable one. Out there we have a rabble, unorganized and as yet leaderless. If myself and Mundus here, with our Germans plus the Palace Guard, were to take them on immediately, I'd be surprised if we weren't able to disperse them.'

'But your Germans number less than two thousand, while the Guards are a mere half of that!' exclaimed the emperor in dismay. 'Against odds of at least a hundred to one, how can you hope to prevail?'

'Serenity – mere numbers count for little against trained soldiers, provided they are disciplined and committed,' replied the youthful general. Tall and handsome, with an air of insouciant confidence, he seemed every inch the dashing cavalry commander (though in this instance in charge of infantry). His infectious optimism made Justinian begin to feel more sanguine. 'Very well, if you really think you can succeed,' the emperor pronounced. 'Then you have my blessing – and my heartfelt gratitude.'

'Oh, we'll succeed all right, Serenity,' put in Mundus,* his flat Mongol features breaking into a grin. 'Our Germans are just spoiling for a fight.'

'But my Palace Guards are not,' declared Marcellus smoothly. 'Their duty is to protect your person, Serenity – not wage war against their fellow Romans. While they are willing to prevent insurgents from entering the Palace, or threatening yourself, Serenity, they cannot be expected to go on the offensive against unarmed citizens.'

'We're better off without you, anyway,' sneered Mundus. 'You'd only get in the way.'

'Yes – we wouldn't want you getting those fancy uniforms dirty,' said Belisarius gravely, shaking his head in mock concern. He turned to Justinian. 'Well, Serenity, with your permission we'll be on our way.'

Shouting Probus' name, the crowds streamed from the Hippodrome and made their way to the senator's house. But that particular bird, having got wind of their intentions, and well aware of the fate awaiting failed usurpers, had already flown. Finding his house empty, barred, and shuttered, the disappointed populace burned it down, then headed for the Palace in a mood of fury and frustration. Intercepted in the Augusteum by Belisarius and Mundus, the mob received a bloody mauling from the German mercenaries. Disconcerted, their

---

* Of Hunnish descent, Mundo – as he was then known – had once been a formidable bandit leader. Since swearing allegiance to Rome, however, he had become one of the most stalwart of Roman generals. A classic case of poacher turned gamekeeper! (See my *Theoderic*.)

ardour suddenly cooling, the people were about to break and scatter, when the situation was unexpectedly reversed.

In a commendable attempt to save lives, a group of clergy, carrying religious symbols, tried to separate the combatants. In the ensuing scuffle, some of the clerics were hurt, and their holy relics, which of course meant nothing to the Arian Germans, got trampled underfoot. Infuriated by such sacrilege, the people recovered their spirit and fought back with redoubled fury, to be joined by sympathetic onlookers, hitherto too frightened to become involved. Fighting stubbornly, the crowds retreated in good order into the twisting streets and alleys of Regions IV and V. With the mood of outrage spreading like wildfire, they were now joined by whole households, the womenfolk hurling roof tiles, buckets full of boiling water, and anything that came to hand, onto the heads of the hated Germans. In the labyrinth of narrow lanes, the mercenaries lost the tactical advantage they had held in the great open space of the Augusteum; the initiative now lay entirely with the urban population. Recognizing the hopelessness of the situation, Belisarius and Mundus called off their men and returned to the Palace.

Meanwhile the people, their mood now both triumphant and vindictive, rampaged through the city, burning down the Churches of the Holy Peace, St Theodore Sphoriacus, and St Aquilina, the Hospitals of Eubulus and Sampson, the Baths of Alexander, and any buildings that could be identified as connected with the government.

'Let's face it, gentlemen – we gambled, and we lost,' said Julianus to the same audience he had addressed the night before, assembled once again in the house of Methodius. 'My advice to you now is that you quietly disappear, pro tempore at least, to country houses if you have them, or to the homes of distant relatives. Thanks to my little speech in the Hippodrome this morning, I am now of course a marked man. Any of you known to have conversed with me these last few days, could well be tainted with –'

'Guilt by association?' broke in a worried-looking councillor.

'I fear so.' Julianus raised his hands in a gesture of helpless apology. 'The Roman Empire may today have more civilized values than in Sulla's time; but is compulsory enrolment in a monastery so vastly preferable to being required to slit one's veins?* I wonder.'

---

* Dictator of Rome from 81–79 BC, Sulla was infamous for his Proscriptions – death lists of political enemies, posted up in public. By Justinian's time, capital punishment, even for murder, was rare; blinding, or confinement to a monastery, the usual alternatives. (See Notes.)

'But surely we don't need to throw in the towel yet,' objected a senator. 'The plebs control the city. The attempt by Belisarius and Mundus to suppress the revolt has failed, and they've been forced to retreat to the Palace.'

'Which remains invulnerable as long as they're inside it with their troops,' countered Julianus. 'So where does that leave us? – stalemate, gentlemen. But that won't last. With Probus gone, and his brothers in the Palace, the people no longer have a focus for revolt. Soon they'll tire of protest and abandon taking to the streets. All Justinian has to do is wait. As for myself, I shall leave you now, my friends, to pack for my return to Italy. It has been an honour and a privilege to –'

He was interrupted by the door bursting open to admit a breathless young man – an 'ear' of Julianus, planted in the Palace.

'Procopius – what brings you here?' the Anician enquired.

'Great news, gentlemen,' gasped the newcomer. 'Fearing treachery on the part of the courtiers and senators within the Palace, Justinian has just this minute forced them all to leave, Hypatius included. We have our new Augustus, after all!'

'Pull yourself together and stop behaving like a headless chicken!' his wife, Maria, shouted at Hypatius, who was pacing the atrium of his villa in the capital, in an agony of indecision. 'We should follow the example of your brother Probus, and leave *now* – while there's still time.'

'But if they find the house untenanted, my dear, they'll burn it down – as they did my brother's. My bronzes, my Rhodian marbles,' the old general wailed, 'my silver crater,* gifted me by Anastasius . . . I can't bear to think of losing them.'

'Better that than losing your life,' his spouse retorted. She held her hand up, her expression suddenly alert. 'Hear that? I think they're on their way.'

A distant hubbub, faint at first but swiftly growing louder, came to the couple's ears. Almost before Hypatius could collect his scattered wits, the building was surrounded by exultant crowds shouting, 'Hypatius Augustus! Hypatius Augustus!'

'You've left it too late,' declared Maria bitterly. 'As usual. It's been the story of our lives. When Anastasius died, if you'd marched at once from Antioch instead of dithering, you could be emperor today.'

---

* Bowl for mixing wine with water. The heavy imperial vintages were usually diluted before serving. A host's generosity or meanness could sometimes be measured by the proportion of water to wine in the mixture.

'Just tell them I'm not here; perhaps they'll go away.'

'Ostrich! You know they won't. For the time being you must pretend to go along with them. Then, at the very earliest opportunity, disengage yourself and make contact with Justinian; he'll understand. After all, he is your friend.' Her manner softening, Maria kissed him gently on the cheek. 'Go now, my love,' she whispered. 'And may God be with you.'

Sick with fear, Hypatius allowed himself to be carried shoulder-high through the darkening streets to a torch-lit Hippodrome, where it seemed the whole of Constantinople was assembled. A jubilant cheer arose from the multitude, and to shouts of, 'Long live Hypatius!', the general was installed in the *kathisma*. Then, for want of a diadem, a golden chain (which someone had been wearing as a necklace) was wound around his head, while a purple curtain, in lieu of an imperial robe, was placed upon his shoulders.

Wishing himself anywhere else but in his present position, Hypatius, as his eyes adjusted to the glare of the torches, noticed that among the cheering citizens – conspicuous by their archaic togas or silken robes of office – were large numbers of senators and councillors, many of them known to him. It dawned on the general that his 'coronation' had been no mere whim of the mob, but had the backing of those who counted in the Empire – the sort of men who alone could provide the stability and leadership essential for any revolution to succeed. This changed everything. Displacing terror, excitement stirred within him; perhaps, after all, he really could become emperor. Suddenly, a cry began to circulate around the stadium, transmuting in an instant, possibility into certainty: 'Justinian has fled!' Soon the words were taken up by everyone, the Hippodrome resounding with triumphant shouts – 'Justinian has fled!' . . . 'The tyrant has gone!' . . . Long live our new emperor – Hypatius Augustus!'

Mixed with relief, a sense of heady euphoria surged through Hypatius. The imperial crown was no more than his due, he told himself. All his life he had worked hard and played by the rules, only to be cheated of the big prizes by lesser men who knew better than he how to play the political game. With his impeccable credentials of noble birth and royal blood, it was *he*, not that barbarian nobody Justin, who should have succeeded Anastasius, as it was *he* who should have been promoted to the top job in the army – *Magister Militum Praesentalis*,* instead of being fobbed off with command of the Army of the East. Even the charge of that remote posting he had twice had to surrender – first, temporarily, to Justinian over that Dhu-Nuwas business, and now, permanently, to that young whippersnapper Belisarius.

* Master of Soldiers in the Presence [of the emperor].

Savouring the moment, Hypatius stood and raised his hand in *adlocutio* – the imperial gesture of address. A hush spread throughout his vast audience.

'Fellow Romans,' he declaimed, '– you have honoured me by making me your emperor. I swear to you before God, that my chief concern will always be to serve you to the utmost of my ability. Also, you have my solemn promise that never again will you have to suffer the brutality of a Eudaemon, the injustice of a Tribonian, or the rapacity of a John of Cappadocia. They will go – as Justinian, their master, has already gone. Good riddance to them all, I say, as together we begin a new and happier chapter in the annals of New Rome.'

The tumultuous applause that greeted his speech was music to Hypatius' ears, wiping out in an instant the many disappointments and frustrations endured throughout a long career.

Meanwhile, in the Palace – virtually empty now that its normal population of courtiers and senators had been dismissed – an eerie silence reigned. Apart from a tiny band of those still loyal to the emperor, its only occupants were now the Palace Guard and German mercenaries waiting in their quarters, a few *silentiarii* stalking the deserted corridors like ghosts, and a downstairs tribe of footmen, maids, and cooks, among whom an air of ribald insubordination to their royal master was beginning to prevail.

In Justinian's *tablinum*, besides the emperor himself, were assembled: Theodora, Belisarius and Mundus, John the Cappadocian, the young lawyer Procopius and the chronicler Count Marcellinus – both experienced stenographers whose function was to record any minutes, and finally, to act as scouts and messengers, two trusted *agentes in rebus*: special agents whose job could cover anything from spying to diplomacy. The sound of cheering from the nearby Hippodrome did nothing to lighten the mood of despondency verging on despair, which hung like a dark cloud over the meeting. One of the *agentes* – a coal-black Nubian named Crixus, had just returned from the Hippodrome to report the 'coronation' of Hypatius.

'Serenity – it takes a wise general to know when he's beaten,' stated Mundus gently, breaking the uncomfortable silence that had followed Crixus' account, and which suggested that few present would disagree with what the general now said. 'Perhaps it's time to leave the field.'

'Mundus is right,' declared the Cappadocian bluntly. 'Grasp the nettle,

Serenity – sail tonight for Heraclea Pontica on the southern shore of the Euxine.* You'd be safe there – for the time being at least.'

'And close enough to the capital, Serenity, to launch a counter-coup when the time is right,' suggested Procopius.

'Thank you, my friend – I appreciate that you're trying to let me down lightly,' responded Justinian in gloomy tones. 'But I think we all know that if I leave, I won't be coming back. I have, reluctantly, to agree with Mundus and the prefect that flight now seems the only option.'

'Before we all decide to write off our chances,' put in Belisarius, 'there is one possibility that may be worth exploring.'

'Go on,' the emperor invited.

'Thanks to Crixus here,' Belisarius went on, to a suddenly animated audience, 'we know that Hypatius is at present holding court in the *kathisma*, enjoying the acclamation of his "subjects". As we know, a short passage leads from the Palace to the spiral staircase which opens into the royal box. If I were to lead a hand-picked group of my Germans along that route to the *kathisma*, we could surprise Hypatius and either arrest or kill him. With its head cut off, the revolt would surely die.'

'I like it!' exclaimed Mundus. 'Like all good plans it's simple, and seems to me to have an excellent chance of succeeding. I think we should accept it.'

'I agree,' said Justinian, perceptibly brightening. He looked around the gathering. 'If you all back Belisarius' idea, which I think is a brilliant one, then let us wish him good luck and God speed.' He turned to Belisarius. 'You have our permission to proceed. Bring back Hypatius alive, if possible.'

If he was quick, Procopius thought, as he hurried through the corridors towards the quarters of the Palace Guard, he'd just have time to warn Marcellus before Belisarius set out with his Germans. So far, things were working out nicely for his plan of revenge against that *meretrix sordida*,** Theodora. Subsisting in exiled poverty in some God-forgotten corner of the Empire, she'd have plenty of time to regret the day she'd turned him down, and given him a nasty bite to boot. The wound had turned septic, taking weeks to heal; he could have lost the hand. Pity his scheme necessarily involved taking down her pathetic lap-dog of a husband too – 'collateral damage', to use army-speak. He bore Justinian no particular ill-will,

* The Black Sea.
** Filthy whore.

but Julianus had promised him Tribonian's job in the event of the coup succeeding. A man had to look out for himself, after all; no one else, for sure, was going to. Starting that false rumour about Justinian having fled was a master-stroke of his, Procopius reflected. Without it, he doubted if that geriatric ditherer Hypatius would have willingly accepted his imperial role. Now however, all could be in jeopardy – thanks to that wretched brainwave of Belisarius. He quickened his pace . . .

'I'm sorry, Serenity,' said Belisarius, looking uncharacteristically crestfallen. 'We found our way blocked by the Palace Guard; they're obviously just waiting for an opportunity to switch sides. To take them on wouldn't have achieved anything; and they'd have been able to warn Hypatius. It's a mystery to me how they found out about our plan.'

'I think it may be time to go, Serenity,' said Mundus, speaking with quiet urgency. 'At least you'll leave in safety; Belisarius and I will make sure of that.'

'I'm touched by your loyalty – by the loyalty of all of you,' Justinian responded, struggling to keep his voice from breaking as he looked around the little group. 'A fallen emperor is fortunate to have such faithful friends. Those who wish to stay may do so with my blessing. The rest of us should now prepare to leave.'

Theodora, who had remained silent throughout the whole meeting, suddenly rose to her feet.

'I know it's not supposed to be a woman's place to speak in a men's council,' she declared in quiet but clear tones. 'However, the present situation allows convention to be waived, I think. You are for flight? Well, there are the ships, there's the sea; life and safety yours for the choosing. But ask yourselves – what sort of life would that be? A life of shameful exile in a distant land. Sooner or later, death must come to us all. Speaking for myself, I would not wish to live deprived of my imperial robe. There is a saying – a true one, I believe – that the purple is a glorious winding sheet.*'

She sat down amid a stunned silence, in which the men avoided each other's eyes in shamefaced embarrassment. Flight, which minutes before had seemed the only option, now, thanks to the galvanizing effect of Theodora's rousing little speech, appeared out of the question.

Soon, an alternative plan was being thrashed out. Leading the Germans in two separate parties, Belisarius and Mundus would circumnavigate the

* See Appendix III.

Hippodrome, then enter via the gates at either end. The obvious risk was that such large bodies of men would be detected and the alarm raised before they could complete the manoeuvre. But desperate situations call for desperate measures.

'I'll just make sure the coast's clear,' murmured Procopius, as the plan's final details were being discussed. 'We don't want anyone learning what's afoot.' And he slipped out of the *tablinum*. Hypatius and his followers must be warned, he thought. He had not gone ten paces however, when he felt his shoulder gripped from behind, then found himself spun violently round to face the *agens*, Crixus.

'Get your hand off me, you black –' Procopius broke off with a gasp of pain, as the other's fingers dug into the soft flesh of his upper arm.

'And just where did you think you were heading?' enquired the huge Nubian softly. 'The Hippodrome, perhaps? I've had my eye on you, sonny. Who tipped off the Palace Guard, I wonder? We'll just go back and join the others, shall we?'

In the flickering torchlight of their great drill-hall, with a frisson of pride and affection Belisarius surveyed his men – blond giants, each protected by *Spangenhelm* (the conical, segmented helmet favoured by Teutonic races) and hauberk of ring-mail or lamellar plates, small bars of iron laced together. All were armed with *spathae*, long and deadly Roman swords, equally effective for cutting or thrusting. Shields were being left behind; these would not be needed. Germans, the general reflected, so long as they were individually recruited, and subjected to Roman discipline and training, made the best soldiers in the world – utterly loyal, fearless, and ferocious fighters. (Federate troops: whole tribes enrolled for Rome under their own leaders, were a different matter. Greedy, treacherous, and unreliable, they had played no small part in bringing down the Western Empire.)

'Right, lads – let's be off,' Belisarius called softly. Followed by the silent files of mercenaries under their *dekarchs* or squad leaders, he led the way out of the Palace, giving the Guards' quarters a wide berth.

Rendezvousing with Mundus and his Heruls (from a particularly fierce Germanic tribe) at the smoking rubble of the Chalke, Belisarius whispered to his fellow general, 'We both count to a thousand, then enter. That'll give us more than enough time to get into position, and allow us both to strike at the same time. All right?'

Mundus nodded, and the two forces – each nearly a thousand strong – set off in opposite directions. Picking their way in the darkness over smouldering ruins without making a sound was no easy task, but Belisarius' Germans managed it superbly. Long before the count was up, he and his men were assembled outside the Hippodrome's Nekra Gate.* From inside the stadium's towering walls arose a deafening hubbub of jubilant shouting.

'Nine hundred and ninety-nine . . . one thousand,' murmured Belisarius to himself. Raising an arm, he pointed to the entrance of the Nekra Gate. Briefed in advance, his men knew exactly what to do; in silence, they filed through the entrance into the torchlit Hippodrome.

As the crowds inside the vast space became aware of the grim ranks of mailed Germans, the shouting died away, to be replaced by a horrified silence – a silence that gave way to screams of pain and terror, as the Germans began their grim task. The crisis had escalated far beyond the point where reason and restraint might have proved effective; now only a lethal lesson could bring the people to their senses.

Trapped in a huddled mass between the troops of Belisarius and Mundus, the citizenry stood no chance. Unlike the street-fighting of the day before, where the mob could escape down narrow alleys to regroup or bombard their opponents from the rooftops, here, squashed together in an open space, they were as sheep for the slaughter. The Hippodrome became a bloody killing-ground, as the Germans – to whom from their youth fighting and slaughter were activities to be relished – steadily advanced, hacking and thrusting with a terrible, machine-like efficiency. At last the two generals called off their men – blood-bespattered, and exhausted by their efforts – allowing the terrified survivors to flee to the safety of their homes, leaving thirty thousand corpses strewn like broken dolls upon the racetrack.

When the sun arose on the smouldering, half-ruined city, no angry crowds appeared on the streets. Cowed and apprehensive, many with wounds being tended by their womenfolk, the citizens of Constantinople remained indoors. In the Palace, Hypatius, white-faced and trembling, was brought before Justinian. When asked by the latter why he had agreed to usurp the throne, Hypatius had no answer. Denial would have been futile; half the city could bear witness to that coronation speech.

'Mercy, Serenity,' babbled the general. 'I allowed myself to be swayed by the vox populi. That was wrong – wrong and stupid. I'd have realized my folly soon enough, and abdicated in your favour.'

---

* So called, because the bodies of charioteers killed in the races were carried through it.

Looking at the broken old man before him, pleading for his life, Justinian felt a stab of pity. Here, surely, was no threat. He had liked Hypatius, coming to regard him almost as a friend. About to pardon him, he caught Theodora's eye; she shook her head in silent warning. As usual, she was right, Justinian acknowledged to himself; any possibility of rivals bidding for the purple must be ruthlessly eliminated. Reluctantly, he gave the order for Hypatius' execution. Pompeius too, would not be spared. Later that morning, the bodies of the two brothers were thrown into the sea. The insurrection was over.

In his private chamber, Justinian broke down and wept, his tears ones of relief, of guilt and sorrow for the deaths of so many of his people; above all of gratitude towards the brave and loyal woman to whom he owed his throne, and – most probably his life.

THIRTEEN

If you do not keep discipline, we shall end up by driving the Africans, who are Romans, into the arms of the Vandals
Procopius (paraphrasing Belisarius' warning to his troops, on landing in Africa), *History of the Wars of Justinian, after 552*

From the Palace, despite his efforts to shut out the sound, Justinian could not prevent himself from hearing the death-carts removing those thirty thousand corpses from the Hippodrome – a continuous low rumbling that lasted for two whole days and nights, and which constituted for the emperor both a painful reminder and reproach, for the blame he shared with others in the root cause of the riots. But though he found it hard to forgive himself, God, he thought, surely would forgive him; the very fact that he had survived (through the intervention of Theodora, God's agent) was plainly evidence that the Almighty had work for him to do, namely the implementing of his Grand Plan: the restoration of the One and Indivisible Empire, together with the establishment throughout his realm, of the One True Faith.

First, however, there must be closure regarding the riots. To satisfy the populace, he dismissed Eudaemon, Tribonian, and John the Cappadocian, while making it clear to all three ministers that theirs was but a temporary suspension, moreover one on full pay; they were too useful to him for their services to be dispensed with permanently. Also, their loyalty was incontestable, and loyalty was a quality that Justinian prized above all others. Despite the urgings of some ministers, he would countenance no savage reprisals against those involved in the disturbance. Some aristocrats of senatorial or consular rank were sent into exile (with the understanding that, conditional on good behaviour, they could eventually be permitted to come back, when their confiscated estates would be returned to them); and the Hippodrome (always a potential focus for disaffection) was closed.* Such were the limits of retaliation by the state; as for the disaffected, although their grievances remained for the most part unaddressed,

---

* But only for a few years. When it reopened, the Green and Blue factions were soon as belligerent as ever, and continued to foment riots periodically.

they were perhaps too relieved by the government's conciliatory stance to indulge in further protest – for the time being at least.

The most pressing priority for Justinian at this time was to express his thanks to God for his deliverance – and in a manner commensurate with the extent of his gratitude. And what greater opportunity for him to do so, than to rebuild Hagia Sophia? (Was its destruction foreordained, the emperor wondered, in order that it might be raised anew in yet more glorious form – a fitting tribute to the Almighty from His Appointed One?)

There were master-builders aplenty in the capital, capable of producing a fine successor to the ruined church – men whose workmanship, based on precedent and rule of thumb, was invariably dependable and of the highest quality. Certainly, such men could build a bigger, more impressive version of the Church of the Holy Wisdom. But like almost every church of any size, it would be based on the *basilica* – a municipal building for the conduct of public business, of rectangular construction, with pillared aisles and a pitched roof: solid, rational, *Roman*. This, however, was not what the emperor wanted. Something suggestive of the meeting-point of this world and the transcendent world of the divine absolute was what was called for. In a word, something more *spiritual*. Justinian had heard of a man, perhaps the only one in his whole Empire, who might answer such a call: one Anthemius of Tralles, a trained engineer and mathematician from a brilliant family of lawyers, physicians, and grammarians. Only a man of quite exceptional talent would be capable of conceiving the bold, ideal vision that Justinian hoped could be realized in stone. Perhaps Anthemius was that man; he would send for him this very day.

'Magnificent,' breathed Justinian in awed delight, as two servitors placed before him on a table in his *tablinum*, a model of the church-to-be. Turning to its maker, he went on, 'That dome – when built, it will be enormous. What are its dimensions?'

'One hundred feet across, Serenity,' replied Anthemius. Small, fat, and bald – the engineer could not have appeared more different from the lean ascetic that Justinian had pictured before their meeting. In fact, Anthemius reminded him of an ivory figurine he had once seen in a shop in the Mesé, representing, as a plump and smiling sage, one Siddhartha,* an Oriental holy man who had lived a thousand years before.

'A hundred feet! Its mass must be incalculable! Surely the pressure must crush its supporting walls, however thick.'

* The Buddha.

'Not so, Serenity. See.' And with a flourish, the little engineer lifted up the model's dome to reveal the interior – exquisitely painted to represent marbles of every hue. 'Those four mighty piers are joined, at a height of seventy feet, by those four great arches on whose apices the dome will rest.'

'Even so . . .' The emperor's voice trailed off in doubt.

'Rest assured, Serenity. The piers and arches won't collapse. The dome, you see, will be constructed from the lightest material imaginable.'

'Wood!' exclaimed Justinian in horror. 'A lightning strike – then up it goes in flames!'

'Not wood, Serenity,' Anthemius chuckled, shaking his head in mild reproof. '*Pumice.* So light it floats on water. Yet tough and durable. It will enable the dome's construction to be thin, but strong; all to be covered with a marble skin, of course. Imagine half an eggshell resting on four child's building blocks.'

'Pure genius!' Justinian smiled, raising his hands in admiration. 'I chose well, Anthemius, when I chose yourself to oversee my project.'

'The scale's too small, Serenity, to let you appreciate the building's chief quality. From the outside, it'll appear impressively big, certainly; and those flanking semi-domes should impart a certain elegance. Otherwise, it won't look all that remarkable. Inside, however, it's a different matter. Standing in the centre of the nave, the spectator will be aware of vistas of space receding into space, while above, the great dome will appear to float in air.' He paused, and his tone, which up to this point had been briskly matter-of-fact, became hushed and solemn as he continued, 'As if suspended by a golden chain from Heaven.'

On almost any day thereafter, the citizens of Constantinople, if passing through the Augusteum could be greeted by the extraordinary sight of their emperor, clad in a workman's linen tunic, clambering about the organized chaos of the great new church's building site, inspecting, exhorting, questioning, his presence both a nuisance and a source of inspiration. Justinian had never been happier.

In that same year, Khusro – the new Great King of Persia (old Kavadh, for so long a thorn in East Rome's flesh, having died the year before) signed a Treaty of Eternal Peace with the Roman Empire. Nothing could have been more opportune for Justinian; now his hands were freed to press ahead with his plans to recover the West's lost provinces for Rome – plans which he had recently been forced to modify.

For a time, it had seemed that Africa could be reunited with the Empire without a blow being struck. The Vandal king, Hilderic – grandson of Gaiseric the conqueror of Roman Africa – had, probably on account of his Roman ancestry of which he was inordinately proud, adopted a remarkably pro-Roman stance, favouring an alliance with the Empire, combined with a hostile stance towards the Ostrogoth regime in Italy. He had even abandoned his Arian faith to become a Catholic. (His mother Eudocia, daughter of the West Roman emperor Valentinian III, was part of the booty which Gaiseric had brought back to Carthage after sacking Rome; subsequently, she had married Gaiseric's son, Hilderic being their offspring.)

All that had changed recently, however. Disgusted with Hilderic and his cosying-up to Rome, the Vandal nobility – anti-Roman to a man – had rebelled, overthrowing Hilderic and replacing him with his cousin, Gelimer, a man after their own heart. Justinian had intervened diplomatically on behalf of his now-imprisoned friend, only to receive a sharp rebuff from Gelimer. No question now of a friendly Africa becoming a launch-pad for an invasion of Italy. On the pretext of restoring Hilderic, the Vandal kingdom must be conquered first. And who better to carry out this task, thought Justinian, than Belisarius – the brilliant young general whose initiative and loyalty had been crucial in ending the Nika affair. Now that peace had broken out with Persia, the emperor lost no time in recalling Belisarius from the eastern frontier.

'This time, my friend, we shall succeed,' declared Justinian warmly, clapping Belisarius on the shoulder. The two were standing on the Palace walls, looking down on the fleet (which had just been blessed by old Epiphanius, the Patriarch) anchored in the Harbour of Hormisdas on the Sea of Marmara. The mighty armada consisted of five hundred ships, four-fifths of them transports, the rest *dromons* – sleek war-galleys armed with deadly rams; aboard were sixteen thousand soldiers, plus thirty thousand sailors and marines. Neither man needed any reminder that the last attempt to liberate Roman Africa from the Vandals – sixty-five years previously – had ended in disaster, bankrupting both empires, and precipitating the fall of the Western one, a mere eight years later.

'On the last occasion, Serenity,' commented Belisarius, 'Basiliscus dithered; some say he was bribed by Gaiseric to do so – anyway, long enough for the wind to change and pin his fleet against a rocky promontory. Then, when the the Vandals sent in fireships . . .' Belisarius shrugged expressively, then went on with a grin, 'Don't worry, Serenity, I'm not about to make the same mistake. A beach-head landing on an occupied coast is a notoriously difficult operation to pull off successfully. But thanks to your brilliant undercover work in Sardinia,* Serenity, I've a good chance of disembarking the army unopposed.'

Setting sail almost exactly eighteen months after the ending of the Nika Riots, and assisted by fair winds, the fleet progressed in stately fashion over the Aegean, around the Peloponnese, then across an unaccustomedly calm Ionian Sea, to make landfall south of Tauromenium** in Sicily, to take on water. It also took on fresh food, for many of the men had fallen sick from eating mouldy biscuit, issued (for profiteering reasons) by a reinstated John of Cappadocia.

While supplies were being loaded onto the ships lying off the beach, an important intelligence mission was entrusted to none other than Procopius. Unsuspected by Justinian of any treachery, and standing high in the emperor's favour, the ambitious young lawyer and aspiring writer had managed to secure for himself the post of military historian for the expedition. Meeting up with a merchant friend in Syracuse, a man with a web of contacts throughout the Mediterranean, Procopius learned from him that the Vandals had not the slightest inkling of Belisarius' expedition; in consequence, their fleet was still tied up in Sardinian waters. (Before leaving Syracuse to rejoin Belisarius, Procopius arranged with his friend – for a sum – that a message be despatched to Carthage . . .)

On receiving Procopius' report, Belisarius – overjoyed by his good fortune, and impressed by the efficiency of the expedition's historian – sailed immediately for Africa via Malta, making landfall at Caput Vada,† a bleak and lonely headland some five days' journey to the south of Carthage. Here, thanks to the general's discipline and organization, the huge and complex task of disembarking thousands of men and horses proceeded smoothly. Once ashore, Belisarius addressed the army, warning the men against doing anything that might alienate the natives. A friendly population would, he pointed out, prove an enormous asset to the Romans in the imminent trial of strength. No sooner had the general dismissed the troops and stepped

---

* Secret agents sent by Justinian had stirred up a revolt by the native Romans against the island's Vandal occupiers, prompting Gelimer to send his fleet to Sardinian waters to put down the insurrection.
** Taormina. Diplomatic negotiations with the Ostrogoth regime in advance had secured landing rights for the fleet.
† Ras Kaboudia.

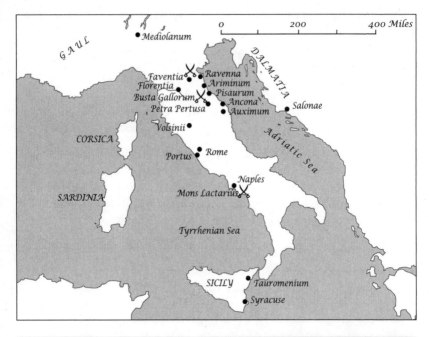

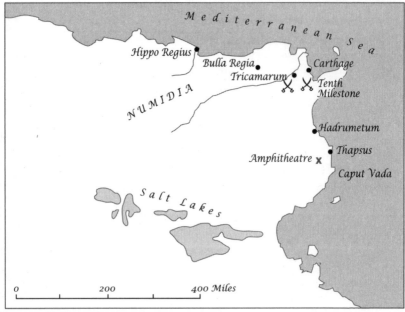

Africa and Italy during the Vandal and Gothic Wars, AD 533–52

down from his tribunal, than a scout on a lathered mount came posting in from the north.

'Sir,' gasped the man, dismounting before Belisarius, 'the Vandals have got wind of your arrival. Gelimer has ordered Hilderic be put to death, and is even now advancing against you with three great armies!'

FOURTEEN

Only in states in which the power of the people is supreme, has liberty any abode
Cicero, *De Republica*, c. 50 BC

Blinking in the bright African sunlight as, in the wake of his Berber guide, he emerged from the darkness of the tunnel, Procopius gasped at the sight that met his eyes: a vast elliptical arena, encircled by tiers of marble seating soaring to a height of a hundred feet or more. At the far end of the amphitheatre,* nearly a hundred and fifty yards away, a figure, flanked by standing spearmen, sat in the *podium*, a raised platform reserved for aristocratic spectators, access to which could be gained only from the exterior of the building. Accompanied by the guide and Aigan – captain of the Hun contingent serving in Belisarius' army – as well as some Huns to act as porters, Procopius advanced towards the *podium*. As he walked, Procopius remembered a conversation with Anicius Julianus, a little over a year and a half before . . .

Responding to a summons from Julianus immediately following the failure of the Nika revolt, Procopius found the senator in his villa, surrounded by trunks and packing-cases.

'Forgive the confusion, dear boy,' said Julianus, sounding remarkably unperturbed considering the circumstances. 'But tempus fugit, as they say, and my ship for Italy awaits the tide.' He handed the lawyer a brimming goblet. 'Nomentan – a reasonable vintage. I've several amphorae of the stuff in my cellars. I recommend you help yourself – before John of Cappadocia's henchmen arrive to confiscate it. Well, to proceed in medias res, as Horace puts it. Regarding Nika – we may have lost the battle, but not, perhaps, the war. At stake is an issue the import of which could not be greater. It is this: unless he can be checked, Justinian will be disastrous for the Empire. Already, his policies, driven by blind ambition verging on paranoia, have brought the state to the verge of ruin. If prosecuted, his plan to reconquer the West from the barbarians will complete that process.'

* The spectacular (and spectacularly well-preserved) Roman amphitheatre at El Jem in eastern Tunisia – the third largest in the Roman world.

'But the restoration of the Roman Empire in its entirety; is that really such a bad thing?'

'The West is finished, my young friend.' The senator turned to some slaves who had entered the room, and issued instructions as to the removal of luggage. When they had departed, burdened with crates and portmanteaux, he went on, 'Any attempt to put the clock back will ultimately prove to be a waste of time, effort, and money. Even if we succeed in driving the barbarians out, other barbarians are waiting beyond the frontiers to take their place: Lombards, Gepids, Heruls, Slavs, to name but some. The effort of reconquering the West will enormously weaken the East, inviting attack from Persia, an empire that is strong, united, and aggressive. And let us not ignore another potential threat – Arabia.'

'A scattered collection of backward, nomadic tribes! Surely, Senator, you can't be serious.'

'Well, perhaps I am being unduly alarmist,' conceded the other. 'I base my suggestion on my observations of the Arab character – ferocious and fanatical when committed to some cause. They caused no end of trouble on the Syrian frontier in Justin's time; some were even rumoured to have drunk the blood of slaughtered Romans.* It would only take a leader of sufficient charisma to unite them, and then . . .' The senator smiled, and shook his head. 'Once, we thought the Huns too primitive to be taken seriously. Then along came Attila, and look what happened.

'But I digress.' Julianus refilled their goblets and went on, 'Some of us who love Rome have, as you know, for you were briefly involved, joined together in a movement called *Libertas*, dedicated to the overthrow of Justinian's regime** and its replacement by a constitutional government. One which will respect the rights of every Roman citizen, rights to be safeguarded by the people's representative body – the Senate – from whose ranks will be drawn a Council, to advise the emperor: both ancient institutions which Justinian, in his overweening arrogance has virtually abolished. Moreover, he who wears the purple will do so only subject to the approval of the Senate, the Army, and the Church. Thus it will be impossible for any such as Justinian ever again to rule the Empire.'

'It all sounds very noble, Senator,' responded Procopius. 'But with the crushing of Nika, Justinian's firmly back in the saddle. He won't easily be unseated, I think.'

* An observation confirmed by Ammianus Marcellinus in Book 31 of his *The Histories*.
** See Appendix IV: *Procopius – Fifth Columnist?*

'Perhaps not; but we must try. At present, thanks to Nika's failure, *Libertas* is seriously weakened, its members dispersed and demoralized. What we all share however, are determination and commitment. Also, we intend to keep in touch, through correspondence and intermediaries, with myself as co-ordinator – leader, if you like. So concerted policy and planning can still be carried on.'

'I don't quite see –'

'– how you fit into this?' Julianus looked keenly at the other. 'You could be invaluable to *Libertas*. You are close to the emperor – a trusted confidant, in fact. When he embarks on his invasion of the West, it shouldn't be too difficult for you to persuade him to involve you in the expedition.'

'In what capacity?'

'Oh, I don't know – observer, go-between; i/c. commissariat; an intelligent young fellow like yourself will think of something. May I take it you'd wish to continue your association with *Libertas*?'

'Perhaps. Depends what's in it for myself.' The lawyer shrugged self-deprecatingly. 'Don't misunderstand me, Senator, I admire what *Libertas* is trying to do. It's just that I'm maybe not so altruistic as your other members.'

'Well, at least you're honest.' Julianus smiled wryly, and topped up their goblets. 'What I would ask of you is this: once Justinian's Western campaign gets under way, that you send regular reports to myself or my agents, apprising *Libertas* of the situation as it stands. Also, you will receive instructions periodically regarding spying, sabotage, acting as an agent provocateur, generating misinformation, et cetera. Such things call for nerve, coolness, and initiative – all qualities that you possess, as you amply demonstrated during your short time with us. In addition, you will be given, on an ad hoc basis, information regarding contacts, drop-off points for messages or letters, safe houses, and the like. Your services will be rewarded by a generous fee from central funds, plus bonuses when merited; most of us, being of senatorial rank, are wealthy, although some will shortly become considerably less so – thanks to confiscations in the wake of Nika. Anything you can do to destabilize Justinian's Western campaign will help to weaken his authority, thus assist in paving the way for his removal. Well, Procopius, what do you say?'

'When do I start?'

'Consider yourself on the payroll as of now.' Smiling, Julianus handed the other a small but heavy bag, that chinked invitingly. He raised his goblet. 'To *Libertas*.'

'To *Libertas*.'

Arriving at the base of the arena's marble wall, beneath the *podium*, Procopius looked up at the seated figure – a massively built man with a great shock of tawny hair.

'The Roman, Procopius, Highness,' called out the guide. Turning to the young historian, he announced, 'Duke Ammatas, *Domine*, brother of King Gelimer.'

The whole mise-en-scène was a childish piece of stage-management on the Vandal's part, thought Procopius with irritation. It was designed to emphasize Ammatas' superior status, and put the Roman on the back foot in any negotiation. Craning his neck in order to address the other face to face, and putting on a false smile, he declared, 'Greetings, Highness; in pursuance of prior arrangements to hold this meeting, I would respect-fully tender the following request. That in return for Hun help to enable the Vandals to defeat their Roman enemy, you agree to pay Aigan here – captain of the Huns in the army of Belisarius *Comes* – the sum of one thousand pounds weight in gold, half to be paid now, the remainder following a successful outcome of hostilities.'

'Ho! ho! – you seek to chaffer like a housewife in the market?' boomed Ammatas. 'Well, Roman, two can play at that game. One thousand pounds? One hundred is surely what you meant to say.'

Gritting his teeth, Procopius joined the other in the tedious process of haggling, knowing full well that an intermediate amount would anyway be agreed upon – eventually. After what seemed an interminable period, the bargaining (conducted in sweltering heat) was concluded, the amount of gold agreed on handed over, and broad tactics regarding the coming en-counter discussed. Ammatas and his Vandals then exited the *podium*, while Procopius' party returned to the entrance of the tunnel (which opened into the passage leading to the Door of Life – the gateway into the arena for performers and wild beasts).

With Aigan's Huns bowed beneath sacks of coin, the little procession retraced its steps along the dank and dripping shaft, lined with massive ashlar blocks positioned there by Roman engineers three centuries before, when Alexander Severus ruled a yet undivided Empire. Emerging from the tunnel at the coast, the party transferred the load to waiting mules, then unobtrusively rejoined Belisarius' army camped nearby.

FIFTEEN

Set up in the reign of the Emperor Flavius Valerius Constantinus; Pious,
Noble Caesar; from Carthage ten miles
Inscription (conjectural, based on ones typical of the period)
on the tenth milestone south of Carthage, c. 330

With the heat of the fierce African sun tempered by a cool sea breeze blowing from the Mare Internum* to its right, the army marched north along a stretch of glorious sandy beaches. Inland, these were fringed by waving clumps of esparto grass topped by graceful feathered seed heads, beyond which olive groves and fields of wheat rolled to the horizon. High overhead, the first migrating birds of early autumn – storks, geese, finches and many other species – speckled the bright blue sky, bound from Europe for the lands beyond the Great Sand Sea.

Walking their horses to the top of a rise, Belisarius and his second-in-command, Dorotheus, a fellow Thracian, looked down on the long cavalry column winding its way below them: horse-archers and lance-armed *foederati*,** mailed *cataphractarii*, the general's personal corps of retainers or *bucellarii*, Hun mercenaries – stocky, skin-clad men with yellowish complexions and flat Oriental faces, mounted on huge ill-conformed brutes, and armed with deadly recurved bows. Miles to the rear, appearing as a multitude of crawling dots, came the infantry.

A rapidly approaching cloud of dust to the fore announced the imminent arrival of a scout. Minutes later, the man drew rein before the two officers. 'Vandals!' the man panted. 'Vanguard's only two miles off.'

'But those Hun outriders told us the enemy was at least a day's march distant!' exclaimed Dorotheus to his superior. 'Strung out like this, our army's at a massive disadvantage. Best we fall back and join the infantry; I'll order the trumpeters to sound "Retreat", shall I?'

'Certainly not,' declared Belisarius. Though projecting an air of breezy confidence, the news had in fact caused him to be deeply worried. Thanks to that faulty information from the Huns, the Romans, at this particular

* The Mediterranean.
** Foreign troops serving under their own leaders.

juncture, were in a poor position to take on the Vandals. Before they could be fully deployed in line of battle, and lacking infantry support, the enemy would most likely be upon them. But the alternative – getting the column to turn around then march back several miles, in a manoeuvre that would be time-consuming, inevitably chaotic, and bad for morale – was even less attractive.

Belisarius was also uncomfortably aware of the fact that the coming encounter would be the first real test of his ability as a commander. Hitherto, his experience of soldiering had been confined to service on the Persian front. Here, he had earned a reputation for energy and dash, but any action had amounted to little more than skirmishing against a civilized enemy who understood the rules of warfare, including knowing when discretion was the better part of valour. The Vandals – Germans with a name for aggressiveness, ferocity, and disregard for personal safety – could prove to be a very different matter. It was to be hoped that a century of life as conquerors in a fat land with a hot climate, had softened them some-what, but it would be foolish to count on it.

'Get the *bucinatores* to sound the "Halt",' he told Dorotheus. 'I'll take the centre with the heavy cavalry, you dispose the archers and light horse on the wings.' And the two galloped off to start the process of readying the troops for battle.

Watching the Vandal advance from a high dune out on the seaward flank of the Roman line, Procopius cursed beneath his breath. The fools were coming on in *three* divisions – all widely separated, thus unable to re-inforce each other. He could see that the foremost was commanded by Ammatas – conspicuous, even at a distance, by his tawny mane. That was counter to the plan. The agreed strategy was that Ammatas, commanding the first two sections as a *single* unit, would, when joined by the Huns, have sufficient weight of numbers to deliver a destabilizing blow to the Roman line; Gelimer, bringing up the rear with the main force, would do the rest. The Roman invasion, like all its predecessors, would be brought to nothing before it had properly begun. Now, thanks to Ammatas' folly, the whole scheme was in jeopardy. What was the man thinking of? fumed Procopius. Probably thought he could defeat the Romans single-handed, so to speak, and thus not have to share the glory with the other Vandal leaders. Typical German.

The scene below Procopius unfolded with a kind of dreadful inevita-bility. The Huns, too cunning to risk throwing away their lives on what they could see was probably now a doomed attempt, held back. From the Roman front, still milling about in semi-confusion as units scrambled to find their place, scattered groups of cataphracts began to emerge; then, swiftly coalescing in a single mass, like drops of oil in the bottom of a skillet, they formed up and thundered down upon Ammatas' force. The mailed horsemen, each armed with a heavy *kontos* – the deadly, twelve-foot lance that could skewer a man like a rabbit on a spit – crashed into the mob of charging warriors, most of whom lacked body-armour. Beneath the shattering impact of the heavy Roman horse, the German formation first shredded at the fringes, then broke up. Once infiltrated by enemy cavalry, infantry is finished; so it proved with Ammatas' Vandals, who were slaughtered to a man, including Ammatas himself.

Now came the turn of the Huns. Anxious to identify with what now looked to be the winning side, they galloped forward and, forming a moving ring around the second Vandal force, proceeded to discharge volley upon volley of arrows into it. Only a few survived that lethal sleet, the Huns only withdrawing when the main Vandal force under King Gelimer arrived upon the scene.

With the advent of the monarch, the scales suddenly began to tilt in the Vandals' favour. Advancing in six enormous *cunei* – close-packed attack columns – the Vandal host, with enormous impetus drove into the still-forming Roman line, causing it to buckle and fall back. Desperately, Belisarius tried to steady his troops, galloping to and fro, exhorting the men in a frantic effort to make them hold their ground. If only, he thought, they could have had just a few more minutes to get into formation . . .

Then, as if the gods (in the heart of most Thracians, Christ had not yet quite supplanted the old Olympian pantheon) had heard his anguished plea and decided to intervene, the Vandal advance inexplicably began to falter; then it stopped. (As Belisarius was to find out later, Gelimer – coming upon the corpse of his brother Ammatas, had been plunged into inconsolable grief, becoming so distracted as temporarily to lose his grip on the demands of leadership.)

It was enough for Belisarius to regain the initiative. Granted those precious extra minutes, he was able to complete the deployment of the Roman line. Immediately thereafter, Roman discipline, combined with superior organization and equipment, began to tell against the Vandals who, in the course of the past century, had had to contend with no more formidable foes than tribal bands of Moors and Berbers. Raw German courage now proved no match against the armoured Roman force, which began to roll forward inexorably, like an unstoppable machine.

With their king no longer directing them, doubt and confusion spread rapidly among the Vandals. Losing heart, they broke, and were suddenly in headlong flight west towards Numidia, bypassing Carthage.

Drenched with sweat – as much from relief as from the exertions of command – Belisarius summoned the expedition historian. He pointed to a milestone beside the Roman road running through the battlefield, which bore the inscription, IMP. CAES. FLAV. VAL. CONSTANTINO: PIO NOB. CAES: A CARTHAGO M. P. X.

'Something for your Chronicle, Procopius. Ready?' The lawyer nodded. Taking out his waxed writing tablets, he scratched with his stylus to the other's dictation, 'Know that on this Ides of September in the year the two hundred and fourth from the Founding of New Rome,* at the tenth milestone south from Carthage, the Romans gained a great victory over the Vandals, ending their one hundred and four years' usurpation of the Diocese of Africa.'

It wasn't quite the end. Although the Romans occupied Carthage and at once set about dismantling the machinery of Vandal administration, Gelimer and the remnants of his army managed to hold out till mid-December, when (Belisarius' Hun contingent deciding to ignore the Vandal monarch's bribes and again stay loyal to the Romans) they were finally routed at Tricamarum, west of Carthage. Africa (now including, besides the mainland diocese, Sardinia, Corsica, and the Balearics) became a praetorian prefecture divided into seven provinces, upon which immediately descended a swarm of officials – and tax-collectors. As for the civilian Vandal population, it was absorbed or killed by the surrounding Romans and Berbers. As a nation the Vandals had been wiped from the slate of history, leaving not a trace of their existence behind, save a memory of cruelty and destruction.

Entering the city through the Golden Gate in the mighty Theodosian Walls, the great procession, flanked by cheering crowds, made its way along the Mesé. At the front, heading his soldiers, marched Belisarius – granted a Roman triumph, the first for centuries; then came Gelimer in chains, but clad, ironically, in royal purple, followed by the tallest and handsomest of the Vandal prisoners, then wagon after wagon loaded with

* 13 September 533.

the spoils of victory, among which was the *Menorah*: the seven-branched gold candlestick which, close on five centuries before, Titus had taken to Rome whence Gaiseric had removed it to Carthage.

The column proceeded through the fora of Arcadius, the Ox, Amastrianum, Theodosius, and Constantine, with all around new buildings rising to replace those destroyed in the riots of two and a half years before. The parade finally halting in the Hippodrome, Belisarius knelt in obeisance before the *kathisma* wherein were seated, surrounded by the great officers of state, Justinian and Theodora.

'"Well done, thou good and faithful servant,"' the emperor quoted from St Mathew's Gospel, his voice warm with emotion, '– conqueror of Africa, and our consul for next year.'*

Next, Gelimer was brought before the imperial pair. Instead of the defiantly scowling savage that he had half-expected, Justinian beheld a gentle-faced man who carried himself with quiet dignity. The thought – 'Thus might Christ have appeared before Pilate,' flitted through his mind.

'Eat the dust, Vandal dog,' growled the officer on escort duty, ripping the purple robe from Gelimer's shoulders, and giving his back a brutal shove. Abasing himself at the foot of the royal box, the last king of the Vandals murmured, in the words of the son of David, 'Vanity of vanities, all is vanity.'

Justinian felt a surge of compassion. There was something touching, almost noble, about a man who, finally surrendering to the Romans after weeks of a wretched existence as a hunted fugitive, had asked for three things: a lyre to accompany himself singing the sad story of his misfortunes, a sponge to wipe away his tears, and a loaf of bread to stay the pangs of hunger.

'Rise, friend,' Justinian commanded softly. 'Your fetters will be removed, your freedom restored, and a fitting residence found for you to pass your days in peace.'**

A sense of triumphant gladness welled up in the emperor's breast. The horror and humiliation of the Nika episode could now finally be put behind

---

* Belisarius' consulship, inaugurated on 1 January 535, was one of the very last; '. . . the succession of consuls finally ceased in the thirteenth year of Justinian [i.e. in 539].' (Gibbon)

** Justinian was as good as his word. Displaying a magnanimity not exactly typical of Roman emperors, he settled the Vandal monarch on a rich estate in Galatia, where he was permitted to practise his Arian faith. In addition, he enrolled surviving able-bodied Vandal males into five regiments of *Vandali Justiniani*.

him. By his great victory over the Vandals, God had indeed confirmed that Justinian was His Appointed. But Africa was only the beginning. As *Restitutor Orbis Romani* – Restorer of the Roman World – he must now embark on the next stage of the Great Plan: the conquest of Italy.

SIXTEEN

The child who had trembled at a schoolmaster's rod would never dare to look upon a sword

Aphorism of Theoderic, c. 500

On an October evening of the same year that Belisarius celebrated his triumph, Cassiodorus – silver-haired elder statesman, Praetorian Prefect of Italy, and Secretary of the Ostrogothic Council – greeted his fellow Roman Cethegus,* the *Caput Senatus* as, from different directions, they entered Ravenna's *Platea Maior*: the main thoroughfare of the city's *civitas barbara*, or Gothic quarter.

'Ave, Rufius. You too have had a royal summons . . . sorry – invitation – to this feast?' enquired the prefect.

'I fear so, Magnus,' replied Cethegus, whose homely features bore a striking resemblance to those of the Flavian emperor Vespasian. 'The royal bratling must have something important he wants us to hear, to have dragged me all the way from Rome. *And* insisted on senatorial dress.' With a wry grin, he indicated the archaic toga in which he was enshrouded. 'I see you too are required to wear your robes of office. I guess Athalaric likes to have the odd tame Roman to show off to his Gothic friends.' And chatting amicably, the pair made their way towards the guards' compound, which the young king (in a gesture of defiance against his mother, the regent Amalasuntha**) had chosen as a venue for his feast, in preference to the royal palace.

The two old friends had risen to high office under Theoderic, the great Ostrogothic leader who (officially as vicegerent of Italy for the Eastern emperor) had proved a model ruler for most of his long reign. His designated heir, Eutharic, husband of Amalasuntha, had predeceased him, leaving Athalaric – son of Eutharic and Amalasuntha – to become king at the tender age of ten, his mother ruling for him until he should come of age.

---

* For the background of these two influential Roman officials, see my *Theoderic*.
** Amalasuntha was the beautiful and learned daughter of Theoderic, who had died eight years before in 526.

'Remind me what's happening at court,' requested Cethegus, as the two strolled through the neat little city, studded with fine new Arian churches built under Theoderic. Protected by its ring of lagoons and marshes, Ravenna had replaced Milan as capital of the Western Empire at the start of the barbarian invasions over a century before. Now, situated in the Ostrogothic heartland of the Padus* valley, it was the administrative centre of Amalasuntha's government. 'As head of the Senate,' went on Cethegus, 'I have to be in Rome for most of the year, so I tend to lose touch with what's going on in the corridors of power up here.'

'Things are pretty tense at present, Rufius,' sighed the prefect, his fine patrician features pursed in cogitation. 'There's a ding-dong power struggle going on between Amalasuntha and the leading Ostrogoths for control of Italy, with young Athalaric a pawn in the game. Basically, the problem boils down to this: Amalasuntha's a woman; she's a Romanophile; she wants – or rather did, until the matter was taken out of her hands – Athalaric to be given a Roman education.** All of which is total abomination to the Gothic nobility. To fierce, patriarchal-minded German warriors, rule by a female is anathema. To them, Romans are an effete and cowardly race, so a Roman education is the last thing they want for their king. Accordingly, they removed young Athalaric from his Roman tutors and switched him to a *German* education. In other words: no more books, no more cane, just learning how to fight, and, unfortunately – drink. Thanks to their enlightened tutelage, the boy, who's now seventeen, has become a drunken wastrel. Round One to them.'

'Somehow, Magnus, I can't imagine Theoderic's daughter taking all this lying down. She's inherited her father's strength of will, I believe.'

'That, my friend, would be an understatement. She got her three chief opponents appointed to frontier commands to get them away from court, then had them murdered. Also, as an insurance policy, she sent her personal fortune across the Adriatic to Dyrrachium in the Eastern Empire, just in case she had to cut and run. It never came to that of course; now, with her three main enemies out of the way, and some leading Goths deciding to back her, she's managing to cling to power – just. So, Round Two to her. However, should Athalaric die – and with his health wrecked by drink, that could happen sooner rather than later – her position, without

---

* River Po.
** A Roman education involved liberal use of the cane. In the opinion of Theoderic, this would cow a boy's spirit, so that when he became a man he would be afraid of battle.

a man to legitimize her rule, would become parlous. As you can imagine, law and order's rather gone to pot, with the *duces* and *saiones** openly flouting the authority of a female regent they resent, and a boy-king they despise.'

'Altogether, a situation you could describe as interesting,' mused Cethegus. 'With Justinian waiting in the wings to take advantage of any crisis that develops. Now that Africa's been brought back into the Empire, Italy has to be his next target.'

'A racing certainty, I'd say.' Cassiodorus shook his head and chuckled. 'As you so rightly observe, the situation's – "interesting". Well, here we are – the old imperial barracks.' And he pointed to a grim Roman building looming ahead, an uncompromising stone box with a massive tower at each corner. Here were housed the *protectores domestici*, the household guards. These were now all Goths, their Roman predecessors having been phased out ten years previously in accordance with Theoderic's principle that only Goths should man the army, leaving Romans to run the administration.

Down the centre of the great drill-hall flanking the *quadratum* extended a long line of trestle tables (none of this effeminate Roman nonsense of lounging on couches) at which were seated the king and his guests – all Gothic nobles, apart from the two Romans, Cassiodorus and Cethegus. This latter pair alone wore Roman dress; the others were clad in Germanic trousers and belted tunics, Roman dalmatics being *streng verboten*. No females were present, for this was to be a *warriors'* feast, where men could brag, guzzle, and swill to their hearts' content, free from the restraining influence of womenfolk. Seated in the middle, the young king, his face blotched and puffy from long acquaintance with the wine-stoup, cut a faintly ridiculous figure. In imitation of what he imagined to have been the garb of his heroic German ancestors, he sported a cloak of wolf-fur, fastened at the shoulder by an enormous enamel-and-gold fibula in the form of an eagle, his head being surmounted by a silvered *Spangenhelm*. Gone was his original short Roman haircut; in its place, flaxen locks now depended to his shoulders. Less successful had been his attempt to grow a Gothic-style moustache, his upper lip adorned by a mere downy fuzz.

Swaying slightly, Athalaric rose and raised aloft his wine-cup. (In contrast to his favouring all things Teutonic over Roman, he had acquired, in

---

* These two categories of Goths corresponded (very roughly) respectively to barons and sheriffs in mediaeval England. 'Dux' was a Roman title for the holder of a high military command, one which Gothic nobles had (rather inappropriately) adopted.

preference to German beer, a liking for the strong Roman vintages, which he drank undiluted.) All followed suit.

'My friendsh . . . friends, fellow Goths and Romans,' the king announced, in tones already slurred, 'in three weeks time I shall be eighteen. An age at which my illushtrious . . . illustrious grandfather, Theoderic, had already made his name, by capturing the great city of Shingi . . . Singidunum. But my mother says I'm not yet fit to rule. The bitch. Well, we'll see about that. Come my birthday, I intend to tell her she is no longer regent, and musht make way for me. I trust I may count on your support.' He paused and looked muzzily around the table. 'I therefore ask you all to drink: to my acsheshun . . . accession.'

Goblets were dutifully drained – except by one venerable greybeard, whom the king unfortunately spotted.

'Hildebrand – you did not drink!' accused Athalaric, his face whitening. 'You, who were my grandfather's cup-bearer. You wouldn't have refused to toasht . . . toast Theoderic, I think.'

'You, Sire, are no Theoderic,' declared the old man bluntly.

'You dare to speak to me like that!' screamed the king. Turning to Cassiodorus he declared, a note almost of pleading entering his voice, 'Tell him I am worthy to be king.'

'Italy is fortunate indeed, to have as ruler a descendant of the great Theoderic,' replied the other smoothly.

'You see!' shouted Athalaric, unaware of the prefect's careful ambiguity. 'Even Cashiodorus – a Roman – thinks that I should shit . . . sit upon the throne. By God Hildebrand, you *will* drink, you . . . you insolent dotard.' And moving down the table, he grabbed the elder by the nose. Forced to open his mouth in order to breathe, the old man was unable to prevent Athalaric from spilling some wine into it.

'Now, leave our presence,' demanded Athalaric, setting down a half-empty goblet. 'You are hereby banished from our court – forever.'

Red-faced and spluttering, Hildebrand nevertheless exited the hall with dignity, an embarrassed silence spreading in his wake.

Awkward and stilted at first, conversation gradually picked up as a harpist began to sing of great deeds by Gothic heroes, and a stream of rude plenty – mainly dishes of beef, pork, and venison – flowed in from the kitchens. (Conspicuous by their absence were elaborate Roman dishes such as flamingoes' tongues with mullets' livers, or sows' udders in tunny sauce.) Toast followed toast, in heavy Roman wines unmixed with water. In contrast to the king, who invariably refilled his goblet, most of the guests, after a time, contented themselves with sipping sparingly each time a health was drunk.

After several hours, with the torches guttering in their sconces and several guests slumped asleep, their heads resting on the boards, Athalaric, cheeks flushed and eyes bloodshot, rose unsteadily to propose a final toast. 'To my beloved mother – Amalashuntha,' he mumbled incoherently. 'May she rot in hell.' Suddenly, he staggered, the goblet slipping from his fingers, and with a loud cry crashed backwards to the floor. Immediately, a doctor was summoned; arriving within minutes, he knelt beside the patient. After a brief examination, he rose and pronounced to the assembled guests, 'Gentlemen – the king is dead.'

SEVENTEEN

If my lord the emperor is dissatisfied, there will be war
Procopius (paraphrasing Peter the Patrician's warning to
Theodahad about the consequences should Amalasuntha
not be reinstated), *History of the Wars of Justinian, after 552*

'Slow down, Serenity,' grumbled John the Cappadocian, as he toiled up the ladder in the wake of Justinian. Unwilling to break his daily routine of checking progress on his beloved project – the building anew of Hagia Sophia – the emperor had summoned his praetorian prefect to join him on the building site, to make his regular report.

Arriving at the topmost tier of scaffolding, adjoining the pendentives linking the arches on which the great dome would rest, Justinian perched himself on the edge of the planking, from which vantage-point he commanded a clear view of the workmen far below, egaged in erecting the green-and-red-veined columns to support the arcades, or encasing the massive piers with slabs of coloured marble – green, red, yellow, and blue. Puffing heavily, John at last joined the emperor, but was careful to position himself well clear of the platform's brink.

'Well, John, things it seems are looking up for us in Italy. A nephew of Theoderic, one Theodahad – Amalasuntha's cousin and next in line of succession after Athalaric – has offered to transfer his liquid assets to Constantinople in return for a position of dignity at court. A strange, unpleasant character. Tries to be more Roman than the Romans. Divides his time between grabbing land in Tuscany, composing Latin verse, and reading Greek philosophy. Amalasuntha herself has been in secret communication with me, hinting that supreme power might be transferred to ourselves. *And* – this has to be significant – my edict concerning transfer of property, addressed to the senators in both Constantinople and Rome, has been accepted by Ravenna, or at least not rejected.' Producing a length of spiced sausage from a knapsack, the emperor cut off a hunk and passed it to his prefect. 'All in all, John, it looks as if Italy could be rejoining the Empire without a blow being struck.'

'Afraid the picture's changed, Serenity,' declared the other, his mouth full of sausage. 'Coming here, I bumped into your ambassador, Peter the Patrician, fresh back from Ravenna and on his way to report to yourself. Told him I'd pass on his news to you, on his behalf. So here it is. Athalaric died in October. In consequence, Amalasuntha was forced to make Theodahad her *consors regni* – co-ruler; you know these Goths, can't stand the idea of a female running things. Well, now that he's become king, Theodahad has suddenly got big ideas, which don't include sharing power with his cousin. From being a committed Romanophile he's now sided with the anti-Roman Gothic nationalists, especially the relatives of the three leading Goths Amalasuntha had murdered, all powerful men with lots of influence.'

Justinian stared at the prefect, his expression bleak. 'This is dreadful, John. And just when things seemed to be going so well.'

'Better brace yourself, Serenity; it gets worse. Theodahad and his clique of leading Goths have staged a coup, deposed Amalasuntha and imprisoned her on an island in Lacus Volsiniensis* in Umbria, where she's rumoured to be in danger of her life.'

'Unbelievable! Theodahad must be warned, in no uncertain terms, that unless he restores Amalasuntha forthwith to her former position, we shall be forced to intervene.'

'Quite right, Serenity. Theodahad needs reminding that, constitutionally, he's the vicegerent of the Eastern emperor – a title and function handed down from Theoderic. It applies of course also to Amalasuntha, only more so. So our Gothic philosopher-king has to toe the line. But so in a sense do you, Serenity. After all, Theodahad *is* the legitimate ruler – if we set aside his usurpation of his cousin's role. So it wouldn't do for you just to march into Italy and take over. That would be universally condemned as naked aggression. What you need is a casus belli. That sausage, by the way, is very good; I won't say no if you're offering some more.'

'Suppose, Serenity, *another* message got through to Theodahad – one different to the one you're proposing to send.' Munching sausage, the Cappadocian shot the emperor a crafty glance.

'Explain yourself, John,' snapped the emperor testily. 'You know I hate mind games.'

'This sausage really is excellent, Serenity – you must tell me where you get it. Well now, just suppose that Theodahad was tipped the wink that, despite your threat, nothing would happen to him if Amalasuntha had, let's say, an "accident". Then suppose Theodahad were to act on that

* Lake Bolsena.

– you'd have a cast-iron case for invading Italy. If necessary, you could always later disown having any part in a second message. Your reason for intervening in Italy would look even better than your excuse for taking over Africa – restoring Hilderic.'

'It's monstrous! I won't hear another word, John – I absolutely forbid it. Do I make myself clear?'

'As glass, Serenity,' the prefect murmured with an enigmatic smile. 'As glass.'

Waylaying Peter the Patrician as (en route to Salonae on the Adriatic, for the crossing to Ravenna) he emerged from Justinian's *tablinum*, Theodora pressed into the ambassador's hand a missive bearing her seal. 'Give this to King Theodahad,' she requested. 'Personally – that's very important. Also, no one, not even the emperor, must know I've given it to you.' She smiled, and patted his hand. 'I know I can trust you, Peter.'

'My lips are sealed, Domina,' replied the other, slipping the letter into his satchel to join Justinian's own message to the Ostrogothic king. Like all servants of the imperial court, he was totally in thrall to the empress's charm and charisma.

The previous day had seen Theodora, in an agony of mind, pacing the little garden where she and Justinian had first met. She recalled the horrified indignation with which the emperor had recounted the Cappadocian's suggestion that Theodahad be given carte blanche to do away with Amalasuntha.

Although her husband had dismissed the idea, Theodora had found herself unable to. Till far into the night, she had wrestled with her conscience. She knew how vitally important the realization of his Grand Plan had become to Justinian. Africa had been a glorious start. But Italy – the very *fons et origo* of Rome's imperial saga – was the prize above all others. Although she cared passionately about the rights of her own sex, was not the sacrifice of a single woman's life justifiable in the great scheme of things? Theodora (despite that snake, Procopius, hinting that Amalasuntha's overtures to Justinian had provoked the empress's jealousy) felt no ill-will towards the Gothic queen; rather, Amalasuntha's courage and resolution in holding out against the chauvinism of the leading Goths had aroused Theodora's admiration and sympathy. But such feelings were disembodied, abstract. She had never met Theoderic's daughter, therefore any guilt she might feel would be impersonal. She was reminded of a conundrum once posed by some philosopher. If, simply by nodding, you would acquire great riches, but at the same time bring about the death of an unknown mandarin in distant China – would you nod?

With a shock of self-disgust, Theodora realized that she had somehow crossed a moral boundary, and was already actively considering how the prefect's sly proposal might be implemented. The steel in her character coming to the fore, Theodora made her decision. Her husband's interests must take precedence. She dismissed the thought that she might be damning her immortal soul; such a consideration would cause Justinian concern, but not herself. Her interest in religious matters was strictly academic, its main solicitude the social penalties of non-conformity. Repairing to her private chamber, she began to draft a letter . . .

'Was the use of Socrates as a character merely a literary device for presenting a philosophical argument?' pondered Theodahad, pen in hand, 'or did it represent Plato's personal views?' Dressed in a Roman dalmatic, and seated at a desk in his *tablinum* (festooned with busts of Greek philosophers and Roman poets) in Ravenna's royal palace, the Gothic monarch was working on a treatise, which he hoped would at last cause others to take him seriously as a scholar and a man of letters. This opus (about the differences between Plato's early dialogues and the middle and late ones) was to be entitled *Crito versus Gorgias*, or perhaps *The Avoidance of Hiatus*. When published, it would, he hoped, impress Cassiodorus to the extent that his eminent *Scriba Concilii** would spread the word, and thus increase his – Theodahad's – status among his Roman subjects. Useless, of course, to expect any Goths to read it; even the few who were literate were hardly likely to have heard of Plato.

He was interrupted by a *silentiarius* (a Goth, the Roman *silentiarii* having been phased out under Theoderic) ushering in, 'The ambassador from Constantinople.'

'Ah – Petrus Patricius,' the king greeted the travel-stained figure who entered. 'Back so soon? Fresh tidings from the emperor, I take it.'

'And from the empress, Your Majesty,' said Peter, removing from his satchel two despatches which he handed to the king.

Theodahad's face paled as he read the first letter, then cleared as he perused the second.

'You may tell His Serenity, Justinianus Augustus, that all is well with Amalasuntha Regina,' he informed the ambassador. 'Far from being under house arrest, she is presently recuperating at a pleasant spot in one of my . . .

* Secretary of the Council.

our estates in Umbria. Her health, you see, has suffered in consequence of her son's untimely death.'

Pacing the study after Peter the Patrician had departed, Theodahad – his markedly Teutonic features furrowed in thought, contemplated his next course of action. Justinian's letter had been unequivocal – return Amalasuntha immediately to Ravenna as queen, or expect the Empire to invade and reinstate her. But against that, the tenor of Theodora's message could hardly have been more different: if Amalasuntha were to be got rid of, Theodahad could rest assured that the emperor would do nothing. The king knew that Theodora's influence over her husband was total; it was well known that he could refuse her nothing. Were she to veto an Italian expedition, then it would be most unlikely to take place. So, on balance, Theodahad felt confident that he could proceed with impunity to do away with Amalasuntha and consolidate his position as sole monarch.

But what was Theodora's motive in sending him the letter? Theodahad decided it was probably jealousy. Suppose a conspiracy of Gothic nobles were to force the queen to come to Constantinople in order to make a personal appeal to Justinian? Amalasuntha was younger than Theodora, and beautiful to boot – probably more so than the empress. Thus, Theodahad reasoned, to Theodora the queen would appear a potential rival, and as such, a target for elimination.

After several hours of swithering, the king at last made up his mind. Murmuring an aphorism of Epicurus, '*Nil igitur mors est ad nos* – Therefore death is nothing to us', he sent for two of his undercover henchmen. When the men arrived – two burly Gepids, a tribe noted for its savagery as well as for its dullness of mind – he proceeded to issue them with instructions, along with a purse of *solidi*. Soon the pair were posting east then south along the Via Aemilia and the Via Cassia – bound for Lacus Volsiniensis . . .

In the fortified villa on the island of Martana assigned by her *consors regni* for her 'recovery', Amalasuntha prepared to take her bath. In the calm of that spring morning,* walking the short distance from the main building to the bath-house, she paused to admire the scenery on the far side of the lake: a shoreline of white rocks making a dramatic contrast to the dark green of pines and cypresses beyond. A flight of ducks planed down onto the tranquil sheet of water, shimmering in the sun's early rays. The sight,

* 30 April 535.

as usual, helped to calm her troubled mind, tortured with uncertainty since her arrest and confinement in this place, in December of the previous year.

The ritual of bathing was one of the few things to give her pleasure in her present existence – a welcome break in the boredom mingled with anxiety which filled her days. First, after depositing her clothes in the *apodyterium* or changing room, a bracing immersion in the plunge pool. Then, a session in the *sudatorium* or steam room to sweat the dirt from every pore, followed by the transit of three cubicles – the *laconium*, *caldarium*, and *tepidarium*, the air in each progressively less hot. Finally, after scraping off the dirt and loosened outer skin with a *strigil*, a period of repose wrapped in a soft dry sheet in the *frigidarium*, when a delicious sensation of perfect well-being would steal over her.

Seated on the wooden bench surrounding the inside of the *sudatorium*, Amalasuntha felt the first prickles of discomfort. The steam was becoming hotter than usual, causing her skin to redden as well as freely to perspire. Clearly, the slaves had miscalculated the amount of fuel to heat the external boiler. She must have a word with the major-domo. For the present, she couldn't bear to remain in the steam room a moment longer; the heat was now intolerable. She tried to push back the sliding door into the *laconium*, but it seemed to be stuck. Fighting down a surge of panic, she pushed harder – still no movement. The door back to the plunge pool she found was likewise jammed. Shouting for the slaves to come to her assistance, she continued to wrestle with the doors – to no avail. Meanwhile, the steam grew hotter and hotter; gushing through the inlets in scalding jets, it caused crops of blisters to erupt all over her skin. Now the vapour was as hot as boiling water: she screamed in mortal agony as the blood began to seethe and bubble in her veins . . .

When the news of the queen's murder broke in Constantinople, Justinian felt simultaneously indignant and exultant. Now, at last, he had the *casus belli* that he needed. Peter the Patrician, who had heard of the incident before taking ship from Ravenna for Salonae, assured the emperor that the deed had caused revulsion against Theodahad's regime, not only on the part of the Roman population, but among many Goths as well. The daughter of the great Theoderic could not be done away with like a common criminal.

Assured of popular support in Italy – at least by the Romans of that peninsula – Justinian commanded Mundus, *Magister Militum* in Illyricum, to invade Dalmatia, and Belisarius to sail for Sicily. The second phase of the Great Plan, the War against the Goths, had begun.

Only later, when he had had time to reflect, did a most disquieting thought occur to the emperor. He had made clear to Theodahad the consequences of maltreating Amalasuntha, yet the king had chosen to ignore the warning. Justinian had (as was his wont) confided to Theodora everything that John the Cappadocian had told him, including the prefect's suggestion that a counter-message reach Theodahad. Could Theodora, to help her husband realize his dream, have sent just such a message? If so, such action spoke of great, unselfish love, also of an iron will, and a ruthless lack of scruple that Justinian had not hitherto suspected. And was it possible that by confiding in Theodora, he had secretly hoped that she would act upon the Cappadocian's suggestion?

Racked with guilt and prey to unnamed fears, the emperor spent the night on his knees in his half-completed great new church, praying for the salvation of his wife's immortal soul.

EIGHTEEN

We have appointed a large part of the soldiers to garrison the forts in Sicily and Italy, which we have been able to conquer, leaving us an army of only five thousand; the enemy are coming against us to the number of one hundred and fifty thousand
Procopius (paraphrasing the opening of Belisarius' appeal to Justinian for more troops), *History of the Wars of Justinian, after 552*

From Procopius Caesariensis – Secretary to General Belisarius and Historian of the Roman Expeditionary Force in Italy, to Anicius Julianus, Senator and *Vir Clarissimus* – greetings.

Dear 'Cato', I write to inform you of events as they now stand here, and of my recent activities on behalf of *Libertas*. Much you'll have already heard of, but it won't do any harm to get things 'from the horse's mouth'. Those extra funds you allocated me came in pretty useful. Before leaving Carthage, I was able to bribe some dissatisfied elements among the troops garrisoning Africa into stirring up a serious mutiny. This caused Belisarius no end of bother, forcing him to return to Africa from Sicily in order to quell the insurrection. While he was doing that, I managed to get a jolly little insurgency going in Sicily, by the same means as above. So by the time he'd sorted *that* out, his plans were badly behind schedule. All in all, I think we can congratulate ourselves on slowing things down nicely. (Pity the Huns reneged on us in Africa – no principles, these people. Even so, the scrap at the Tenth Milestone was a close-run thing.)

Well, thanks to our beloved emperor's tight-fistedness, poor old B. – with only *five thousand* troops at his disposal (the same number are pinned down on garrison duties) has his hands tied. So I've been forced to write (following B.'s instructions) to Justinian himself appealing for reinforcements. Even with such a tiny army, B. has, unfortunately, performed wonders – taking Naples, then Rome itself, before the Goths were able to muster their host. The position at present is as follows.

True to form, Theodahad dithered – switching allegiance between his own people and Constantinople, depending on whichever side seemed at the moment most likely to win. Predictably, the Goths eventually lost patience with their Platonist monarch, and have now replaced him with one Witigis – not a noble scion of the royal Amal line, but a tough, experienced commander. Which is excellent news from our point of view. By the way, I took steps to prevent Theodahad staging a possible comeback. (Had that happened, he might have ended up handing Italy to Justinian on a plate.) Discovering that the deposed king planned to lick his wounds in Ravenna, I was able to inform an old enemy of his (plenty of those to choose from) who intercepted him en route on the Flaminian, and put him out of his misery. For the nonce, B. is holed up here in Rome. He and his staff (which of course includes myself) are comfortably enough quartered in the old imperial palace on the Pincian Hill. Meanwhile, Witigis has invested the city with a force of a hundred and fifty thousand Goths.

B. is quite the blue-eyed boy, everywhere at once: on the walls directing *ballista* fire against the enemy, cheering up the troops, organizing raids and sorties, smuggling in convoys of food, encouraging the citizens . . . With that mile-wide smile of his, and a comradely hand always ready to clap a man on the shoulder, the soldiers will do anything for him. Everyone in Rome is queueing up to sing his praises, proclaiming how brave, generous, compassionate, and inspirational is their Great Deliverer. Positively sickening. I *almost* managed to get him killed the other day, which would have been a splendid coup for *Libertas*. He led a sortie in person (I ask you – what modern Roman general does a thing like *that*?) from the Flaminian Gate, mounted on a conspicuous bay horse with a white face. I got word to the Goths through a man on my (our) payroll; B. immediately became the target for a veritable blizzard of arrows and javelins, but by some miracle escaped unscathed. Which of course has only enhanced his already sky-high reputation.

The good news is that Witigis, apart from cutting the aqueducts, has managed to blockade the port of Rome,* and seal off the supply routes from Sicily and Campania. So the siege may yet succeed, forcing B. to surrender or withdraw, tail between his legs.

* This was no longer Ostia, which had become silted up in the course of the previous century (and whose spectacularly well-preserved remains today rival those of Pompeii), but an altogether humbler facility – Portus.

As arranged, I shall leave this missive by the Tomb of Cecilia Metella on the Via Appia at the place you know of, to await collection by your *agens*; the city walls are not so closely watched that a man of mine can't smuggle it out. Vale.

Written at the Domus Pinciana, Roma, *pridie Kalendas Septembris*, in the year from the Founding of New Rome the two hundred and eighth.*

Post Scriptum.

How exactly *is* one supposed to date a letter these days? With no Western consuls appointed for the last three years, and no Eastern one for this year, consular dating may soon be a thing of the past, especially as our dear overlord has intimated that in future, the office may devolve on him alone. Imagine dating one's correspondence, 'in the —th consulship of Justinianus Augustus'. Perish the thought! So, for want of any better system, I shall stick meanwhile to dating A.R.U.C.**

From Anicius Julianus, Senator, to Procopius Caesariensis, Chronicler, greetings.

My dear 'Regulus', friend in *Libertas*, your letter arrived safely by the hand of the trusty 'Horatius'. My congratulations on your excellent work in Africa and Sicily. As for B.'s popularity, and thus his influence concerning the citizens of Rome, I don't think you need be too concerned. Just wait till famine bites, as the siege by Witigis begins to take effect. With priority regarding food of necessity being given to the army and its mounts, B.'s image will become severely dented. Take my word for it; in my youth I saw that happen with Odavacar at the siege of Ravenna, when Theoderic had him penned up inside the place.

As for myself, I sit here in Fanum† on the Mare Adriaticum – 'like a great spider in the centre of its web', as 'Cincinnatus', my second-in-command, put it (rather unkindly, I thought). Still, the simile is apt enough. My base here, at the junction of the Flaminian and Aemilian Ways, is the focus of routes north and south in Italy,

---

* 31 August 537.
** *Anno Regiae Urbis Conditae* – From the Founding of the City (i.e. of Constantinople in AD 330).
† Fano.

and being directly opposite Salonae (now in imperial hands again) on the Adriatic's eastern coast, enables me to keep in touch with my contacts in the Empire. One of these, 'Catullus', is an influential senator at court. (Yes, they're all back in the Palace, as though Nika had never been.) You say that B. is desperate for reinforcements. Why don't I get 'Catullus' to work on Justinian to send General Narses with more troops? If he can bring that off, we can, I think, sit back and watch the fun. Where Belisarius is all dash and brilliance, Narses is slow and exceedingly cautious – rather like Fabius Maximus of old. The two are bound to clash. With B.'s authority likely to be challenged, and the Roman command thus hopefully divided, the Goths may well recover the initiative and the Italian Expedition end in failure – or at least in stalemate.

By the way, last year Theodahad (now defunct thanks to your initiative) was nearly panicked through the eloquence of Peter the Patrician into handing over power to Justinian. Well, we couldn't allow that to happen, so I arranged for poor Peter to be 'taken out', as they say. Not terminally, you understand (*Libertas* has principles), just clapped in prison for the nonce. My agents persuaded the new, pro-Gothic Pope, Silverius, to 'lean' on Theodatus (as Theodahad Romanized his name) sufficiently for him to have Peter incarcerated. I'm assured he'll be released ere long. Meanwhile, keep up the good work. Look for further instructions at Cecilia Metella in the last week of this month. Vale.

Written at Insula Meridiana, Porta Flaminia, Fanum, VIII Ides Septembris, A.R.U.C., ducenti et octavo.*

---

* 6 September, 537.

NINETEEN

Solomon – I have surpassed you!
Justinian (referring to Solomon's great Temple in
Jerusalem) at the consecration of Hagia Sophia, 537

The day after Christmas of the same year that Belisarius took Rome and
Witigis invested it, Justinian and Theodora, accompanied by Menas, the
new Patriarch, and followed by a glittering train of courtiers and clerics,
set out from the Imperial Palace for the consecration of the new Hagia
Sophia, risen Phoenix-like from the ashes of the old.

As the procession crossed the Augusteum (or Augusteon, as the great
square was coming to be called, Greek fast replacing Latin in the capital),
the emperor reflected on the events of the three years that had elapsed
since the triumphant conclusion of the Vandal War. There had been a
few unforeseen setbacks and anxieties: the mutinies in Africa and Sicily;
the shock of hearing from Belisarius that the war might be lost for lack
of reinforcements (the speed and apparent ease of victory in Africa, had
perhaps caused him to assume too easily that Roman discipline and tactics,
even with modest manpower, was a combination that would always beat
barbarians); the Gothic resurgence following the replacement of the timid
and vacillating Theodahad with the formidable Witigis; the tug-of-war
between himself and Theodora over who should be Pope.

But in the end, most problems (or at least those that could be loosely
termed political) had been resolved: a relief force of tough Isaurians and
Thracians under an experienced general (rejoicing in the appellation John
'the Sanguinary') had entered Rome and re-opened lines of communication, forcing Witigis to prepare to abandon the siege; Theodora's choice for
Pope – the pro-Monophysite Vigilius – had triumphed over his Orthodox
rival Silverius. (Perhaps it had been for the best, the emperor conceded to
himself, his basic sense of justice enabling him to realize that the recent
revival of persecution of the Monophysites was as lacking in humanity
as it was unproductive.) All considered, the success of the Grand Plan
seemed tantalizingly close to completion. In Italy, the tide was turning in
his favour; a few more months should see the whole peninsula in Roman

hands (with Spain, Gaul, and perhaps one day even Britain, to follow?), especially as he had decided to send an experienced general – Narses, with a fresh army – to help Belisarius. The second version of his and Tribonian's great Code* had been published to universal acclaim and satisfaction. While the goal of religious uniformity might seem for the moment to be elusive, with goodwill, patience and perseverance, that too, Justinian believed, could eventually be achieved.

However, like those fabled Apples of the Hesperides – fair to the eye but which turned to ashes in the mouth – a secret fear lurked ever at the back of Justinian's mind, threatening to dash the cup of triumph from his lips. There had been times when, if he were being honest with himself, he had experienced 'a dark night of the soul' concerning his attitude towards his wife. Deeply though he loved Theodora, there had been moments when he had been tempted to see her, not as his Divinely Chosen colleague, but as an agent of the Evil One with whom he had weakly colluded: a figure like Medea, the enchantress in the fable, who, to gratify her love for Jason slew her own brother. Such a moment had come to pass when the thought occurred to him, 'Had Theodora sent the letter to the Gothic king that had resulted in the murder of Amalasuntha?' Another had been prompted by rumours that the recent Pope, Silverius, an enemy of the Monophysites (whose cause Theodora had championed), had been done away with at her orders. At such times, the old corrosive fear that he might be cursed, that he was somehow bad for others (a fear that for long he had believed buried) had returned to haunt him. To the roll of shame: the deaths of Atawulf and Valerian, the near-fatal hesitation to speak up for his uncle in the Senate, that self-inflicted blow in the Cistern of Nomus the mark of which he bore to this day – to these perhaps could now be added the names of Amalasuntha and Silverius.

As, resplendent in the robes and diadem of a Roman empress, Theodora processed across the Augusteum beside her husband, she reflected on the tumultuous events of the past eighteen months regarding the Monophysites, whose well-being was (next to the lot of her own sex) the cause dearest to her heart.

As a result of pressure from a reactionary Pope, Agapetus, who, on a visit to Constantinople had been horrified to find the Monophysites in the ascendancy (largely through the efforts of Theodora on their behalf), not only in the capital but as well throughout the Empire, Justinian had been forced

* The version we possess today.

to renege on his granting of favoured status to the Monophysites. Squeezed between the Scylla of the Pontiff and the Charybdis of Monophysitism, Justinian had yielded to the former – who was in an extremely strong bargaining position. Agapetus had hinted that he might use the immense power that he wielded as Pope to tell the Romans in Italy not to co-operate with Belisarius and his army of liberation, unless the emperor agreed to his demands. These were: the deposition of Anthimus, the Monophysite Patriarch of Constantinople, and the excommunication of all leading Monophysites in the capital.

Realizing that his cherished aim of recovering Italy for the Empire (the key constituent of his Grand Plan) could be put in jeopardy, Justinian had reluctantly yielded to what, in effect, was Pontifical blackmail. Anthimus was duly deposed, and replaced by Menas – an ultra-Orthodox Chalcedonian* – who immediately and with brutal thoroughness began a crackdown on Monophysites throughout the Empire, especially in their heartlands of Syria and Egypt, where a reign of terror was unleashed. The death of the aged Agapetus did nothing to improve the lot of the persecuted sect, Silverius – a principled conservative – being consecrated by the electoral college in Rome as his successor.

Theodora however, wholehearted in her loves as in her hates, was not the sort of person meekly to accept defeat. She had an ally in the corridors of power: Antonina, wife of Belisarius, a strong-willed woman who had even more influence over her husband than did Theodora over hers. Via correspondence, the two women (who were bosom friends) concocted a plot. Antonina would put pressure on her husband (now installed with his tiny army inside Rome, a city which the Goths, led by their new king, Witigis, proceeded to besiege) to have Silverius deposed in favour of Theodora's choice for Pope, Vigilius, an unscrupulous, ambitious deacon from an illustrious Roman family. Vigilius had sworn that, in the event of his being elected, he would reverse the anti-Monophysite regime of the Patriarch Menas. To undermine Silverius' position, forged letters purport-ing to be messages from him to Witigis offering to throw open the gates of Rome to the Goths, were to be 'discovered' . . .

Torn by shame and indecision, Belisarius paced the marble floor of a reception chamber in Rome's Pincian Palace. He had sent a summons to Pope Silverius

---

* To refresh the reader's memory: the Chalcedonians believed that Christ had two natures – human *and* divine (the view accepted by Orthodox Catholicism), while the Monophysites held that Christ had only one nature – divine.

in the Lateran Palace on the opposite, southern side of the city, and was now awaiting his arrival. It was a meeting the general was not looking forward to. Under orders from Antonina (acting on instructions from that she-devil of a friend of hers, the Empress Theodora), he was to present the Pope with an ultimatum: issue a statement supporting the Monophysites, or face the consequences.

Belisarius hated the role he had been forced to play – a second Pilate compelled by circumstance to act against a good and innocent man. He liked and respected Silverius, the man who, in the face of considerable opposition from more cautious souls in both the Senate and the Vatican, had opened the gates of Rome to Belisarius' army. Now, he was to pay back that generous act by betrayal.

'Come!' he shouted with uncharacteristic violence, as a rapping on the door interrupted his thoughts. A frightened-looking servant entered. 'S-Sir,' the man stammered, '– the Domina would wish to see b-both yourself and the Holy Father – should your d-discussion not succeed.'

'Understood,' replied the general in more kindly tones, dismissing the messenger with a gesture. Soon after, the Pope – a frail-looking figure with an open, guileless countenance – was ushered into the chamber.

'Welcome, Your Holiness,' declared Belisarius, waving the other to a seat. 'There is a proposition I must put to you,' he went on awkwardly, continuing to pace the floor, '– one which I hope you will feel able to accept. It is –'

'– that I must go along with what the Empress wishes on behalf of the Monophysites,' continued Silverius with a wry smile; 'or surrender Peter's throne. Something on those lines, I assume?'

'Precisely, Holiness,' responded the general, sounding relieved. 'You've saved me from having to spell it out.' He seated himself opposite the Pontiff. 'For God's sake, man!' he cried, in his agitation forgetting to observe the correct mode of address, '– just do as she requests. If *you* don't, then someone else will; and we both know who that someone is – a time-serving lickspittle called Vigilius.'

'I can appreciate you're in an awkward position, General,' replied the other. 'I suppose you've no choice but to put the Empress' case to me. But you must understand that I cannot compromise my principles by agreeing to her demands. If that makes things difficult for you,' he went on gently, 'then I am sorry. But I have to answer to my conscience rather than an earthly power. What was it that Christ said? – 'Render unto Caesar the things which are Caesar's; and unto God the things that are God's'.'

Giving a resigned shrug, Belisarius conducted Silverius to his wife's suite. Assembled in the *triclinium* were a number of officials and servants, also a beautiful woman, extended on a couch like a great, sleek cat. Beside her stood a smooth-faced man, clad in the rich apparel of a noble rather than a deacon's simple gown – Vigilius.

'Come, my love – sit by me,' commanded Antonina. Obediently, the general perched himself on the floor beside the couch. Turning to Silverius, she waved a clutch of documents in the air and declared in icy tones, 'You would betray us to the Goths, it seems, Your Holiness. "At the first hour on the Kalends of next month, I shall cause the Asinarian Gate to be opened",' she read from one of the missives. 'Your own words, Holiness. What have you to say?'

Silverius smiled and spread his hands, as if to imply that the question did not merit any answer.

'Traitor – by your silence you condemn yourself,' sneered Antonina. 'If further proof of guilt were needed, the fact that your residence, the Lateran Palace, is hard by the Asinarian Gate, supplies it.' She nodded to two of the officials who, stepping forward, tore the pallium from the Pontiff's shoulders then forced him to exchange his papal vestments for the habit of a monk. A barber then advanced, and, producing a razor, unceremoniously scraped the hair from Silverius' scalp to form a tonsure.

The unfortunate man was hustled from the palace (from which his waiting retinue was curtly dismissed) and put on board a ship bound for the east. Next day,* Vigilius was consecrated Pope, groups of Belisarius' soldiers standing by to discourage hostile demonstrations.

Arriving in the Empire, Silverius was confined in a monastery near Patara in Lycia, a coastal province of south-west Anatolia. Chancing to hear of his distinguished 'guest', the bishop of Patara visited Silverius, from whom he heard the whole sorry saga of deposition and abduction. Outraged, the bishop wrote to Justinian informing him of Silverius' plight. For the emperor (prepared though he was on most occasions to turn a blind eye to the machinations of his wife) this was too much. Indignantly, he had Silverius freed and put on board a ship for Rome, with instructions that the case against him be re-opened and the charge of treason re-examined. When he heard the news, Vigilius was terrified (should Silverius be cleared and reinstated, what would happen then to him?) and at once appealed for help, to Antonina and Theodora . . .

* 29 March 537.

Off Naples, the ship carrying Silverius to Rome was intercepted by a fast galley or *liburna* and boarded by four rough-looking individuals. Showing the captain a letter of authorization bearing the seal of Belisarius, their *caput* demanded that Silverius accompany them. The skipper and the former Pope had little choice but to comply. Two hours later, the *liburna* beached on a rocky islet and Silverius was bundled ashore. 'Your new See, Holiness,' chuckled the *caput*. Then the craft stood out to sea, dwindled to a distant dot, and vanished.

The awful truth dawned on Silverius. Here, on this tiny island, he had been left alone to die. A hasty examination of his 'new See' confirmed his fears: the place consisted of bare rocks from fissures in which sprouted a few hardy shrubs. It was totally devoid of shelter, fresh water, or edible substance – in short, of anything that might sustain life. A horrible, lingering death from thirst and hunger awaited him. Unless . . .

The son of another stout-hearted Pope, Hormisdas, (before the latter entered the priesthood), Silverius had grown up on the coast of Calabria.* Like all his boyhood companions, young Marcus, as he had then been known, had taken to swimming almost as soon as he could walk. But that was sixty years ago. Old and in failing health, could he now attempt the sort of distances he had swum with ease in his youth? He looked east across the blue Tyrrhenian, to a steep and barren coastline perhaps five miles distant. On the far horizon a tiny, purple cone was etched against a sky of palest azure – Vesuvius.

Never one to shirk a hard decision, Silverius rapidly made up his mind. If he remained on the island, he faced inevitable death – barring unlikely rescue by some passing craft. Death too, probably awaited him if he attempted to swim to shore, but at least it would come quickly. Stripping off his monkish habit, he waded into the sea and began to swim.

It being summer, the water was not cold and he managed to make slow but steady progress; his old skills had not completely atrophied. After what he estimated to be an hour, Silverius noted to his gratified surprise, that the coast was appreciably closer. Though tiring, he was far from exhausted; provided he could escape the onset of muscle cramps and did not encounter adverse currents, there might, he thought, be a possibility that he could actually reach shore. And then? With luck, he could surely beg some local peasant to provide him with clothing and sustenance for his immediate needs. He could then make his way to Rome where he

* Then situated where Apulia – the 'heel' of Italy, is today; Calabria is now the 'toe' of Italy – anciently Bruttium.

had many friends among both Goths and Romans, men of integrity and influence who would help him live 'underground' as it were, until . . . Until Justinian and Belisarius (both decent, well-intentioned men, but as potter's clay in their wives' hands) developed enough backbone to call off Theodora and Antonina. And that, Silverius was realist enough to acknowledge, might not be for a very long time. Still, better a life of precarious obscurity than imprisonment in a remote monastery, or slow starvation on a sea-girt rock.

Now, on the approaching shore he could make out individual features such as rocks and trees; he must have covered at least two-thirds of the distance. Silverius felt a surge of optimism. Against all the odds, it looked as though he might in fact survive. Then he spotted something that caused hope to shrivel in his breast, to be replaced by a cold knot of terror – a dark, triangular fin slicing through the water fifty feet ahead of him.

The great shark dived deep below the swimmer, then, with powerful sweeps of its crescent tail, shot upwards with the speed and impetus of a missile from an *onager*.

Feeling a jarring thump against his leg but as yet no pain, Silverius reached downwards – and experienced a thrill of disbelieving horror as his groping fingers encountered a stump of shredded flesh and jagged bone, felt a pumping flow of blood from a severed femoral artery. Then pain struck; Silverius' scream of agony was mercifully cut short as the monster hit again, crushing his torso to a jelly in its massive jaws . . .

With its scaffolding now removed, Justinian could see the exterior of the great church clearly for the first time. As Anthemius had warned him to expect, though impressive through sheer scale, it was not otherwise especially arresting. However, entering from the narthex into the ambulatory and thence into the vast central space, Justinian (who had deliberately refrained from visiting the building in the final stages of construction, the more to savour this moment of revelation) was reduced to stunned silence, awed by an overwhelming sense of space and light. And everywhere, such colour: marble richly veined in varied hues, softly glowing mosaics, the gleam of gold and silver.

Justinian raised his eyes, caught his breath at the sight of the vast dome high above, appearing, just as Anthemius had said it would, to float in air – 'as though suspended by a golden chain from Heaven'. A sense that he had touched the Infinite, the Transcendental, overcame the emperor. Through these mute stones, he felt, God was assuring him that he was indeed His Chosen One, as Theodora was divinely authorized to be his helpmeet. His doubts and fears evaporating like the mists of morning on the Bosphorus, Justinian fell upon his knees and whispered, 'Solomon – I have surpassed you!'

TWENTY

As far as may be advantageous to the public service
Rider to Justinian's commission to Narses enjoining
obedience to Belisarius, 538

From the citadel of Ancona – Italy's chief seaport on the Adriatic and recently captured from the Goths* – Belisarius looked down on the vast semi-circular harbour into which were sailing the transports conveying a fresh army under the command of General Narses. Belisarius supposed he ought to feel delighted by the prospect of yet more reinforcements, but admitted to himself that he had mixed feelings. The arrival of John the Sanguinary with his Isaurians and Thracians in November of the previous year had completely altered the tactical situation, tilting the scales decisively in favour of the Romans. Witigis' lines of communication had been threatened when, on Belisarius' orders, John had seized Ariminum,** south of Ravenna, the Goths' capital, and a chain of fortified positions had been established across the Apennines, protecting Roman gains in the south of the peninsula, also the vital route from Rome to the Adriatic. As a result, Witigis had been forced to abandon the siege of Rome and withdraw his army (a shadow of the mighty host that had invested the place a year before, thanks to disease and endless sorties by Belisarius' crack cavalry) to the Gothic heartland of the Padus valley. The coming of thousands more Roman troops (they were actually Heruls, from the same Germanic tribe that had supplied Mundus with his force at the crushing of the Nika revolt) meant putting an additional strain on the local Italian population, regarding billeting and feeding. And the presence of another senior commander in the shape of Narses, a man much older than Belisarius and standing high in the favour of Justinian, was not entirely welcome, raising as it did the possibility of a challenge to his authority, with the concomitant risk of dividing the command.

What did he know of Narses? Belisarius asked himself. Not much, beyond the fact that he was an Armenian and a eunuch (castration was

---

* In March 538.
** Rimini.

168

illegal in the Roman Empire; Narses hailed from the Persian zone of Armenia), and had a reputation for steadiness and reliability. Belisarius recalled that he had met the man briefly when, in the aftermath of Nika, Narses had done a quietly efficient job patrolling the streets to ensure that the insurgency did not flare up again. As for the Heruls he now command-ed, they were notoriously troublesome and insubordinate, refusing to obey any officers bar the ones they were accustomed to. Still, there was no point in anticipating trouble where none might actually exist. Determined to put a positive face on things, Belisarius set off down the hill towards the waterfront to welcome the new general, whose fleet was even now dropping anchor beside Trajan's Mole, the immensely long breakwater constructed in the reign of that emperor more than four centuries before . . .

In the auditorium of the citadel's Praetorium, where Belisarius had summoned a council of war, the staff of the two generals were assembling. Belisarius had called the meeting, firstly to plan the next stage of the campaign against Witigis, secondly as a means of introducing Narses to Belisarius' own officers, and giving the other a chance to express any views that he might have.

After extending a formal welcome to the newly arrived general, Belisarius advanced to the front of the auditorium and faced his audience. With a pointer, he traced on a large easel-mounted map of Italy a line from Rome north-east across the peninsula to Ancona. 'This, gentlemen, is our present front line. To the south of it we have cleared the land of Goths, so half of Italy is in our hands. We are now in a very strong position, one which enables us to launch a major push against the enemy. My plan is this: we move forward slowly, taking stronghold after stronghold – Sena Gallica, Urbinum, Pisaurum, et cetera.* An iron frontier too strong for the Goths to break through, creeping relentlessly north to pen them at last into their heartland of the Padus plain. Then we will close in for the kill.'

A murmur of approval swept round the chamber, accompanied by a nodding of heads.

'What about old "Blood-and-Guts", sir?' asked a fresh-faced *tribunus*.

'John the Sanguinary, you mean?' laughed Belisarius. 'Well, he's still in Ariminum. But with Witigis pulling back towards the north, he's now dangerously exposed; in fact Witigis' advance troops have already begun to invest the town. I'm about to order John to withdraw to the safety of Ancona, while he still can.'

* Senigallia, Urbino, Pesaro.

Narses stood up: a slight, delicate-looking figure with fine-drawn Armenian features, as unlike the popular stereotype of the plump, sly eunuch as it was possible to imagine. 'With respect, General, I think that would be a mistake.' Though he spoke quietly, Narses projected an air of unassuming certainty that commanded the close attention of all present.

This was the first time that Belisarius had been flatly contradicted by a fellow officer, and he felt at a loss as to how to respond. Up till this moment his charisma and breezy confidence had always proved enough to carry others with him. To be put in a position where he must defend and justify his decisions was a new and disconcerting experience. 'Perhaps, General, you could explain,' he replied, in as polite a tone as he could muster.

'Your plan, insofar as it goes, is sound enough,' conceded Narses. 'But with respect, it lacks imagination. Also boldness – a quality without which no campaign was ever won.' His gaze swept the chamber, establishing eye contact with his audience. 'With John in Ariminum,' he went on, 'you have established an excellent forward position – a marker, if you like, for future gains.' His voice dropped, which somehow had the effect of heightening the urgency and conviction of its tone. 'My Heruls have a name for it: *Blitzkrieg* – Lightning War! It depends on forward momentum – flying columns moving rapidly ahead of the main force, which follows, occupying the territory thus claimed before the enemy can rally his resources. If we let the Goths have Ariminum, we surrender what would be a key advantage.'

A collective buzz of enthusiasm showed how completely Narses had captured the interest of his hearers.

'*Blitzkrieg*', thought Belisarius, in bewilderment tinged with resentment. The Armenian was talking a different language to himself, strategically speaking. It was ironic, he thought, that he, Belisarius, with a reputation for dash and élan, should find himself accused of lack of boldness. By instinct, he was all for swift attack, of taking the battle to the enemy. But in the past year he had learned, through hard-won experience, that the Goths, unlike the Vandals, had huge powers of resilience, recovering rapidly from reverses that at the time had seemed crushing. Hence his present policy of consolidating gains made before risking further moves against the enemy.

'Perhaps the conqueror of Africa has lost his nerve?' Uttered in tones of sneering mock politeness, the taunt came from a *vicarius* noted for his surliness, but who hitherto would not have dared to question the decisions of his commanding officer. The intervention of Narses, acting like some malign alchemy, had somehow changed all that, Belisarius felt. His old, easy authority had now been challenged and might not be easily regained.

'That was uncalled for,' rapped out Narses, subjecting the *vicarius* to a disapproving stare. 'Let us have no more such aspersions. By falling out we simply play into the hands of the Goths. A disagreement as to tactics should not lead to rolling in the mud.' Turning to Belisarius he said, 'However, General, I think you should reconsider your decision to recall John from Ariminum, and instead relieve the place.'

'Oh you do, do you?' declared Belisarius, nettled. 'Perhaps you're forgetting, Narses, who is in overall command here.'

'My commission indeed states that I owe obedience to yourself,' replied the other smoothly. He paused, then added, giving the words a quiet emphasis, '– *as far as may be advantageous to the public service*. It is not my wish to embarrass you before your officers, Belisarius,' he went on, 'but I must insist on your compliance in this matter.'

Belisarius felt betrayed and humiliated, sick at heart – as though someone had kicked him violently in the stomach. But the rider to Narses' commission, though imprecise, was unequivocal. The interpretation as to what constituted 'advantageous' lay with the Armenian. Justinian at least had made *that* clear. His loyalty to his emperor winning out over his sense of hurt and anger, Belisarius heard himself declare, 'Very well, General – as soon as we disperse, I shall begin my preparations for the relief of Ariminum.'

From Procopius Caesariensis, Chronicler, to Anicius Julianus, Senator, greetings.

Dear 'Cato', your plan to have 'Catullus' persuade J. to send Narses to the aid of B. has succeeded beyond expectations! N.'s arrival has really set the cat among the pigeons; to mix my metaphors, the general staff here are fighting like ferrets in a sack – some supporting B., some N. In consequence, the Golden Boy's lustre is now badly tarnished; he's had to give way to N. (who has our Dear Leader's ear, it would seem), and lead a force to Ariminum to relieve John 'the Sanguinary'. (Honestly – the names these Germans give themselves; he's the nephew of General Vitalian, a Goth who, you'll remember better than myself, once tried to bring down Emperor Anastasius, then threw his hat in the ring when the old man became a god, as we used to say.) How odd that B. and N.

should, thus far, be acting against type – N. all for pushing on, B. for holding back. Unfortunately, B. performed quite brilliantly at Ariminum – quite his old dashing self – and forced Witigis to call off the siege.

Though far from being finished, Witigis has rather gone to pieces since being forced to pull back from Rome. You know these barbarians – easily demoralized when things go wrong. His judgement's been affected; in a fit of *furor Teutonicus* he's had some important Roman hostages killed – a batch of senators he's been carting around with him as a sort of mobile insurance policy. Which is bad news for us as, predictably, Roman opinion is hardening against the Goths. That venerable old Roman, Cassiodorus, has even resigned in protest from his post of Secretary to the Gothic Council. He's what you'd call a 'national treasure', so unfortunately his opinion carries considerable clout throughout Italy.

News just in – *Mediolanum** is in Roman hands once more. Without consulting N. (which means he's in hot water again), B. sent a seaborne column up the west coast to Liguria, to harry the Goths from the rear. Though little more than a reconnaissance-in-force, they've managed to capture Italy's second city without a blow being struck. It seems the citizens – inflamed by the anti-Gothic feeling sweeping Italy thanks to the murder of those senators – threw open the gates to them. Witigis is reported to be furious, breathing fire and slaughter and denouncing the Mediolanese as traitors (against Goths?). With the help of a Frankish army from Gaul (what's he playing at? – the Franks are simply looking for an excuse to extend their territory), he's now besieged the place, vowing to put all inside to the sword. So perhaps Golden Boy has bitten off more than he can chew; let's hope so.

'Horatius' knows to collect this from the drop-off point – by the Arch of Trajan near the waterfront. A short trip for him; your base at Fanum's not thirty miles up the road from here. Vale.

Written at the Praetorium of Ancona, IV Kalendas Augusti, A.R.U.C. the two hundred and ninth.**

Post Scriptum

Narses' Heruls are a gift – picking endless fights with B.'s Greeks,

* Milan.
** 29 July 538.

whom they regard as a bunch of softies. The *centenarii** have their hands full keeping the two lots apart. Ferocious fighters the Heruls may be, but in combined operations they're a total liability, refusing to obey orders from any officers other than their own. What fun!

'I hear you've given orders for a relieving force to set out for Mediolanum!' Narses accused Belisarius as the two generals, followed by their staff, filed into the officers' mess in Ancona – now the permanent headquarters of the Roman Army in Italy.

'The city *must* be relieved, Narses – its people are starving; we can't not help.' Taking his place beside the Armenian at the dinner table, Belisarius went on, a note of desperate appeal entering his voice. 'Surely you can see that. We can't allow the place to fall – especially as Witigis has threatened to massacre the inhabitants. I assumed I could take your permission for granted when I gave the order. If, by omitting to do so I've given offence, then I apologize.'

'Your conduct goes beyond a mere breach of good manners, Belisarius,' replied the Armenian in coldly formal tones. 'In matters of strategic planning I insist on being consulted. You will cancel the order immediately.'

'But – by now the expedition will be nearing Sena Gallica!' cried Belisarius disbelievingly.

'A mere twenty miles; send a fast rider to recall them.'

'This is intolerable!' shouted Belisarius, giving way to a rare burst of fury. 'Only months ago, you insisted – against my judgement – that I relieve Ariminum. Now, you try to stop me doing the same for Mediolanum. I'm beginning to think, Narses, that this is more about personal animosity towards myself, than anything to do with military requirements.'

Casual conversation around the table died away into fascinated silence, as the other officers became aware of the spat developing between their two commanders.

'That's rubbish, and you know it,' replied the other evenly. 'By relieving Ariminum we not only retained the initiative, we were able to push forward our front line. With Mediolanum, the situation's completely different. The place is two hundred miles north-west from here. To hang on to it, we'd have to stretch our lines of communication to breaking-point. In effect, it would mean having to start up a second front.'

'So much for your theory of *Blitzkrieg*,' retorted Belisarius bitterly.

* Sergeants – not to be confused with *centuriones*, a much higher, but by this time, obsolescent rank.

'Now you're being deliberately obtuse,' sighed Narses. 'Lighting war involves pushing forward from an already advancing front. Until we've consolidated our position in Central Italy – Auximum and Faesulae* especially, need to be reduced – that won't be possible.'

'So – you're happy then to see Mediolanum given over to fire and sword. With the slaughter of its innocent inhabitants on your conscience, I hope you'll be able to live with yourself.'

'*My* conscience? I would remind you, Belisarius, that this is a problem solely of *your* making.' With a steady hand, Narses poured himself a goblet of wine. Taking a sip, he went on, 'But we are wasting time. Will you send that order for the recall of your force, or would you prefer that I pull rank on you and do so for myself?'

From Anicius Julianus, Senator, to Procopius Caesariensis, Chronicler, Ave.

Dear 'Regulus', friend in *Libertas*, with B.'s capture of Ravenna in a bloodless coup, it would appear, on the face of it, that *Libertas* has failed: half the Western Empire recovered and Justinian still on his throne – stronger than ever, it might seem.

I suppose, with hindsight, we succeeded *too* well with Narses. The squabbling and backbiting that resulted from his transfer to Italy worked spectacularly well, resulting as it did in a fatally divided command. The ensuing paralysis caused Mediolanum to fall to the Goths (half a million put to the sword and the city razed to the ground!), which, unfortunately, caused J. to think again and have N. recalled. Since when, as we know, with his leadership no longer challenged and the field to himself, B. was able to polish off Witigis – since pensioned off by J., like Gelimer. (Doesn't it make you sick the way we treat defeated barbarian leaders these days? When Rome *was* Rome, Witigis would have been crucified like Spartacus, or strangled in public like Vercingetorix.) That was a master-stroke of B. – pretending to go along with W.'s suggestion that provided he split with J. and called off the war, the Goths would recognize him as Western emperor in a power-sharing deal. Once B. was allowed into Ravenna and showed his true colours after the Goths surrendered, it was of course too late for poor old W. – who'd had the wool well and truly pulled over his eyes.

I said above that *Libertas* might *appear* to have failed. It would

* Osimo and Fiesole.

however be premature, I think, to throw in the towel – for two reasons. Firstly, B.'s success in Italy may be built on sand. The Goths have not been defeated *militarily*, only tricked into surrender. Even with Witigis now out of the picture, there are other potential Gothic leaders waiting in the wings – Urais in Ticinum* and Hildebad in Verona, for example, neither of whom have yet lain down their arms. With Belisarius (accompanied by yourself, of course) recalled from Italy, leaving General Vitalius, a competent second-rater, in charge, a Gothic resurgence can by no means be ruled out. Congratulations by the way on your 'poison pen' campaign. Your letters to our beloved emperor suggesting that B. seriously toyed with accepting Witigis' offer to recognize him as Western emperor – like Julius Caesar when Anthony offered him the crown – had the desired effect. They planted the *seed of suspicion* in J.'s mind (always fertile ground for doubt to germinate), to the extent of persuading him to withdraw B. – just in case . . .

My second reason for suggesting that the cause of *Libertas* may not be dead is this. Last year, as my spies found out, Witigis, seeing defeat staring him in the face, made a desperate appeal to Khusro, the new Great King of Persia. His envoys carried the message that if Italy were reconquered by Belisarius, the Roman Empire would then be strong enough to renew hostilities with Persia – notwithstanding that the Treaty of Eternal Peace was still in force. In other words, W. was suggesting that Khusro launch a pre-emptive strike against the Empire, while Rome still had its hands full in Italy. Even with W. now gone and Italy in Roman hands again, the war might well flare up once more, as I've pointed out. So W.'s appeal could still make sense in terms of what's in it for Khusro.

All in all, my dear Procopius, the Friends of *Libertas* may yet have all to play for, and, who knows, you may find yourself ere long back in Italy with B. I have entrusted delivery of this missive to 'Gracchus', who will no doubt find you ensconced within the Imperial Palace at Constantinople.

Written at Fanum, Flaminia et Picenum (once more a province of the Roman Empire!), IV Ides Februarii, in the Year of the Consul Basillus.** (Wonder of wonders, it looks as if J. may have

* Pavia.
** 10 February 540. (See Notes.)

undergone a change of heart regarding consigning the consulship to history.)

'Does the capture of Ravenna, Lord, mean that You look with favour on Justinianus, Your unworthy son? With Italy as well as Africa now Roman once again, Your servant has recovered half the Western Empire. Much still remains to be done, of course – the barbarians cleared from Gaul and Spain, and the light of Your true faith, Orthodox Catholicism, made to triumph over the false creeds of the Monophysites and Arians, throughout the Empire. If, as Constantine and Augustine averred, the mission of the Imperium Romanum is to spread and safeguard Christianity over all the world, then perhaps I can dare to hope that You have indeed chosen me, to be the humble instrument for furthering Your great design for the salvation of mankind.' Cold and stiff, Justinian shifted his aching knees on the marble floor of Hagia Sophia's nave, where he had spent the night in prayer.

'There have been times, Lord,' the emperor intoned, continuing his orisons, 'when I feared that You had withdrawn your favour from me, that I was indeed in some way cursed: as if the Furies of legend – those dreadful winged maidens whose locks are twisting serpents and whose eyes drip blood – had been sent by Fate to prescribe the course that I must follow. For example, Lord, when I sent Narses to aid Belisarius in Italy, and their quarrel resulted in the destruction of Milan and the massacre of its people. Have I, Lord, been indirectly guilty of the death of half a million souls? At times I think I must have been, for my conscience continues to torment me. Through timidity and hesitation, Lord, the faults that cost the lives of Atawulf and Valerian my friends, I would have let the Goths keep Italy from the Padus to the Alps, had not Belisarius turned a deaf ear to my instructions to abandon the siege of Ravenna and make terms with Witigis. And was I wrong, Lord, to listen to rumours reported to me by Procopius, that Belisarius thought to make himself Emperor of the West – rumours that caused me to recall him? Have I thereby been guilty of a grave injustice against one who is a good and faithful servant?

'Perhaps I am a weak and broken vessel, Lord, one who is unworthy to be emperor. I think at times of Amalasuntha and Silverius. And then I wonder, Lord, if I should renounce Theodora, my beloved wife, who, as woman, is tainted with the sin of Eve, and whose transgressions I connived at. If however, Lord, You have indeed chosen Justinian, despite his manifest and many frailties, to be Your Appointed Instrument, I would humbly pray that you vouchsafe to him a sign – as once You did to Constantine of blessed memory.'

Justinian opened his eyes and waited, in an agony of hope and doubt. From outside the church, the faint stir of the awakening city came to the emperor's ears. The creak and rumble of the vendors' carts told him that the gates in the Wall of Theodosius had been opened. It must be dawn; the realization was confirmed by the dim radiance beginning to suffuse the nave's interior.

Then, suddenly, the sun's rays burst through the windows surrounding the base of the great dome, to bathe the kneeling figure in golden light. Here was his sign, Justinian told himself, sobbing with relief and gratitude. He – Justinianus Augustus, *Restitutor Orbis Romani* – was indeed God's Chosen One.

But perhaps, as the emperor Commodus – at the height of his power foreseeing his own downfall, observed – the gods were laughing. In Persia, Khusro was contemplating ending the Treaty of Eternal Peace with Rome; in Italy, an unknown young Goth called Totila determined to resist the Roman conquerors; and in far-off Aethiopia, carried in the fur of rats, a tiny creature spreading death and desolation on an unimagined scale began its journey down the Nile towards the Roman diocese of Egypt.

PART IV

HUBRIS
AD 540–552

TWENTY-ONE

Embrace, O king! the favourable moment; the East is left without defence,
while the armies of Justinian and his renowned general are detained in the
distant regions of the West
                              Appeal of Witigis' envoys to Khusro, 539

In the throne room of the great royal palace at Dastagerd on the Euphrates, a tall, handsome young man gazed intently on a bust of Emperor Justinian. 'We are rivals you and I,' Khusro, Great King of Persia, murmured to himself, 'although you may not know it yet. In the age-old contest between Persia and Rome, it is surely Persia that is destined to emerge superior. Let us weigh up your strengths and weaknesses, my enemy.'

The young king peered closely at the bronze features, whose likeness to their subject's the sculptor had captured with amazing skill from coins and medals bearing the emperor's image brought back from a Constantinople celebrating the triumph of Belisarius. 'I see kindness there, and will; also ambition and a desire to rule justly and well. But what you imagine to be best for your people may not be what they themselves desire. You are determined to recover Rome's Empire of the West, and to establish one Orthodox faith throughout your realm. But in striving for these ends you risk two things. Firstly, overstretching your resources, thus weakening your Eastern Empire; secondly, dividing your subjects into two warring camps – Orthodox and Monophysite. Persia, on the other hand, has no such problems: we have no lost empire to waste treasure in reconquering, nor are we plagued by divisive religious policies. Zoroastrians, Jews, and Christians, at liberty to follow their own creeds, all have enriched our realm by the free exercise of their varied talents.'

Khusro chuckled to himself at the thought of how an observer watching his monarch address a mute lump of bronze might react. He continued to study the metal face, looking to discern further character traits. 'I see self-doubt, I think. Which suggests that your drive to achieve will be compromised by uncertainty. In the coming struggle, Justinian, it is I, Khusro, who will prove to be the winner. Your character is flawed, your realm riven by potential fault-lines. Old age is waiting in the wings, and soon the years will sap your strength and your resolve. It will be a contest between a young lion and a tired old bull.' Smiling in anticipation, Khusro fondled the jewelled pommel of his sword. Drawing the weapon, he stood it upright between his knees, a sign to his generals, who would soon be arriving, that they should prepare for war.

Entering the chamber, Khusro's captains knelt before the three symbolic thrones which, at a lower level, faced the one on which the monarch sat. One was for the Roman emperor, one for the chief ruler of the Central Asian khanates, the third for the emperor of China – against the time when these potentates would come to pay homage to the King of Kings.

'Rise,' commanded Khusro. 'As you see, the sword is drawn. We will make war again against our ancient enemy.'

'Would that be wise, Great King?' enquired the elderly *Surena*,* Isadh-Gushnasp, the only civilian in the group, whose wisdom and experience alone entitled him to express his views without reserve. 'The Treaty of Eternal Peace still stands; it should not, perhaps, be lightly broken.'

'"The word of a Persian noble is his bond",' the king responded, quoting a maxim of the ruling caste, whose guiding principles were honour, truthfulness, and courtesy. 'That is true – on a personal level. But at times relations between rival states demand a more, let us say, 'flexible' approach. And any ending of the Peace need not be permanent – only long enough for certain pressing issues to be resolved.'

'These issues – the disputed territories of Lazica, Armenia, Mesopotamia, and Syria**?'

'Precisely, my *Surena*. It is my view, as it has long been that of my predecessors, that the balance of power in these regions has for too many years been tilted in Rome's favour. Once the scales are readjusted to an even level, Rome and Persia can sign the treaty once again.'

'But give the word, Great King!' exclaimed a grey-haired general, 'and we shall raze Constantinople and bring you the hide of this Justinian – as once we served Valerian.'†

'We do not seek to conquer Rome, Shahen, old fire-eater,' chuckled Khusro fondly, 'merely remind her that our Empire of Iran is not to be

---

* The title of the Shah's chief minister and plenipotentiary.
** How curiously the wheel of history revolves. All these territories (for Lazica read Georgia, for Mesopotamia, Iraq), for centuries mere pawns in the 'Great Game' between powers such as Rome, Persia, Russia, Britain, the Ottoman Empire, and more recently, America, are all now independent nations. (Perhaps, in the case of Iraq, that should be 'semi-independent'!)
† See Notes.

trifled with. Persia needs Rome – both as a training-ground where our young men can learn the arts of war, and as a source of subsidy in times of peace.' Addressing the whole group, he went on, 'Ravenna may have fallen to the Romans, but the situation there is still precarious. Before they can bring back their forces from the West, let us – as the envoys of Witigis have already suggested – surprise them while the Eternal Peace still holds, and launch a strike against their eastern frontier. I have a legitimate claim to Justinian's throne.* But despite that, as I mentioned, conquest is not our aim – what does Persia need with more territory, when our realm extends from the Euphrates to the Himalayas? Instead, by holding their wealthy cities of Syria to ransom, we can extract huge indemnities to swell our Treasury.' Turning to the *Surena*, he went on with an ironic smile, 'I trust this does not meet with your disapproval, Izadh-Gushnasp?'

The minister bowed his head in mute assent. 'I would only point out, Great King, that with Italy now Roman once again, Belisarius may soon be posted to the east.'

'Then we must lose no time. Prepare your various commands for war,' he declared to his generals. 'I myself will lead the army. We march for Syria in three days' time.'

'My instructions, from the emperor himself, are that you break off any negotiations you may have begun with Khusro, and immediately make ready for a siege.' The speaker – Count Prudentius, an influential courtier just arrived in Antioch from Constantinople – was addressing Germanus, Justinian's cousin, whom the emperor had designated plenipotentiary in Antioch, in response to Khusro's invasion of Syria. The two men faced each other in the main reception hall of Antioch's *Praetorium*: Prudentius – florid, running to fat, sweating heavily in his official robes which, despite the June heat, he seemed to think it necessary to wear; Germanus – spare, with sharp, intellectual features, clad in a light tunic.

'That's madness!' exclaimed Germanus, his face creasing in concern. 'Megas, bishop of Berrhoea,** has just reported back to me after seeing Khusro. He says the king is willing to spare Antioch in return for a thousand pounds of gold. A small price, it seems to me, to save "the Crown of the East".'

'Giving in to blackmail,' sneered Prudentius, mopping his face with a silken handkerchief. 'Since when did Rome condescend to bow the knee

* See Notes.
** Aleppo.

to Persia? Shame on you, Germanus. Before he became emperor, Justin, as commander of Rome's eastern army, saw off the Persians when they invaded Oriens. His nephew is prepared to do no less.'

'But the two situations aren't remotely comparable,' protested Germanus, his heart sinking at the sight of the other's stolidly impassive expression. 'Justin was an inspirational leader, opposed by a mob of unblooded conscripts. There's just no one of his calibre in Antioch at present. The city faces the prospect of investment by a new type of army: a huge force of volunteer professionals, battle-hardened in campaigns against fierce steppe nomads like the Turks and Hephthalites,* and commanded by Khusro himself – a charismatic leader to whom they show fanatical loyalty.'

Prudentius blew out his cheeks then expelled his breath in a contemptuous puff. 'Excuses,' he declared dismissively. 'Antioch's protected by massive walls, with many wells and granaries within their circuit; she could withstand a siege of months. Belisarius will soon be on his way with a powerful army. And meanwhile, you have already been reinforced by six thousand Roman troops, just the first of more to come.'

'They will come too late!' cried Germanus desperately. 'Can't you understand what's going to happen? Six thousand men's a tiny force with which to defend the immense circuit of the city walls. The Persians will eventually break in, then, in revenge for having been put to the trouble of besieging the place, start to massacre the population. It's what always happens.' He added bitterly, 'But perhaps you're just too blind or stupid to appreciate that.'

'How dare you!' retorted the ambassador, a rosy flush rising up his neck. 'Don't think I won't report your insolence to the emperor.'

'Do you really suppose I care?' replied Germanus wearily. He prepared to make a last appeal to the other. 'Look,' he declared in a conciliatory tone. 'I shouldn't have said that; I got carried away. But I wouldn't be doing my duty if I didn't point out the realities of the situation. Khusro may be ruthless, but he's also a man you can do business with, as they say. 'Pay up and you'll be left alone' is his message to the Syrian cities. Hierapolis handed over two thousand pounds of silver and was spared, Berrhoea didn't and was burned. I've no reason to suppose that Antioch will be an exception. Clearly, Justinian has failed to grasp just how serious things are on the ground here. Victory in Italy, and the fact that Belisarius is now free to intervene in the east, must have made him over-confident. Go back to

---

* Or White Huns. (Gibbon refers to them as Nephthalites.)

him and point out that calling Khusro's bluff simply won't work. I imagine you've enough influence to make him see sense. I suggest that meanwhile we pay off Khusro, and thus avert catastrophe.'

By the supercilious lifting of the other's eyebrows, Germanus knew that his appeal had failed. 'I do believe that you're naive enough to think that I might act counter to the orders of our emperor,' Prudentius declared, in terms of mild amusement.

'Do as you will,' responded Germanus in resigned disgust. The man, he saw, was a career politician, incapable of acting other than from narrow self-interest. 'As for myself, I intend to withdraw to Cilicia; Khusro shall not have the glory of capturing a kinsman of Justinian.'

Even before Germanus' departure for the north, Prudentius made known to the garrison and citizens of Antioch the wishes of their emperor. The six thousand reinforcements, experienced in the harsh realities of war, greeted the announcement with dismay, the people with a wild elation born of ignorance, and a rash sense of superiority inherited from their proud Seleucid ancestors.

While the citizens made ready to defend the walls, Prudentius (secure in the knowledge that his ambassadorial status gave him diplomatic immunity, a tradition scrupulously honoured by both Persia and Rome), retired to the pleasant suburb of Daphne to await the Persian host.

Macedonia was awakened by a thunderous knocking on her Daphne villa's outer door opening onto the street. Simultaneously, an agitated major-domo entered her *cubiculum*, bearing a lamp.

'Domina,' the man gasped, 'the Persians are here. An advance party, I think; the main force is not expected till tomorrow.'

'Let them in,' Macedonia instructed, striving to sound calm despite the pounding of her heart. 'Tell the staff to behave with courtesy, and do nothing to antagonize them. If necessary, offer them refreshment.' Hurriedly throwing on some clothing, she proceeded to the *atrium* which, by the dim light of dawn, she could see was already occupied by a dozen wild-looking irregulars in filthy sheepskins, and frightened members of her household cowering against the walls.

Grinning evilly, one of the strangers advanced on Macedonia. Grabbing her by the arm, he began roughly to drag her back the way that she had come. The major-domo rushed to her aid, but was brutally felled by a blow from her assailant's buckler. 'Don't try to help,' Macedonia called in a trembling voice to her visibly shocked staff. 'Anything I may have to suffer would be nothing compared to the death of any of yourselves.'

In the semi-darkness of her *cubiculum*, Macedonia found herself being thrust backwards onto her bed. Easily pinning her down with one hand, the soldier ripped apart her dress with the other. She gagged with disgust as a rank stench of stale sweat, unwashed skin and rancid breath filled her nostrils. With a mounting sense of horror, she realized that she was helpless to prevent what was about to happen, as he thrust his knees between her legs, prising them effortlessly apart. That this brutal coupling was being forced upon her by a *man* made it all the more repugnant.

Suddenly, the soldier gave a choking gasp. He stiffened; blood gushed from his mouth, drenching Macedonia, then his inert body rolled aside from his intended victim . . .

Macedonia came to, her spinning brain registering the elements of the scene that met her eyes: the corpse of her would-be rapist face down on the floor, a bloody puncture in his back; a man – clearly an officer from the quality of his armour and accoutrements – standing beside the bed, a reddened sword in his hand.

'A thousand apologies, Lady,' declared the officer in halting Greek. 'That a man under my command should have behaved so bestially is a stain upon my honour and my conscience.' He shifted uncomfortably. 'Did he . . .' he began.

'Rest assured, sir,' Macedonia replied tremulously, covering her semi-nakedness with a blood-spattered sheet. 'You intervened in time.'

'Bactrian scum,' declared her rescuer, an edge of bitter anger in his voice. 'We recruit them for their horsemanship and scouting skills, but I sometimes wonder if they're not more trouble than they're worth. In charge of a billeting party of them in advance of the king's main army, I was careless enough to leave them unattended while I checked the stabling for my horse. I should have known better. I hope you can forgive me, Lady, for I find it hard to forgive myself.'

After promising to arrange for armed protection for her house when the army should arrive, the officer departed with his troop – chastened after receiving a savage tongue-lashing.

The first intimation of the Persians' approach was a wall of dust extending along the horizon to the north-east. At last the van could be distinguished – company after company of cataphracts in glittering armour; before it, borne by white-clad priests, flew the *Drafsh-i-Kavyan*, the huge Sassanian royal flag, its gold and silver cloth encrusted with gems.

For hour upon hour the Persian host streamed onto the level ground before the city, not being finally assembled until mid-afternoon, its presence indicated by a sea of tents extending from the banks of the Orontes to the fringes of the coastal plain. Khusro himself, accoutred as a cataphract (following the custom of Persian commanders), his silvered carapace of articulated plates blazing in the sun, advanced with his entourage of satraps, generals and attendants to the suburb of Daphne. Here, villas had already been commandeered by advance parties for their residence, and Prudentius and his staff were already installed.

The latter group, plus the citizens of Daphne (which included Macedonia, whose house was now under guard, as the Persian officer had promised), were invited to meet the Great King. Fearful yet curious, they obeyed the politely veiled command, finding the king seated on a throne before his retinue, a short distance from the city walls, its ramparts crowded with excited Antiochans. The throne was flanked on one side by a curious iron tripod, on the other, ominously, by a gibbet.

A formal exchange (couched in terms of flowery politeness) followed between Prudentius and Khusro. The Roman informed the king that, in obedience to Justinian's command, the people of Antioch were determined to resist any Persian attempt to take their city. Khusro thereupon gave assurances that should the Antiochans change their minds and pay the thousand pounds of gold agreed upon, the city would be spared. He would give them until the following morning to decide. The inhabitants of Daphne (unless they chose to join their fellow citizens inside the walls) would not be affected by the consequences of any siege.

Persian intermediaries, mingling with the citizens of Daphne, then asked them (in Greek and with impeccable courtesy) if they had any requests or enquiries to make of the king. Macedonia, full of gratitude towards the Persian officer who had saved her, commended him warmly for his timely action. A short time later she was summoned to appear before the king himself. Suddenly nervous and regretting her impulse to speak out, she found herself facing a strikingly good-looking young man, whose welcoming smile helped to put her at her ease.

'What unit was this officer in charge of, Kalligenia*?' the king asked politely, in the purest Attic Greek.

* One-who-is-born-beautiful – a complimentary mode of address. (The title was originally bestowed on the priestess supervising certain ancient Greek rites.)

'I think he said his men were Bactrian scouts, Your Majesty.'

The king rapped out an order to one of his attendants who instantly departed, then, turning back to Macedonia said, 'I can only apologize for the failure of one of my officers to keep better discipline among those whom he commanded. Failure for which you nearly lost your virtue. Rest assured, he will be duly punished.' And he inclined his head in dismissal.

Macedonia, who had assumed that the officer was to be congratulated or promoted, was shocked. Opening her mouth to protest, she was confronted by an official who placed a warning finger to his lips, then led her from the scene.

Soon after, the unfortunate officer was conducted under escort to the iron tripod, to be questioned brusquely by the king. Khusro then issued a command, whereupon two brutal-looking menials seized the officer by the arms and hustled him roughly to the gibbet. His hands were bound behind his back, a noose whipped round his neck, and, before the horrified gaze of the assembled Romans, he was hauled aloft, kicking frantically as the cruel rope choked his life away.

Next morning, the Daphne Gate was opened and, to the jeers of the Antiochans and the laughter of the Persians who opened ranks to let them through, the six thousand Roman reinforcements sent by Justinian fled, heading north for the Cilician border. Persian heralds then rode up below the walls and repeated the terms that Khusro had specified to Prudentius. On these being greeted with yells of defiance, the heralds withdrew and the Persian host rolled forward to commence the siege.

First to the attack, advancing to the beat of drums and cymbals, were the *Jan-avaspar* – 'the men who sacrifice themselves' – assault troops carrying scaling-ladders. Time and again the ladders were sent crashing to the ground, spilling their human cargo, the defenders shoving the topmost rungs from the ramparts with long, forked poles. But so vast was the perimeter of the walls that it proved impossible to repel all such attacks, and gradually the Persians began to infiltrate the city, meeting desperate resistance from the citizens who knew that they were fighting for their very lives.

Meanwhile, Persian miners dug tunnels beneath the fortifications from which they began excavating galleries. Listening for the tell-tale clink of picks on rock beneath their feet, the citizens dug counter-mines, breaking into some of the subterranean passages where, in pitch-blackness, they fought bloody hand-to-hand battles with the enemy. But they could not detect every man-made cavern; in the largest of these, the Persians ignited the wooden beams supporting the roof. Minutes later, with a rumbling crash, a section of wall collapsed in a vast pall of dust and smoke.

Into the gaping breach charged a mass of cataphracts, scattering any defenders foolhardy enough to contest their passage. The heavy cavalry was followed by the Sogdian Brigade. These mailed giants from beyond the Hindu Kush were armed with heavy battle axes that inflicted fearful damage on the Antiochans, severing heads or limbs with nearly every stroke. With the cutting edge of the Persian army driving all before them, a torrent of infantry now poured through the gap and began a systematic slaughter of the citizens, suddenly reduced to a demoralized mob possessed of but one thought – escape. However, for the fleeing, huddled crowds and screaming women and children corralled inside the bulwarks, there could be no escape. For the remainder of that day and through the night, the killing continued, the Persians hunting down every man, woman, and child that they could find . . .

Several mornings later, accompanied by Prudentius whom he had 'suggested' might care to join him, Khusro looked down upon Antioch from the wooded slopes of Mount Casius. Fanned by a strong wind blowing onshore from the sea, fires now raged throughout the city, the distant crackle of flames and the crash of falling masonry mingling with a faint hubbub of despairing cries, as the slaughter carried on unchecked.

'Stop them, Great King!' cried Prudentius, aghast, his previous complacency destroyed by an object-lesson in the grim realities of war, and now replaced by disbelieving horror. 'In the name of humanity, I beseech you – put an end to this.'

Khusro shrugged and spread his hands in a gesture of helplessness. 'Even I, the *Shah-an-Shah* of the mighty Empire of Iran, am not omnipotent. My soldiers' blood is up, and their fury must be allowed to run its course. If I commanded them to desist, would they obey me? As well instruct a tiger not to rend its prey.' He smiled and shook his head with a smile of gentle irony. 'You see, my friend, unlike Justinian, who has God upon his side, I am but a man, who must act within his human limitations.' He gestured to the conflagration below. 'You seem to imply that this is somehow my fault. Perhaps you should reflect,' he went on in tones of mild reproof, 'that it could so easily have been avoided, if only . . . Well, I'm sure I need not recapitulate.'

'To see Antioch destroyed!' cried Prudentius in a stricken voice. Choking back a sob, he whispered, 'It is unbearable.'

'Courage, friend.' Khusro placed a reassuring hand on the other's shoulder. 'Antioch will rise again. For those who survive this unfortunate event, I shall build a new city on the banks of the Tigris, where they may live in peace and freedom as honoured guests of Persia. Greeks have long been welcome in my realm – an ornament to our society, like those professors from Athens when Justinian closed the Schools.'

When the blood-lust of his soldiers was eventually slaked, Khusro continued his progress through northern Syria, exacting tribute from city after city (all paid promptly, encouraged by the fate of Antioch), returning to Persia in the autumn,* well-pleased with the fruits of his campaign against the Romans. These included promises by Justinian to pay an annual subsidy in gold towards 'protection' – ostensibly for both Romans and Persians – against the nomads of the steppes.

Accompanying the mighty host as it headed homewards beside the Euphrates was a long, long train of captives (among them Macedonia) – the survivors of the Sack of Antioch.

* Of the year 540.

TWENTY-TWO

The ground over a wide area being thus waterlogged . . . had turned the
whole area into a quagmire . . . covered by swarms of gnats and flies
Ammianus Marcellinus (referring to terrain near the western end of
the Naarmalcha Canal*), *The Histories*, c. 390

As the booming of the horns signalled the end of that day's march, the
long line of captives shuffled gratefully to a halt. To their left – a ribbon of
gold in the late sun – rolled the broad Euphrates, to their right, thanks
to the network of irrigation channels, fields of standing crops, bordered
in the distance by a line of low and arid hills. Accompanied by Pelagia,
a strapping kitchen-maid, and a tough old nun called Sister Agnes,
Macedonia joined one of the queues forming at the various distribution
points where rations (usually barley or wheaten bread, and dried fish)
for the next twenty four hours were being issued.

The three women, who had all lost friends, colleagues, or loved ones in
the destruction of their city, had become close companions in the course of
the long journey south-east from Syria. They were now in the Persian zone
of Mesopotamia, having left Roman soil two days previously after passing
the border city of Circesium. Unlike the majority of their fellow captives
(who had reacted with relief and gratitude to the news that they were to be
given a new home in Persia), the three friends, each for their own personal
reasons, had formed a pact to escape from the column and make their way
back to Roman territory. Pelagia was betrothed to a young baker in Apa-
mea (one of the cities spared by Khusro after it had paid the ransom price);
to Sister Agnes, the thought of breathing sacrilegious air for the remainder
of her life was anathema; while Macedonia could not bear to contemplate
never seeing again the love of her life, Theodora.

Their plan, based on Macedonia's knowledge (gained from conversations with suppliers in her previous business) of the terrain they would
eventually traverse, was, like all the best schemes, simple. Three hundred
miles downstream from their present position, the Euphrates entered a

---

* This important waterway connected the Tigris with the Euphrates south of Ctesiphon
(whose site is very close to where Baghdad now stands).

marshy region – a vast area of reed-beds and waterways, which should offer an excellent chance for the trio to slip away undetected. As the captives were neither to be ransomed nor sold into slavery, their value to Khusro was not commercial, rather a measure of his great-heartedness; thus the glory of his soubriquet – Nushirvan, 'the Just' – would be augmented. In consequence, the Antiochans were only lightly guarded, more in fact for their own protection against lions* or the occasional band of brigands, than to prevent escape. After entering the marshes, the three would then head back to Roman territory, keeping to the marshland for a time in order to avoid detection, then following the Euphrates upstream back to the Syrian border. For food against the journey, they had regularly saved part of their daily rations; water, thanks to the initial topography and the excellent irrigation systems maintained by the Persians, which they would encounter thereafter, should not be a problem – barring the risk of infection. Pelagia, however, had managed to pilfer a strike-a-light and pannikin; provided they could find dry fuel, they would be able to boil their water.

Twenty days after leaving Circesium, the column reached the marshes, the road here replaced by a broad causeway laid over a foundation of piles and sunken earth. On the morning of the second day's progress through this fenny area and before the day's march had begun, the three friends slipped away from the causeway and concealed themselves in a patch of reeds. Soon, roused by the booming of the horns, the column was on its way. Some time after the rearguard had passed out of sight, the three judged it safe to rise and take stock.

Macedonia felt excited, her exhilaration tinged with awe and apprehension. To be free! That was wonderful, yet at the same time challenging. All around stretched a strange and (bar the whine of insects and the croak of frogs) silent world of pools, lagoons, and reeds. Keeping to solid ground where possible, at times forced to wade thigh- or even waist-deep, the trio began to make their way north-west by keeping parallel to the causeway, staying far enough from it, however, to avoid being spotted should any pursuit come looking for them. (Though no roll-call was maintained, a rough count of the captives was made daily at the various stations where rations were issued. If noticed, any escape would be held to lessen the prestige of the Great King; so efforts to recapture any fugitives could be expected to be rigorous.)

* See Notes.

Progress through the waterlogged terrain was slow and exhausting – the humidity, August heat, and biting insects adding to the travellers' discomfort. Around noon, to their inexpressible relief, they came to a deserted village on an artificial island, cunningly created from bundles of reeds rammed one atop the other into the yielding mud. The reed huts had mostly collapsed, but one habitation (a guest-house?) more stoutly built than the rest, provided grateful shade from the sweltering conditions. After sleeping for several hours, the companions embarked on a tour of the village, where they made two invaluable discoveries: a boat, and a trident for spearing fish. The craft was long, of shallow draught, with centre beam and ribs of poplar, covered with a skin of thin planks waterproofed with tar. Immersion in a pool discovered a few rifts which let in water. Once these were caulked with strips torn from clothing, the vessel was refloated, when it was pronounced to be (almost) leakproof.

Next morning they embarked in the boat, taking turns to propel it through the maze of watery channels (some clearly of artificial construction), using a long poplar pole salvaged from the central support of the 'guest-house'. From the number of abandoned and semi-submerged villages they encountered, it was clear that the whole area had once been populated; a rising water-table, perhaps resulting from a succession of exceptionally wet summers, may have caused the inhabitants to leave, Macedonia speculated.

The finding of the boat and trident transformed their lives. Gone was the energy-sapping ordeal of struggling through sucking, clinging mud. Instead, a slight push of the pole was all it took to send the craft smoothly through the water. So began an idyllic period (its perfection only slightly marred by ubiquitous mosquitoes) of gliding through a world of green-gold reeds, and long pools powder-blue from a reflected sky, in which pink flamingoes waded while overhead sailed pelicans and giant herons. Thanks to the trident, their diet was now supplemented with carp and catfish grilled over a fire of dried reeds or palm leaf stalks, of which a plentiful supply was always to be had at the abandoned villages where they spent the nights.

In the evenings, they regaled each other at first with accounts of their past lives then, when these were exhausted, with traditional stories, such as staples like 'The Seven Sleepers of Ephesus'.* In addition: Macedonia had a plentiful supply of travellers' tales garnered from merchants and

---

* For an account of this tale, see Chapter 33 of Gibbon's *Decline and Fall*.

suppliers she had dealt with in her business ventures; Pelagia, who had absorbed the old Greek legends at her mother's knee, recounted the exploits (embellished by a lively imagination) of Jason and the Argonauts, Perseus who slew the Gorgon, of Herakles and his twelve heroic Labours, Theseus who rid Cnossos of its terrible Minotaur, et cetera; Sister Agnes delighted in telling of the martyrdom of saints – the grislier the better – preferably featuring virgins of spotless innocence and virtue being torn with red-hot pincers, tortured on spiked wheels, pulled apart by horses, thrown to wild beasts in the arena . . .

One night Macedonia suggested that, for a change, they make up a story, each continuing from the point at which the previous teller left off. The suggestion being received with enthusiasm, she offered to be the first.

'Once upon a time,' she began, 'on an island to the east of Taprobane,* there lived a poor fisherman. One day he found in his catch an oyster, which yielded an enormous pearl. It was as big as a –'

'Pomegranate?' suggested Pelagia.

'Foolish girl,' scoffed Sister Agnes. 'Everyone knows that's impossible; a grape would be more like it.'

'Perhaps something in between,' said Macedonia tactfully. 'An apricot. Anyway, the fisherman, knowing that his pearl was worth a fortune, realized that he could greatly ease life for his family if only he could sell the pearl. But who would buy it? There was no one on the island anything like wealthy enough to offer a fair price. So this is what he did.' Macedonia turned to Pelagia with a smile. 'I pass the baton on to you.'

'Hearing of the wondrous pearl, a prince of Araby determined to acquire it for himself,' gushed Pelagia, her eyes shining with excitement.

'There you go again,' sighed Sister Agnes. 'You haven't told us *how* the prince heard about the pearl.'

'Oh, I don't know,' retorted the girl impatiently. 'Let's say the fisherman told his fellow fishermen to spread the news among any ocean-going vessels they encountered. Will that do?'

'Admirably,' put in Macedonia. 'Carry on, my dear.'

'Well, the prince told his boldest sea-captain to try to find the island and, after rewarding its owner, to bring him back the pearl,' continued Pelagia, and went on to relate how, after various adventures – surviving storms, near-shipwreck, attack by pirates and so on – the captain reached the island and bought the pearl. 'However, just as he was setting sail for

* Ceylon/Sri Lanka.

home –' Breaking off, the girl turned to Sister Agnes. 'Your turn, Sister,' she invited.

'For their love of filthy lucre and the vain object it could buy, the Lord decided to punish both the prince and the fisherman,' declared the nun, clearly relishing the opportunity to wreak divine retribution (if only in imagination) on weak and worldly sinners. 'And so He commanded Porphyry* to leave the Bosphorus and swim to the island, where –'

'But how would it get from the Mediterranean into the Indian Ocean?' interrupted Pelagia. 'There's no entry into the Red Sea.'

'To the Lord, Who split asunder the Red Sea to allow the Children of Israel to pass, all things are possible,' replied the nun loftily.

'That won't do,' objected Pelagia. '*I* had to explain how the prince found out about the pearl. What's good for the goose . . . Porphyry would have to swim round Africa; but we don't know if that's possible.'

'This is supposed to be story, not a Geography lesson,' laughed Macedonia. 'Actually, it probably *is* possible – if Herodotus was right in claiming that an Egyptian called Necho circumnavigated Africa about a hundred years before his time. Anyway, let's assume Herodotus was right and that Porphyry reached the island. What then?'

'The monster waited until next the fisherman put out to sea, then, with a swish of his mighty tail, he sank the vessel, and devoured the man. After that, he appeared, just above the surface, beside the ship in which the captain was returning with the pearl. Thinking the back of Porphyry to be a small island or strange rock and curious to know more, the captain and his crew rowed out and landed on it. Whereupon the monster dived, leaving the men to drown.' Having despatched the erring mortals in the tale, Sister Agnes sat back with a leer of satisfaction at a job well done.

'Now you've gone and spoiled the story!' complained a disappointed Pelagia. 'I wanted to find out what happened to the pearl, and the fisherman's family, and everything . . .'

'Come, pet, it's only a story,' soothed Macedonia, with a rather forced laugh, and casting a reproachful look at Sister Agnes. 'We'll tell it again some other time and you can make up a different ending.'

For something so trivial, the abrupt and gloomy ending of the story

---

* The name of a real 'sea-monster' (probably a killer whale) that for years terrorized fishermen in the Bosphorus at this time. When finally washed ashore, it was found to measure forty-five feet by fifteen.

seemed to cast a disproportionate pall on the mood of the evening. Conversation dried up, and shortly after, the three lay down to sleep on mats of sedge and rushes.

Almost as though the story of the pearl and the fisherman had been the cause, Fortune – which thus far had seemed to smile upon the trio's bid for freedom – now turned her face against them. The following day, a strange unearthly light suffused the skies at first. These then darkened, the weather breaking in a series of thunderstorms and torrential down-pours. Macedonia suddenly fell sick from fever, with chills, sweats, and fits of violent shivering, caused, they thought, by the poisonous miasma supposedly arising from the marsh.* Her condition worsening, they were forced to make semi-permanent camp in one of the marshland's deserted villages whose 'guest-house' (as usual, of stouter construction than the ordinary huts) provided adequate protection. Here, rest, and shelter from the incessant rain would, it was hoped, aid Macedonia's recovery.

One morning, the rain having eased somewhat, Pelagia was foraging along the island's 'shore' for wind-blown palm-fronds to dry for fuel. A heavy drop of water struck her cheek, warning her that the lull in the weather was destined not to last – a message reinforced by a sudden darkening of the skies, accompanied by a rumble of thunder. As she was bundling up her spoils, Pelagia became aware of an unfamiliar noise close by, its source invisible behind dense screens of reeds. The noise grew louder – a large animal, to judge by the splashing and loud snorting. Terrified, Pelagia stood stock-still, scarcely daring to breathe, almost tempted to believe that the pounding of her heart must give away her presence.

The reeds before her trembled, then parted, to reveal a monster from the realm of nightmares: a huge bull-like creature, with shiny dripping muzzle, patches of bare brown polished hide showing through bristly black hair, and a pair of enormous, curving back-swept horns. The creature stared at her balefully from little red-rimmed eyes.

Suddenly, a crack of thunder sounded and the sky lit up, as a jagged bolt of lightning struck a palm not twenty feet away. Pelagia's nerve broke; with a scream, she dropped her bundle, turned and began running. Maddened by the thunderclap and lightning flash, the girl's flight was the trigger for the buffalo to go into attack mode. With an enraged bellow, it raised its head and charged. Docile enough when domesticated, water-buffalo quickly revert to a feral state if returned to the wild. This must have been

* See Notes.

such an animal – abandoned by its owner in whatever crisis had caused his community to migrate.

Pelagia stood no chance. In seconds the huge beast was on her. With a sound like a snapping branch, her back broke beneath a vicious swipe from those terrible horns. Her screams of agony and terror died swiftly as, butting and trampling, the creature proceeded to reduce her body to a tattered pulp . . .

Some hours later, Sister Agnes found Pelagia's remains. Recovering fast from her initial shock, the old nun, no stranger when it came to dealing with the dead, covered the corpse with vegetation and stuck in the ground near the head, a cross crudely fashioned of stalks from the girl's discarded bundle. A poor apology for a committal, she thought sadly, but under the circumstances the best that could be done. After muttering a prayer, she returned to her patient in the 'guest-house'.

Two days later, despite Sister Agnes' unremitting solicitude, Macedonia passed away. Just before the end she woke from a delirious slumber, and in a clear voice said to the nun, 'Would you, dear friend, go to Constantinople for me. Tell Empress Theodora that I truly loved her, and ask her sometimes to remember Macedonia? It is much to ask, I know; but you will be amply recompensed.' She clasped the other's hand; her grip tightened – then suddenly relaxed in death.

Love between women is an abomination, the Bible condemns it, thought the nun. Nevertheless, for the sake of her friend, she would fulfil her dying wish. Lacking tools to dig a grave, she removed the body to one of the huts. In this makeshift sepulchre, she prayed long for the souls of her companions, and in the morning pushed on westward in the boat, armed only with an iron will and an indomitable faith.

TWENTY-THREE

The King of Kings looks down on such petty acquisitions [the cities of Syria];
and of the nations vanquished by his invincible arms, he esteems the Romans
as the least formidable
Taunt of Khusro to Justinian (via an ambassador), 541

Conveyed by a broken Prudentius, the news of the fall of Antioch and the massacre of its population came as a shattering blow to both Justinian and Theodora, though it affected them in different ways. With the success of Belisarius in Africa and Italy, Justinian had begun to assume that Roman arms, as in the glory days of Trajan, were invincible, especially since they constituted the main instrument by which his Grand Plan was being achieved. A Plan, moreover, which, Justinian believed, enjoyed divine approval. However: the capitulation of Berrhoea's Roman garrison to Khusro, and the disgraceful flight of the six thousand Roman troops that he, Justinian, had personally sent to Antioch, suggested that perhaps, this might no longer be the case. Even Khusro's magnanimous gesture in providing a new home for the surviving Antiochans seemed calculated to rub salt into Justinian's wounded pride, emphasizing his powerlessness and vulnerability in the face of Persian might.

Suddenly, the emperor's glittering self-image as God's Appointed Vice-gerent upon Earth seemed less convincing than it had a few short months before. His old demons of self-doubt, which he had thought banished forever, began once more to stir within the dark recesses of his mind. And with self-doubt revived his old fear that he was in some way cursed, that the price of allegiance to Justinian was – as with Milan and now with Antioch – fated to be catastrophe and death.

The news about Antioch threw Theodora into an agony of uncertainty as to the fate of her beloved Macedonia. Had she perished in the slaughter? Or was she among the captives taken into exile in Persia? If the latter, then a personal appeal by a Roman empress to the Great King would surely be effective in securing her release. Convincing herself that Macedonia was now safely in Persia, she was about to send an ambassador to Khusro, when her hopes were cruelly dashed.

An aged nun, weary and travel-stained ('bearing urgent news for the empress' ears alone', according to the *Comes Domesticorum* who interviewed her), arrived one day at the Imperial Palace and was granted an audience with the empress. Theodora's anguished howl of misery when she heard that Macedonia was dead was audible in every part of the palace close to the audience chamber. Sister Agnes, departing with a handsome 'dowry' (her entrée to the *Metanoia** of which she was to become Mother Superior), would say nothing when asked about the cause of Theodora's distress. For days, the empress stayed immured within her private suite, unapproachable even by the emperor, her only contact an expert limner. Between them, the empress and the artist created a likeness of Macedonia for delivery to the mosaicists adorning the Church of Sanctus Vitalius in Ravenna (then under construction, to celebrate the reintegration of Italy into the Roman Empire) with two panels depicting separately, Justinian and Theodora together with their suites. The instructions accompanying the portrait – showing a pretty, heart-shaped face, full of compassion and a lively intelligence – stated that it was to be the model for the female figure immediately to the left of the empress in the panel. 'And so, my love,' Theodora murmured sadly, all her tears long since wept out, 'now you and I will be together for all time.'

When at last she emerged into public life once more, many noted that the empress had changed – afflicted from then on by some secret sorrow. Some later went so far as to suggest that the seeds of the sickness that would in a few years strike her down were sown at this time.

With Belisarius now posted to the east, Justinian's morale began to recover. His all-conquering general would surely teach that presumptuous young puppy, Khusro, a lesson he would not easily forget. Meanwhile, Gubazes, king of the disputed territory of Lazica** (encouraged by the collapse of Roman prestige as a result of Khusro's Syrian campaign, and resentful of the efficiency of Roman tax-collectors), had invited the Great King to replace Roman with Persian sovereignty. Khusro was only too willing to oblige; a Persian army swept through Lazica,† defeated the Roman forces there, and captured the fortified port of Petra, giving them an outlet on the Black Sea.

* Or Convent of Repentance – a refuge, founded by Theodora, for women forced into prostitution.
** Georgia.
† In the spring of 541.

But with Belisarius at the head of a mighty Roman army (swollen with troops no longer needed in Italy) advancing into Persian Mesopotamia, it looked as if the Great King's rashness in challenging the might of Rome was about to incur its just deserts. And for a time, this seemed indeed to be the scenario that was destined to unfold. On swept the Romans unopposed, past Nisibis whose huge garrison dared not emerge to challenge them, to take the great fortress city of Sisaurana on the Tigris. And then, just as it seemed poised to descend on Lazica, the Roman advance stalled . . . To everyone's amazement and consternation (none more so than the emperor's), Belisarius now proceeded to march his army back to Roman territory!

Speculation as to the reasons for the general's withdrawal was rife, wild, and fevered. The consensus was that distressing news had reached Belisarius concerning the conduct of his wife, Antonina. Normally, she accompanied him on campaign, but on this occasion, so the story went, had chosen to remain in Constantinople, in order to resume a long-standing and passionate affair with a young man called Theodosius (her own adopted son!) – a liaison that Belisarius had fondly imagined to have run its course. His forbearance tested beyond endurance, the general, it was thought, had finally snapped, and was now determined to confront his wife and discover the truth, or otherwise, of the rumours concerning her.*

To Justinian, it began to seem that God had indeed decided to withdraw His favour from His former Chosen One, especially as the stalemate on the eastern front coincided with the downfall of Justinian's invaluable finance minister, John of Cappadocia (engineered by his arch-enemy Theodora, who managed to link his name with a plot against the emperor**). The Cappadocian's genius for raising money had helped provide the enormous financial resources needed for Justinian's campaigns. Thus his disgrace and dismissal constituted both a major political defeat for the emperor (inflicted by his wife!), and a severe blow to his confidence. After much soul-searching however, he was able to comfort himself with the reflection that the major constituent of his Grand Plan – namely the recovery of Africa and Italy for the Roman Empire – was solidly intact.

But that reassuring consolation was about to be shattered . . .

---

* They proved, alas, to be only too well-founded.
** For this, also Antonina's unbelievably steamy and tangled affair with Theodosius, see Notes for Chapter 19.

TWENTY-FOUR

Recover for us dominion over Italy
Plea of the Goths to Totila on electing him their king, 541

'Know anything about this new king the Goths have just elected for themselves?' Artabazus – commander-in-chief of the Field Army of Italy (an Armenian, as his olive complexion and delicate aquiline features hinted) – asked Bessas, his second-in command. The latter was an elderly Goth from Thrace, a veteran of many campaigns stretching back to Anastasius' clashes with the Persians. The two men were seated in the commander's pavilion near Faventia in Tuscia,* overlooking a smiling landscape – undulating hills clothed in forests of chestnut, valleys chequered with vineyards and olive groves. Around the pavilion the tents of the army stretched in orderly rows, the soldiers sleeping, cleaning kit, preparing supper, or, in the case of the younger ones, just skylarking.

'Not much,' grunted Bessas in reply, his battle-scarred old face framed by grizzled locks, worn long in the German fashion. 'Except that he's the nephew of Hildebad, the king the Goths chose after Belisarius left Italy eighteen months ago. Didn't last long. Jealousy among the Gothic leaders, I heard, led to his assassination last year. Replaced by one Eraric, who wasn't even a Goth, but a Rugian.'

'And *his* reign was even shorter,' observed Artabazus with a grin. 'Murdered after five months. That was when the Goths found out he was planning to cede their newly recreated kingdom to Justinian – in return for a fat pension and being allowed to settle in Constantinople as a patrician. Shades of Gelimer and Witigis. Anyway, what about this nephew of Hildebad?'

'Young man, name of Totila. Scarcely out of his teens.'

'This just gets better and better,' chuckled Artabazus. 'I'd give him even less time than Eraric. To a Goth, being ruled by an untried boy is only marginally better than being ruled by a woman. And *that's* total anathema. You've only got to think of Amalasuntha and her poisonous offspring, Athalaric.'

* Faenza in Tuscany.

'In the case of Totila, I wouldn't be too sure,' mused Bessas. 'They say he's mature beyond his years; also he seems to have held some sort of command under his uncle. The Goths appear to think highly of him. And, what's perhaps more worrying, so do many Romans, who have yet to be persuaded of the benefits of being back in the Empire. And who can blame them? What with Justinian's army of tax-collectors hell-bent on making up for lost time, and our soldiers forced to turn to looting to supplement arrears of pay. If Totila succeeds in stamping his authority on his people, we could be in trouble. Both from the Goths *and* the Romans.' The old warrior frowned and shook his head. 'Whatever was Vitalius thinking about to let the Goths start up their kingship once again? Once you've beaten him, the one thing you *don't* do with a German is give him a second chance. I should know – I'm German myself.'

'Perhaps Vitalius wasn't in charge long enough to stop the Goths regrouping,' the other pointed out. 'Or perhaps he thought that letting them elect their own King Log* would be enough to keep them quiet for the nonce. Our emperor's crazy plan of switching around the top command hasn't exactly helped. He was terrified, you know, that Belisarius would accept when the Goths offered to recognize him as Western emperor. Hence Justinian's present policy of divide and rule regarding his generals. The man's paranoid, afraid of his own shadow; you didn't hear me say that, by the way. You yourself were appointed *Magister Militum* for a time, after Vitalius. Now it seems it's my turn. Well, one thing I am determined to do before *I'm* phased out, is to nip this Gothic resurgence in the bud – before it has a chance to become a real threat.'

'Totila's army's only ten miles north from here, according to the scouts' report. You mean to take him on?'

'I should say! A scratch force of only a few thousand Goths?' Artabazus laughed scornfully. 'He's serving himself up to us on a plate. We should be able to bring him to battle tomorrow, when the Army of Italy will make short work of him. Then we can put an end to this nonsense of a renewed Gothic kingdom, once and for all.'

That night, Totila encamped his five thousand Goths – all that were brave (or desperate?) enough to follow him – at the head of a valley overlooking the Romans' position.

'At least three times our number,' murmured Aligern, looking down

---

* A king who is merely a figurehead. (See Aesop's *Fables*.)

at the distant rows of 'butterflies' glowing in the late sun – the eight-man leather tents the Romans carried on campaign. Aligern was an elder statesman, kinsman of the murdered Hildebad, and loyal supporter of that monarch's nephew and successor. 'It will take cunning as well as courage on our part, if we hope to have any chance of beating them.' He glanced keenly at the tall, golden-haired young king standing beside him. 'It may be Sire, that – for the present – discretion is the better part of valour. There would be no shame in withdrawing in order to build up our forces against a future, more evenly matched encounter. If we choose to fight them now, and are defeated –' Aligern shrugged, then added with a grim smile, 'It would be the end of the Ostrogothic nation. Think well, Sire, before deciding.'

Cunning as well as courage, Totila repeated to himself. Courage – his men had that in overflowing measure. If bravery alone could win the day, victory was theirs. As with all Germans, every Gothic male was a warrior, schooled in the use of arms, nurtured on a tradition of heroic deeds and contempt for danger. But, again like all Germans, each Gothic warrior was eager for *personal* glory, and impatient of discipline. A trait that could have spelt disaster when, as his uncle's swordbearer in his first command, he had taken Trabesium,* the only Roman-occupied fortification north of the Padus. He remembered when he had led his men against that mighty fortress on its rock two years ago . . .

Perceiving some inner quality of self-belief or leadership in his nephew, Hildebad had let the boy take charge of the assault. Totila had found himself cajoling tough warriors two, or even three times his own age, into abandoning their desire to launch a head-on attack on the place – an action that would have proved suicidal against the town's strong garrison and massive walls. Instead, with a blend of tact, humour, and firmness, he had persuaded them to accept an alternative manoeuvre – ascending, under cover of night, a steep path leading to an unguarded postern gate. The enterprise called for courage (clearly, the garrison thought the postern not worth the trouble of defending, thanks to its being sited above a precipitous ascent), teamwork, and, the hardest thing of all to instil in Germans – discipline. In addressing his men, Totila discovered that he had that most precious of gifts a leader can possess – charisma, the quality that makes men *want* to follow another, someone who can, by enthusiasm and example, unite his followers into a band of brothers sharing a common goal.

* Treviso.

The operation had proceeded without a hitch, with Trabesium falling to the Goths.

'I have decided, Aligern,' Totila replied to his senior lieutenant. 'Tomorrow, we must fight them. If we retreat now, our men will lose heart and begin to disperse. Any reputation I possess would soon be lost, and I'd probably end up sharing the same fate as my uncle or Eraric. Besides, I don't believe the odds against us are as great as they might seem. The Army of Italy certainly outnumbers us – greatly so. But what of its quality? Belisarius has taken the cream of his troops to the east, leaving mainly mercenary units behind. Men whose only motive is gain, and who value their hides far above whatever cause they fight for. A hundred and sixty years ago, our ancestors defeated a vastly superior Roman army at Adrianople. Let us emulate their tactics.'

'Which were?' Aligern's tone sounded somewhat less pessimistic than before.

'Essentially, the following. Instead of the usual wild charge, the Goths – under their leader, Fritigern – formed a defensive line against the Romans, who advanced in close order. A suprise cavalry attack by the Goths smashed into the Roman left wing, causing confusion and disorder with men being pushed back into each other, so that they were unable to manoeuvre. The Gothic line now advanced against the Roman ranks, jamming them even more closely together. Result – slaughter, then rout. So, what we must do is this . . .'

'Archers,' groaned Aligern to Totila the following morning, as a long line of unarmoured men formed up in front of the Roman army. In what seemed almost a casual, unconcerned manner, they advanced in open order up the valley towards the Gothic line – a double row of spearmen forming a wall of shields flanked by woods, across the valley's head. Clad in undyed linen tunics with indigo government roundels at hip and shoulder, bows and quivers slung carelessly on backs, the Roman archers looked curiously unthreatening. Yet both Gothic leaders knew just how devastating and demoralizing arrow-fire could prove, unless countered effectively.

'Once that lot starts shooting, it's going to take all your authority to stop our fellows from going after them,' observed Aligern. 'Which, of course, is what the Romans hope we'll do.'

'They must just stand and take it. As long as the men stay behind their shields, they'll be all right – barring a few inevitable casualties; we must accept that. So long as we don't react, they'll call off their archers soon enough.'

So long as we don't react, the young king repeated to himself. Everything depended on the Goths maintaining discipline, something that ran counter to their nature, but whose importance he had striven with every fibre to make them understand. While the shield-wall stayed intact, the enemy would be unable, on a narrow front, to bring his advantage of superior numbers to bear. Then, provided we can hold him . . .

A hundred paces in front of the Goths' formation, the archers halted then formed up in an extended line. Unhurriedly, they strung their bows – powerful, recurved, composite affairs of laminated wood and horn – nocked arrows, raised their shooting-arms to a steep angle, and drew the shafts to an anchor-point at the chin. Suddenly, they no longer looked innocuous, but deadly.

With a soft, whirring sound a flight of arrows arced towards the Gothic line, racing its speeding shadow on the ground to strike the wall of shields with a ripple of thuds. One or two *andbahtos* – retainers – cried out in pain or slumped to the ground; the great majority remained unharmed. After enduring several volleys however, the Goths began to grow restive, their line showing the first signs of losing cohesion, as individual warriors fought their instinct to rush forward and close with these cowards who dared fight only from a distance. Sensing the danger, Totila, golden hair swinging about his shoulders, strode along the line urging restraint, an arrow clanging off his *Spangenhelm*, while two others smacked into his shield. His words had the desired effect; everywhere, the shield-wall firmed and straightened.

Except at one point near the centre. Here, a group of Goths rushed forward. With the incline in their favour, they could expect to catch their tormentors before the archers could run back to the protection of their army. Instead there came a blur of movement in the Roman ranks, which opened to allow passage for a cloud of horsemen. Though only light cavalry, they were more than capable of dealing with an isolated group of the enemy.* Galloping through the scattering archers they were among the Goths in a flash, thrusting and slashing with their long *spathae* till not a man remained alive. It was a chilling, and salutary, object-lesson. Thereafter, no one in the shield-wall needed further encouragement to stay in line.

A trumpet sounded, recalling the archers and the horse. Now the Roman infantry rolled forward – rank upon rank of mailed soldiers, moving

* Belisarius had taken the heavy cavalry with him to the east, leaving behind only light horse – suitable for scouting or skirmishing, but useless against enemy en masse.

as one like some grim machine, or monster clad in iron scales. With a deafening clash the two lines came together, when began a deadly shoving-match, with victory destined for the side that did not break. The Goths – big fair-haired men – had the slope in their favour, while the woods at either end of their line meant that they could not be outflanked. Against this, their formation was only two deep compared with the Romans' six; most were unarmoured, relying for protection solely on their oval wooden shields. Gradually, the greater weight of the Roman line began to tell; slowly, fighting stubbornly every yard of the way, the Goths found themselves being forced back.

Then, just when it seemed that a Roman victory was inevitable, the surprise that Totila had planned all along was sprung. Away to the flank, concealed from view until the moment it was needed, was the cream of Totila's force – a body of heavy lancers, several hundred strong, armoured and equipped from the armoury of Trabesium, after that city's capture. Now, thundering up the valley from its mouth they smashed into the Romans from behind, inflicting massive carnage and causing widespread confusion. Desperately pushing forward to escape those terrible lance-points, the rear ranks caused the ones in front to become jammed together. Soon the whole army had become a close-packed, struggling mass, in which men were unable to lift their weapons, or, losing their footing, were trodden underfoot to suffocate. In such a situation panic spreads like wildfire, and this scenario was no exception. With shocking suddenness, the Roman army broke and fled, not stopping in their flight until reaching safety behind the strong walls of Faventia.

For the Goths it was a famous victory.* News of it spread rapidly; men flocked to join Totila's standard and within days his army had quadrupled in strength. Badly mauled though still intact, the Roman army withdrew south towards Florentia,** via the long Mugello valley. Here, Totila ambushed them, winning a second – and decisive – victory. Too distracted and demoralized to send out scouts, strung out in a straggling column along the length of the defile, the Romans fell easy prey to the Goths charging down upon them from the heights. Having sustained serious losses, the Roman army now broke up into separate sections (each commanded by a different general), which proceeded to take refuge in the fortresses of central Italy. Here, apprehensive and rudderless, they remained bottled up to lick their wounds.

* The Battle of Faventia/Faenza was fought in the spring of 542.
** Florence.

Meanwhile, nothing less than a social revolution was sweeping the peninsula. All over Italy, those who had suffered the consequences of Justinian's 'liberation': the merchants, the urban middle classes, and the peasants – ground between the upper and nether millstones of Alexander 'the Scissors' ruthless tax machine, and the casual plundering of East Roman troops – hailed Totila as a saviour. Like a second Spartacus, the young monarch divided up the great estates among the tenants, sweeping away crippling rents and corvées; freeing the slaves, who willingly enrolled in his army; cleansing the civil service of the corrupt and greedy officials who had run the administration very much with an eye to their own profit, and staffing it instead with humble Romans. Within a few short months, apart from Rome, Ravenna, and a few towns on the coast or in the central Apennines, the whole of Italy had fallen to the Goths. Only the senatorial class held out against Totila. To these, the young 'barbarian' continued to extend an olive branch (for he hoped eventually to bring them round), treating with kindness and respect all aristocrats who fell into his hands. Meanwhile the expulsion of landlords, freeing of slaves and ending of abuses went on apace, with ordinary Romans everywhere enthusiastically supporting their charismatic new champion.

Shock and consternation clubbed Justinian when he received the news of what was happening in Italy. His Grand Plan, it seemed, was fast unravelling; perhaps, he conceded to himself, it had been a mistake to alternate the command among his generals. Radical steps must be taken to stop the rot before it was too late. Belisarius, unfortunately, could not be spared, what with a newly aggressive Persia under Khusro threatening the eastern frontier. His generals in Italy, even tough old veterans like Bessas, had proved a sorely disappointing lot. None of them, it appeared, was capable of taking on this Totila. But perhaps there *was* one man, presently here in Constantinople, who might be equal to the task – a certain Maximinus.

Maximinus, a senator and courtier, had recently come to the emperor's attention by the sound advice he had offered to officials at the Treasury – advice which had helped to fill the void in fiscal policy resulting from the departure of John of Cappadocia. Wit, poet, man of culture and sophistication, to say nothing of his administrative skills, this second Petronius Arbiter possessed the sort of over-arching intelligence that perhaps made him the ideal person to tackle the Hydra-headed crisis that had blown up in Italy. The more he thought about it, the more Justinian convinced himself that Maximimus was the man to send. Granted, he lacked military experience, but perhaps, given the recent woeful performance of the generals, that might even be an advantage; Maximinus would be coming to the job with a fresh, objective outlook, and no baggage.

But before The Prodigy could be dispatched to Italy, calamity – on a scale unprecedented in its reach and terror – struck the Empire's eastern provinces . . .

TWENTY-FIVE

*During these times there was a pestilence by which the whole human race
came near to being annihilated*
Procopius, *The Wars of Justinian*, after 552

'They say the pestilence 'as got to Syria,' declared a lighterman to the
patrons of Damian's, a wine shop near the Harbour of Phosphorion at the
entrance to the Golden Horn.

'Stale news, mate,' chipped in a packer from the *horrea*, the rows of
warehouses for storing grain that lined the wharves. 'It's now in Phrygia.
Three hundred miles to go, and then it's our turn.'

'The Bosphorus'll stop it,' murmured a coppersmith hopefully.

'Oh, really,' scoffed a seaman. 'If it's come a thousand miles from Egypt,
stands to reason a puddle of water won't make any difference.'

'Repent, all ye – for the Day of Judgement is at hand!' bawled Scripture
Simon, a burly stevedore celebrated for his extempore hellfire harangues.
'That dread day, when the Last Trump shall sound and the graves give up
their dead, and Christ shall divide the sheep from the –'

'Stuff a sponge in it, Simon,' sighed the bartender. 'What with the
pestilence and the End of the World coming, we'd best not waste any more
drinking time. Next orders, gentlemen.'

'In view of the fact that the pestilence is now in Chalcedon, a mere mile
across the Bosphorus,' Cyril, *princeps* or head of the University of Constantinople, addressed his staff assembled in a lecture hall, 'I have decided, for
obvious health reasons, to close this institution. I trust you all concur.'

There followed a general nodding of heads and mutter of agreement.

'Do we know anything about the causes of the pestilence?' enquired
the Chair of Law, 'or what precautions can be taken to reduce the risk of
infection?'

'The answer to both your questions is, sadly, "no",' replied Cyril, whose
sturdy frame and ruddy complexion suggested more a prosperous peasant
than an academic. 'All I can tell you, you most likely know already. Namely,
that it seems to be quite indiscriminate and arbitrary as to whom it strikes.

That thus far it has caused death on a devastating scale wherever it has spread, with whole towns and villages depopulated. That beyond total isolation from one's fellow-men, there is no known safeguard against catching the disease. Nor is there any cure; one either recovers, or, in the case of at least two-thirds of those affected, succumbs. As to its cause – some subtle distemper in the air?; "cadaveric poisoning" or touching of a corpse? One can only guess.'

'The writer John of Ephesus suggests there may be some association with rats,' observed a grammarian. 'He relates how large numbers of the rodents have often been seen in places affected by the plague.'

'Coincidence, I'd say,' replied the *princeps*. 'The pestilence is naturally most prevalent in densely populated centres where risk of contagion, if that is indeed how it is spread, is highest. *Id est*, in towns and cities, whose refuse dumps attract rats in large numbers. Anyway, only a tiny proportion of plague victims could have received a rat bite, which virtually rules out any direct connection.'

'I've heard that, prior to infection, some sufferers have had dreams of headless figures sitting in bronze boats and holding bronze staves, moving across the sea towards them,' put in the librarian.

'Sounds as if they had too much wine with a heavy dinner,' responded Cyril, to general laughter.

'I was only repeating what I'd *heard*,' countered the librarian defensively. 'By what symptoms then, should we recognize the onset of the disease?'

'Like yourself, I can only repeat hearsay. Apparently, a mild fever is followed by the appearance of *bubones* – gross swellings in the groin and armpits, or black pustules breaking out all over the body. In the latter case, or in the event of the *bubones* turning gangrenous, the patient swiftly dies. But should the *bubones* discharge pus, the inflammation is relieved and the patient soon recovers.'

'Perhaps the Almighty has a lesson for us here, whose meaning we should endeavour to interpret,' declared a professor of Theology – one of a new breed of appointees, chosen as much for their subscription to strict Chalcedonian Orthodoxy, as for their professional qualifications.

'Oh, for goodness sake!' snapped Cyril, a classically educated rationalist of the old school. 'Let's stick to facts, not bring in mumbo-jumbo.'

'I don't imagine the emperor or Patriarch would be impressed by *that* remark,' retorted the professor, colouring.

'I rather think they'll soon have more urgent matters to occupy their minds,' said Cyril wearily. 'As will we all. I therefore bring this meeting to a close, and hope to see you all again when, God willing, the pestilence shall have run its course.'

In the summer of that year,* the plague leapt across the Bosphorus and battened on the capital. In the maze of close-packed houses, especially the poorer quarters, it spread like wildfire seemingly through contagion, the appearance of the swellings usually amounting to a death-sentence. The symptoms were invariably the same, and most of those infected died in agony within a few days, or even on the same day that the symptoms manifested themselves.

The death-rate escalated swiftly – from five thousand in a day, to ten thousand, to sixteen thousand on the worst day of all. Disposal of the dead became a nigh-insuperable problem. To deal with this distasteful task, Justinian appointed an imperial private secretary named Theodore. Theodore's solution was to dig vast burial pits at the suburb of Sykae across the Golden Horn. But so relentless was the torrent of fresh corpses that these rapidly filled up; in desperation, Theodore then resorted to pulling off the roofs of the towers of the suburb's walls, and filling them with the dead. In consequence, whenever the wind blew from the north, an appalling stench from Sykae pervaded Constantinople, whose inhabitants cowered in their houses, too terrified to venture out in case they caught the plague. Countless homes throughout the city became charnel houses, in which their dead inmates lay rotting for lack of anyone brave enough to bury them.

And then, just when it seemed that things could get no worse, the emperor himself became infected by the plague. Justinian was hardly popular. Many recalled with bitterness the harsh government policies which had provoked the Nika riots, and the brutality with which these had been suppressed. And the tax burden to sustain the wars in Africa, Italy, and Persia had borne heavily on almost everyone. But as Roman emperor, who was also Christ's vicegerent upon earth, he was seen by Roman citizens as their champion against the forces of evil and barbarism that constituted an ever-present threat to the survival of the Empire. In allowing the pestilence to strike down their emperor, had God withdrawn His favour from the Romans? And if this could happen to Justinian, the highest in the land, then what hope was there for anyone? If scent could be an attribute of prayer, then the odour of the orisons arising for the safety of their emperor would have overwhelmed the stink of rotting corpses from across the Golden Horn.

* 542.

With Justinian confined to a sick-bed and expected to succumb, to Theodora devolved the running of the Roman world. A woman distracted by grief over the death of a lover she adored, concerned for a husband gravely ill, and inexperienced in the conduct of high politics, now found herself in charge of an empire extending from Atlantic to Euphrates, from the Alps to Aethiopia, and numbering (prior to the pestilence) perhaps a hundred million souls.

From Procopius Caesariensis, Chronicler, to Anicius Julianus, Senator, greetings.

Dear 'Cato', friend in *Libertas*, although I have heard nothing from you in all the time since Ravenna fell to Belisarius (ending what has turned out to be only the first phase of the Gothic War), I allow myself to hope and trust a) that you are safe and in good health, and b) that I may soon hear from you again in your capacity of head of *Libertas*, now that Totila is sweeping all before him. Assuming both will prove to be the case, I shall inform you of those matters relevant to the Cause which I am competent to comment on that have transpired since last we corresponded. Much of what I have to tell you I daresay you'll have heard about already, but to insure against lacunae I shall omit nothing of substance.

Justinian unfortunately did not die (his death from pestilence would have made *Libertas* virtually redundant!), but during the months that he was sick Theodora, bless her, inadvertently gave our Cause a tremendous boost. How? By emasculating Belisarius, the one man who could have stopped Totila! (The plague having spread to Persia, Khusro suspended hostilities with Rome, thus ending the need for B's presence on that front.) Allow me to elucidate.

As very few recover from plague (this visitation is estimated to have killed 300,000 in Constantinople alone – a third of the capital) everyone assumed Justinian was going to die. So it was only common sense on Belisarius' part, as one of the Empire's movers and shakers, to plan ahead against developments arising from the emperor's demise. Having (quite rightly) little faith that Theodora would make a sensible choice of successor, he let it be known that the appointment of an emperor could only happen with the concurrence of himself and the army commanders – otherwise there would be a very real risk of civil war. Of course Theodora, the silly bitch, who can only ever see things from a *personal* point of view, construed this as an insult and proceeded to confiscate B's fortune, dismiss his corps of personal retainers, and all but have him flung in gaol (which is what she did to poor old Buzes, B's second-in-command).

Even after he turned the corner healthwise, Justinian had to convalesce and let Theodora carry on as regent. With Belisarius available but in disgrace, the emperor, lacking the guts to contravene Theodora, was forced to send his original choice, Maximinus, to Italy in order to sort out Totila. Well, although a disaster for Justinian, Maximinus proved a perfect gift for us. An indecisive ditherer, he let Totila run rings round him, allowing the Goths to capture Naples, thus giving Totila a port and power-base of immense strategic value for the whole of southern Italy.

By this time, Justinian had recovered sufficiently to take up the reins of power once again. Finding at last the courage to override Theodora, he reinstated Belisarius (much to the empress' chagrin), recalled the hapless Maximinus, and despatched B. (with yours truly in tow) to Ravenna to try to rectify the situation in Italy. Predictably, our wise and far-sighted emperor had neglected to provide the general with sufficient troops or supplies to achieve anything, forcing B. to appeal to J. for reinforcements, and to the Romans to abandon their allegiance to Totila and come over to his side. A plea which, in view of the 'benefits' conferred by Roman reoccupation, needless to say fell on deaf ears. While B. cooled his heels waiting for reinforcements to arrive, Totila was able to take the last few fortresses in central Italy and go on to besiege Rome itself.

Meanwhile, you'll be interested to know, while my superior was fuming impotently in Ravenna, I contrived to stir things up in Africa again. Via my contacts in the diocese, I persuaded Guntarith – a Roman general of Vandal origins (whose troops, surprise, surprise, were in arrears of pay) – to combine with rebel Moorish chiefs to mount an insurrection against Roman rule. Knowing you'll honour my pledge when you resume command of *Libertas*, I took the liberty of promising to back any revolt with funds. I'm pleased to say they took me at my word, with the result that Artabanus, *Magister Militum* in Africa, now has his hands full with mutinying soldiery and Moorish insurgents. As for the war in Italy, I'll spare you the details – a dreary catalogue of sieges, counter-sieges, sorties, and manoeuvrings, the consequence of Belisarius taking to the field again as a result of his long-awaited reinforcements eventually arriving. Suffice to say that the campaign is taking a terrible toll on the civilian population and the land itself, with many areas reverting to uncultivated waste, and starvation becoming endemic. (The plus side of all this misery, from our point of view, is that it's fast turning Justinian into a hate figure.)

I've saved the best till last. Again, as a result of promises of payment on my part, via contacts inside Rome, I persuaded a unit of Isaurian soldiers (minus pay, as usual) to open the Porta Asinaria.* In rushed the Goths and, I'm pleased to report, the Eternal City is now in Totila's hands.

In full confidence that I will hear from you ere long, I shall leave this at our old collection-point at Cecilia Metella on the Via Appia, for your *agens* to pick up. (This, I imagine, is what you would expect me to do, assuming me to be in the vicinity of Rome with Belisarius.) Vale.

Written at Portus** XIII Kalendas Januarii, in the year from the Founding of New Rome the two hundred and seventeenth.†

Post Scriptum

My cover, by the way, seems rock-solid. At the height of his sickness, I was summoned by the emperor who told me that he wished to reward those who had stood by him at moments of crisis. (I suppose he was thinking – ha! ha! – of my 'services' during the Nika affair.) He said (speaking in a dreadful croaking whisper) that after the war, when my services as official historian could be relinquished, he would make me Prefect of Constantinople. Or, should he die, he had left instructions as to my promotion. I confess that I was touched, also that I felt almost sorry for the old fox to see him lying there – a wasted skeleton, like one of those hideous things in the catacombs of Rome. I was also, being in close proximity to one of its victims, absolutely terrified of catching the plague. But you can't ignore an imperial command. Theodora too (who, to her credit, had nursed him faithfully throughout his sickness) looked at death's door – hollow-eyed and ravaged from worry, also lack of

---

* The Asinarian Gate was opened on 17 December 546.
** Now Porto, at the mouth of the Tiber.
† 20 December 546.

sleep – and, this is just guesswork on my part, perhaps some hidden malady that was sapping her constitution.

From Anicius Julianus, Senator, to Procopius Caesariensis, Chronicler, Ave.

Dear 'Regulus', most loyal, courageous, and efficient of colleagues, I write in haste, a) to thank you for your sterling efforts on behalf of *Libertas*, b) alas, to inform you that *Libertas* itself is now dissolved, and c) to warn you to destroy instanter any correspondence relating to our Cause. My cover, as they say, is 'blown'. Justinian's *agentes* have at last caught up with me, and I am ordered to report to the monastery of Saint Catherine on Mount Sinai, there to do penance for my 'treason' for the remainder of my days. I am as sure as I can be that your connection with *Libertas* is at present unsuspected and will probably remain so, provided you are circumspect.

Before the net closed in on me (and my senior lieutenants), I was able to honour the pledges you had made to our friends in Africa and Rome. Good Fortune attend you always. We may have failed, but at least we struck a blow for Roman values. Vale.

Written at Ancona, Nones Februarii, A.R.U.C., the two hundred and eighteenth.*

Post Scriptum

We shall not meet again, dear friend. The climate on Mount Sinai I suspect I'd find most disagreeable, and the monastic life insufferably tedious. So, in the best Roman tradition, I intend to open my veins in the bath (no doubt while reading some uplifting stanzas of Horace or Catullus).

* 5 February 547.

TWENTY-SIX

There are two natures of Christ united in respect of His one hypostasis*
Leontius of Jerusalem, *Against the Monophysites*, 532

The triple calamity of pestilence, the phenomenon that was Totila, and insurgency in Africa had put on hold that other aspect of Justinian's Grand Plan – the establishment of religious uniformity throughout the Empire. But, with Belisarius now back in Italy, thanks to the resumption of (no doubt temporary) Eternal Peace with Persia,** General John 'the Troglite' – Anastasius' successor – beginning to turn the tide of insurrection in Africa, and the plague having spent itself, the now fully recovered emperor looked forward with relish to confronting the challenge (thus far un-resolved) of bridging the gulf between the rival creeds of Chalcedonian Orthodoxy and Monophysitism.

In his mind, Justinian reviewed the field of battle as it looked at present. The successful machinations of Theodora and Antonina had secured the throne of Peter for Vigilius, a Monophysite sympathiser,† thus 'planting' a potentially heretical pontiff in the ultra-Chalcedonian West! In the East, apart from Constantinople (where the Patriarch, Menas, was staunchly Chalcedonian), much of the Empire, especially the wealthy and important dioceses of Egypt and Oriens, the latter comprising Syria and Palestine, were passionately Monophysite. To an emperor more cynical and less idealistic than Justinian (a man, say, of Khusro's stamp), this potentially schismatic situation might have been shrugged off – a tiresome but essentially un-important dichotomy. But Justinian was no cynic, and he was nothing if not idealistic. If the situation were allowed to drift, the Empire, in his opinion, was in danger of splitting into two mutually irreconcilable camps. It was his duty, as both emperor and Christ's vicegerent upon earth, to ensure this did not happen. To help him in his search for a solution, he sent for Theodore

---

* i.e. two elements combining in a single entity – 'as fire and iron come together in a red-hot ingot', as Leontius puts it.
** The treaty was renegotiated in 545.
† See Chapter 19. To remind the reader: the Monophysites held that Christ had only one, divine, nature; the Chalcedonians that He had two natures – both human *and* divine.

Ascidas, Metropolitan of Caesarea, an ambitious, worldly, and intelligent cleric, who loved nothing better than the cut-and-thrust of intellectual debate . . .

'You're in a fix, Serenity,' chuckled Ascidas, pouring himself a chaliceful of communion wine from the flagon on the altar. The two men were in Saint Irene's in the capital, consecrated a dozen years before. 'In Africa and Italy,' went on the bishop, a well-fleshed individual with a pleasant, lived-in face, '– especially Italy, what with Totila making things hard for Belisarius, you can't afford not to keep the Romans on side. Not if you hope to hold the West, once you've reconquered it – again. And to *keep* those West Romans on side, you've got to be seen to be the champion of Chalcedonian Orthodoxy. For which you absolutely have to have the support of the Roman Church establishment, an institution that has largely filled the power-vacuum created by the absence of a Western emperor. Let the Romans of the West suspect you for a moment of going soft on the Monophysites –' Ascidas took a swig from the jewelled, silver cup and beamed at the emperor. 'Then your credibility's gone. I trust I'm making myself clear, Serenity.'

'Only *too* clear,' confirmed Justinian glumly. 'I hear what you say, Ascidas, but unfortunately I can't afford to crack down too hard on the Monophysites. Not since this firebrand priest, Jacob Baradaeus, has stirred up the Monophysite majority in Egypt, Syria, and Asia Minor to defy the Chalcedonian hierarchy. Why, in Alexandria alone, demonstrations against Zoilus, the Orthodox Patriarch, forced the man to flee. And there's not a thing I can do about it; not unless I want a revolution on my hands. And, to make my position even more invidious, this wretched Jacob has the backing of my wife.' The emperor paced the nave distractedly, before sitting on the lowest tier of concentric stone benches that formed the nether portion of the church's apse. 'But I asked you here to help me find some answers,' he went on, with a reproachful glance at Ascidas, 'not just present me with a string of problems.'

'Patience, Serenity. Diagnosis comes before the cure. What we must do is find some common ground on which both Chalcedonians and Monophysites can unite.'

'Common ground?' The emperor laughed bitterly. 'Something I've been searching for since I put on the diadem. If you can find *that* for me, I'll be forever in your debt.'

'Think, Serenity,' invited the bishop with a reassuring smile. 'The Blues and Greens are even more divided than are Rome and Alexandria, yet once they did make common cause.'

'You mean, during the Nika riots – against myself? Don't bother to spare my feelings, will you?'

'Apologies, Serenity – nothing personal intended. But you take my point. The most effective way of uniting opponents is to find a common enemy. Allow me therefore to explain the Ascidas Plan – something which could be fittingly entitled, "The Condemnation of the Three Chapters" . . .'

In an auditorium of Rome's Lateran Palace, hard by the Asinarian Gate,* Stephen, the Pope's *apocrisiarius* or legate, a tall, commanding figure with a great eagle's beak of a Roman nose, stood to address the mass of clergy he had hastily convoked. In his hand he held an Edict, just arrived from Constantinople.

'His Holiness, Pope Vigilius, is unable to attend,' announced the legate, 'because he is en route to Constantinople, by invitation of the emperor.' He glared sternly round the assembly. 'The reason for the summons, I suspect, is so that Justinian can exert direct pressure on Vigilius to get him to agree to *this*.' Angrily, Stephen waved the Edict in the air. 'This is the emperor's latest trick to force us to compromise with the Monophysites.' He paused, then went on, his voice rising to a shout, 'Well, he must imagine that we're idiots, to think we're going to fall for it! The content is: a condemnation of certain century-old writings – 'Chapters' he calls them – by Theodore of Mopsuestia, Theoderet of Cyrus, and Ibas of Edessa.'

'The significance of which is – what exactly?' enquired a puzzled-looking deacon.

'The three writers were all Nestorians,' replied Stephen. 'For the benefit of those of you whose knowledge of ancient ecclesiastical history may be sketchy, I shall endeavour to explain. Back in the time of Emperor Theodosius the Second, one Nestorius, a Patriarch of Constantinople, propounded the doctrine that Christ was essentially a man, but a man onto whom God grafted a divine nature, making Him a single entity you could call a God-man. After the Council of Chalcedon, such a doctrine was naturally obnoxious both to Chalcedonians for whom Christ has two natures, human *and* divine, and also to the Monophysites, who believe that Christ has only one, divine, nature.'

---

* Both Palace and Gate are still extant. (See Notes.)

'So, if I've understood you aright, *Apocrisiarius*,' put in a presbyter in tones half-disbelieving, half-exasperated, 'in condemning the writings of these three disciples of Nestorius, who was anathema to Chalcedonians and Monophysites alike, Justinian's hoping to curry favour with both sects. How? By reheating a forgotten controversy from the past, on which, at the time, they both happened to share the same view. Surely that does absolutely nothing to resolve the fundamental *differences* between the two creeds? This Edict seems to me just a crude attempt to paint over the cracks.'

'Couldn't have put it better myself,' concurred Stephen warmly.

'This is classic Justinian,' fumed a bishop. 'All smoke and mirrors, designed to obfuscate what he's *really* trying to do – make concessions to a foul Egyptian heresy. Well, I for one refuse to subscribe to such a shabby ruse.'

'And I! . . . And I! . . .' An angry chorus of agreement erupted throughout the chamber.

'Who the hell does Justinian think he is, laying down the law on matters of theology?' shouted a fiery-eyed lector. 'That's for the Pope and the Patriarch of Constantinople to decide. This whole charade's a blatant con, designed to fob us off!'

Which pretty well summed up the mood of the assembly, and, when news of the Edict reached the streets, of Rome itself, eventually of all of Italy and Africa. Within a few weeks, the Condemnation of the Three Chapters had become, so far as the West was concerned, as dead a letter as the Laws of Hammurabi, the Edict viewed as a Trojan Horse to sneak in concord with Monophysitism by the back door.

In the East, the Edict was received with scarcely more enthusiasm than in the West. What the Monophysite clergy (now in the ascendant, thanks to the evangelizing clout of Jacob Baradaeus) wanted, was not the condemnation of Nestorius but the creed of Chalcedon itself. However, made subject, by Geography, to direct pressure from Justinian and Menas, the strongly Chalcedonian Patriarch of Constantinople, most of them reluctantly gave their assent to the imperial decree – a surrender which, in Menas' case, resulted in his excommunication by a furious and disgusted Stephen.*

Arriving in Constantinople,** Vigilius was welcomed at the harbour

* Rome, rather than Constantinople, Antioch, or Alexandria, was held to have the final say in matters of theology.
** On 25 January 547.

by Justinian himself. Treated with respect and cordiality as an honoured and distinguished guest, the Pontiff nonetheless soon found himself under pressure (relentless though courteously applied) from his imperial host – and in a quandary. Vigilius, a covert Monophysite, owed his election as Pope to the machinations of Theodora who, as a quid pro quo, expected him to promote the Monophysite cause in the West: a virtually impossible commission, considering the loathing in which the staunchly Chalcedonian West Romans held the eastern creed. An arch-trimmer and survivalist, Vigilius, however, had brought off a tricky balancing act. Keeping his Monophysite sympathies to himself, he had avoided offending the Western clergy, while at the same time keeping Theodora at bay with endless excuses regarding the delay in proselytizing on behalf of Monophysitism.

But now, a virtual prisoner in the eastern capital with both emperor and empress holding him to account, the wily Pope could vacillate no longer. Yielding to the inevitable, Vigilius handed to Justinian and Theodora* a signed statement declaring his condemnation of the Three Chapters. Fully aware that if this became public knowledge in the West his authority as Pope would disappear, he managed to persuade the imperial couple that his signed statement should remain secret until he, Vigilius, had had time to hold a final enquiry into the views expressed in the Three Chapters. Breathing a huge sigh of relief at obtaining this all-important concession, Vigilius set about preparing his case against the moment of truth when he must reveal his stance regarding the Three Chapters – whatever that stance should turn out to be.

In his luxurious suite in Constantinople's Palace of Placidia, Vigilius stared at his reflection in the looking-glass. What had happened, he wondered, to that sleek young deacon who, eleven years before, had – thanks to Theodora and Antonina – found himself the occupant of Peter's Throne? That his promotion had involved the deposition and subsequent 'disappearance' of Pope Silverius had not cost the ambitious cleric any sleep; climbing the ladder of success necessarily involved stamping on others' fingers on the rungs. What *had* put lines on those once-smooth cheeks and thinned a luxurious mop to a few greying strands on a balding pate, was the strain of constantly having to maintain a precarious balance between fobbing off Theodora and keeping up a pro-Chalcedonian front for the benefit of Western bishops.

* On 29 June 547.

In practice, what this had entailed was endless procrastination regarding his promise to Theodora, involving the fabrication of convincing reasons as to why it was never quite the right time to keep his side of the bargain. For let the clergy and people of Italy once suspect him of compromising with what they saw as heresy, the ensuing uproar could bring about his downfall. And that, he was determined, he would never allow to happen. He relished the feel of the pallium about his shoulders far too much to let another take it from him.

Yet there was a very real and present risk of precisely that happening. Time had finally run out for Vigilius. For today he must address the synod formally convoked to enquire into the views expressed in the Three Chapters. And, in addressing the synod, composed of seventy bishops from the West, he must finally reveal that he had signed that statement condemning the Three Chapters – news that would be as welcome to the bishops, as a side of bacon in a synagogue. It would take all of his negotiating skills to tread a safe path through the maze of theological pitfalls that awaited him.

'. . . and after diligently perusing the aforementioned Chapters of Theodore, Theoderet, and Ibas, and carefully weighing up the views expressed therein, I came to the conclusion – a surprising one to me, I must confess – that these were in fact extremely dangerous men whose ideas, unless anathematized, could lead men into heresy. Consider this, my friends.' Looking round the seventy attentive faces in the audience chamber, Vigilius assumed an expression of meekness and humility, then went on, 'Nestorius, whose views these men subscribed to, held that the Virgin Mary was *not* the Theotokos or Mother of God, but the mother of the man Jesus only, not of the divine Christ. I ask you, as a humble seeker after truth, can such a view be tenable?' (In fact, Vigilius hadn't the faintest idea if it was tenable or otherwise. He had never read the works of Theodore et al., and was simply parroting the words of the ecclesiastic assigned by Justinian to 'enlighten' him.)

From the speculative murmur that broke out following his question, Vigilius felt that he had at least sown a seed of doubt in the minds of his hearers. He sensed that the atmosphere in the chamber had subtly changed from suspicion verging on hostility at the inception of the meeting, to one of interest that was not unsympathetic. Their entrenched opposition to condemning the Three Chapters was perhaps beginning to erode. Sufficiently, at least, to allow his own position in the matter (or rather the position he had been forced to adopt) to be accorded a fair hearing. Vigilius began to entertain the hope that he might even win them round. A hope, however, that was destined to be dashed.

A hand was raised, and on Vigilius' nod a huge figure rose – Facundus, bishop of Hermiane in Africa and a famous scholar. Outstanding in appearance on account of his great size and coal-black skin, Facundus seemed to radiate an indefinable air of presence and personal magnetism. Most African Romans were of Berber or Italian stock, the latter mainly descended from settlers who had arrived following Rome's victory against Carthage in the Punic Wars. But a few hailed from Africa the continent, rather than the diocese: from Nubia or Axum, even from beyond the Great Sand Sea. Such a Roman citizen was Tertius Facundus.

'My thanks, Your Holiness, for granting me permission to speak in this august assembly,' acknowledged Facundus, speaking in a richly booming rumble that someone had once described as 'like thunder laced with cream'. Smiling, he addressed his audience. 'Vigilius, with admirable clarity, has summarized the stance taken by Nestorius regarding the relation of the Virgin Mary to the Son. Was she Theotokos, the Mother of God, or simply the mother of Jesus the man? If the latter, then His Divinity must have been conferred by God alone.' The bishop paused, then lowering his voice, went on, 'No doubt what I now have to say will sound to some of you controversial, nay, heretical even. But I put it to you: does this issue of the status of the Virgin Mary really *matter*? To my mind, it seems in essence a distraction, an irrelevance which obscures what we should chiefly be concerned about: the true nature of the Christ himself. Of infinitely greater importance in the teaching of Nestorius has to be the fact that he acknowledges the dual nature of Christ – that He was both human *and* divine. Which is the very essence of our Chalcedonian creed – something that Ibas of Edessa in especial, homes in on in his Chapter, a Chapter to which the Council of Chalcedon itself gave its approval.'

A tense and prickling silence reigned throughout the chamber as Facundus surveyed his rapt audience. 'Wake up, my friends!' he declared in ringing tones. 'This Edict is nothing but a shabby cover-up. If we condemn the Three Chapters, we condemn the very faith which every one of us holds dear – Chalcedonian Orthodoxy!'

All over the great room bishops leapt excitedly to their feet, shouting their approval of Facundus' words: 'Down with the Edict! . . . Down with Justinian! . . . Up with the Three Chapters! . . . Long live Facundus! . . . Shame on you, Vigilius! . . .'

With a surge of panic, Vigilius realized that any hope he might have entertained of persuading the bishops to condemn the Chapters was now dead beyond recovery. Obeying his instinct to play for time, he declared the meeting at an end – a statement greeted with noisy resentment. Raising his voice to be heard above the hubbub, he cried, 'Fellow bishops, you have made your feelings plain. Rest assured, I shall take due cognizance of this when, in due course, I announce my verdict. Depart in peace, my friends, and may Christ's blessing be upon you all.'

The bishops departed – not in peace, but in a bitter mood of fury and frustration.

In his official judgement or *Judicatum*,* Vigilius (as, under pressure from Justinian, he was bound to do) roundly condemned the Three Chapters. But, in a desperate attempt to salvage some scraps of credibility with the Western clergy, he included in the document an addendum avowing his unshakeable attachment to the findings of the Council of Chalcedon – the very assembly which, as Facundus had pointed out, had stated its approval of those selfsame Chapters! Vigilius' attempt to square this particular circle met with utter failure. Throughout the West, outraged clergy demanded the withdrawal of the *Judicatum*, the General Synod of African Bishops going so far as to break completely from communion with the Pope until he should agree to do this.

Far from establishing the unity that Justinian desired, his Edict, in combination with the Synod, then the *Judicatum*, had created a yawning gulf between the Churches of the East and West that now seemed nigh unbridgeable.

'Well, we did our best, Serenity,' said Ascidas to Justinian in conciliatory tones, 'But we failed. It seems there are some battles we are destined not to win, however hard we try. Best perhaps that we accept that, and move on.' The two men were once again inside Saint Irene's, a venue that, for some reason, Justinian found soothing to his troubled state of mind.

'I hear what you say, Ascidas,' replied the emperor. 'But in this matter, failure cannot be allowed to be an option. The Three Chapters *must* be universally condemned.'

'Even now, Serenity,' said the cleric gently, 'after the Western bishops have forced Vigilius to withdraw his *Judicatum*?'

'You don't understand!' cried the emperor, a note of desperation entering his voice. 'As Christ's vicegerent upon earth, it is my duty not only

---

* Issued on Saturday 11 April 548.

to reunite the Roman Empire, but to ensure unity of faith within that Empire. To achieve the first without the second would be a meaningless accomplishment.' He stared intently at the other. 'You can understand that, can't you? Vigilius must not become a broken reed. I have made him swear an oath, backed up by a signed statement, that he will revisit this whole matter of the Three Chapters with a view to ensuring their condemnation. As a concession to religious sensitivities, however, I have given my permission for the oath to remain secret – for the time being.'

At that moment, a man attired in palace livery burst into the church. 'Serenity,' the official blurted out, 'the physician urges that you come immediately to the Palace. The Augusta has been taken gravely sick!'

TWENTY-SEVEN

Enter into thy rest, O Empress! The King of Kings and Lord of Lords calleth thee
Salutation of the master of ceremonies at the funeral of
Theodora, 548

Hurrying through the Palace corridors en route to Theodora's bedchamber, Justinian was intercepted by Theoctistus, the imperial physician.

'What ails the Empress?' cried Justinian distractedly. 'I had no idea anything was amiss. I – I came immediately I received your message.' Grabbing the other's arm, he stared with wild-eyed panic into the man's face. 'How is she?'

'The Augusta sleeps, Serenity,' replied the *medicus*, a grave-faced man of calm demeanour. 'I have increased her medication. She is very sick, I fear. But, to spare you from worrying, she has insisted these past months, while secluding herself in her summer palace of Hieron, that you were told nothing. Until now, that is.'

'Until now! What does that mean?'

'Her sickness is terminal, I fear, Serenity. She has a cancer in her back – beyond my skill to operate.'

Theoctistus, formerly the army's most brilliant surgeon, had saved the life of many a soldier whom other physicians had despaired of helping. When such a one declared a case hopeless . . . Nevertheless, Justinian found himself clutching at straws. 'A cancer – can that not be cut out?' he gabbled.

'Not in this case, Serenity. It is too deep. Besides, it has now spread,' he added gently, his face creased with compassion, 'The best that I can do is ease her pain with a potion I've prepared: an infusion of mandragora – *poein anasthesian*, as we say – to dull the pain. I should warn you, though; its effectiveness will soon diminish rapidly.'

'How long?' whispered the emperor, a terrible sense of impending loss replacing his initial shock.

'A month at most, Serenity.'

'Will she experience much pain, Theoctistus? Please be frank; I have to know.'

'Very well, Serenity. She is already suffering bouts of severe pain at intervals, which she is enduring with commendable fortitude. These, unfortunately, will increase in frequency and severity. Towards the end, the pain will be unbearable. Unless –'

'Unless! You said "unless", Theoctistus! Does that mean what I think it means?'

'I can supply the means, Serenity, to ensure that death comes swiftly and without pain. As a physician, I am constrained by my Hippocratic oath which begins, "First, do no harm", from administering it myself.' Glancing keenly at the emperor, he added softly, 'But perhaps another may.'

'For her sake, I must be strong; I must be strong,' Justinian repeated to himself as he entered the bedchamber. But, at the sight of that beloved face drained of all colour to a waxy pallor, his resolve crumbled and he broke down.

'You cannot, must not leave me,' he sobbed. 'I myself, the Patriarch, all Constantinople, will pray for you. God, the All-Powerful, will surely heed our intercessions and restore you to health.'

'Don't torture yourself with false hopes, my dear,' murmured Theodora, summoning a tremulous smile. 'My time has come. I have accepted that, and so must you. We have been fortunate, you and I. Our married life together has been long and good; not many are so blessed. Besides, our parting will not be forever. Soon, I must be in Heaven, but you will join me there in God's good time.' Suddenly, she took a sharp intake of breath and winced, biting her lower lip with such force as to draw blood. After a few moments she relaxed, then whispered, 'The pain – it strikes suddenly, without warning; but it is gone now. For a while.'

Cursing himself for being so blindly obsessed with implementing the religious aspect of his Grand Plan that he had been unaware that his wife was sick – Theodora, who had nursed him so devotedly while he lay stricken with the plague, his loyal helpmeet through thick and thin these twenty-three years – Justinian could only hold her hand and gaze at her with helpless love from tear-blurred eyes as she drifted into sleep.

The time had come. His heart pounding, his breathing shallow and constricted, Justinian was seized with a fit of trembling so violent that he could scarcely hold the phial that Theoctistus had made ready. It contained, in addition to Theodora's usual medicine, a substance called *arsenikon* – in a quantity sufficient to cause the patient 'to pass peacefully away within an hour', as the *medicus* had assured him. The memory of the terrible agony he had witnessed Theodora enduring in the last few days had nerved the emperor at last to carry out the task he knew he must perform.

'Time for your morning dose, my love,' said Justinian in a broken voice, tears streaming freely down his cheeks. Had she guessed? he wondered, as he poured the phial's contents into a cup which he held to her lips. Steadying his shaking hand with hers, she drained the vessel in a single draught.

'Don't weep, my love,' she murmured, her head falling back on the pillow. 'We shall meet again in a place where there will be no more tears nor pain, but only joy and peace.' Her eyes began to close, then opened suddenly. With a smile and a hint of her old spirit, she declared in a low but clear voice, 'You and I – the barbarian from Thrace and the bear-keeper's daughter from the Hippodrome, together we showed the world, did we not?'

'We surely did, my dear,' whispered her husband in choked tones. 'We showed the world indeed.'

Stirring awake, Justinian took a few seconds to come to himself. Exhaustion from shock and the strain of the past days must have temporarily overcome him, he told himself. Then he realized that the little hand he held in his was cold. In sudden panic, he bent his ear to her lips, could detect no sound nor sign of breath. The awful truth hit him: Theodora was dead!* – had died while, unforgiveably, he had slept. He felt as though the central pillar of his life had suddenly been knocked away, leaving him, at sixty-six, bereft and utterly alone. The remainder of his life seemed to stretch away before him like a bleak and barren desert. What meaning had his Grand Plan now, when there was no Theodora to share it with?

A great cry of grief and loss burst from the emperor. To have taken Theodora from him, God must surely have abandoned him – no longer His vicegerent upon earth. The old morale-sapping conviction that he was somehow cursed came flooding back; those who had been close to him had always come to harm – now including Theodora. The dreadful thought occurred to him that, being the instrument of her passing, in the eyes not only of the law but of the Church, he was guilty of the cardinal sin of murder. That he had acted out of love and pity made no difference. For such a terrible deed there could be no absolution. Therefore, for him no entry into Heaven, and thus no prospect of a joyful reunion with Theodora to

* She died on the 28 June 548.

comfort his declining years. But was not God a kind and loving Father, who would surely stay His Hand from punishing one who had always striven faithfully to serve Him? And had not Christ His Son declared that he who repented should not perish? As he had done before, he would pray to God to give him a sign. On that occasion, his prayer had been answered; surely, this time it would be again. Hope and dread mingling with overwhelming sorrow, he kissed his wife's cold forehead. Then, after summoning Theoctistus, he made his way towards his private oratory.

'. . . and all my life, Lord, I have tried to do Your bidding,' intoned the emperor. 'I have set about recovering the West for Rome, the Roman Empire being the vehicle for the spreading of Your Word over all the world. Though the work is yet unfinished, Lord, much has been achieved. Also, I have striven to establish one single faith throughout the Empire, to the end that You be worshipped in a true and fitting manner. I freely own, Lord, that I have not yet succeeded in accomplishing this latter task, but with perseverance and Your aid, hope eventually to illuminate the darkness that presently obscures the minds of many of my subjects.

'And lastly, Lord, I confess to having ended the life of my beloved spouse Theodora. I tell myself I did so out of love, to end her pain. But is it possible, Lord, that I acted out of weakness – to spare myself the distress of witnessing her suffering? If that should be the case, Lord, I truly repent of my great sin, and ask You to look with compassion on Justinian, Your unworthy servant. And that I may truly know You have forgiven me, vouchsafe to me a sign, I beseech You, O Lord.'

The shadow of the cross upon the altar grew shorter as it moved towards the base, merged briefly with it, then, appearing on the other side, began to lengthen. The distant rumble of the vendors' carts as they headed for the city gates before they closed signalled the approach of evening. When the light within the oratory grew so dim that the kneeling emperor could no longer read the frieze of prayers inscribed around the window's architrave, he knew at last no sign would be forthcoming. But perhaps to have hoped for a sign was delusion in the first place, the emperor pondered, as a terrible sense of hopelessness and doubt began to permeate his mind. What if the Resurrection was, after all, a myth, and Jesus just a heap of mouldering bones in some forgotten tomb in Palestine? 'If Christ be not risen,' Paul had said, 'then is your faith vain'. Justinian felt as if a tide of black despair were closing over his head.

In the Triclinium of the Nineteen Couches, in a long, long line the Roman Empire's great and good filed past the bier on which Theodora lay: Menas, the Orthodox Patriarch, with a retinue of monks and bearded priests; Pope Vigilius, accompained by his nuncio and Stephen his *apocrisiarius*; bishops from both East and West; toga-clad senators; patricians; prefects in their robes of office; high government officials; magistrates; generals; and finally, Justinian himself. His vision half obscured by tears, the old emperor looked for the last time on that beloved face – marble-pale, from which all ravages of pain and sickness had, as if by a miracle, disappeared, leaving her countenance serene and beautiful. Was this at last His sign? Justinian wondered, with a surge of desperate hope. With trembling hands he placed around her neck a parting gift – a necklace of magnificent jewels to wear inside the tomb. Then, unable to contain his grief, he burst into uncontrollable sobs, suffering himself to be gently led away from the bier. Mastering himself with a huge effort, he signed to the bearers, who lifted up the bier. In a loud voice, the master of ceremonies called three times, 'Go forth, O Empress! The King of kings and Lord of lords calleth thee.'

In slow and solemn procession, the mourners followed the bier down the length of the great hall, out of the Palace, through the Augusteum, along the Mesé thronged with silent citizens, through the Fora of Constantine and Theodosius, to the empress' last resting-place – the Church of the Holy Apostles. Here, while a choir of clergy sang the Office for the Dead, Theodora's small body was lifted from the bier and gently placed within a porphyry sarcophagus. 'Enter into thy rest, O Empress!' declaimed the master of ceremonies, and the enormous lid of the sarcophagus was lowered by pulleys into place. The congregation then dispersed, and Justinian returned to his empty Palace, broken and in tears.

TWENTY-EIGHT

As he rode he hurled his javelin into the air and caught it again . . . then
passed it rapidly from hand to hand . . . with consummate skill
Procopius (commenting on Totila's display of martial skill before the
Battle of Busta Gallorum), *The Wars of Justinian*, after 552

Seating himself on a marble bench in a little garden in the Palace grounds
whither he had been summoned, General Narses awaited the arrival of the
emperor. Rumour had it that this was the spot where Justinian had first
met, then wooed and won, Theodora; also that, since her death two years
before, it had (no doubt on account of its fond associations) become a
favourite retreat and a venue for informal interviews.

Why had Justinian arranged this meeting? Narses wondered. It could
hardly be to ask him to take command on any military front. Belisarius (together with the official war historian, Procopius) had recently been recalled
from Italy to keep an eye on Lazica, where trouble had again flared up. But
he had been replaced by an able general, Germanus, cousin* of Justinian,
and his heir-designate. And in Africa, John the Troglite was successfully
grinding down Moorish resistance. Perhaps Justinian just wished to have
Narses' views on the way strategies were being handled. If so, the Armenian
general had plenty to say about the conduct of the war in Italy.

In Narses' view, it had been utter folly on Justinian's part to have recalled
Belisarius. Any semi-competent general could deal with Lazica, but in Italy,
where Totila had been making all the running, you needed the best military
talent you could find to counter him. The brilliant young Gothic leader had
captured a string of strong points across the peninsula, consolidating his
support among the Roman population, and raising a powerful fleet. This
last had enabled him to capture Sicily, enriching his war-chest with a vast
quantity of booty, and ravage the coastal cities of Dalmatia; for the first time
the Goths had seriously challenged Roman sea-power, previously unassail-
able. Meanwhile, Belisarius, starved of resources by the imperial government
despite increasingly desperate appeals for reinforcements, had barely been
able to hold his own.

* Or nephew, according to Gibbon.

The situation fairly reeked of muddle and incompetence. What *should* have happened, it was clear to Narses, was for Belisarius to have been given sufficient troops; he would then have been able to regain the initiative, perhaps even to the extent of landing a killer blow on his adversary. Instead, despite being recalled to deal with Lazica and appointed Master of Soldiers in the East, he had, incredibly, been kept in the capital as commander of the Palace Guard!

Things in Italy following the appointment of Germanus as Belisarius' successor had been even more bizarre, reflected Narses. Germanus was married to Matasuntha, widow of Witigis, and daughter of Amalasuntha whose father had been Theoderic. The plan was that the Western Empire be restored, with Germanus, popular with troops and citizens alike, as its emperor. Also, that some sort of power-sharing deal with Totila's Goths be negotiated, whereby as well as for the first time sitting in the Senate, Goths would man the army, protecting Italy from invasion by Lombards, Franks, and Alamanni. Any son born to Germanus and Matasuntha would, as a matter of course, become in turn the Western emperor, half-Roman and half-Goth, preserving through his mother the old Amal royal line. Should all this come to pass (and it seemed to Narses there was nothing to prevent it doing so), then, the general thought in disgust, the whole Italian war had been for nothing – a colossal waste of manpower and resources, resulting in the destruction of the country's infrastructure and the ruin of her people. With Italy the permanent homeland of barbarians, who would also have a major say in running it, Theoderic's ghost would have surely triumphed. But then, reflected Narses, ever since Theodora had died, Justinian's grip on affairs had seemed to falter, his policies increasingly lacking in coherence and consistency.

'Thank you for coming, General,' announced Justinian, breaking in on Narses' thoughts. He seated himself beside the general. Narses was shocked to notice how much the emperor had aged, the once-handsome face now gaunt and lined beneath a thinning fuzz of lint-white hair, the neck all scrawny and wattled like a vulture's. Although older than the emperor by a good five years, Narses reckoned he himself must look at least a decade younger.

'How would the idea of returning to Italy appeal to you, old friend?' enquired Justinian. 'You once served me well in that same theatre.' He added with a gentle smile, 'Although I seem to recall, on that occasion yourself and Belisarius had views that, let us say – "diverged".'

'You could say that, Serenity,' acknowledged Narses wryly. He shot the other an appraising look. 'Of course I'm honoured by your suggestion, but, to be frank, I think it's a bad idea. I suspect I'd get along with Germanus even less well than I did with Belisarius. With Totila's star in the ascendant, the last thing you need at this stage is a divided command.'

'Germanus is dead,' declared Justinian sadly. 'After driving from the Balkans a huge force of Slav invaders, he suddenly fell sick and died at Sardica.* What an emperor he would have made! – as Augustus of the West uniting Goth and Roman, then, upon my death succeeding to the Eastern throne, leaving his son to become the Western emperor.'

Masking his huge relief that this nonsense of a reconstituted Western Empire-cum-Romano-Gothic entente was now dead in the water, Narses enquired, 'You wish me then to take over as supreme commander in Italy?'

'Precisely.'

'Then I gladly accept, Serenity. 'However,' he went on, a note of steel entering his voice, 'there are conditions.'

'Conditions?' Justinian's eyebrows lifted. 'You forget yourself, I think, General.'

'I'll be blunt, Serenity. I leave for Italy only when I have sufficiency of troops. And *Roman* troops at that, drawn from regular units of the field armies. Not a ragbag collection of personal retainers, mercenaries, and barbarian federates, such as Belisarius was fobbed off with. Before you recalled him, that is.'

'My hands were tied!' protested Justinian. 'You must see that, Narses. With revolt in Lazica threatening to destabilize the whole eastern frontier, I needed a strong general on the ground to contain a crisis that could escalate.'

'I understood that Belisarius was no further east than Constantinople.'

'Granted he may not physically be *in* Lazica, but his very presence in the capital has been enough to make the Lazi draw their horns in. As to your military demands –' Justinian shook his head and spread his hands in a gesture of helplessness. 'Impossible, I fear. The financial resources of the Empire are severely over-stretched – suppressing insurgency in Africa, countering Totila in Italy, building a chain of forts across the Balkans against Slav invaders,** relocating troops to meet this new threat in the East, the cost of rehabilitation following the plague . . . You'll just have to make do with whatever extra forces can be scraped together, I'm afraid.'

---

* Sofia.
** The remains of these impressive works can still be seen. Their deterrent effect is questionable – as Germanus discovered to his cost.

'Then, Serenity, I must decline your offer,' declared Narses with icy self-restraint. 'Find some pliant nobody to do your bidding – a yes-man who won't object to taking up lost causes.' He rose and bowed. 'With your permission Serenity, I'll take my leave.'

'Oh for God's sake, Narses, do sit down!' snapped Justinian. 'I daresay we can come to some arrangement that'll keep you happy.'

Sensing victory, the general re-seated himself. 'My request's a simple one, Serenity,' he said with a conciliatory smile. 'Give me the men; I'll give you Italy.'

To meet Narses' ambitious targets, with chilling efficiency the full might of the Roman tax machine now bore down on all parts of the Empire, including Italy (or at least those parts of it not under Totila's control) and Africa, now largely pacified by John the Troglite. Men, equipment, ships and money were raised in ever-increasing quantities, creating a force of awesome power such as Rome had seldom mustered. Narses, tirelessly involved on a tour of military establishments based mainly in Thrace and Illyria, at last declared himself satisfied.

A realist who was also both humane and clear-sighted, the Armenian knew that the surest way of mitigating the cruel consequences of war was to defeat the enemy as swiftly and decisively as possible. Men like Belisarius, Totila and Germanus, the general reflected, obsessed with outmoded ideals of restraint towards an enemy they respected and admired were anachronisms – more suited to the Trojan War than to this modern age of realpolitik. Their peculiar code of honour had allowed the war in Italy to drag on for nearly twenty years, laying waste vast swathes of the peninsula and inflicting untold suffering on the civilian population. What was needed was a speedy victory. And this could only be achieved, Narses told himself, by taking on the Gothic host with a force of such overwhelming power as to utterly annihilate it. That this inevitably meant the wiping out of most male Goths of fighting age was unfortunate. But in the end it was more merciful than waging a campaign of slow attrition, which ultimately must bring about the same result, as well as prolonging the country's economic misery and incurring the death of many thousands of non-combatants.

At last, the great expedition fully mobilized, Narses set out northwards from his headquarters at Salonae* and, the fleet keeping level with the army, rounded the head of the Adriatic and descended upon Italy.

* In April 552.

On the last day of June of that same year, Totila, pushing up the Via Flaminia from Rome, halted his army (the bulk of which was cavalry) near the village of Tadinae, midway between Ariminum to the north and Perusia to the south.* Accompanied by his chief general, Teia, he rode out a further mile to survey the terrain on which he would most likely have to fight the Romans – a bleak plain surrounded by the high peaks of the northern Appennines. The place, so Totila's scouts had informed him, was called Busta Gallorum – 'The Tomb of the Gauls' – site of a great Roman victory against that people, fought eight centuries before.

'Good cavalry country, Sire,' observed Teia, a tough veteran who had vainly tried to halt Narses' advance, flooding the Padus valley by breaching the dykes of that river and its tributaries – a move that Narses had circumvented by marching his army along the coast, crossing the delta's mouths by means of pontoon bridges.

'Provided they choose to fight us on the level,' muttered the young king (he was not yet thirty), noting with dismay the Roman dispositions. Narses had drawn up his army, which far outnumbered the Goths', on rising ground at the northern end of the plain, which was surrounded by steep and broken slopes, ruling out all but a frontal attack on their position – save at one spot. This was a gully to the right** of the low ridge on which the Romans had encamped, constituting a possible route by which they might be outflanked. Pointing out the feature to Teia, Totila said, 'Today we rest. Tomorrow, by which time our expected cavalry reinforcements should have joined us, we will try to force the gully and attack the Romans from the rear.'

Though making himself sound calm and positive, Totila in fact felt close to despair. In the ten years since his great victory at Faventia, he had fought the Romans to a standstill, occupied the greater part of the peninsula, taken Sicily, achieved naval superiority in western waters, won over the Roman people to his side, and come within a hairsbreadth of securing an honourable peace by which Goth and Roman would share the government on equal terms. Yet it had all been for nothing. With the sudden and unexpected death of Germanus, the picture had changed completely. That terrible old man in Constantinople had recovered his resolve and, prompted by Narses, mobilized the full might of the Roman Empire against Totila's people. Even at the height of his success, Totila had known he could never achieve full victory against the Romans; a

* Rimini and Perugia.
** i.e facing Totila; it would of course be to the Romans' left. (See Plan.)

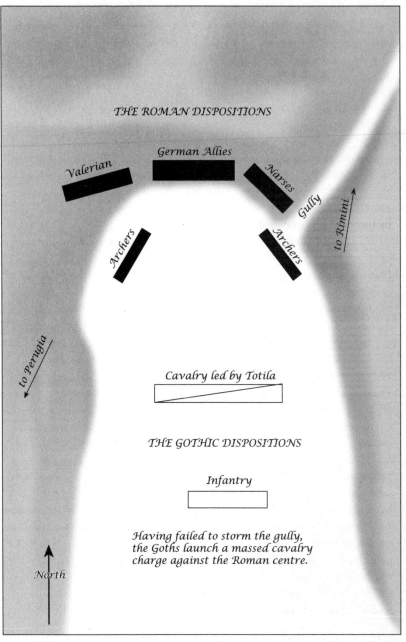

THE ROMAN DISPOSITIONS

Valerian

German Allies

Narses

Gully

to Rimini

Archers

Archers

to Perugia

Cavalry led by Totila

THE GOTHIC DISPOSITIONS

Infantry

Having failed to storm the gully,
the Goths launch a massed cavalry
charge against the Roman centre.

North

The Battle of Tadinae/Busta Gallorum, 1 July(?) AD 552

compromise settlement was the best that he could hope for. Their Empire was simply too strong, their resources too vast, for him to match. Clearly, between them Justinian and Narses had decided finally to bring matters to a head in an attempt to finish off the Goths for good. The fate of his nation, Totila told himself, depended on whether he could push through that gully on the morrow.

The Kalends of July dawned grey and overcast. From his own position on the left wing of the Roman line, Narses surveyed the arrangement of his troops. All were dismounted, the right wing (Romans like his own command) under an experienced general, Valerian; in the centre, Lombard, Herul, and Gepid allies – stout warriors of Germanic stock. Before each wing was ranged a screen of archers – all expert marksmen, armed with powerful recurved bows of laminated wood, horn, and sinew.

Narses had never shared the prevailing Roman bias which favoured cavalry over infantry, believing that well-trained *pedites* were (as in Rome's glory days) superior to *equites* every time. The Ostrogoths on the other hand, from having in the past been mainly foot-soldiers, had gradually changed to fighting principally on horseback, perhaps in imitation of Belisarius' tactics, or perhaps reverting to an earlier tradition. Centuries before, migrating from northern Germania to the steppelands of the Euxine littoral, their way of life had changed to that of mounted herdsmen. As such, they had been absorbed into the Empire of the Huns, supplying Attila with formidable cavalry shock troops, which had almost turned the tide in his favour at the great Battle of the Catalaunian Plains.*

Narses was satisfied that his position was a strong one. Numerically, his army was far superior to Totila's, and the ground was in his favour. The only potential weak spot was a narrow, steep-sided valley to the left of the Roman line, which the enemy would probably try to penetrate in order to turn Narses' flank. It must be securely blocked, and held – at all costs.

It was. The battle opened with a fierce assault by Gothic cavalry on the Romans guarding the ravine in an attempt to dislodge them. But the steep and broken nature of the terrain (unfavourable to horsemen) made it relatively easy for the defenders to beat off such attacks, which continued throughout the morning.

The sun, glimpsed at rare intervals through a screen of low clouds and drizzling rain, had passed its zenith when a huge force of mounted warriors, the main part of Totila's host, advanced to the middle of the plain,

* See my *Attila*.

leaving behind, near the Goths' encampment, a much smaller infantry contingent. A lone rider, magnificent in gilded armour, now cantered out before the Gothic host, and proceeded to put on a dazzling display of horsemanship, making his mount circle and caracole while tossing up and catching his javelin, then throwing it from side to side. The long golden locks escaping from beneath the rider's *Spangenhelm*, together with the splendour of his armour, identified him as none other than Totila.

A pall of dust on the horizon heralding the approach of the Gothic reinforcements, Totila rejoined his army to wild applause.

'What now, Sir?' one of the staff officers grouped around Narses enquired of the general.

'Thank God they used cavalry to try to clear the gully,' remarked Narses in heartfelt tones. 'If they'd sent in infantry, we might not still be standing here. That leaves Totila with only one throw of the dice, poor devil. He'll be forced to use the same tactics he employed successfully at Faventia.'

'A cavalry charge?'

'Exactly. Only this time, it won't work. At Faventia, he took the Romans in the rear and by surprise. This time, we're ready for him. Best we advance the archers now, I think. Tell the *bucinatores* to give the signal, would you?'

As the trumpets boomed out, the archers moved forward ahead of the divisions on each flank, ready to provide enfilading fire.

The Gothic cavalry, now augmented by the reinforcements, began to move forward, gradually accelerating from a trot to a canter, finally to a full gallop. Down swept a forest of lances as the huge mass of horsemen thundered up the low incline bounding the limit of the plain, towards the Roman centre. Nothing, it appeared, could stop the centre from being swept away like chaff before the wind. Then an extraordinary thing happened. At the last moment, the seemingly irresistible Gothic charge stalled, the van milling about in confusion, confronted by a rock-steady frieze of spearpoints presented by the Lombards, Heruls, and Gepids. The endless hours of training in repelling cavalry, which Narses had insisted on, now paid off handsomely. Faced with the terrifying sight of charging horsemen, a footsoldier's instinct is to drop his spear and flee. But if he can learn to hold his nerve and, in concert with his fellows, stand his ground, he will find that horses (endowed with a far greater sense of self-preservation than men) will not press home a charge against sharp blades, no matter how much their riders urge them on. And so it proved.

Suddenly, the sky darkened as the archers on the flanks let fly. A storm of arrows drilled into the bucking, rearing horsemen, causing carnage on a massive scale and increasing the confusion. Volley after volley took their bloody toll, until it became more than flesh and blood could stand. The Gothic cavalry broke and fled – ploughing through their own infantry in their haste to escape those deadly shafts. Now the Romans, mounting their temporarily abandoned steeds, galloped in pursuit, scything down the flee-ing Goths in their thousands . . .

Busta Gallorum proved a great and conclusive Roman victory, especially when the corpse of Totila – conspicuous in its gilded armour – was found among the dead; 'The Tomb of the Gauls' had become 'The Tomb of the Goths'. The power of the Goths was broken, permanently. Though Teia (immediately chosen as the new king) and a few Gothic leaders continued to hold out for a little longer, they were eliminated one by one, the final battle of the war being fought at Mons Lactarius in October of the same year as Busta Gallorum. Thereafter, all that remained to be done was a little mopping-up. With all its leaders and most of its fighting men killed, the nation of the Ostrogoths had ceased forever to exist.

The ending of the Gothic War meant that a major part of Justinian's Grand Plan had been accomplished. With Africa, Italy and southern Spain (seized from the divided Visigoths in the year of Busta Gallorum in a lightning campaign waged by Liberius* – an enterprising Roman general of eighty-five) now reintegrated into the Imperium Romanum, the Roman Empire had regained more or less the same dimensions it possessed at the time of Julius Caesar, prior to his expedition against Gaul.

But the knowledge brought little satisfaction to Justinian, to whom the 'triumph' was as dust and ashes in the mouth. Narses' reports were starkly honest. Alongside total victory in Italy must be weighed the cost: destruction of the country's infrastructure and economy along with count-less towns and villages; displacement of people on a massive scale; huge casualty figures for both soldiers and civilians; venerable institutions like the Senate swept away (taken hostage, most senators had died in acts of retribution in the final bitter stages of the war); and, by no means least, the annihilation of a worthy enemy who might have played a valued part in the building of a new nation. Even if, by some miracle, the recovery of

---

* The same Liberius who, nearly sixty years earlier, had masterminded the division of land in Italy between the Romans and Theoderic's Ostrogoths – an immensely challenging and delicate task.

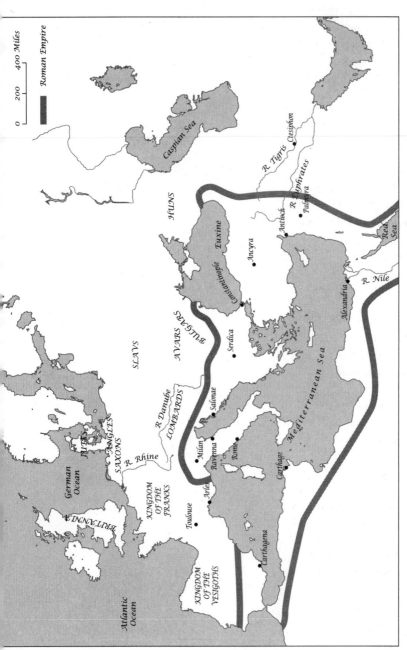

The Roman Empire at the death of Justinian, AD 565

the West had been achieved with little bloodshed, any joy it might have afforded would have eluded the now aged emperor. For without Theodora to share it with, life had lost all savour.

But life, nevertheless, had to go on. There was still an Empire to run (one vastly bigger than when he had first assumed the purple), still the thorny issue of religious unity to be resolved, and in Italy – apart from the immense and daunting task of reconstruction – slaves to be returned to their masters and *coloni* to be evicted from the estates they had commandeered from landowners. With iron in his soul, 'the Sleepless One' proceeded to immerse himself in the thousand tasks involved in the administration of his realm, in an attempt to fill the emptiness of his existence.

PART V

THE SLEEPLESS ONE
AD 552–565

TWENTY-NINE

Now this country of silk lies beyond the remotest of the Indies, and . . . is
called Tzinitza [China]
Cosmas Indicopleustes,* *Christian Topography*, c. 540

In the year that witnessed the destruction of the Ostrogoths at Busta Gallorum and Mons Lactarius, two Nestorian monks from Persia who had sojourned in China sought an audience with Justinian.

'The monks are here, Serenity,' a *silentiarius* announced to the emperor, seated as usual at his desk in his *triclinium* or private study. Here, rather than in rooms of state or the chambers of the Council, the administration of the Empire was increasingly carried out, by the 'many-eyed' emperor – 'the Sleepless One' himself – working alone at night till dawn.

'Ah, Paul,' murmured the emperor, looking up with a smile from the codex he was scanning, 'a little bird tells me you're composing a poem – a description in hexameters of our Church of the Holy Wisdom.'

'The bird speaks correctly, Serenity.'

'Then I look forward to a private reading on completion of the work. You may admit our visitors.'

'Fathers Hieronymous and Antony,' announced the usher and withdrew, flushing with pleasure at the emperor's recognition of his opus.

Two black-robed figures entered the *tablinum* and bowed. 'We much appreciate your granting us an interview, Serenity,' declared the foremost, a man of burly build with a large bald head, fleshy hooked nose and a pair of lively black eyes. 'Father Hieronymus,' he went on, clapping a hand to his chest. 'Father Antony.' And he indicated the other, a birdlike figure with a nervous smile.

'But – I understood that you were Persians,' said Justinian, looking mildly puzzled. 'These are Roman names.'

'Our abbot requires us to take the names of Roman Fathers, in honour of the Founder of our Order – the great Nestorius,' explained Father Hieronymus.

'I see. Well, Fathers, how may I help you? Or perhaps I should be asking

* The Indian navigator.

243

your help. As Nestorians, you may be able to assist me in untying a doctrinal Gordian Knot, that is proving to be particularly, ah – knotty. It concerns my Edict regarding certain writings by three followers of Nestorius, which I'm attempting, with considerable difficulty, to get my subjects to accept; the Edict, not the writings, I should say.' And he regarded the pair invitingly.

'Alas, Serenity, the purpose of our visit is not to do with matters spiritual, but rather concerns Mammon,' said Father Hieronymus. 'If I were to ask you, Serenity, what was the Empire's most valuable luxury item, what would be your answer?'

'Silk,' replied the emperor without hesitation. 'It's required for robes of state for officials and high clergy, also for diplomatic gifts to foreign potentates. And of course it's highly prized by women of the upper class. The cost, however, is prohibitively high. Thanks to our control of the Straits of Bab-el-Mandeb leading into the Red Sea, we can get some silk from China, our shippers buying it from merchants based at Taprobane.* The trouble is, Persian traders are strongly entrenched there and usually manage to buy up all the silk before we can get our hands on any. Which leaves the overland route – the 'Silk Road' – from China via Central Asia to Persia and the Mediterranean. Our *commerciarii* buy it from the Persians at scheduled frontier posts.'

'Putting the Persians in a perfect position to extort monopoly prices,' observed Father Antony.

'Exactly!' retorted Justinian with some heat.

'So – wouldn't it be splendid if silk could be produced *within* the Roman Empire,' said Father Hieronymus.

'It would indeed,' concurred Justinian, adding wryly, 'We can all dream, I suppose.'

'It need be no dream,' said Father Hieronymus in earnest tones.

'Go on,' prompted Justinian, his interest quickened.

'When Father Antony and I served in China as missionaries, based in the great city of Nanking,' went on the monk, 'we were able to observe, among many other things, how silk was manufactured. Hatching from an egg, the caterpillar of the silkworm moth feeds on the leaves of the mulberry plant; then, when it has attained a certain size, it secretes around itself a cocoon of fine thread – silk, in other words. Inside the cocoon it prepares for metamorphosis – the change from grub to moth. Before this can happen, the grub is killed by steam or hot water. The silken filaments

* Ceylon/Sri Lanka.

from several cocoons are then unwound together, being spun into a silken thread. After which, once the thread is cleaned, the normal process of weaving and dyeing – as with cotton, wool, or linen – can take place.'

'Fascinating, truly fascinating,' enthused Justinian. 'There's just one small detail you've omitted though. While the Empire has no dearth of mulberry plants, the silkworm moth is not a native species, and is nowhere to found inside our realm.'

'A want which can be rectified,' said Father Hieronymus, beaming at the emperor and tapping the side of his nose. 'Suppose Father Antony and I were to travel to China, smuggle out silkworm eggs, then bring them back into the Roman Empire – would you be interested, Serenity?'

'Would I be interested! But won't smuggling out the eggs be hideously dangerous? Their silk industry is bound to be a jealously guarded secret. I shudder to think what your fate would be if your theft were to be discovered. Their methods of execution can be, let us say, inventive.'

'We have thought of a means of transporting the eggs, Serenity, which virtually eliminates the risk of detection,' put in Father Antony. 'Examine, if you will, our walking-staves.' And he held out his long, stout staff of ash. 'See, Serenity, the top unscrews, revealing the inside of the staff to be hollow – the perfect receptacle for concealment of the eggs. When the top is screwed back on, the join is undetectable.'

'Brilliant,' breathed the emperor, shaking his head in admiration. 'What can I say? If you are willing to undertake this mission, Rome will be eternally in your debt, and your reward commensurate. Now, for your journey you will need –'

'There's something else we could bring back with us from China,' broke in Father Antony excitedly, 'something whose importance, I believe, far exceeds even that of silk.'

'Be quiet, fool!' hissed Father Hieronymus savagely. 'You do not interrupt an emperor.' Turning to Justinian, he declared, 'A thousand pardons, Serenity. He has an obsession that makes him forget his manners at times.'

'Let us hear him, anyway,' responded Justinian with a patient smile. 'Obsessions can be interesting.' Turning to Father Antony, he went on in courteous tones, 'Pray continue, Father.'

'The Chinese have a means of reproducing books,' said Father Antony eagerly, 'that does away with the tedious and time-consuming labour of copying each page. Using a sharp tool, a page of writing is carved, in reverse, onto a block of pear-wood, the field being removed, leaving the letters in high relief. The block is then smeared with ink and pressed onto a sheet of a material similar to our papyrus, but finer and less brittle. When the block is removed, lo and behold – there is the page perfectly reproduced! The process can be repeated an infinite number of times, thus making the dissemination of knowledge cheap, and available to all with the ability to read. Think, Serenity,' the monk continued passionately, '– Holy Writ and the writings of the Christian Fathers such as Augustine, Eugippius, and Salvian could become available to millions throughout your Empire and beyond, who otherwise could never afford to read them!'

'An intriguing idea, certainly,' declared Justinian. 'My own seal performs a function not dissimilar, many times a day. I have one objection, though. If I were to allow your Chinese invention to be adopted, many thousands of skilled copyists working for the book-dealers, to say nothing of the clerks in the imperial chancery engaged in reproducing promulgations, would lose their livelihoods. I would not have that on my conscience. At the present time, a book is a rare and precious thing. Perhaps it should remain so, especially if it deals with matters of Divinity. Now – preparations for your journey,' he went on briskly. 'Where were we?'

'Well, we did it!' Father Antony declared, as the two monks looked back at Jiayuguan, the imposing gateway at the end of China's Great Wall, 'the mouth' that marked the western limits of the Celestial Kingdom.

Thus far, the mission had proceeded without a hitch. The year-long journey to China, in the train of an ambassador of the Son of Heaven, had been tedious but safe, the task of collecting the precious eggs requiring only vigilance and caution. Two holy men from Rome's distant Empire aroused respectful curiosity but not suspicion. Now, beyond the security of an ordered state, they were faced with an arduous odyssey through harsh terrain, beset with perils from brigands and wild beasts, until they reached the Persian frontier and civilization once again. After that, the remainder of the journey through the well-policed Empire of the Shah-an-Shah to the Roman ports on the eastern Euxine coast should be smoothly uneventful. Meanwhile, being part of a small caravan of merchants bound for Persia with a freight of spices, jade and silk offered a measure of security. To defray expenses, they could draw on generous funds supplied by the imperial Treasury – the beautiful gold coins of Justinian, recognized as international currency everywhere, from Beijing to Britannia, from Gaul to Zanzibar.

The first stage of the journey, on the western fringes of the Gobi Desert, lay through a dreary tract of red earth seamed with gullies and pimpled

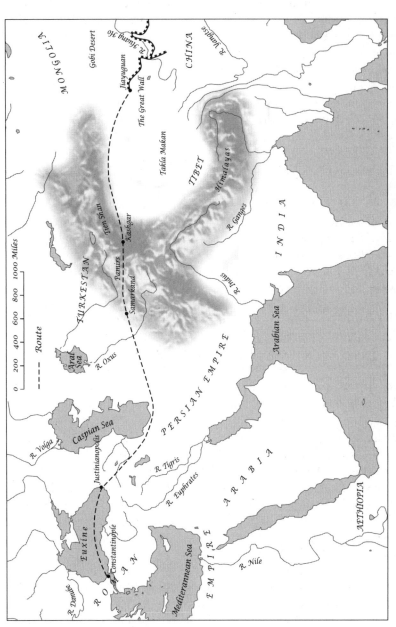

The journey of Fathers Hieronymus and Antony from Jiayuguan to Constantinople

with low, stony hills. After several weeks, this arid emptiness gave way to scanty pastureland: a corridor of tawny steppe running between the Tien Shan – 'the Heavenly Mountains' to the north – and to the south the feared Taklamakan, the desert 'You Enter and Never Return' in the language of the Uighur, the wild, nomadic local people.

The days passed in a blur of repeated rituals. First, after a scanty breakfast of dried apricots and leathery strips of dried mutton, loading up the camels – evil-tempered, shaggy brutes with two humps; then, several hours plodding through steppeland relieved occasionally by stands of pine or willow, the haunt of wolves and wild boar; a midday meal followed by an extended rest period against the hottest part of the day; and another march in the late afternoon till camp was pitched an hour before the setting of the sun.

There were occasional breaks in the monotony of the journey: stopovers at the towns which punctuated the Silk Road – Turpan, Korla, Kuqa, Aksur, each with its colourful market filled with noisy crowds, and traders selling everything from spices and harnesses to rock salt, skins, and cummin. Once, they witnessed a game of *buzgashi* – a ferocious tussle between mounted herdsmen for the carcass of a sheep.

At last they came to the oasis town of Kashgar, where the route divided – one path leading north and east for Samarkand and Persia, the other south for India. Taking the northern route, the caravan struck up a treeless valley into the Pamir Mountains, a bleak wasteland of barren crags and stony defiles, dominated by the distant, towering mass of Mush-taq-ata*, its snow-clad peak soaring above a tangle of saw-toothed ridges. Here, animals had grown huge as a defence against the cold – outsize yaks, sheep with five-foot horns, a dread species of enormous bear.

One night, the caravan, camped on an alluvial plain beside a glacial lake, was disturbed by a commotion in the camel lines. Rushing to the spot, the merchants were confronted, in the flickering light of the camp fire, by a horrifying sight – a bear of vast size attacking the tethered beasts, two of them reduced to shredded corpses. Standing on its hind legs, the creature, jaws agape revealing rows of vicious fangs, reared high above the terrified camels; even as the merchants looked on in helpless horror, another beast was clubbed down, half-decapitated by a blow from the monster's paw armed with razor claws. Breaking loose, the remaining camels charged off into the night, their frantic braying fading at last into silence.

* Mount Kongur.

The bear now turned its attention to the men who, retreating to the fire, managed to fend off its furious lunges with blazing brands. At last, as though satisfied with the carnage it had wrought, the creature abandoned its attack and lumbered on its way.

In the morning, the shocked and devastated merchants recaptured three of the six fugitive camels (of the others two had fallen into a gully and broken their necks; the third was never found) and recovered what could be salvaged of their scattered merchandise – much of which was damaged beyond repair. Cacheing this, they bade farewell to the two monks and sadly turned their faces to the east, intending to return when they had built up another caravan in China.

The two monks now faced the daunting prospect of crossing the high Pamirs alone. Weeks later, starving, exhausted, and suffering from frostbite, they staggered into Samarkand as penniless beggars, having been relieved en route by bandits of their funds (but fortunately not their staves). In the bustling metropolis they were able to join another caravan bound for Persia, their medical skills enabling them to earn their passage money. The remainder of the journey, through Transoxiana, Turkestan, and Persia to the Euxine coast where, at the great new Roman port of Petra Justinianopolis* they took ship for Constantinople, was uneventful. A year almost to the day since leaving China, they disembarked at the quayside of the Golden Horn.

The mission proved an unqualified success. Under the close and expert supervision of the monks, the eggs were hatched at the proper season by the heat of dung, and a thriving industry was rapidly established, soon producing silk of a quality to equal China's, but costing infinitely less than the imported cloth.

---

* Formerly just Petra, it was renamed and extended after being captured from the Persians, who had occupied Lazica. (See Chapter 23.)

THIRTY

With this sign, you shall conquer
Message accompanying a vision of the Cross, which appeared
to the emperor-to-be, Constantine, before his victory over
Maxentius at the Milvian Bridge, 312

At Damian's wine shop in the harbour area between the Bosphorus and Golden Horn, the talk was all about a terrifying crisis that had suddenly, it seemed, blown up out of nowhere. A barbaric horde of mounted nomads originating from the steppes of Central Asia had crossed the frozen Danube, swept through the Balkans into Thrace, looting and killing as they went, smashed through the Long Walls* (damaged in a recent earthquake), and were even now advancing on the capital itself. Daily, panic-stricken refugees crowded into the city, creating a major problem for the authorities to lodge and feed them, and sapping the morale of the citizens.

'They say the Huns have crossed the river Athyras,' declared a burly coppersmith. 'Christ, that's less than twenty miles away.'

'They're not Huns, you know,' corrected a youth from the University, 'slumming it' in Damian's with some of his fellow students. 'They're Kotrigurs – led by one Zabergan, their chief.'

'Same difference, mate. Slant-eyed yellow bastards, with these ruddy great pigtails down their backs. They eat Roman babies for breakfast, so I've heard.'

'And I looked, and behold a pale horse: and his name that sat on him was Death!' bellowed Scripture Simon. 'And Hell followed with him. And power was given unto them over the fourth part of the earth, to kill with sword, and with hunger, and with death, and with –'

'Shut it, Simon,' sighed the bartender. 'There's a noggin on the house with your name on it – but only if you keep your trap shut.'

'What's the emperor doing about it – "Cottigers" did you call them?'

---

* Not to be confused with the Theodosian Walls protecting Constantinople (and which can still be seen). The Long Walls constituted a further line of defence, running across the peninsula thirty miles west of the capital – a sort of Maginot or Siegfried Line.

grumbled a pot-bellied carpenter with sawdust in his hair. 'That's what I'd like to know.'

'Nothing, chum,' commented a brawny porter. 'Bloody nothing. Oh, he can sort out Italy and Africa but when it comes to us poor sods at home – doesn't want to know, does he? Too taken up with this latest religious wheeze of his to bother about the likes of us.'

'Aphthartodocetism – that's the new doctrine you're referring to,' pronounced the student, smirking knowingly at his friends.

'Aphtha –; what the hell's that when it's at home?' growled the porter.

'Aphthartodocetism holds that the body of Christ was incorruptible – ergo, His sufferings were only apparent.'

'Well!' exclaimed a floury-armed baker. 'Sounds to me like something the Patriarch'll take a dim view of – *very* dim indeed, I'd say.' Sensing from the interested hush that he had the floor's attention, the man went on portentously, emphasizing points with an admonitory finger. 'According to Chalcedon, Christ is both human *and* divine. Strikes me that this Apartho-whatever stuff is suggesting He's only got the *one* nature – which puts it squarely in the Monophysite camp. Looks like His Serenity has screwed up badly over this one.'

Keen amateur theologians, like all Constantinopolitans, the patrons of Damian's immediately became engaged in passionate debate about the merits or otherwise (mostly otherwise) of this latest theological dogma, which seemed to have about it an exciting whiff of heresy . . .

Seated as usual at his desk in his *tablinum*, Justinian racked his brains as to how best to tackle this appalling business of the Kotrigurs. No sooner had he finished the momentous task of restoring the West to the Imperial fold, he told himself, than the Danube frontier – despite being reinforced with a line of massive fortifications – started springing leaks, allowing a seemingly endless tide of barbarians to come flooding in. If it wasn't Bulgars it was Slavs, if it wasn't Slavs it was Utigurs, if it wasn't Utigurs it was Kotrigurs. These last two – fierce Mongol tribes related to the Huns – he had managed, in time-honoured Roman fashion, to play off against each other for an extended period. Now, however, they seemed to have patched up their differences, resulting in the present crisis. With all Roman armies away in Italy or the east, the problem of how to defend the capital was acute. Also, it was becoming personally embarrassing. As 'Little Father to his People', an emperor was expected to ensure protection for his subjects in times of peril. Should he, Justinian, be found wanting, his status as

God's Appointed would inevitably be called in question. Meanwhile, the one man who might have been able, if anyone could, to deal with the situation, was absent. Belisarius, now retired, was nowhere to be found, and had left no word as to where he could be contacted . . .

In his dream, more radiantly beautiful even than she had been in life, Theodora advanced towards Justinian. Taking him by the hand, she led him silently through the Triclinium of the Nine Couches, out of the Palace, and into the Augusteum. Pointing to the huge bronze equestrian statue of the emperor, arrayed in the panoply of a conquering Roman general, that had recently been installed in the centre of the great square, she turned to Justinian with a smile and murmured, '*In hoc signo vinces* – With this sign you shall conquer.'

Stirring awake, the emperor felt a sharp pang of loss and disappointment. The dream had been so *real*; in his memory it seemed as though Theodora had actually spoken to him. Suddenly, these sad reflections were replaced by a surge of excitement, as a thought flashed into Justinian's brain. '*In hoc signo vinces*': the words that, accompanying a cross in the sky, the symbol of the Christians, Constantine had seen in a vision before going on to defeat his rival Maxentius at the Battle of the Milvian Bridge. At last, God had given him his sign! – the sign that he had prayed in vain for, following the death of his beloved wife. The message of the dream was clear: he, Justinian, was to lead an army in person against the Kotrigurs, an encounter from which he would emerge victorious!

But where was the army to come from? Justinian's mind raced. With the enemy almost at the gates of the capital, there was no way that any units could get here from their distant postings in time to intervene. There were the Palace Guards of course; but a token force of a few hundred parade soldiers could achieve little against fierce nomad hordes. There was only one solution: he must appeal directly to the citizens of Constantinople and raise a volunteer army – as Fabius had done, in the dark days when Hannibal had wiped out the flower of Rome's legions. Never mind that for more than a hundred and fifty years, no Roman emperor had commanded troops in battle,* or that he was now seventy-seven; age had not dulled his mind nor sapped his resolve. Summoning the captain of the guard, he strode to the armoury to select the right accoutrements in which to lead his people into battle.

* Theodosius I at the Battle of the Frigidus in 393; Justinian took the field against the Kotrigurs in 559.

'Belisarius!' En route to address his subjects in the Forum of Constantine, Justinian uttered a cry of joyous welcome at the sight of his old general riding towards him at the head of his bodyguard – tough German *bucellarii* or personal retainers.

'Came as soon as I heard the news about the Kotrigurs, Serenity,' declared Belisarius. 'Been away on a hunting trip in Phrygia, so rather incommunicado, I'm afraid.'

The two embraced warmly, Justinian feeling a rush of affection and gratitude towards this man who, more than any other, had made the dream of a reconstituted Empire into a reality. He also experienced a stab of guilt for ever having listened to Belisarius' detractors; time and again – as he was indeed demonstrating at this moment – the general had proved his unswerving loyalty towards his emperor.

Entering the great circular forum, dominated by the porphyry column bearing a statue of the city's founder, the pair, imposing in muscle cuirasses and crested helmets, mounted the tribunal for reviewing troops. The vast crowd assembled in the forum (Palace messengers had been busy spreading the word that the emperor wished to address the citizens) fell silent.

'People of Constantinople,' declaimed Justinian, experiencing an exhilarating flow of confidence, 'I need hardly remind you that we stand today in peril from a savage enemy, both numerous and cruel. Our armies are too far off to help us, so it is to ourselves that we must look for the defence of our city and our families. That you will rise to the occasion I have every confidence, for you are Romans of New Rome, stout of heart and strong of spirit, who will never allow barbarian feet to trample the pavements of our capital. All fit males between the ages of sixteen and sixty, report now to the Arsenal where Belisarius – who, as you see, has joined us in our hour of need – will form you into companies and see that you are issued arms. That done, assemble at the Golden Gate, where Belisarius and I will lead you out against these heathen Kotrigurs. With God upon our side, we cannot fail to be victorious.'

For a few moments silence filled the vast enclosure; then thunderous applause erupted from the audience, moved and uplifted by the sight of their aged emperor and his great general come to their deliverance.

'Amazing!' breathed Justinian in admiration, looking at what appeared to be a huge army, arrayed along a ridge of high ground overlooking a tributary of the Athyras. 'Congratulations, general – a really splendid job. From here, I can't tell which are real and which are dummies.'

'Let's hope Zabergan thinks the same,' said Belisarius, looking pleased by the emperor's reaction to his subterfuge. 'Only one in twenty's an actual soldier; the rest are made of bundled straw with wooden poles for spears. Well, we'll soon find out,' he went on, pointing to a distant pall of dust. 'That'll be Zabergan's van approaching.'

Minutes later, scouts came posting up, confirming Belisarius' observation. Soon, the Kotrigur host was near enough to enable Justinian to make out details: squat, powerfully built men with flat, Oriental faces, mounted on huge, ill-conformed brutes; on the back of each warrior was slung a powerful-looking bow and a quiverful of long arrows. Obviously unwilling to engage the formidable Roman 'army' threatening their flank, the river of horsemen made a wide detour to the side into the tributary's valley – as Belisarius had intended. Overweight and middle-aged he might be, but the retired general had lost none of his military flair.

'They've fallen for it!' exclaimed the general, slapping his thigh in glee. 'Let's spring our trap, Serenity.'

Spurring along the lip of the valley ahead of the slow-moving enemy column, the two Roman leaders arrived at where the river's enclosing walls narrowed and steepened to become a gorge. Here, armed with darts and javelins, was stationed a large body of the citizen-militia recruited earlier. Piles of boulders, together with sheaves of extra missiles, had been arranged along the canyon's edge. Despite his age, and hardly ever having set foot outside the capital these fifty years, Justinian found that he was enjoying immensely this challenging adventure.

Waiting for the Kotrigurs to come in sight, an air of tense expectancy built up among the Romans to a nerve-jangling degree. At last, from around a bend in the river, the nomad van appeared, and soon a densely packed mass of horsemen was drawing level far below.

'Right lads,' called Belisarius, 'let 'em have it!'

A storm of stone and iron burst upon the Kotrigurs. Dropping from the heights, the huge rocks acquired enormous impetus, smashing men and horses to a bloody pulp, while volleys of sharp-tipped shafts skewered their helpless targets by the score. Unable to respond, the nomads milled about in desperate confusion; at last, on retreat being sounded by a horn-blast, they turned and streamed back up the valley, leaving hundreds of casualties strewn upon the floor of the defile.

In a gesture of infinite regret, Zabergan spread his hands, a wry smile creasing his broad Mongol face. 'My young men – so headstrong, so high-spirited,' he said to Justinian in apologetic tones. '"A spot of cattle-rustling in Thrace", was all they wanted, so they said. Things got a little out of hand, I fear; I found myself unable to control them.' And he sighed and shook his great head.

That was rich, thought Justinian, coming from a ruthless despot as feared among his followers as by the targets of his depredations. The two men were seated on cushions in the chief's yurt, furnished in barbaric splendour with eastern rugs and hangings, weapons of the chase and war, furs, and looted vessels of silver, gold and bronze. Anyone less unable to control his men would be difficult to imagine.

'Well, let us call your, ah . . . "visit" an unfortunate misunderstanding,' said the emperor, torn between inner mirth and indignation. 'So, now you wish to take the *foedus*,* for your people to become Friends of Rome?'

'Indeed, My Emperor. It will be a privilege indeed to serve one whose feats of arms are known throughout the world.' Zabergan added slyly, 'And whose generosity to his allies is equally legendary.'

'The labourer is worthy of his hire, I suppose. Mind you, I expect results – no Utigurs, Slavs, or Bulgars to cross the Danube into Roman territory. An annual subsidy of, say, fifty pounds of gold; would the Khan of the Kotrigurs find such a sum acceptable?'

Justinian was well satisfied with the outcome. Zabergan duly led his Kotrigurs back across the Danube and seemed prepared to earn his subsidy, for no further raiding parties crossed the river. Not everyone agreed with his methods of maintaining peace beyond the frontiers, Justinian knew. His generals to a man (Belisarius included) regarded the stratagem of paying barbarians to keep the peace or to police other barbarians as shameful appeasement, unworthy of a Roman emperor. Which did not trouble Justinian one whit; his policy *worked*, and that was all that mattered.

After a tour of inspection of the Long Walls against ordering a programme of urgent repairs, Justinian and Belisarius returned to Constantinople at the head of their tiny army. As they rode past market gardens and fields of sunflowers, the emperor reflected on the main events occurring since the termination of the Gothic War. Apart from the start of silk production in the Empire, and barbarian incursions into the Balkans – now hopefully halted thanks to his deal with Zabergan – those seven years had seen: the death of Pope Vigilius and his replacement by Pelagius (a most reluctant

* Oath of loyalty, requiring the swearer to become a *foederatus* – federate.

'convert' to Justinian's Edict condemning the Three Chapters, acceptance being the price for Peter's Throne), with the goal of religious unity however, seemingly even more remote than before; a series of destructive earthquakes (one of which had caused the dome of Hagia Sophia to collapse); a recurrence of the plague – mercifully less lethal and of shorter duration than its terrible predecessor; a renewal of the so-called Eternal Peace with Persia; and a wary alliance forged with yet another formidable tribe of steppe-nomads, newly arrived in Trans-Caucasia from Mongolia (the survivors of a massacre masterminded by the Chinese) – the Avars.

Of his friends and close advisers none remained, thought Justinian with sadness. John of Cappadocia, his one-time right hand man, following his disgrace at the hands of Theodora had taken Holy Orders, and died some years before. Narses, ever-efficient and still on active service in Italy though in his eighties, was however, never a man the emperor found that he could warm to. Popes, bishops, generals, and civil servants – all had come and gone, most serving him with competence, some brilliantly, without ever touching his heart. Wait though, he was forgetting; there *were* two faithful servants he could count as friends – Belisarius and Procopius, of course. Both had stood by him at that supremely testing time – the Nika Riots. Belisarius had shown unswerving loyalty throughout a long career, and Procopius – almost alone of his officials – had been brave enough to visit him when stricken with the plague. So, following Theodora's death, he was after all not quite so alone as he had thought.

Constantinople came in sight: behind the mighty Walls of Theodosius stretched a vista of low hills rising one behind the other, studded with domes, towers, and tall columns topped by statues of past emperors, with – in the far distance – the looming mass of Hagia Sophia, shrouded now in scaffolding against the reconstruction of its fallen dome.* Entering the city from the north by the Charisius Gate, the procession was greeted by a deputation of senators and dignitaries headed by Procopius, now city prefect (duly promoted to the post – as Justinian had promised on his sick-bed). As it advanced past the Cistern of Aetius then through the ruined Wall of Constantine, the column was cheered to the echo by ecstatic crowds who had assembled to welcome home their emperor and favourite general, together with their little band of citizen-militia. True, no wagonloads of booty or lines of chained captives accompanied the victors, but Roman arms had triumphed and Roman honour been upheld.

* The project was undertaken by Anthemius' son. By increasing the curve, he succeeded in making the new dome even more impressive than the original.

When it reached the Church of the Holy Apostles the procession halted, Justinian dismounting to enter and light candles before Theodora's tomb. As he rose from his knees after offering a prayer, the emperor experienced a sudden, overwhelming conviction. His victory against the Kotrigurs had proved the sign appearing in his dream to be no false illusion. God had indeed forgiven him, and confirmed that he, Justinian, truly was His Chosen One. He would enter Heaven after all, to be forever reunited with Theodora.

Rejoining the procession, another realization struck Justinian that further raised his spirits. In taking on the Kotrigurs, he had, at last, exorcised those demons of self-doubt and hesitation that had plagued him all his life, resulting in: the deaths of Atawulf and Valerian; his self-harming in the Cistern of Nomus, the mark of which he carried to this day; his near-fatal hesitation to speak up for his uncle in the Senate; his vacillating concerning Belisarius; his failure to support Silverius or send troops adequate to protect Antioch. At last, those phantoms from the past could finally be laid to rest. As the column made its way beneath the towering arches of the Aqueduct of Valens, the emperor felt calm, and happier than at any time since Theodora had died.

But his new-found serenity and peace of mind were destined not to last . . .

THIRTY-ONE

Revenge is the poor delight of little minds

Juvenal, *Satires*, 128

Procopius, one of whose duties as city prefect was to ensure the flow of water to the public baths and fountains, nodded to the water engineer. That official turned the handles of a long iron rod projecting from the roadway to open the sluice-gate of a subterranean tunnel leading from the Cistern of Aetius. The assembled group of workmen looked on anxiously, then burst into a ragged cheer as, after a few moments, sparkling jets of water spurted from the fountain.

'Well done, lads!' laughed Procopius. 'You've earned your bonus; clearing that channel must have been a mucky job. Take a short break now, then meet me at the Mocius Cistern in an hour.'

Grinning cheerfully at the prospect of that extra drinking money (Procopius was a popular prefect), the maintenance crew, accompanied by the engineer, departed – except for one man, a tall individual with an air of quiet self-possession that marked him out from his fellow workers, Procopius had observed.

'A word in private, Prefect?'

'Very well.' Impressed by something in the other's manner and bearing, Procopius suggested they walk to the Necropolis, situated coveniently near to the Cistern of Saint Mocius. A stroll through an expanse of low-density housing interspersed with vegetable gardens, between the Walls of Constantine and those of Theodosius, brought them to the City of the Dead, a strange and haunting area of mortuary monuments – tombs, urns, obelisks and statues, many of exquisite workmanship, their whitewashed surfaces or gleaming marble contrasting with the sombre greens of cypress, box, and yew.

'Will this do?' asked Procopius, and went on with a smile. 'A bit crowded, but at least they can't hear us.'

'We haven't met, Sir,' said the stranger. 'But we both, as "Friends of *Libertas*", served the same great man – Gaius Anicius Julianus, alias "Cato". You'll have heard of me as "Horatius" – a go-between who collected and delivered messages. And you, Sir, I believe were known as "Regulus".'

Procopius inclined his head in acknowledgement. 'Well, Horatius – something you wish to tell me?'

'We both know, Sir, that *Libertas* has been disbanded, and all its leaders – Cato, Catullus, Cincinnatus et al., dead or forced to take Holy Orders. However, something has arisen which – if we can ensure it goes ahead – would amount to a final blow being struck for the Cause.'

'Go on.'

'Justinian is in a quandary regarding the succession. Because of his advanced years, he knows that he can't for much longer avoid naming his successor. Yet he fears to do so, because he thinks he would then be perceived as yesterday's man, with the reins of power slipping from his grasp. For someone like the emperor, who can't bear the idea of not being in control, that would be intolerable. So he's let the matter drift.'

'Even though it's an open secret that the succession's almost bound to pass to one of two men,' the prefect commented. 'There's Justin the son of Germanus who commanded in Italy before his untimely death. And there's another Justin, son of Justinian's sister – a modest, capable fellow, of a type usually referred to as "a safe pair of hands". Of course the fact that no preference has been made public has led to wild speculation on the part of the citizenry.'

'Exactly, Sir. Which brings me to my point. All this uncertainty has created an atmosphere of disquiet and instability, the perfect breeding-ground for riots – stirred up, of course, by the Greens and Blues. Also plots. Most of these are hatched by bungling amateurs and come to nothing. But one or two have to be taken seriously – like the one your *vigiles* put down two years ago.'

'You mean the Theodore affair? – when the *curatores** George and Aetherius tried to elevate to the purple the son of Peter the Patrician, of all people?'

'That's the one, Sir. Compromised by security leaks, as I recall. However, I've got wind of a fresh conspiracy – this time one that's been planned with meticulous care, and, in my view, stands a much better chance of succeeding.'

'How come you know this?' asked Procopius, both astonished and piqued that his own efficient network of *delatores* – informers – had failed to hear of such a plot.

'Before I was recruited by *Libertas*, Sir, I was an *agens in rebus* for the state, which meant I had to be ready to take on any role from diplomat to

---

* Civic dignitaries. The plot was investigated in 560, but the case fizzled out for lack of evidence. None of the mud stuck to Peter himself, for we find him in post as Master of Offices throughout that year, and in 562 negotiating a Fifty Year Peace with Persia.

spy. And, though I say it myself, Sir, I was good. Which is why Cato took me on. When it comes to keeping an ear to the ground to learn the "buzz", there's no one can match yours truly, Sir.'

'You say this plot could succeed. Your reasons?'

'It's being masterminded by a pair of senators, Marcellus and Ablabius – intelligent, cool-headed types. They're on the guest list for a banquet celebrating the re-dedication of Hagia Sophia, to be given by the emperor and held in a fortnight's time – on the Ides of October. At a given moment during the feast, they, together with another senator, will draw their daggers – hidden till then beneath their robes – and despatch Justinian. Their men – already stationed in the vestibule and porticoes – will then announce the death of the tyrant, and excite sedition in the capital. Given the present mood of discontent, that shouldn't be a problem. I learned all this from the third main accomplice, Sergius, a friend of two officers of Belisarius. I had made it my business to strike up an acquaintanceship with Sergius, and managed to convince him that I was sympathetic to the plot. Which of course, because its purpose is identical to the primary aim once held by *Libertas*, is no more than the truth. As a one-time Friend of *Libertas* yourself, Sir, I thought you'd like to be put in the picture.'

'Would I, indeed! My thanks, Horatius – you've done well to tell me this. I'd appreciate it if you'd keep me informed of any future developments.'

'My pleasure, Sir. A word of caution though.'

'Explain.'

'We wouldn't want the plot to be aborted, would we, Sir? Best keep what I've told you to yourself; it wouldn't do for any of your *vigiles* to act in any way which might arouse the suspicions of the plotters. You get my drift, Sir?'

'Rest assured, Horatius. This conversation will remain between ourselves.'

'I'll be off then, Sir; I see your workmen beginning to arrive at the cistern over there. I'll keep you posted, never fear.'

The plot, of course, must not be allowed to succeed, thought Procopius, as he made his way down from the Necropolis towards the great shining square that marked the Cistern of Saint Mocius, one of the three that were open to the air. Usurpation – though a frequent occurrence in the old Western Empire – had never succeeded in the East, though the Nika Riots had come pretty close. Should the conspiracy be foiled by others than the prefect and his *vigiles*, then he, Procopius, would appear in a most unfavourable light – incompetent at best, implicit in the plot at worst. If, on the other hand, the coup succeeded, what then? As a favoured appointee of the murdered emperor, he might well find himself proscribed by the new regime as politically tainted. Alternatively, one or both of the two Justins might launch a counter-coup. Should Justinian's usurper be deposed as a result, Procopius, as former prefect responsible for law and order in the city, would be blamed for failing to forestall him in the first place.

That he, Procopius, might harbour such reservations, would not have occurred to someone like Horatius – clearly a blinkered idealist who probably imagined all Friends of *Libertas* to be as altruistic as himself. Anicius Julianus on the other hand, being a man of the world had understood that, while one might be prepared to support a noble cause, there was nothing wrong with expecting due compensation for providing that support, or for not being willing to make the ultimate sacrifice on behalf of the cause. Not for him that '*Dulce et decorum est pro patria mori*'* hogwash. His undercover work for *Libertas* had, for sure, been dangerous at times; but it had been well rewarded, the risk adding spice to the campaign of sabotage which he had waged, not altogether unsuccessfully, against Belisarius.

Meanwhile, he would pretend to go along with Horatius, learning from him all he could about the details of the plot. Then, in a pre-emptive strike, he would arrest the conspirators before they could carry out their intention. He, Procopius, would be the hero of the hour, no doubt to be suitably recompensed for his boldness and professionalism. *Libertas* was a cause lost many years before; a sensible man accepted that and moved on. Then a sudden happy thought occurred to him. There *was* something to be salvaged from the wreck of that abandoned dream – something that would provide enormous satisfaction, while incurring not the slightest risk . . .

Meeting regularly with Horatius at the Necropolis in the course of the next two weeks, Procopius learned the following. Marcellus, Ablabius and Sergius had arranged with the master of ceremonies (no doubt some coin changing hands) for their couches at the feast to be the ones nearest to Justinian's. The third accomplice, Sergius (from whom Horatius obtained his information), had received assurances from his two officer friends that, in support of the coup, they would call out a large number of the Palace Guard, disgruntled over recent cost-cutting measures regarding donatives and privileges.

* Horace, *Odes*. 'It is sweet and fitting to die for one's country.'

Procopius now confided to Horatius that he had just stumbled upon reliable information that Belisarius was privy to the plot, and (though his position prevented him from openly declaring it) intended to lend it his support. The general's huge authority and popularity would, Procopius pointed out, virtually guarantee the coup's success. Of course, he, Procopius, had no such secret knowledge; it was merely a fabrication to implicate Belisarius. Planted in Horatius' mind, the seed would germinate and grow. Passing by osmosis to Sergius, then to Sergius' two officer friends, it would serve to cast suspicion on the general in the event of anyone 'talking' under interrogation in the aftermath of the plot's exposure.

What a delicious way to settle an old score, thought the prefect. Now, he stood to be paid back in overflowing measure for all those mind-numbingly tedious hours when, as official war historian compiling his account, he had been forced to listen to Belisarius enlarging on his deeds of derring-do. The man was an unashamed glory-hunter, a romantic dreamer who loved war for its own sake, who had seemed to treat campaigning as a game, where opponents like Witigis or Totila were regarded more as sporting rivals to be treated with respect and courtesy than as deadly enemies to be eliminated by whatever means were most effective. *That* was something Narses understood; a professional soldier to his fingertips, he had finished off in months a war that Belisarius had allowed to drag on for nearly two decades, resulting in destruction and suffering on an incalculable scale.

Should Belisarius' 'involvement' in the plot come to light, it would cause the general acute embarrassment at the very least. More likely it would incur public humiliation, with loss of office, wealth, or even liberty, while his 'betrayal' would come as a bitter blow to Justinian, who regarded the general not only as a valued servant, but as a trusted friend. *Libertas* may have failed, Procopius reflected, but at least the tyrant and his minion would not escape entirely a measure of just retribution.

On the fifteenth day of October, the Palace, especially its kitchens, hummed with activity concerning preparations for the banquet to be hosted by the emperor. Cleaning, tidying, arranging, checking lists, scores of menials and slaves, chivvied by *silentiarii* implementing the instructions of the *Magister Officiorum* – Peter the Patrician – transformed the *Triklinos* or state banqueting hall into a space of glittering magnificence, with couches of rare woods decked with silken cushions, elegant tables supporting dishes, flagons, bowls, and goblets, all of solid gold and finest workmanship, and everywhere swags and garlands of sweet-smelling flowers.

Mid-afternoon, and Justinian's guests – the great and good of Constantinople, resplendent in their robes of office – began arriving: senators, patricians, generals, bishops, the Patriarch. After being announced by the master of ceremonies, these were shepherded to their places by *silentiarii*. Smiling, affable, welcoming to all, Justinian was the very model of a gracious host, his mood serene and happy following the morning's service of re-dedication in Hagia Sophia, its restored dome more glorious even than before.

Course followed course of exquisite food, each accompanied by the appropriate wine; then, when the lamps had been lit and the last course finished, the master of ceremonies proposed a toast to, 'Flavius Anicius Justinianus – our Thrice-Blessed Augustus, Restorer of the Roman World.'

All rose and raised their goblets. Then a collective gasp of horror burst from the assembled guests as three senators, placed nearest to the emperor, drew daggers from beneath their robes and stepped towards Justinian. But before they could strike, they were surrounded, overpowered, and disarmed by *vigiles* disguised as servants. Bursting free from his captors, one of the would-be assassins grabbed a carving knife from a table and, before he could be re-apprehended, drew the blade across his throat. Spouting in scarlet jets from severed arteries, blood fountained through the air, splashing Justinian's purple robe.

In a dungeon deep in the bowels of the Praetorium, the remaining two conspirators in manacles – Marcellus being the one who had died by his own hand – stood before the seated prefect. The room's other occupants were a dozen *vigiles*, and a *carnifex* or torturer, who stood beside a table on which, like a set of surgeon's instruments, was ranged the grisly tool-kit of his trade. In a corner, an array of rods and pincers projected from a glowing brazier.

'Just tell me all you know,' said Procopius in pleasant tones. 'You'll talk anyway – eventually. So why suffer unnecessarily?'

Both men remaining silent, the prefect nodded to the torturer. The man approached the pair, bearing in gloved hands an iron rod with white-hot tip. This was applied to the backs of the prisoners, these being restrained securely in the grip of burly *vigiles*. A sickening stench of burning flesh filled the dungeon. Ablabius remained silent, blood dripping down his chin from where he had bitten through his lower lip, but Sergius screamed aloud in agony. 'No more!' he sobbed, as the iron was withdrawn. 'I'll tell you everything.'

It all came out: the announcement to be made that the emperor was dead; the part to be played by Sergius' two officer friends in persuading a section of the Palace Guards to back the coup; the information that Belisarius himself supported the conspiracy. All this was confirmed when the two officers in question were arrested and interrogated. (Horatius meanwhile had disappeared – provided with a bag of *solidi* and instructed to escape.)

Disdaining flight (suggested by his friends) as admission of complicity in the plot, Belisarius indignantly refuted before the Council the 'evidence' produced against him. Nevertheless, he was judged guilty and, though his life was spared in consideration of his forty years of loyal service, he was put under house arrest, and his wealth confiscated. However, no hard proof emerging that he was involved in the conspiracy, the following year Belisarius was released and restored to favour. Too late; his heart broken by grief and resentment, the great general – perhaps the greatest Roman general of all – died a few months later.

Shock and sadness over what he perceived as betrayal by his oldest friend changed to remorse and bitter self-recrimination on Justinian's part as he came at last to see that Belisarius was no traitor, but the innocent victim of malicious rumour.

Revenge, as a Greek philosopher once said, was indeed a dish best eaten cold, reflected Procopius as, lauded and heaped with honours by a grateful emperor, he basked in his new-found reputation as the saviour of the monarchy.

THIRTY-TWO

Nothing is lost; destruction is only a name for a change of substance
Lucretius, *On the Nature of Things*, c. 50 BC

The funeral, as befitted one of the best prefects Constantinople had known, was a grand and solemn service. A moving eulogy, delivered by Paul the Silentiary,* paid tribute to a distinguished public servant who had graced the world of scholarship and letters with his great *History of the Wars of Justinian*, having himself taken part in many of the campaigns he wrote about so eloquently. Above all, the Roman world owed an incalculable debt to one who, only a few short months before, had, by his expertise and boldness, foiled a monstrous plot to assassinate the emperor. All Constantinople had, it seemed, turned out to pay its last respects to the great Praefectus, as the cortège proceeded from the Praetorium to the Church of Saint Irene, where the body of Procopius was laid to rest.

Returning to the Palace, Justinian retreated to the garden where he and Theodora had first met and which, increasingly, had become a place of refuge where he could be by himself with his deepest thoughts. At last, he was quite alone, the emperor reflected sadly. In turn there had been taken from him: first Theodora, both cornerstone and central pillar of his life; then Belisarius, the friend and faithful servant he had wronged; and now, Procopius – whom, in some ways, he had loved like the son he had never known. Were all things transitory, he wondered, with loss and change the only certainties? All his life he had striven to establish good things that would endure: a Roman Empire that would last forever, serving to implement God's Plan for the light of civilization and True Faith to shine in time throughout the world; laws that would guide men's conduct down the ages; great buildings of a design and structure to defy the ravages of time . . .

But perhaps it had all been for nothing. Everywhere, blind, uncaring forces seemed to be threatening all he had achieved. Ferocious Lombards were already casting greedy eyes on Italy, ravaged and weakened by

---

* Whose poem extolling the glories of Hagia Sophia had recently been recited at the re-dedication of that church.

twenty years of war; Slavs, Bulgars, and now this new threat from the East, a race more terrible even than the Huns – the Avars – menaced the Danube frontier. His attempts to forge religious unity between East and West – Monophysite and Chalcedonian – had foundered on the rocks of ignorance and stubborn wilfulness. When he passed away (and, at eighty-one, that time could not be distant, Justinian reminded himself), would all that he had worked for fade and vanish also, as ripples from a pebble cast into a pool were briefly seen then disappeared? Was his new-found interest in Aphthartodocetism – the doctrine that held Christ's body to be incorruptible – merely a reflection of a longing for assurance that some things did not change, were immutable and permanent? Insidiously, a terrifying thought slid into the emperor's brain. What if the very faith he had striven all his life to understand and serve were nothing more than empty superstition?

In the midst of these gloomy cogitations, Justinian was interrupted by a servitor bearing a book – not an old-fashioned set of papyrus rolls or *volumina*, but one of the newer kind with parchment *paginae*.

'In his Will, Serenity, the prefect stated that he wished you to have the first copy of his final work.' Bowing, the man handed the *codex* to Justinian, then departed. Inscribed in gold on the beautiful calf-leather binding was the title – *Secret History*. Welcoming this distraction from his mood of sombre introspection, the emperor opened the book and eagerly began to read . . .

'Justinian's family was illiterate, boorish, descended from slaves and barbarians . . . he [Justinian] was the son of a demon . . . Justinian's senseless wars and persecutions . . . during his reign the whole earth was drenched with human blood . . . without hesitation he shattered the laws when money was in sight . . . was like a cloud of dust in instability . . . never paused for a thorough investigation before reaching a decision . . . was never able to adhere to settled conditions, but was naturally inclined to make confusion and turmoil everywhere . . . while Justinian ruled no law remained fixed, no transaction safe, no contract valid . . . an evil-doer and easily led into evil . . . she [Theodora] could win over her husband quite against his will to any action she desired . . . she would lie with all her fellow diners the whole night long; when she had reduced them all to a state of exhaustion she would go to their menials, as many as thirty on occasions, and copulate with every one of them, but not even so could she satisfy her lust . . .'

With a cry of horrified disgust, Justinian dropped the book, unable to read on, each poisoned phrase seeming like a dagger-thrust to the heart.

From what deep well of resentment had issued this astonishing outpouring of hate and malice? Shaken to the core of his being, Justinian felt, not anger – only sorrow, hurt, and incomprehension that a man he had always regarded as a friend, should see him (and Theodora) in such a baleful light. A black depression settled on the emperor, from which, for many days he was unable to be roused.

'Serenity – Tan-Shing, the Chinese sage I told you of is here,' announced Paul the Silentiary, standing at the entrance of Justinian's *tablinum*. 'Shall I admit him?'

'Let us receive him by all means, Paul,' replied the emperor with a wan smile, 'though I doubt that anything he has to say can lift my spirits.'

The silentiary ushered into the emperor's study, an elderly Chinese, upright of bearing, with a keen, good-humoured face, and clad in a saffron-coloured robe. He seated himself at the emperor's invitation.

'I am told your mind is troubled,' the visitor declared in perfect Greek. 'Excuse my bluntness, Serenity; unlike most of my countrymen I never learned the art of how to be discreet. To me, a spade has always been a spade, never an agricultural implement. Some members of your household – who shall be nameless, by the way – out of concern for your well-being have asked me to make contact with you. So, here I am. To help in any way I can.' And Tan-Shing gave the emperor a beaming smile.

'Some members of your household,' thought Justinian, touched rather than offended by what others might interpret as presumption. That would include Paul the Silentiary and Theoctistus his physician, functionaries in whom solicitude for their employer transcended efficient performance of their duties. Clearly, some attribute possessed by this stranger had impressed such men sufficiently to make them send him here.

'Well, Tan-Shing,' replied the emperor, 'I appreciate your offer. But if even my physician cannot cure my – sickness of the spirit, let us call it – I can't see how –' Close to shameful tears, Justinian trailed off, moved that there were some who cared sufficiently to wish to help him, but oppressed by a terrible sense of hopelessness that nothing anyone could do would avail. With an effort, he pulled himself together and said with forced brightness, 'Your Greek is excellent. I had feared we might have need of an interpreter.'

'I have several tongues, Serenity. Apart from my native Mandarin, I speak Hindustani, Urdu, Persian, even Greek, as you were kind enough to mention. You see, in a past life, before I became a wandering monk, a

Seeker after Enlightenment, I was a wealthy merchant who travelled the Silk Road many times.'

'Enlightenment – what is that?'

'It is not easy to define, Serenity. True Enlightenment can only be experienced rather than expressed in words. We who seek to find it, think of it as a mystic vision of the Truth, the All, the Infinite, the Transcendental – there are different words. It is to be attained through meditation and self-discipline, involving ultimately the annihilation of the Self in identification with the Soul of the Universe. The state of mind when this is achieved is called Nirvana. The *Saddhus* – the holy men of India – seek Enlightenment via a particularly ferocious form of ascetisism. Lord Gautama,* who lived a thousand years ago, prescribed a gentler way, one based on meditation and inner holiness through correct behaviour. His is the Path that I myself attempt to follow.'

'This is all most interesting,' said Justinian, who had indeed found the other's discourse fascinating. 'Your words remind me of our own Desert Fathers – Antony, Jerome et al. – who sought through abstinence and contemplation to find communion with God. However –,' he smiled at the sage and shook his head in mild puzzlement, 'I can't quite see how any of this applies to myself.'

'I am about to embark on a pilgrimage, Serenity. To the Church of Saint Michael, at Germia near Ancyra** in Galatia. You see, the Path does not require you to be an adherent of any particular religion or philosophy over another. The priest at Germia, Father Eutropus, a most remarkable man, has gathered about him a dedicated following of . . . seekers after Truth, I suppose you could call them, who engage in contemplation and religious discussion. It's not officially a monastery; there's no formal organization as such. Basically, it's a loose community where minds can stimulate and react with other minds, perhaps thereby to reach a deeper understanding of the Nature of God. I confess to having a great curiosity to experience for a time the way of life at Germia.' Tan-Shing paused and regarded Justinian earnestly. 'Why not come with me, Serenity?' he urged. 'Germia may not provide an answer to your problems, but at least it could perhaps enable you to see things from a fresh perspective – which could only be a good thing, surely.'

One month later, having travelled three hundred miles due east from Constantinople, Justinian and Tan-Shing – the former on muleback, the

* Buddha.
** Yerma, near Ankara.

latter, aided by a sturdy pilgrim's staff, on foot – forded the Sangarius river and climbed up into a beautiful plateau of rolling grassland, stippled with flocks of sheep and herds of goats. Two further days of easy travel brought the pair to Saint Michael's Church, an imposing multi-domed edifice in the midst of outbuildings surrounded by cultivated plots.

As they approached the complex, Justinian reflected on the journey (in the course of which, as 'Brother Martin' – a wandering monk, clad in a simple habit, he had never once been recognized). Tan-Shing had proved an ideal travelling-companion: silent when Justinian wished to be alone with his own thoughts, cheerful and talkative at other times, well-informed on a multitude of subjects, including the religious and philosophical systems as well as the literature of China, India, Persia and Rome. He was also endlessly resourceful when it came to finding lodgings for the night, supplementing their diet from Nature's bounty, or haggling for foodstuffs in local markets. From the sage Justinian learned more about the Way suggested by Lord Gautama (the goal of which seemed to be the transcending of Self, linked to ultimate escape from an endless cycle of rebirth), and the 'noble eightfold path' which its disciples sought to cultivate: right views, right aspirations, right speech, right conduct, right livelihood, right effort, right mindedness, and – most importantly – right rapture. Whether it was the Chinese sage's stimulating company, the healthful open-air lifestyle (so different from the sedentary Palace routine of receptions, ceremony, and administration), or the changing landscapes that each day's travel brought, or by a combination of all of these, by the time the journey neared its end, Justinian was – he acknowledged to himself – in a calmer and happier frame of mind.

Father Eutropus proved to be nothing like the saintly scholar Justinian had vaguely imagined. Diminutive, rotund, with a bright indignant eye, and clad in a brown cassock, he put the emperor in mind of nothing so much as a fierce little robin. 'Visitors are welcome, provided they're prepared to work, and forego their former status,' declared the priest, glaring at the two arrivals, as if they were pedlars proffering goods of suspect workmanship. Justinian was duly assigned to helping in the kitchens, Tan-Shing to maintenance and cleaning duties.

At mealtimes, held in common in a refectory, talk flowed freely among the guests whose backgrounds varied widely: artisans, senators, clerics, a retired general, a pair of Indian Brahmans, a Persian noble . . . No subject was off limits. Passionate discussions about the Nature of the Trinity, the relationship of Christ to the Father, the doctrine of reincarnation – namely 'varna', the Indian theory of rebirth from a lower to a higher caste through leading an unblemished life – all took place in an atmosphere which, though often charged, was always one of mutual respect. (Anyone tending to express their views too hotly could expect to be chastened by a bellowed reproof from Father Eutropus.)

For the first time, Justinian found himself unable to impose his views by the fiat of imperial decree. Initially, he found this disconcerting, but soon, as 'Brother Martin', he began to relish the cut-and-thrust of debate, of having to defend his ideas by argument alone. In the process, he became – unconsciously and imperceptibly – more tolerant of views that differed from his own, less certain of ones previously held by him with unshakeable conviction. Gradually, the differences between Chalcedonian Orthodoxy and Monophysitism, which once he'd seen as irreconcilable, began to seem less absolute, almost like different facets of a single canon.

Especially was this the case, Justinian thought, when viewed from the standpoint of Aphthartodocetism – the doctrine that held Christ's body to be incorruptible and which, in recent years, had begun to interest the emperor profoundly. Here, perhaps, lay hopes of finding a *via media* between the two opposing creeds, which might lead eventually to resolution.

'Read *De Rerum Natura*,'* suggested Tan-Shing, when Justinian broached the matter with the sage. 'By Lucretius – one of your Roman poets from the time of the late Republic.'

In the commune's well-stocked library, Justinian located a copy of the work in question – a poem in six books, each consisting of a separate scroll. A long read. Settling himself in a comfortable chair, the emperor unscrolled a section of the first *volumen* . . .

'It's bleak – bleak and terrible!' cried Justinian to Tan-Shing some hours later. 'He postulates that all we are consists of an infinite number of tiny particles – each called *atomos*. The whole disintegrates when we die, leaving nothing of ourselves but the dispersed atoms – not even a soul!'

'You are distressed, Martin,' the sage responded calmly. 'You have glimpsed the Truth, and it has frightened you. That is only natural, to be expected.'

'But if Lucretius is right, it means I will not see Theodora again!'

'Not in the sense, perhaps, that you and she will meet as individuals in some afterlife,' replied the other gently. 'She is already part of the Infinite, as you yourself will be eventually – both of you absorbed and re-united in

* *On the Nature of Things.*

God, the Universe, the All – in Heaven, if you like. Is not that an infinitely greater and more liberating prospect than one that only sees the limited, imperfect Self?'

'I'll have Father Eutropus excommunicated, anathematized!' exclaimed Justinian. 'His community will be broken up, his Church of Saint Martin deconsecrated!'

'I do not believe that,' said Tan-Shing with a patient smile. 'There speaks Justinianus Augustus only. But already, as "Brother Martin", you have moved on, experienced a tiny transformation – if you like, a foretaste of the Infinite. As Epicurus says, "We can never step into the same river twice". Today, I leave Saint Michael's to resume my pilgrimage. Meanwhile, dear friend, I offer a farewell suggestion: meditate on these wise words of Lucretius, "Nothing is lost".'

Saddened by the departure of Tan-Shing, whom he had come to regard as a cherished comrade, and oppressed by a nameless sense of bewilderment and dread, Justinian set off from the commune into the countryside later that same day, in an attempt to clear his mind. Scarcely aware of his surroundings, he walked for miles, confused thoughts whirling in his brain, until, coming to a cliff edge, he was forced to stop. Exhausted, he sat down and contemplated the view.

Immediately before him, a precipice dropped hundreds of feet to an expanse of undulating pastureland. Peering over the edge, he spotted on a ledge far below, a large untidy nest in which two downy chicks were stirring. Moments later, an eagle, a tiny lamb gripped in its talons, alighted at the eyrie. Repelled yet fascinated, conscious of the mother ewe's distress at the loss of her offspring, Justinian watched the eagle's young tear at the offering with hooked and greedy beaks. For creatures to live, other creatures must die. Like Tan-Shing's endless cycle of rebirth, transformation was the order of the Universe – if Lucretius was right, that is. Nothing was lost, the poet had affirmed. Could a practical example illustrate that? the emperor wondered. Take a river – its volume lessened as it flowed into the sea. But the surface of the sea evaporated in the sun, to form clouds which, blowing from the sea back over the land cooled as they rose, turning to rain, which restored the river's volume. Therefore nothing was lost. The cycle was complete.

Was there a parallel here with Aphthartodocetism? as Tan-Shing had suggested. If, as Lucretius proposed, the individual atoms of which the body was made up dispersed after death yet remained constant – *in quantity*, then nothing, after all, was lost. In this sense, Christ's body could indeed be held to be incorruptible. 'If Christ be not risen, then is your faith vain,' said Paul. But, even if one accepted Lucretius, the Ascension into Heaven could still be said to have occurred, only in a way not previously conceived. Justinian found the thought strangely comforting. In a state of mental excitement akin to an epiphany, he returned to Saint Michael's, determined to think through the enormous implications of this most challenging of revelations, and to try to form from it some coherent doctrine. It would, he realized, have to be framed in language which, in order to be acceptable to Christians throughout the Roman Empire, must not offend or affright traditional believers. Like Paul on the road to Damascus, he felt as though the scales had dropped from his eyes, enlarging his perception to a terrifying yet exhilarating degree. As that same Paul had said in his First Epistle to the Corinthians, 'For now we see through a glass darkly; but then face to face: now I know in part; but then shall I know even as also I am known.'

Back in Constantinople, Justinian lost no time in promulgating the new doctrine of Aphthartodocetism. Even if his subjects might not fully comprehend its meaning (as he himself did but 'in part'), he felt it was important that, at least on trust, they should accept it; complete understanding could follow later. Throughout that thirty-ninth year of his reign,* Justinian wrestled with refining and clarifying the new dogma, studying and comparing texts, taking endless notes. Night after night, lights burning in the Great Palace testified to the Sleepless One's unceasing efforts for the spiritual welfare of his people. They were still burning when, on the night of the fourteenth of November, Callinicus, Praepositus of the Sacred Bedchamber, entered the emperor's *tablinum* and found him dead, sitting upright at his desk. On his face was an expression partly startled, part enraptured – as though he had suddenly grasped the meaning of some tremendous yet elusive truth.

* 565.

AFTERWORD

Occupying much of what has been called 'the last Roman century', Justinian's reign, in terms of the chief aims he set himself (restoration of the West Roman Empire in parallel with the establishment of religious unity), has to be adjudged a failure, though a failure of heroic dimensions. For within a few generations of his death, the mighty realm which he had inherited and, with the conquest of Africa, Italy and southern Spain, greatly expanded, had, under the onslaught of Lombards, Avars, and militant Islam, shrunk to an Anatolian rump with a scattered archipelago of minor outposts in the West. And his mission to create religious unity by attempting to resolve the differences between the Monophysite East and the Chalcedonian West (through the Edict condemning the Three Chapters, and the later one regarding Aphthartodocetism), merely resulted in driving the two sides even further apart. Anyway, the epic struggle between the two opposing creeds (which had given rise to so much angst and persecution during the fifth and sixth centuries), suddenly became – with the Arab conquest of Roman Africa, Egypt, Palestine, and Syria – an obsolete irrelevance, as did, due also to Islamic occupation (of the Great King's realm this time), the eternal tug-of-war between Rome and Persia.

Yet despite so much of his life's work running into the sands, Justinian has left us an enduring legacy in one important field – that of law. His and Tribonian's great *Institutes* provided the foundation for the legal systems of many countries (e.g. Scotland and Holland) at the present day. In addition, we owe to Justinian the existence of a number of magnificent churches, above all Hagia Sophia – the apogée of Roman architectural and engineering genius. If this sublime building were Justinian's sole memento, the world would still owe him an immeasurable debt.

In a telling metaphor in his perceptive and thought-provoking *The World of Late Antiquity*, Peter Brown imagines a traveller by train realizing 'at the end of a long slow journey that the landscape outside has altered – so in the crucial generations between the reign of Justinian and that of Heraclius, we can sense the definitive emergence of a medieval world'. The world into which Justinian was born was still a fully Roman one. By the year of his death, 565, the signs that Antiquity was ending (e.g. a pre-occupation with religious issues at the expense of rational philosophy, of which the closing of the Schools of Athens is a marker) were beginning to appear. It is perhaps not without significance that, almost coincidentally with Justinian's passing, was born (c. 570) the man whose legacy would bring about the passing also of Justinian's world – Mahomet.

AUTHOR'S NOTE

By far the most valuable source of information for Justinian and his times is *The Wars of Justinian* by Procopius of Caesarea – a lawyer who became official war correspondent for Justinian's great general, Belisarius. Procopius accompanied the latter on his African campaign against the Vandals, and for much of the long Gothic War in Italy, many of the incidents he describes being written from first-hand experience. Admirably detailed and objective, it is very much in the classical vein of Greek and Roman historians such as Thucydides, Polybius, Tacitus and Ammianus. In glaring contrast to *The Wars* (which on the whole paints a favourable picture of Justinian) is Procopius' *Secret History* – a savage attack on the emperor and his wife Theodora, portraying them in the most scurrilous of terms. Too biased to be helpful in describing the imperial pair, in other respects it is a useful supplement to *The Wars*. Some other useful contemporary sources are the ecclesiastical histories of Evagrius and John of Ephesus, and the chronicles of John Malalas, John of Antioch, and Count Marcellinus.

Regarding modern sources, Gibbon, to my mind, stands supreme when it comes to giving us a sweeping overview of the Justinianic era. His ability to fashion from a complex, often tangled, sometimes obscure mass of facts a clear, colourful, and coherent narrative, is surely unrivalled. His only fault – if such it can be called – lies in his impatient dismissal (which I've touched on in the Notes) of the Christological controversies which occupied so much of Justinian's time and energy. Also essential as background reading is the magisterial *The Later Roman Empire* by my old lecturer, the great A.H.M. Jones. I am enormously indebted to my publisher, Hugh Andrew, for lending me many of his books. Especially useful were the following: *The Cambridge Companion to the Age of Justinian*, edited by Michael Maas, a veritable quarry of information regarding all main topics for the period; Robert Browning's masterly *Justinian and Theodora*, which provides penetrating insight into what motivated Justinian and the people he was involved with; and *Theodora*, a marvellous little book by Antony Bridge, which paints a warmly sympathetic picture (and, one feels, a true one) of the bear-keeper's daughter who became a Roman empress.

For the sake of drama and clarity, I have (as mentioned in the relevant sections in the Notes) gone in for some abridging and telescoping of events in places, without, hopefully, distorting essential historical truth. Anyone who has ever wrestled with the Christological subtleties of the Three Chapters controversy, or tried to form a coherent overview of the Gothic War from the endless (and frankly, often tedious) catalogue of sieges, counter-sieges, marches, counter-marches, blockades, sorties, ambuscades, ruses de guerre, et cetera of Belisarius' and Narses' campaigns in Italy, will understand my reasons for doing so.

The Dramatis Personae are, for the most part, real people. The majority needed little fleshing-out on my part, the records being sufficiently detailed for clear individual profiles to emerge, regarding, for example: Belisarius, Narses, John the Cappadocian, Theodora, and, of course, Justinian himself. A richly complex character, the great emperor comes over as a well-intentioned but ultimately tragic figure; someone who, by his own lights tried to do good things, but whose efforts resulted in the impoverishment of the Empire, the ruin of Italy, and a final parting of the ways between the Churches of the East and West.

In telling the story I have, wherever possible (and allowing for a modicum of artistic licence), stuck to the known facts, only giving rein to my imagination where lacunae in the records permitted me to do so. For example, we don't know if Justinian was personally involved in the Dhu-Nuwas campaign, but – as (theoretical) commander of the eastern army – he was certainly in a position to be so. Again, my making Procopius an agent provocateur dedicated to destabilizing Belisarius, although fictitious, is entirely consistent with his views about the general, plus his location alongside Belisarius in various places during the campaigns in Africa and Italy, as well as in Constantinople when he was prefect of that city.

APPENDIX I

THE ETHNIC AND LINGUISTIC BACKGROUND OF JUSTIN
AND JUSTINIAN

Historians have tended, perhaps too uncritically, to accept Procopius' assertion that Justin and his nephew Justinian were of Thracian stock. I would suggest that this needs some re-examination.

Gibbon points out that Justinian's original name, and that of his father – *Uprauda* (Upright) and *Ystock* (Stock) respectively – were Gothic; evidence, surely, that their owners were also Gothic. Settler-groups of Goths (a Germanic tribe), known as 'Moeso-Goths', had been established in the northern parts of the Eastern Empire long before the great Gothic migration across the Danube in 376. (It was for his countrymen living in the East Roman province of Moesia Secunda that Ulfila translated the Bible into Gothic c. 350–60.) Justinian's and his father's home village, Tauresium, could well have been such a community (especially considering the pair's likely Gothic origins), a Gothic enclave within the Latin-speaking province of Dardania. As Justinian's uncle, Justin, hailed from Bederiana (the district in which Tauresium was located) and very possibly from Tauresium itself, he too could well have been of Gothic, rather than Thracian, stock. Also, I strongly suspect that Justin was not his original name. ('Justinus' is an eminently appropriate appellation for a Roman emperor; but for a peasant?* It's as though Thomas Hardy had named his yeoman character, Gabriel Oak, 'Marmaduke' Oak!) Hence my borrowed, and Gothic, name for him – 'Roderic'. I suggest that Justin, and later his nephew Justinian, would have first arrived in Constantinople speaking, in addition to their mother-tongue of Gothic, basic Latin, but no Greek.

I have suggested that Justinian had slave progenitors. In his *Anekdota*, Procopius affirms that Justinian was descended from slaves and barbarians; but the *Secret History* is such a biased source, and one so motivated by malice, that its findings have to be regarded with the greatest suspicion. However, in *Chambers' Encyclopaedia* of 1888–1892, the article 'Justinian'

* The names of his companions on that youthful journey to Constantinople were Zimarch and Dityvist.

contains a statement that the future emperor was 'of obscure parentage, and indeed slave-born', citing, *inter alios*, the scholars Isambert and G. Body. On the strength of this, I felt justified in making slave parentage a feature of the story. The article also mentions that Justinian's 'original name was Uprauda', confirming Gibbon's observation.

If (as on the evidence seems likely) Justin's sister Bigleniza was married to a Goth living in a Gothic community, it is not unreasonable to suppose that she too was of Gothic origin – an inheritance that would be shared by her brother. (Admittedly, 'Bigleniza' is not a particularly Gothic-sounding name, which is why I have hinted in the story that she may have had some Thracian blood.) In the end, perhaps, any attempt to define Justin as either a Goth or a Thracian runs into the sand. As Robert Browning says in *Justinian and Theodora* (in the context of Belisarius' birth c. 505), 'Romanized Thracians were much mingled with Gothic stock by this time' – which allows me, I think, to present Justin in the story as of Gothic rather than Thracian origin.

APPENDIX II

The Nika Riots of 532: was there ever, in the whole of history, a more exciting and momentous set-piece? Had the revolt succeeded in toppling Justinian (as it very nearly did), subsequent history might have been very different; at the very least, Istanbul today would be without Hagia Sophia, one of the world's sublimest buildings, and Justinian's reform of Roman Law (the basis of the legal systems of many nations at the present day) would never have been finalized, and may well have been passed over and forgotten.

For dramatic reasons, I have gone in for some fairly radical telescoping and condensing regarding some of the incidents connected with the riots. This was to preserve, as far as possible, a sense of the urgency and tempo of the actual events, without, I hope, sacrificing essential historical truth. These changes will become apparent to any reader who cares to compare the relevant pages in the text with the timetable shown below.

While there is broad agreement as to the chronology of events relating to the riots among most authorities, some sources show minor variations between themselves. The following scenario is probably pretty accurate.

Saturday, 3 January to Tuesday, 6 January
Street disturbances (in which some people are killed) resulting from un-popular government policies, broken up by city prefect's police. Arrests made; some of those detained charged with murder.

Thursday, 8 January
Trials of accused; seven condemned to death.

Sunday, 11 January
Two of those condemned survive bungled execution – a Green and a Blue, given sanctuary in Church of St Lawrence. Prefect posts armed guard around church to prevent rescue.

Monday, 12 January
Tension mounts in the capital; stalemate regarding the two in St Lawrence.

Tuesday, 13 January – the Ides
Hippodrome opens for races. Greens and Blues join forces to demand release of St Lawrence pair, but Justinian refuses to reply; spectators become frustrated and defiant, eventually leaving Hippodrome with shouts of 'Nika!' to surround Praetorium. Failing to force the Perfect to listen to their complaints, they break into the building, release prisoners, killing police who try to stop them, then set Praetorium ablaze. Mob then burns Chalke, Hagia Sophia, and other prominent buildings.

Wednesday, 14 January
Races resume in the Hippodrome. Despite Justinian agreeing to the people's demands for the dismissal of unpopular ministers, the mob becomes more militant. Egged on by members of the upper class (senators et al. who want regime change) it goes to the house of Mundus (one of the three nephews of the emperor Anastasius, and thus a possible candidate for the throne) to try to make him emperor. Finding him absent, they burn down his house in frustration, then threaten the Palace, but the building is protected by German mercenaries under generals Belisarius and Mundus. (The loyalty of the Roman Palace Guard is, at best, uncertain.)

Thursday, 15 January
Belisarius and Mundus sally forth from the Palace to try to suppress the revolt, but can make no headway when the fighting moves to the narrow streets. They withdraw their Germans to the Palace. Stalemate ensues.

Friday and Saturday, 16 and 17 January
Mob goes on rampage, burning down many public buildings. Fearing treachery, Justinian expels from the Palace almost all the courtiers and senators – including Pompeius and Hypatius, the two other nephews of Anastasius! (This, as soon becomes clear, is a bad mistake.)

Sunday, 18 January
Justinian again appears before the people in the Hippodrome. Despite offering a general amnesty and more concessions, he is shouted down by a hostile crowd. As Justinian retreats to the Palace, the mob learns of the expulsion of Pompeius and Hypatius and forces the latter to be crowned as emperor. Reluctant at first, Hypatius accepts the role once he realizes that the mob has senatorial support. In the Palace, Justinian and a small band of faithful followers, convinced that all is lost, prepare to flee. But, perhaps rallied by a stirring exhortation from Theodora (see Appendix III), they change their minds and decide to fight back. After an attempt to 'spring' Hypatius from the royal box in the Hippodrome is thwarted by the Palace

Guard, Belisarius and Mundus manage to lead their German troops un-detected to the Hippodrome, where they launch a surprise attack on the crowd. The ensuing bloodbath and arrest of Hypatius break the spirit of the rebels.

Monday, 19 January
To prevent further rival bids for the purple, Hypatius and Pompeius are executed. This marks the end of the insurrection.

APPENDIX III

DID THEODORA REALLY MAKE HER 'WINDING SHEET' SPEECH?

To suggest that Theodora's famous speech ending with the words, 'the purple is a glorious winding sheet', is actually a piece of propaganda fabricated by Procopius, might cause many to react with scepticism, disbelief, disappointment, or even outrage. However, in the interests of objectivity, a writer of historical fiction (with some allowance for artistic licence) has, I think, an obligation to stick broadly to historical truth – even when this risks upsetting cherished beliefs by airing controversial facts or theories. (No doubt many were upset when it emerged that the saintly Thomas Jefferson had sired a child by one of his female slaves.)

In *The Cambridge Companion to the Age of Justinian*, Leslie Brubaker makes a case for Procopius penning Theodora's speech as a 'rhetorical set-piece', rather than as factual reportage – an accepted literary device on the part of ancient authors. (Witness the famous speech that Tacitus puts into the mouth of the Caledonian leader, Galgacus – 'They create a desert and call it Peace'.) According to Brubaker, the crisis for Justinian resulting from Hypatius' apparently successful coup was so bad that in order to invest it with maximum dramatic effect, Procopius reverses the natural order, 'with men quaking like women and a woman speaking like a man'. In this, Procopius was expressing a typically 'Roman' attitude (some would say prejudice) regarding gender roles: women were supposed to be gentle, modest, submissive and dedicated to home and family; men were expected to be courageous, strong, just and wise.

To those who like their historical heroes and heroines consistently heroic, I would emphasize that the above is just a theory, developed only very recently. That Theodora herself made the speech has in the past been regarded as 'kosher' by almost all historians. To those who prefer their history 'warts and all', Brubaker's argument is reinforced by reference to convincing theories, based on solid research, presented by Elizabeth Fisher and Averil Cameron in the late twentieth century.

The question remains: if not Theodora, then who *did* galvanize the demoralized little band loyal to Justinian into mounting the operation that ended the Nika revolt?

APPENDIX IV

PROCOPIUS – FIFTH COLUMNIST?

Although *Libertas* (see Chapter 14 *et seq.*) is fictional, it is tempting to speculate that a secret resistance movement on similar lines could have existed, and that Procopius might somehow have been involved. Certainly, the time could not have been more ripe. At the time of Nika and its immediate aftermath, Justinian (as hopefully the text makes clear) was extremely unpopular with all classes of society – especially among those of senatorial rank, who alone could provide the leadership, wealth, and organizing know-how necessary to promote change. Men like my character Anicius Julianus, who was suggested by a real person – Anicia Juliana, daughter of the West Roman emperor Olybrius, a member of the immensely rich and powerful Anician family, part of the West Roman diaspora settled in Constantinople, and whose son was one of the senators exiled after the revolt. None of the grievances which had provoked the Nika Riots had been resolved, nor was there any sign that solutions would be forthcoming. In the past, discontent with the rule of tyrants and incompetents had led to the toppling (often by a combination of senior army officers and senators) of emperors such as Nero, Commodus, and Valentinian III.

Incidentally, the Roman Senate (and that includes its East Roman incarnation) has often been portrayed as a toothless tiger, whose only function was to rubber-stamp the diktats of an autocratic emperor. Such a picture is deceptive. For it is a fact of history that rulers who continued to flout the mores of S.P.Q.R. were invariably removed from office – 'with extreme prejudice', to use a deliciously bizarre euphemism once favoured by the American Secret Service. Even in the dying days of the Western Empire, the Senate still had enough clout to have the emperor Avitus 'disposed of' for adopting too accommodating a stance towards the barbarians. Though the power of the Senate as an institution was severely weakened by Justinian, the class from which its ranks were drawn continued to be an influential sector of society, one which any emperor would be foolish to ignore or alienate.

Allowing, for the sake of argument, that an organization on the lines of *Libertas* could have existed (and, all things considered, it would perhaps be surprising if some form of underground resistance against Justinian had *not* arisen after *Nika*), then Procopius would have fitted perfectly into such a scenario – as spy, double agent, or fifth columnist. Cast in that sort of role, he becomes an absolute gift to the writer of historical fiction. We know that he detested and despised Justinian. ('Without any hesitation he shattered the laws when money was in sight', is one of the milder aspersions against the emperor in *Secret History*.) Given the opportunity to do him harm, it is hard to believe that he would have refrained from doing so. And an organization such as *Libertas* would have provided just such an opportunity, with Procopius (as part of Belisarius' staff* in the African and Italian campaigns, and later as Prefect of Constantinople) ideally placed to cause maximum disruption. How else to account for the following?

i) Who started the drip-drip of malicious rumours about Belisarius, causing Justinian to harbour suspicions about his general regarding his conduct during the Vandal campaign,** and later, leading to his recall from Italy?

ii) Who almost persuaded the Huns to switch sides to the Vandals in Africa?

iii) Who supplied Totila with secret information enabling him to generate a resurgence of Gothic power in Italy?

iv) Who fomented mutiny in Africa, following its reconquest?

v) Who spread false rumours that Justinian was dead, which led to a constitutional crisis?

vi) Who was behind the hatching of a plot to assassinate Justinian?

None of the above directly points the finger at Procopius. Taken collectively however, they could be significant. On every occasion connected with these queries, Procopius – in an inversion of T.S. Eliot's famous line about McAvity – *was* there. Which, if nothing else, does perhaps serve to 'put him in the frame'.

---

* Procopius had little respect for Belisarius (as evidenced in *Secret History*, where he refers to the general's 'contemptible conduct') so presumably wouldn't have scrupled to betray him.

** '. . . private despatches maliciously affirmed that the conqueror of Africa . . . conspired to seat himself on the throne of the Vandals . . . Justinian listened with too patient an ear; and his silence was the result of jealousy rather than of confidence.' (Gibbon.)

Prologue

Ammianus Marcellinus

This Roman officer-turned-historian paints a marvellously colourful and detailed picture of the late Roman world in the second half of the fourth century, covering – besides a wealth of fascinating domestic issues such as witchcraft trials and snobbery among the nouveaux riches in Rome – campaigns in Germany, Gaul, Britain and Persia. He ends on a sombre note – the destruction of a huge Roman army by the Goths, at Adrianople in AD 378. Though he could not foresee it, this disaster would precipitate a chain of events that would culminate in the fall of the Western Empire a century later.

this year of the consul Paulus

Normally, two consuls – one from Constantinople, the other from Rome – were chosen each year, the year being named for them. This practice continued even after the fall of the West, Western consuls being nominated by the first two German kings of Italy – Odovacar, then Theoderic – in their capacity as vicegerents of the Eastern emperor, who held the power to ratify or ignore their choice. A less common way of dating events was from the Founding of the City (of Rome, in 753 BC) – *Ab Urbe Condita*, or A.U.C. Dating from the birth of Christ was only introduced in 527, at the instigation of one Dionysius Exiguus, but was not generally adopted before the age of Charlemagne and King Alfred. Dating for the interim period between the lapsing of consular dates (the office was abolished in 539) and the adoption of the Christian Era c. AD 800, was from the supposed Creation (according to one Julius Africanus) on 1 September, 5,508 years, three months, and twenty-five days before the birth of Christ. (See Gibbon's note at the end of Chapter 40 of his *Decline and Fall of the Roman Empire*.)

elephants and cataphracts

Alexander encountered (Indian) elephants in his Persian and Indian campaigns, and elephants (African ones) were famously used by Hannibal against the Romans. For a limited period after the end of the Punic wars, elephants were even employed by late Hellenistic armies, before falling out of fashion. Persia, as Ammianus Marcellinus eloquently testifies, was still using war-elephants in the later fourth century, but seems to have abandoned them by the seventh, as they are nowhere mentioned during the East Roman emperor Heraclius' war against Persia in AD 622.

Cataphracts, or *cataphractarii* – heavily armoured cavalry – appear to have been a Persian invention, but were extensively copied by the late Romans. Strictly, the term 'cataphract' should apply only when the rider, not his horse, was armoured; *clibanarius* – literally (and appropriately!) 'oven man' – is the correct term when both were armoured. 'Cataphract' however, was freely used to describe both types. Cataphracts, despite a superficial resemblance in appearance, were *not* the ancestors of the European mediaeval knight, although often referred to as such. Knighthood was a strictly feudal development, in which military service was an obligation incurred by a grant of land from a feudal superior.

Scipio's tactics against Hannibal

Roderic and Victor were not the only ones to benefit (in their case, fictionally) from the great Roman campaigner's ideas. General 'Stormin' Norman' Schwarzkopf studied and applied Scipio's tactics with great success in at least one battle in the first Gulf War.

standard regulation issue

From archaeological and representational evidence, we have a clear idea of the equipment of the typical East Roman soldier (both officer and other ranks) of the fifth and sixth centuries. The marvellous Osprey series about armies and campaigns (on whose illustrations in *Twighlight of the Empire* etc., I've based my descriptions) is invaluable for visualizing fighting men of the period. The gear of late Roman soldiers of the Eastern Empire tended to be very conservative. It often featured typically 'Roman' helmets (actually based on Greek 'Attic' helmets of Peloponnesian War vintage) that would not have looked out of place on Trajan's Column.

an immensely long pike

The fearsome *sarissa*, or twenty-foot long pike, enabled Alexander to conquer much of Asia with the famous Macedonian phalanx – an invincible formation, provided iron discipline was maintained and enemy archers neutralized in advance. In various guises the pike-phalanx kept reappearing throughout history: as the *schiltron* in the Scottish Wars of Independence, and in the massed formations of Swiss mercenaries and *Landsknechte* of the Renaissance period and of the English Civil War, where battles could sometimes be decided by 'push of pike'. The formation's weakness of course was its vulnerability to archery, and later to musket fire. However, in combination with the firearm, the pike as an individual weapon lives on in the shape of the bayonet, proving its value in close combat fighting in campaigns stretching from Blenheim to Afghanistan.

a rigid code of loyalty and honour
Sharing something of the ideal values of Periclean Athens, Republican Rome, mediaeval chivalry, and the code of *Bushido* of Japanese *samurai*, the moral standards of Persian aristocracy were shaped by scrupulous observation of consideration and politeness (often taken to absurd extremes), truthfulness, fidelity and respect for superior rank.

N.B. Beyond telling us that he was a good and conscientious soldier, the records don't explain how it was that 'Roderic' came to be awarded, in the words of Gibbon, 'the dignity of senator, and the command of the guards'. So I felt I had to invent a situation which would allow Roderic to show himself, through action, as the kind of man we believe him to have been. Though fictional, the incidents in the Prologue are (very) loosely linked to real events. The Persians did invade Oriens during the reign of Anastasius, but on the initiative of Kavad* himself, not one of his generals; they eventually withdrew, not because of a decisive Roman victory but because the campaign became bogged down in a bloody stalemate; Kavad was under the influence of a powerful personality – not a general, however, but a religious impostor called Mazdak – who may or may not have encouraged him to embark on a military adventure against the East Roman Empire; the defeat of Tamshapur's force is borrowed from an incident occurring in 622, when the East Roman emperor Heraclius routed the cataphracts and infantry of the ferocious Persian general Shahrvaraz, 'the Wild Boar', who actually did burn prisoners alive on crosses, and who was my model for Tamshapur. The scene of his defeat was suggested by the location of Petra (minus the rock-carved buildings) – a long, sandstone defile, exceedingly narrow in places.

Chapter 1
an Edict of Emperor Theodosius
Passed on 24 February 391, this draconian enactment – which was enforced with fanatical thoroughness by the minions of the emperor and his partner in zealotry Bishop Ambrose of Milan, banned *all* pagan practices within the

* Variously given as Cabades, Cobad, Kavadh.

Empire at a time when many Roman citizens still clung to pagan beliefs. Henceforth, all religious creeds, other than Orthodox Catholicism, were to be deemed illegal, including the Arian form of Christianity – the faith of almost all Germans. But this created a massive inconsistency. Owing to a severe shortage of Roman recruits, Theodosius took the dangerous step of enrolling into the army whole tribes of (Arian) Germans enlisting under their own chieftains. Clearly, there could be no question of trying to make these federates relinquish their Arian belief in order to conform to the Edict; in their case, a blind eye had perforce to be turned. However, this exception did not extend to isolated Gothic communities long settled in the Empire (sometimes referred to as 'Moeso-Goths', from the province of Moesia Secunda where many of them had made their homes) of which the Goths of Tauresium may have formed an example.

Born 31 August in the year . . . 482
This is necessarily conjectural; we know that Uprauda was born in either 482 or 483, but not the exact date. In Roman times, dates within any given month were calculated by counting the number of days occurring *before* the next of the three fixed days dividing the Roman month: Kalends, the first day of the month, the Nones on the 5th or 7th, and the Ides on the 13th or 15th. (In March, May, July and October, the Nones fell on the 7th and the Ides on the 15th, in the remaining months on the 5th and 13th respectively.) Thus, the Ides of January happening on the 13th of that month, the next day would be termed by a Roman not the 14th, but the 19th *before the Kalends of February*, reckoning inclusively, i.e., taking in both 14 January and the 1 February; and so on to the last day of the month which was termed *pridie Kalendas*. In this particular entry, 'in the year of' is understood, ablative absolute construction being used to give, 'Trocundus and Severinus being consuls'.

Legio Quinta Macedonica
Thanks to representational evidence (carvings of the fifth and sixth centuries), we have a very clear idea of the appearance of soldiers of this unit: oval shield decorated with 'sunflower' motif; scale armour or chain mail hauberk; 'Attic' helmet (sometimes shown with crest); spear and long sword (spatha) in the case of infantry; short recurved bow but no shield in the case of horse-archers. (See *Twighlight of the Empire* in the excellent Osprey series.)

Chapter 2
a vigorous bout of harpastum
Beyond the fact that it appears to have been some sort of competitive

ball-game, I've been unable to discover any details about how *harpastum* may have been played, so have had to fall back on invention. Sidonius Apollinaris – Bishop of Clermont in the fifth century – refers to a game with teams of ball-players throwing and catching balls with swift turns and agile ducking. Could this have been *harpastum*?

that first sight of the city

Among the landmarks mentioned by Petrus, the Walls of Theodosius (at present being restored to something like their original glory), the Golden Gate, and the Aqueduct of Valens are still to be seen – all in a remarkable state of preservation.

the tall column that rose in the middle of the square

Commemorating a bloody pogrom of the Goths in Constantinople in AD 400, the Column of Arcadius was an ugly example of state-sponsored chauvinism. (Shades of the inscription on Sir Christopher Wren's Monument in London, laying the blame for the Great Fire on the Catholics!) Although, apart from the base, the column was demolished in 1715, we know what it looked like from a drawing made earlier.

the Cistern of Nomus

Nomus was a real person (when Master of Offices during the wars with Attila, he bought time for the Eastern Empire by unobtrusively strengthening the defences of the northern frontier), but the cistern I've named for him is a composite invention. Readers may recognize parts of it from scenes in Istanbul: in the James Bond film, *From Russia with Love*, in the TV series, *Francesco's Mediterranean Voyage*, by Francesco da Mosto, in the Basilica Cistern (Yerebatanserai), which still impresses visitors today.

the Department . . . controlled by the city prefect

'The principal departments [of the city prefect] were . . . the care of [inter alia] . . . the aqueducts [and] the common sewers . . .' (Gibbon, *The Decline and Fall of the Roman Empire*, Chapter 17.) This passage refers to Rome, but Gibbon goes on to say, 'a similar magistrate was created in that rising metropolis [Constantinople], for the same uses and with the same powers.'

Chapter 3

the capital's prestigious Eleventh Region

This was one of the city's most desirable districts: relatively open, elegant, containing the largest proportion of free-standing houses (*domus*) of all the regions, patronised by the aristocracy, and containing the fashionable church of the Holy Apostles – a bit like Edinburgh's Morningside or Grange! The best regions were I and II around the Imperial Palace. Regions IV to VIII were the least salubrious, being the areas where labourers, artisans, and the unemployed lived – along the Mesé, and around the fora and the harbours.

an overrated pastime

There is a considerable amount of evidence suggesting that some men of power or genius (intellectual, artistic, scientific, military, etc.) have shown little interest in sex – perhaps because their overriding drive/passion/ obsession displaced or sublimated it. Examples are: Thomas Carlyle, Ruskin (who may have died a virgin), Isaac Newton, Erasmus, Michaelangelo. Henry VIII, despite his famously priapic reputation and his ill-starred passion for Anne Boleyn, would appear to have been less interested in sex *per se* than as a means of securing dynastic progeny; the same observation probably also applies to Napoleon. Hitler, despite lurid speculation of the 'tabloid headline' variety would appear to have been uninterested in sex, except perhaps on a semi-abstract, idealized plane.

Justinian comes over to me as very much a man of the above type – an intellectual and obsessive workaholic, to whom (as I've hinted in the story) sex would have been a time-wasting distraction, and may even have been physically distasteful. Which may seem a ludicrous conclusion in view of his marriage to the (allegedly) promiscuous and oversexed Theodora. That they genuinely loved one another seems certain; however, as I've suggested in later chapters, their love may have been more to do with a 'meeting of minds', than anything based on physical passion.

indicating their support for 'the Blues'

Dominating popular entertainment in Constantinople was the sport of chariot-racing, held in the Hippodrome. Supporters of the two rival teams – known as 'the Blues' and 'the Greens' (from the colours worn by the opposing racing drivers) – extended their mutual rivalry far beyond the realm of sport. (Shades of Celtic v. Rangers fans in West Central Scotland!) In a pre-democratic age, these factions could be the voice of the people, and woe betide the emperor who failed to take notice of their complaints or demands, as voiced in the Hippodrome; Justinian very nearly lost his throne in the Circus faction Nika Riots of 532. The Blues tended to represent wealthy businessmen and landowners, while the Greens drew support from traders and artisans, many of Syrian origin. The Blues' 'Establishment' credentials were further strengthened when they were backed by Justinian, whose patronage enabled them to terrorise the streets of the capital with impunity. Known as 'Partisans', their leaders, dressed in Hunnish fashion, were engaged in perpetual gang warfare with their rivals, the Greens: a situation with striking parallels to the urban gang culture in many cities today.

our 'little father' has been taken from us
The soubriquet has nothing to do with Anastasius' stature, but was a popular endearment conferred on many Eastern emperors from Marcian on, whose generally benign régimes helped to create an image of the emperor as the loving Protector of his people. (In contrast to the policy of appeasement towards Attila of the feeble Theodosius II, his successor Marcian's resolute stand against the Hun leader gave him popular hero status.)

Blinding or death
To forestall any possibility of his becoming a future focus for disaffection, a defeated rival for the purple was invariably either executed or – as a 'humane' alternative – mutilated by blinding or amputation of the nose. Disfigurement constituted an automatic bar to becoming emperor.

the most powerful post in the Empire
The powers of the Master of Offices were very great. He was in effect the head of the Empire's central administration. In modern terms, his position would combine the roles of most senior cabinet ministers, excluding that of the Chancellor of the Exchequer.

a damaging schism
At the Council of Chalcedon, near Constantinople, in 451, the belief, put forward by Pope Leo, that Christ had two natures – both human and divine – was established as orthodoxy for the Church in the Western and Eastern Roman Empires. Chalcedonism was violently opposed by the Monophysites (mainly in Syria and Egypt) who believed that Christ had only one, divine, nature. As the Monophysites were now officially heretical, the effect of Chalcedon was to create religious strains within the Empire, which could threaten to degenerate into schism unless handled with tact and diplomacy. Thus, in Egypt (the source of the Eastern Empire's vital grain supply), a blind eye had perforce to be turned to Monophysitism. After the fall of the Western Empire in 476, relations between Italy (ultra-Chalcedonian, although her German rulers were Arian) and the Eastern Empire cooled (in what became known as the Acacian Schism), because of the pro-Monophysite sympathies of Emperors Zeno and Anastasius. However, the accession of the strongly Chalcedonian Justin ended the

schism, and this paved the way for Italy to become reintegrated into the Empire under Justinian.

Chapter 4

stage menials rushed around the orchestra
In the Ancient Greek theatre, the stage (a long narrow platform upon which the actors performed) was fronted at a lower level by a semi-circular space called the *orchestra*, in which the chorus sang and danced. The Romans (often using the same theatres that the Greeks had constructed) reversed the functions of stage and orchestra.

Eratosthenes . . . who had measured the earth's circumference
By observing the difference between the angles of the sun at two places a measured distance apart (north-south), Eratosthenes was able to calculate the angle subtended by that distance. The number of times the angle would divide into 360 degrees multiplied by the distance, gave him the answer – which was amazingly close to our own measurement of 24,000 miles. Pure geometry, pure genius!

you can't just send me away
Beyond the fact that he was appointed governor of the Pentapolis, and that Theodora accompanied him there as his mistress, we know nothing about Hecebolus or why he should have turned her out of his house, piling insults on her as he did so (thus causing me to resort to invention). Procopius, of course, exploits poor Theodora's predicament with prurient relish. In the *Secret History* he writes, 'she was at a loss for the necessities of life, which she proceeded to provide in her usual way, putting her body to work at its unlawful traffic.'

Chapter 5

The terminus of the cursus publicus
The imperial post was one of the glories of Roman administration, with staging-posts every eight miles on the main highways where horses or vehicles could be hired, operating on a relay system. In the West, it functioned (unevenly post c. 400) almost to the end. In the East, it was discontinued early in Justinian's reign as a cost-cutting exercise – barring, for military reasons, the road from the capital to the Persian frontier. From the time of Constantine, clerical dignitaries were accorded special travel privileges on the post.

admitted to the bishop's presence
I've had to invent scenarios introducing Theodora to Timothy and later to

Severus, as we don't know how they met. But meet them she did (which seems almost incredible considering her background, and which speaks volumes for her determination and power of personality). Not only that, she formed a deep and fruitful friendship with both men – two of the finest minds in the Roman world, from which she gained a grounding in rhetoric, a taste for intellectual conversation, and a lasting respect for the Monophysites. Altogether, her experiences in Alexandria amount to something like a Damascene conversion.

the Graeco-Roman mind

The passionate concern displayed by people of late antiquity about the nature of Christ may seem to us today to be both incomprehensible and pointless – mere sterile Christological hair-splitting. But less so perhaps, if we view this obsession as stemming from the Graeco-Roman cast of mind that sought to discover the truth via reason and logic, the two great fruits of which are (as I've had Timothy point out) Greek philosophy and Roman law. And lest we become too dismissive of such concerns, we should perhaps remind ourselves that our own times have witnessed preoccupations no less abstruse. Forests have died to produce endless tracts devoted to dialectical materialism, Marxist-Leninism, existentialism, etc.; while the quest to arrive at a satisfactory definition of the Trinity continues to exercise and baffle the minds of bishops at successive Lambeth Conferences. Impatience with ambiguity is what drove these late Roman theologians. The true heirs of Athanasius and Augustine may be Charles Darwin and Richard Dawkins (by way of Peter Abelard, Thomas Aquinas, John Locke and David Hume) rather than Cardinal Newman or Ronald Knox.

a kindness Theodora . . . would repay a thousandfold

Once married to Justinian, Theodora – as a result of the kindness shown her in Alexandria by Timothy and Severus – persuaded her husband (who could deny her nothing) to call off the persecution of the Monophysites. Not only did this happen with immediate effect (making Theodora enormously popular with the sect) but the Monophysites actually became a favoured minority at the imperial court, with Severus himself being invited to a conference between the leaders of both the Orthodox party and the Monophysites, intended to settle their differences.

Chapter 6

gazing adoringly at her lover's face

History has many examples of strong-willed, intelligent women who, loving their own sex as well as, or in preference to, men, have had sufficient force of character to ignore the strictures of society and live according to their nature. Examples are: Sappho, Aphra Behn (that amazing polymath and early champion of women's rights and racial equality), perhaps Queen Anne and Catherine the Great, Anne Lister – Regency landowner, diarist and proud lesbian, Colette, Radclyffe Hall, Virginia Woolf, Vita Sackville-West, Violet Keppel (Trefusis), Frida Kahlo and many individuals associated with the Women's Liberation movement of the 1960s and 1970s. With her intellectual interests, sturdy independence of mind, and passionate proto-feminism,* Theodora comes over to me as being very much cast in the same sort of mould as the above women. Which is not to say of course that she necessarily shared their sexual proclivities. Still, when you can tick three out of four boxes indicating traits in common, there's a temptation also to tick the fourth, even when the answer is 'unknown'. There's a tantalizingly vague phrase in Gibbon which may or may not shed some light on the matter: 'Her secret apartments were occupied by the favourite women . . . whose . . . passions she indulged'. It's hard to know what to make of this. Gibbon doesn't name his source; it's certainly not Procopius, who would have had a field day in his *Secret History*, exploiting any kind of lesbian activity on Theodora's part, had he got wind of it. And none of his contemporaries, as far as I've been able to find out, mentions anything that Gibbon might have been referring to. So, for want of any hard evidence one way or the other, to the question of whether Theodora was bisexual or lesbian, probably the least unsatisfactory answer has to be that good old Scots Law verdict, 'Not proven'. Which allows me, I think, sufficient artistic licence to portray Theodora and Macedonia as lovers.

addressed to a certain 'Petrus Sabbatius . . .'
Antony Bridge in his splendid *Theodora* states, 'Before returning to Constantinople she went to Antioch for a time, where she made friends with a celebrated dancer named Macedonia'. He goes on to speculate, 'that it may well have been through her [Macedonia's] instrumentality that Theodora . . . met the man who was destined so radically to change her fortunes' [i.e. Justinian]. He confirms, as do other sources, including Gibbon, that on her return to the capital she earned a modest living spinning wool – an enterprise which I've had Macedonia take a hand in. The name 'Petrus Sabbatius' had

---

* She got Justinian to enact edicts freeing prostitutes from virtual slavery to brothel-owners, and enhancing women's legal rights; she championed women's rights (often over those of men) at every opportunity, and converted a palace into a hostel for the prostitutes she had liberated, where they were helped to begin new lives.

now been changed officially to 'Flavius Justinianus', for as such he is listed in the consular *Fasti* for the year 521, the other consul being one Valerius. 'Flavius' indicates favoured status as part of the imperial family, perhaps a hint that he was already being groomed as Justin's successor.

Chapter 7

John the Cappadocian

I have introduced him rather prematurely, as he seemed the ideal person to grasp the significance of 'the Arabia Felix Question', and to explain its complexities to others in a clear manner. In real life originally a clerk in the office of the local Cappadocian military commander, rather than in one of the imperial *scrinia* (as in the story), he was actually chosen by Justinian, not Justin. Coarse and offensively outspoken, he was also loyal, efficient and incorruptible. As praetorian prefect, he made himself indispensable to Justinian through his administrative reforms, cost-cutting exercises and tax-raising measures – the last two of which made him extremely unpopular with many citizens, and were largely the cause of the Nika Riots of 532 (of which more hereafter).

Dhu-Nuwas has invaded Arabia Felix

For convenience in plotting, I've had the invasion of Yemen start a little earlier than was actually the case, and telescoped the events of the subsequent counter-attack into a somewhat shorter time-span. Two historical facts enabled me conveniently to involve Justinian in the expedition. Firstly: as Robert Browning in his brilliant and most readable *Justinian and Theodora* suggests, Justinian may have personally contacted Ella Atsbeha (Elesboas) in response to his appeal. Secondly: we know that about this time Justin offered his nephew command of the Army of the East. Paucity of information concerning Justinian's doings at this period therefore allowed me to speculate that he *might* have gone to Ethiopia in a military capacity. (We know that the Romans supplied a naval force to help the Ethiopians. Whether they also sent ground troops is uncertain, although considering the importance of 'the Arabia Felix Question', they must have been prepared to do so, if necessary – in which case, it would have fallen to the Army of the East to provide the required contingent.)

As for the expedition itself, beyond the fact that its outcome was successful, little is known about the actual campaigning – which allowed me to use my imagination to chart its progress. In hindsight, it seems a pity that the Romans neglected to exploit the Ethiopian victory over Dhu-Nuwas – a victory which surely offered them a golden opportunity to extend their influence in Arabia, Ethiopia, and the Horn of Africa, with perhaps in time the possibility of opening up a 'Second Front' in the struggle against Persia. Another, and most relevant consideration (one of those intriguing 'what ifs' of history) is this: had the Romans followed up the recapture of Yemen with an expansionist policy in the region, then Islam might never have come to pass.

Chapter 8

cut from a 'living' animal
James 'the Abyssinian' Bruce, Scottish 'Renaissance Man' and explorer (he discovered the source of the Blue Nile in 1770), published an account of his travels in Abyssinia (Ethiopia) in 1790. Many of his claims in this work – e.g. his reference to a steak being cut from a living cow, seemed so extraordinary that they were generally disbelieved, although subsequently vindicated *in toto*.

crowned by the ramparts of a mighty fortress
Magdala was taken and destroyed by a British expedition under Sir Robert Napier in 1868. The campaign was mounted in response to a public out-cry, after several British subjects were imprisoned in Magdala by the mad Abyssinian emperor, Theodore.

The great machines . . . were duly being assembled
Some idea of the fearsome power and destructive capability of Roman catapults can be gained from the following passage in Josephus' *The Jewish Wars*. 'One of the men . . . had his head carried away by a stone [and] shot . . . to a distance of three furlongsv. . . More alarming even than the engines was their whirring drone, more frightful than the missiles was the crash.'

N.B. In Chapters 7 and 8, I've relied mainly on imagination and evidence from later periods in depicting Ethiopian warriors, as there is a dearth of contemporary material regarding their appearance. In arming them with spears and rawhide shields (standard equipment for as far back as records show) I imagine I'm on pretty safe ground. But having some with swords? Nilotic warriors have used European-looking swords well into modern times (e.g. as brandished by the Khalifa's army in that splendid film of 1939, *The Four Feathers*). But how far back did the practice go? Some have suggested that it stemmed from acquisition/copying of Crusaders' swords. If so, I can see no reason why the date should not be extended even further back – to the long, cutting *spatha* of late Roman times.

Chapter 9

a cruel surprise awaits the poor, duped girls
Sadly, a problem which – thanks to 'people trafficking' from Eastern Europe
and Asia – the West is only too familiar with today.

Justinian was visibly impressed
In his *Justinian and Theodora*, Robert Browning states that, 'she quoted
the orator Isocrates [to Justinian] with electrifying effect'. I've used this
incident to suggest that it marked a turning point in their relationship: the
moment when he fell in love with her – *for her mind.*

a Seneca to my Nero
Lucius Annaeus Seneca (c. 4 BC–65 AD), philosopher, man of letters, and
a noble, upright character, was entrusted with the education of the young
Nero. For a time Seneca was able to exert a salutary effect on the boy; when
Nero became emperor however, his essential viciousness of character came
to the fore, and he degenerated into the monstrous tyrant he is remembered as today. Disillusioned, Seneca allowed himself to become involved
in a plot to murder Nero. But, on the plot failing and his part in it being
discovered, he committed suicide.

compensation for brothel-owners
The amount eventually settled on was five *nomismata* – about thirty
pounds in present value.

I love you . . . in the sense that Plato means
Despite Procopius' attempt (in his *Secret History*) to portray Theodora
as a raging nymphomaniac, I remain strongly of the opinion that the
love between her and Justinian was – as I've suggested in the Notes for
Chapter 3 – more about a meeting of minds than anything physical,
while their wedded state remained strictly monogamous. Even Procopius
can find no evidence that she was anything but faithful to Justinian after
their marriage. There is some evidence that they may have produced a
daughter, who died young. If so, she was their only offspring – although
there doesn't appear to have been any physical reason why they should
not have had more children. All of which suggests that sex may well have
been a low priority for both of them. Justinian comes over as an ascetic
intellectual for whom sex may even have been mildly repugnant. (Again,
see Notes for Chapter 3.) As for Theodora, occasional prostitution dictated by economic necessity, combined with her experience as the mistress
of Hecebolus may well (as has been recorded concerning many women

with similar experience*) have put her off sex – at least with men. (See Notes for Chapter 6.) Her total commitment to the causes she espoused on behalf of prostitutes, women in general, and the Monophysites, suggests that her sex drive may have been sublimated into, or replaced by, the energy she devoted to these all-consuming passions.

I'll pay you back for that
Procopius of Caesarea (c. 500 to after 562), a lawyer by training, was military secretary to Justinian. As such, he was an eye-witness to many of the events which he describes, with commendable objectivity, in his *The Wars of Justinian*. However, in addition he wrote the *Secret History*, a vicious and scurrilous attack on Justinian and Theodora – particularly Theodora. Just why he should have taken against her so venomously is a mystery; I'm tempted to think that something like the incident I've described may have been the cause.

Chapter 10
an invitation from the Peacock Throne
For dramatic reasons I've slightly put back the date of Damascius' and Simplicius' acceptance. They (plus five other Athenian professors: Eulamius, Priscian, Hermeias, Diogenes and Isidore) set off for Ctesiphon after the new Great King – Chosroes (Khusro) – had invited them following his enthronement in 532.

You can't touch me – it's against the law
Up to this time there had existed, as Robert Browning says in his *Justinian and Theodora*, 'general immunity' from corporal punishment for the upper classes. He then goes on to relate how John of Cappadocia's subordinates 'dared to imprison and flog men of high social position for non-payment of taxes'.

devastated by a terrible earthquake
In the interests of simplification, I have conflated the terrible earthquake of 526 (in which, according to Procopius, many public buildings were flattened, and 300,000 people killed) with the less severe one of 29 November 528.

to ferry her across the Bosphorus
To enable Theodora to reach her destination expeditiously, I have contracted

---

* An extreme example would be that of Aileen Wuornos, a prostitute (with a young female lover) who embarked on a killing spree of her male clients, whom she clearly despised.

the time the trip would have taken. By the shortest route, Hieron was above four miles from the nearest harbour in Constantinople.

a complete reform of Roman Law
This hugely ambitious and historic project (which still has relevance to-day) was achieved with incredible speed, with no sacrifice of scale or thoroughness – thanks to the energy, expertise, and organizing ability of Tribonian, the great jurist commissioned by Justinian to see it through. The *Code* of 529 was followed in 533 by the *Digest*, a carefully edited and condensed compilation of all the responses of jurisconsults (such as Gaius and Papimian) of the classical period – a mind-boggling task involving the reduction of three million lines of text to one hundred and fifty thousand! To enable lawyers easily to comprehend and utilize the great new legal corpus, a training-manual for law students – the *Institutes* (in use until the twentieth century) – was published in the same year as the *Digest*. Today, Tribonian's great work forms the basis of the law of many European countries, especially that of Scotland and Holland.

free to love each other outwith marriage
A rather liberal interpretation on Macedonia's part, of one aspect of certain secret rites exclusive to unmarried women in the classical Greek period, in which Sapphic practices took place. (In her fascinating television series about ancient Sparta, Bettany Hughes refers, in this context, to 'girl on girl' liaisons.)

the two hundred and third from the Founding of New Rome
Events in the Eastern Empire were now increasingly being dated from the founding of Constantinople – *anno regiae urbis conditae*, rather than by the consuls (whose office anyway was soon to be abolished) for a particular year. The system of dating from the founding of Constantinople (AD 330) can be seen in the *Chronicle* of Marcellinus Comes (not to be confused with the fourth century historian Ammianus Marcellinus) – an invaluable source of information for the early Justinianic period. The Chronicle ends in 534, but was continued in an *Additamentum* (covering the years 534 to 548) by an anonymous '*Continuator*'.

Chapter 11
appointed as quaesitor
The office was actually created by Justinian a few years later, in 535. But as its purpose was to deal with public order offences, it seemed appropriate to introduce it here.

Chapter 12

more civilized values than in Sulla's time

Which made the executions of Sunday, 11 January all the more shocking, especially as the government was widely blamed for provoking the disturbance in the first place. In England, as recently as the early nineteenth century, there existed close on two hundred capital offences (mainly for crimes against property), some of them bizarrely harsh: 'stealing anything whatsoever from a bleaching-field', 'cutting down young fruit-trees *at night*' (my italics) etc. By comparison, Justinian's Empire seems, in this context, a model of enlightened humanity – capital punishment, even for murder, being rarely carried out.

In Justinian's tablinum . . . were assembled

In addition to those persons mentioned in the text, Narses was also present. However, as his part in the ensuing events was peripheral, I have not included him. On the evidence available it seems unlikely that Procopius was actually present; Count Marcellinus, on the other hand, might well have been, especially as he is known to have been a loyal supporter of Justinian. The two *agentes* are conjectural. For the purposes of the plot, I have included Procopius at the meeting, portraying him as a sort of double agent – 'an ear of Julianus planted in the Palace'. Artistic licence; but his private loathing of the royal couple (as clearly demonstrated in his *Secret History*) makes such a role entirely in character. The false rumour that Justinian had fled was actually started by one Thomas, an imperial secretary, due to a misunderstanding.

Chapter 13

based on the basilica

Notable examples of this type of church still standing are: S. Apollinare Nuovo, in Ravenna, Sta Sabina and S. Paolo fuori le Mura, in Rome, Constantine's Church of the Holy Wisdom, in Bethlehem – to name but four.

marbles of every hue

A contemporary poet, Paul the Silentiary, describes in a poem, *Descriptio Sanctae Sophiae*, the various stones and marbles used to decorate the interior of the church: the *Carystian* – pale, with iron veins; the *green marble of Laconia*; the *Carian* – from Mount Iassis, with oblique veins, white and red; the *Lydian* – pale, with a red flower; etc.

Chapter 14
Some of us who love Rome
The tendency of people in modern times to see the citizens of the East Roman Empire as somehow not being 'real' Romans, was certainly not shared by those citizens themselves. As Antony Bridge in his brilliant book *Theodora* says of them, 'They were . . . intensely conscious of being an heir to the eternal world of Rome . . . their pride in themselves as Romans became even greater than it had been before the barbarians began to encroach upon the Empire . . . Their role as defenders of civilization often seemed a very lonely one'.

Emerging from the tunnel at the coast
In the seventh century, the Berber princess Al-Kahina was besieged in the amphitheatre by Muslim forces. A strong tradition has it that the building was connected by a tunnel to the coast, enabling Al-Kahina to taunt the besiegers by waving fresh fish from the topmost tier of seats. But could the tunnel story be just that – a story, perhaps deriving from the fact that an underground aqueduct leads to the amphitheatre? Whatever its origins, I felt that the legend was too good not to use.

Chapter 15
the long cavalry column
In the text, I have simplified the appearance of the units in the column, so as not to overload the reader with information. On the march, cataphracts would have stowed their armour in a case behind their saddles. In addition to spare horses, riders would have taken the following impedimenta: small tent or extra cloak (a heavy one) for bivouacking, 20–30 lbs. of hardtack, flour, or other provisions, water-bottle, cooking utensils, cloak, javelin cases, spare horseshoes or, if the horse was unshod, a hoof-cleaning tool. *Strategikon* – a sixth century military manual by one Mauricius – is a mine of information for such details.

stocky . . . men with yellowish skins and flat Oriental faces
The Huns – who burst upon the scene in the late fourth century, forcing the Goths to take refuge in the Roman Empire (an event which set off a chain reaction resulting, a century later, in the Fall of the Western Empire) – were most likely of Mongol stock from Central Asia. Some scholars equate the Huns with the Hsiung-Nu who long terrorized China, and Gibbon, referring to Jordanes' famous description of Attila, affirms that it corresponds in all details to that of 'a modern Calmuck'. The Kalmucks,

according to *The New Penguin English Dictionary*, are 'a group of Mongolian peoples inhabiting a region stretching from W China to the Caspian Sea'.

Chapter 16
Theoderic . . . had proved a model ruler
Given a Roman education in his youth as a hostage in Constantinople, Theoderic succeeded his father as king of the Ostrogoths, a Germanic tribe who had settled in the East Roman Empire. Emperor Zeno persuaded the Romanophile Theoderic to lead his people to Italy which he would take over as the emperor's vicegerent (in reality to rid the Empire of a potentially dangerous threat). There was just one problem – Italy was *already* under the rule of another German monarch, Odovacar, who had seized control in AD 476 after sending the last Western emperor into exile. Nothing daunted however, Theoderic defeated Odovacar, to become for most of his long reign of thirty-three years (493–526) one of the best rulers Italy ever had, establishing a system of benevolent apartheid for Goths and Romans. Towards the end of his life he became justifiably suspicious that Italian senators were plotting with Justinian (éminence grise to his uncle, the emperor Justin) for Italy to be reintegrated into the Roman Empire. As a result, his final years were darkened by acts of savage retribution. (See John Moorhead's excellent *Theoderic in Italy*.)

Goths should man the army . . . Romans . . . the administration
Despite some scholars (e.g. Ensslin, *Theoderich*) insisting otherwise, the rule was not set in concrete. A few Romans, such as a certain Cyprianus and Count Colosseus served in the army, while Wilia the *Comes Patrimonii*, Triwila the *Praepositus Sacri Cubili* and the senator Arigern were Goths. All the above were, however, exceptional.

Chapter 17
his markedly Teutonic features
Coins from Theodahad's short reign (534–536), especially a bronze forty-nummi piece depicting the king in profile wearing a *Spangenhelm*, show an archetypally Germanic physiognomy – an image that surely would have gladdened the heart of Hitler. However, as an exemplar of some Aryan über race, Theodahad would have proved a sad disappointment to *der Führer* – timidity, vacillation, greed, and self-delusion being the Gothic monarch's predominant character traits.

The ritual of bathing
I have based my description of a Roman bath-house on the reconstructed one at Wallsend, the remains of one at Chesters (both sites on Hadrian's Wall), the famous complex at Bath, and (because Turkish baths are the direct descendants of Roman ones, with which they are virtually identical) the Turkish baths at Portobello, Edinburgh – where the old Roman terminology: *caldarium*, *tepidarium*, etc. is alive and well today! In a typical Roman bathing suite, a steam room (*sudatorium*) was not obligatory, but would have been an optional extra. ('There were many variations on the sequence . . . cold and hot, moist and dry . . .'. Philip Wilkinson, *What The Romans Did For Us*.)

In the steam room at Portobello, the temperature of the steam is in the region of 50° C. If heated to 100° C, I was assured it would cause the blood to boil, death occurring after around twenty minutes to half an hour. ('The steam rising from boiling water in an open vessel is of the same temperature as the water – viz. 212° F; but notwithstanding this, it contains a great deal more *heat*'. *Chambers' Encyclopaedia*, 1888.)

Some sources say that Theodahad had Amalasuntha strangled, others that he had her murdered in her bath – which allowed me, I think, to despatch her in the way I have described.

Today, Bolsena (anciently Volsinii) is a favourite stopping-off point for tourists en route to Orvieto with its famous cathedral. The circular lake (a crater lake set in a basalt plateau ringed by mountains) is popular with swimmers, who can be joined by remarkably tame ducks, its waters being pleasantly cool thanks to an altitude of c. 1,000 feet. The area, noted for its association with the powerful Farnese family, is rich in Etruscan remains. On the triangular-shaped island of Martana, the remains of the *castellum* where Amalasuntha met her end, can still be seen. A tourist attraction with less grisly associations is the Capodimonte porcelain factory, situated near the lake.

Chapter 18
Dear 'Cato'. 'Cato', 'Regulus' et al.
in the spirit of *Libertas*, these noms de guerre are borrowed from celebrated Romans noted for their staunch championing of Republican values. (Shades of 'Jacques One, Two, and Three' in Dickens' *A Tale of Two Cities*.)

events as they now stand
In the text, a detailed account of the dreary catalogue of marches, sorties, sieges, attacks and counter-attacks (including the mutinies in Africa and

Sicily), which make up the initial phases of the Gothic War, would, I suspect, have tested the patience of most readers. To avoid this, I resorted to that well-worn (but handy) device of summarizing the key points by means of an interchange of letters.

the Tomb of Cecilia Metella

This huge brick-built drum from the Augustan period, situated outside Rome on a well-preserved section of the Appian Way (built by the censor Appius Claudius from 312 BC), was converted into a castle in the fourteenth century.

I'm assured he'll be released ere long

Some hope! – his imprisonment lasted altogether four years. After his release, Peter continued a long and distinguished career, becoming Master of Offices, and carrying out important diplomatic missions into the 560s.

Chapter 19

the two women . . . concocted a plot

When it comes to ruthless scheming and the ability to manipulate members of the male sex, especially husbands, Antonina and Theodora make the likes of Lucretia Borgia and Cleopatra look like amateurs. (Their 'framing' of John of Cappadocia to bring about his downfall is a classic revenge plot worthy of the Mafia.) Although Theodora could be devious and unscrupulous in striving to achieve her goals (witness her likely connection with Amalasuntha's murder), she was driven by motives in themselves commendable – ferocious loyalty towards her husband and her friends, unselfish concern for the welfare of her protégés.

Antonina's character, on the other hand, is not redeemed, as far as can be ascertained, by any trace of altruism. Self-gratification seems to have been her chief motivation, and she showed no shame or scruple in her attempts to satisfy it. One example will suffice to illustrate this. With breathtaking brazenness, she seduced her and Belisarius' adopted son, Theodosius (a youth half her age), and carried on the affair right under her husband's nose while accompanying him on campaign in Africa, Sicily and Italy. Even when discovered *in flagrante delicto*, she managed to pull the wool over the eyes of the doting Belisarius. On one occasion, she was denounced to Belisarius, with clear evidence of guilt, by servants; on another by her own son Photius (from a liaison preceding her marriage to Belisarius). In each case, the whistleblowers were rewarded for their pains by execution and imprisonment, respectively. When eventually (the presumably exhausted) Theodosius fled to a monastery to escape the demands of his insatiable lover, Antonina – with the assistance of her devoted friend, Theodora – tracked him down and had him re-installed in the bosom of the family. (Soon afterwards, according to Gibbon, 'Theodosius expired in the first fatigues of an amorous interview'!)

Regarding the plot to have Silverius replaced by Vigilius, I have telescoped some of the events, and taken one or two liberties with the (probably true) account of his death by starvation on an island west of Naples. But the facts as I have presented them in the story are substantially those that history records. None of the four main protagonists emerge from the affair with any credit. The worst that can be said of Justinian and Belisarius however, is that they were weak – meekly going along with their wives' demands, against the dictates of their consciences.

The stories behind the Silverius/Vigilius plot, Antonina's affair with Theodosius, and the fall of John of Cappadocia are recounted in graphic and fascinating detail by Antony Bridge in his *Theodora*. Ironically, after being shoehorned into the Vatican, Vigilius proved a sad let-down to Theodora. Unwilling to offend the staunchly Orthodox clergy and people of Italy (and thus weaken his position as Pope), he procrastinated endlessly about implementing her wishes. The impasse was eventually overtaken by events of a catastrophic nature – as will be seen in later chapters.

a dark, triangular fin slicing through the water
While sharks that are dangerous to man are mostly encountered in tropical waters, they are, or were until recently, not uncommon in the Mediterranean – including the fearsome Great White Shark (which actually prefers temperate seas to warm ones). This species tends to cruise in shallow water near the coast, which of course would have put Silverius in danger as he approached the shore. Shark attacks in the Mediterranean on humans have been recorded from Ancient Greek times onwards.

Chapter 20
dropping anchor beside Trajan's Mole
This enormous structure – 2,000 feet in length – can still be seen, as can a triumphal arch erected for the same emperor.

he's still in Ariminum
In fact, John refused to evacuate Rimini when ordered to do so by Belisarius. This flagrant act of disobedience received the backing of Narses, who

proceeded to tell Belisarius to relieve the town – thus adding insult to injury!

when the old man became a god
Prior to Constantine under whom Christianity became the official religion of the Roman Empire, emperors, on dying, were deemed to become gods, acquiring thereby the title '*Divus*'. This was a piece of state propaganda that probably few people, especially among the upper classes, took very seriously – witness the remark of one expiring emperor: 'I believe I am turning into a god!' Shades of the god-emperors of Japan, a status surviving into modern times.

the spat developing between their two commanders
The clash between the two generals (arising from the extraordinary rider to his commission which enabled Narses to outrank Belisarius whenever he felt it appropriate to do so) created a poisonous atmosphere of acrimony and dissent, which at times virtually paralyzed the progress of the war, and was directly responsible for the failure to relieve Milan.

B.'s capture of Ravenna in a bloodless coup
Displaying a failure of nerve that was not untypical, Justinian ordered Belisarius to abandon the siege of Ravenna (which the emperor had been led to believe was virtually impregnable) and make the best terms he could with the Goths – in case troops had to be diverted to the east in the event of Persian aggression. Italy would then be divided between the Romans, who would retain the land south of the Po, and the Goths, who would keep the rest – mainly consisting of their heartland, the Plain of Lombardy. Belisarius however, was made of sterner stuff than his emperor. Ignoring the order, he pretended to agree with a secret proposal of the Goths that he become Western emperor in return for a power-sharing deal with them. He was then allowed to enter Ravenna with his army, whereupon the Goths surrendered – only to discover that they had been tricked. Belisarius, who had no intention of honouring the deal, informed the Gothic leaders that he was occupying Ravenna in Justinian's name and that the Ostrogothic kingdom was no more. (Gibbon suggests that Ravenna was captured late in 539, rather than 540 – the year most sources give.)

half a million put to the sword and the city razed
The population of Milan – then as now Italy's second city – has been estimated to number c. 500,000 at the time. Displaying his usual common sense, Gibbon (in contrast to most historians) is highly sceptical about

the notion of total genocide and destruction being visited on a conurbation of this magnitude. He suggests that dividing the *reported* number slain (300,000 males alone) by ten, and assuming that the city's walls rather than its buildings were levelled, would give a more credible picture. Though inclined to agree with Gibbon, for dramatic reasons I have, in the story, stuck with the generally accepted version of the fate of Milan.

the Year of the Consul Basilius

After a lapse of several years, a consul, Basilius, was elected for the year 540. His diptych shows him in his consular robes, beside him – hand on his shoulder – an allegorical figure of Rome. Basilius wears a most apprehensive expression – caused by worry about the colossal expense of throwing his consular Games, or concern regarding the imminent demise of the office he represents? He was in fact to be the very last consul. (*The Cambridge Companion to the Age of Justinian* suggests a date of 541 for Basilius. As, however, Gibbon gives 539 as the final consular year, I decided to split the difference and settle for 540.)

as once You did to Constantine

Justinian is referring to the famous incident – one of the most important single events in the history of Christianity, when Constantine, about to do battle with his rival Maxentius for mastery of the Roman Empire, beheld in the sky a cross (cloud formation?) – the emblem of the hitherto persecuted Christian sect. Interpreting the vision as a sign from God, he instructed his soldiers to paint the symbol on their shields. In the ensuing battle at the Milvian Bridge (still in use) outside Rome in 312, Constantine was victorious and the rest, as they say, is history . . .

Khusro was contemplating ending the treaty

For dramatic reasons, I have deferred Khusro's invasion of Syria until Chapter 21, so as not to spoil Justinian's moment of triumph on hearing the news of the capture of Ravenna – which must have seemed to bring the Gothic War to a glorious conclusion. In fact, according to most sources, the news arriving in Constantinople of Khusro's 'putsch' preceded – just – the tidings that Ravenna had fallen (March and May 540 respectively). If, however, we accept Gibbon's argument that Ravenna in fact fell in late 539 rather than in early 540, then the order of events as I've presented them can stand. (See Gibbon's footnote on the capture of Ravenna in Chapter 41 of his *Decline and Fall*.)

Elsewhere in Chapter 20, in order to present a reasonably coherent picture from the shifting pattern of sieges, blockades, reliefs, reductions and 'pushes' which constitute the main strategic events in Italy for the years 538–540 (a crucially important period in the first phase of the Gothic War), I have gone in for some pruning and telescoping without, I trust, distorting the essential facts.

Chapter 21
the age-old contest between Persia and Rome
If we broaden the term 'Rome' to 'the Greeks and Romans', and 'Persia' to include successively: the empire begun by Cyrus in 537 BC, the Parthian state which lasted from 246 BC to AD 218, and its successor the Sassanian Empire, then, by the reign of Justinian, the Graeco-Roman world had been at war with Persia for over a thousand years – allowing for an interregnum (329–246 BC) when the country had come under the sway of Alexander and his successors. For a time – in the 610s and 20s – it looked as if Persia might overrun the East Roman state, but in 628 the tables were turned decisively in Rome's favour when the emperor Heraclius utterly crushed Khusro II. Then, just when it seemed that Rome had emerged the final victor . . . (For the 'Final Solution' to the millenium-long struggle, see Afterword.)

as once we served Valerian
In AD 260, the Roman emperor Valerian, along with his 70,000-strong army was captured by the Persians, who for many years displayed his skin as a grisly trophy of war.

a legitimate claim to Justinian's throne
This astonishing assertion was not without an element of justification. Near the end of Justin's reign, when Khusro (the third and favourite son of the Great King, Kavad) was a young boy, plans (part of a diplomatic entente between Persia and Rome) were drawn up whereby young Khusro would be adopted by the childless Justin. The boy had actually started on the journey to Constantinople when – on the advice of hardliners, particularly the quaestor Proclus – the scheme was cancelled. Had it not been . . . (It is fascinating to speculate what might have been the implications for the succession on Justin's death, if the plan had been implemented.)

their proud Seleucid ancestors
One of the most splendid cities of the ancient world, Antioch was founded c. 300 BC by Seleucus Nicator (in honour of his father Antiochus), one of Alexander's generals. He began the Seleucid dynasty, whose territory included most of the eastern portion of Alexander's empire.

Antioch will rise again

'After his [Khusro's] return he founded, at the distance of one day's journey from the palace of Ctesiphon, a new city, which perpetuated the joint names of Chosroes and of Antioch. The Syrian captives recognised the form and situation of their new abodes; baths and a stately circus were constructed for their use, and . . . a liberal allowance was assigned to these fortunate exiles . . .' (Gibbon.) A quixotic (but staggeringly generous!) gesture by one of history's most enigmatic and intriguing personalities. In contrast to Justinian, Khusro was motivated by pragmatism rather than idealism, and possessed both a streak of cruelty and a sense of humour – traits not shared by his great rival.

Chapter 22

thanks to the network of irrigation channels
These, once ubiquitous throughout Mesopotamia, have long fallen into disuse. As a result, most of what is now Iraq has largely reverted to desert.

protection against lions
Ammianus Marcellinus, the fourth-century soldier-turned-historian, mentions (in his *The Histories*) seeing lions in this area.

a . . . silent world of pools, lagoons, and reeds
I trust I may be forgiven for having transposed the world of the marsh Arabs (whose way of life is said to go back to the time of the Sumerians) a few hundred miles north-west from the confluence of the Tigris and Euphrates. This is not as capricious as it may sound. Ammianus mentions marshy terrain beside the Euphrates, in the area west of the Naarmalcha Canal (i.e. south of present-day Baghdad) – something that is still the case, as John Keegan in his masterly *The Iraq War* confirms: 'Manoeuvre along this stretch of the Euphrates [near Karbala, south of Baghdad] was difficult. The river banks were high, the surrounding ground marshy'. So, my depiction of the topography of this area is more, perhaps, a case of judicious borrowing and augmentation rather than unalloyed invention.

The marsh Arabs had, in the course of many centuries, succeeded in creating an environment in which human activity and nature achieved a perfect balance – a unique, unchanging, and arrestingly beautiful world, which aroused the admiration of many environmentalists, as well as explorers such as Wilfred Thesiger. (See his *The Marsh Arabs*.) To a monster like Saddam Hussein, such an ideal scenario was of course intolerable, and he set about destroying it (by drainage on a massive scale) with brutal efficiency. Since the fall of his regime however, the area is beginning to recover, and there is hope that the way of life of a unique community may yet be saved.

the poisonous miasma supposedly arising from the marsh
The true cause of malaria was unsuspected at that period, and remained so until the beginning of the twentieth century, when (based on work by Laveran, Sir Ronald Ross, Bignami et al.) breakthrough research showed that the disease resulted not from 'bad air', but from the bite of the anopheles mosquito.

a huge bull-like creature
Originating in the East Indies, water-buffalo were domesticated in India thence introduced into the Middle East, Egypt, eastern Europe, and, by the sixth century, Italy. Adapted for marshy situations, buffalo are used as beasts of burden mainly in areas where water is a major feature of the terrain – such as paddy-fields, or the homeland of the marsh Arabs. The most notable difference between the Asiatic and the African buffalo is in the horns. In the Asiatic buffalo, the massive horns are long, curved, and lie back towards the shoulders. In the African buffalo, the horns – equally massive – nearly meet on the forehead in a huge boss, and are markedly recurved with upward-turning points. Though less aggressive than its African cousin, in a wild state (or if returned to the wild from domestication) the Asiatic buffalo is savage and dangerous, capable of unprovoked attack. Even in a domesticated state it is apt to resent injury – an attitude extremely characteristic of the African buffalo (which has never been domesticated).

Chapter 23
a pretty, heart-shaped face
This does indeed describe the countenance of the figure immediately to Theodora's left in the famous San Vitale mosaic panel. But she almost certainly does *not* represent Macedonia, of whose fate we remain ignorant. So, a piece of, hopefully permissible, artistic licence on my part. (There has been considerable speculation that the figure, in fact, represents Antonina, wife of Belisarius.) Like the other mosaic portraits in the panel, that of Theodora is thought to be a good likeness, its 'fragility and air of physical delicacy [suggesting] that perhaps the disease that was eventually to kill her may have already at work in her'. (Antony Bridge, *Theodora*.) For the purposes of the story, I have commissioned the mosaics a few years earlier than was actually the case.

Chapter 24
impatient of discipline
A fatal weakness. Despite their great size and strength, plus ferocious courage, Germans were invariably defeated by Roman troops (provided these were properly led), thanks to Roman discipline and superior equipment. The only exceptions to this were when Germans attacked in overwhelming numbers – as on the last day of 406 when a vast confederation of barbarian tribes crossed the frozen Rhine, or when a leader of exceptional quality, capable of imposing discipline and teamwork, took charge. Examples of such Germans are extremely rare: Hermann/Arminius who led a confederation which wiped out three legions in the Teutoburger Forest in AD 9; Fritigern, under whom the Goths destroyed a huge Roman army at Adrianople in 378; perhaps Alaric; and of course Totila. Otherwise . . . ? (Although he was undoubtedly a great military leader, Theoderic can't be included, as his victories were against barbarians, not Romans.)

a band of brothers
Besides Totila, some other charismatic leaders capable of inspiring huge personal loyalty are: Alexander, Caesar, Alfred the Great, Robert the Bruce, Henry V, Joan of Arc, Napoleon and (unfortunately) Hitler.

staffing it [the administration] . . . with humble Romans
Theoderic's system in Italy whereby the Goths manned the army, and the Romans the administration, had worked well. Native Romans had by this time lost their taste for fighting, whereas every Gothic male was a warrior. Romans, on the other hand, alone possessed the know-how to manage the complexities of the civil service. The only change here that Totila made was to staff the administration with Romans from a lower social stratum than heretofore.

this second Petronius Arbiter
Petronius, 'Arbiter Elegentiae' (memorably played by Leo Genn in the film *Quo Vadis?*), was a sort of intellectual and cultural guru at the court of Nero. His brilliant satire, *Trimalchio's Feast* (the centrepiece of a fragmentary work, *The Satyricon*), gleefully trashes the pretensions of Roman nouveaux riches. You wonder how he might have responded to today's celebrity culture – perhaps with a satire entitled, *Party at Beckingham Palace*?

Chapter 25
the causes of the pestilence
Ignorance as to what caused the bubonic plague of the 540s (the same

disease as the Black Death of 1348–49 and the Great Plague of 1665) prevailed, as with malaria, until the early twentieth century. It was then established that the disease is caused in humans by the bacterium *pasteurella pestis* entering the bloodstream via the bite of a flea – *Xenopsylla Cheopsis* – whose favourite mode of transport was the warm fur of black rats. It is thought that the rats – moving down the Nile valley from plague-ridden Ethiopia – reached the Egyptian port of Pelusium, whence, spread by ships, the plague became a pandemic, spreading west as far as Wales and east perhaps as far as China. The crowded conditions of most East Roman towns and cities – especially Constantinople – together with rotting piles of refuse outside city walls, provided ideal breeding grounds for rats, which helps to account for the terrifying speed with which the plague spread. (Infection was caused not by contagion but by transfer of fleas, which in crowded conditions virtually amounted to the same thing.) Procopius' description of the plague's symptoms and effects is both detailed and commendably accurate.

Competition with brown rats eventually caused a severe decline in the population of the black rat, and thus of the plague itself.

some association with rats

I plead guilty to selective omission here, as John of Ephesus, commenting on the plague, mentions other animals besides rats. However, the fact that he mentions rats at all gives food for intriguing speculation. If physicians of the time had come to associate the plague with rats *specifically*, then a connection of the disease with rat-borne fleas might eventually have been made, enabling measures of control and avoidance to be taken.

headless figures sitting in bronze boats

John of Ephesus reports people experiencing such visions in areas affected by the plague. Could he have been implying that these were hallucinations?

one of a new breed of appointees

Rather as political and professional advancement in Soviet Russia depended on your being a card-carrying Communist, professing adherence to Marxist-Leninist dogma, so in Justinian's Empire, subscription to Chalcedonian Orthodoxy was a prerequisite to obtaining a teaching post. A sign (of which the closing of the Schools of Athens was another) that the classical world, with its traditions of intellectual freedom and rational enquiry, was coming to an end.

Chapter 26
this firebrand priest
Despite Theodora's passionate championing of their cause, by 540 ferocious persecution (directed principally by Menas, Patriarch of Constantinople, backed by Justinian) had reduced the Monophysites outside Egypt to a state of cowed powerlessness. Then, in 543, everything changed. In that year, one Jacob 'Baradaeus' (meaning 'ragged' from his favourite disguise as a beggar) was permitted to be consecrated Monophysite bishop of Edessa. (Delicate political considerations involving the Monophysite king of an Arab buffer-state dictated that the concession go ahead.) For the Chalcedonian establishment, this proved to be a fatal mistake; they soon found they had unleashed a whirlwind. Imagine a personality imbued with all the toughness, resilience, charisma and sheer power of leadership of a combined Robin Hood-Zorro-Che Guevara-Mahatma Ghandi figure, and you have Jacob Baradaeus. Travelling incognito throughout the eastern provinces, ordaining priests and bishops and running rings around the imperial agents assigned to catch him, he succeeded, almost single-handedly, in re-kindling the dying fires of the persecuted creed. By the time Justinian issued his famous Edict of late 543 or early 544, the Monophysites were once again ascendant in the east.

Both Palace and Gate still extant
Re the Lateran Palace, mediaeval fabric has mostly replaced Roman; the Baptistery however is entirely fifth-century work. The Asinarian Gate – perhaps the finest in the whole circuit of the Aurelian Walls – survives in all its original glory.

a condemnation of certain century-old writings
In the text, I have done my best to outline (as simply as possible, in order to spare the reader) the basic issues involved in the apocalyptic row known as the Three Chapters controversy. The Three Chapters: it sounds innocuous enough. But once I started to scratch beneath the surface and are confronted with: '. . . while the Divinity of the Logos is to be distinguished from the temple of the flesh, yet there remained but one person in the God-man . . .', or, '. . . while granting the true Divinity and humanity of Christ, he [Nestorius] denied their union in a single hypostasis . . .', I began to suspect that I had tangled with something in which I could soon find myself out of my depth. Hoping for illumination, I turned from primary sources to more modern ones. As a true son of the Enlightenment, Gibbon treats the subject with magnificent disdain, dismissing it in three contemptuous lines: '. . . the East was distracted by the Nestorian . . .

controversy, which attempted to explain the mystery of the incarnation, and hastened the ruin of Christianity in her native land . . .' So, not much help there, then. Antony Bridge (in his *Theodora*), Robert Browning (in his *Justinian and Theodora*), and Claire Sotinel (in her article 'Emperors and Popes in the Sixth Century' – Chapter 11 of *The Cambridge Companion to the Age of Justinian*), all struggle valiantly to explain the theological metaphysics of Nestorius, Theodore, Theoderet and Ibas. To them I owe a debt of gratitude for whatever (limited) understanding I've been able to glean concerning the Three Chapters.

For the sake of clarity and pace, I've somewhat telescoped the main events of the controversy, and emphasized the roles played by the *apocrisiarius* Stephen (whose denunciation of Justinian's *Edict* I have, for dramatic reasons, relocated from Constantinople to Rome), and Facundus, bishop of Hermiane. (Vigilius' self-serving vacillation needed no underscoring on my part!) This approach is justified, I think, for the following reason. Without some selective highlighting and streamlining in its presentation, the whole Three Chapters topic (which is important for our understanding both of Justinian and of his times) could appear to the average reader as an impenetrable thicket of Christological subtleties.

Chapter 27
Theoctistus – formerly the army's most brilliant surgeon
Procopius (in his *The Wars of Justinian*) describes in graphic detail an incident that took place during the siege of Rome, in which Theoctistus successfully treated a soldier horrendously wounded by an arrow between the nose and the right eye, 'the point of the arrow penetrating as far as the neck behind', whom other physicians were reluctant to operate on, in case they caused the patient's death. Roman medical practice, especially in the army, was highly sophisticated and efficient – of a standard unrivalled until modern times. The tool-kit of a Roman *medicus*, with its array of needles, probes, catheters, lancets, forceps, scissors, etc., would be instantly recognizable to a surgeon of today. Though often brilliant in their ability to cope with 'accident and emergency' type injuries, the Romans' competence in the field of invasive surgery was limited, being primarily confined to lithotomy, the removal of fistulae and the excision of some cancers, provided they were not too deep. Though of course knowing nothing of infection caused by germs, Roman doctors were aware from experience that cleanliness could aid recovery. Roman hospitals, especially army ones, were probably a good deal more hygienic than any operating at, say, the time of Waterloo.

Chapter 28

become in turn the Western emperor

Thus reviving Diocletian's neat but somewhat arid constitutional device known as the Tetrarchy: two 'Augusti' (one for the East, one for the West), with two 'Caesars' – emperors-in-waiting, who would replace the Augusti in due course. That was the theory; in practice it could break down, when power-hungry usurpers ignored the formula.

leaving his son to become the Western emperor

Germanus' son (by Matasuntha) was in fact born posthumously.

I'll be blunt, Serenity

In an age of subservience and protocol, Narses was noted for speaking his mind to Justinian – and being listened to (probably because his advice was invariably sound, and Justinian, unlike many Roman emperors, was, at bottom, a reasonable and fair-minded man).

pushing up the Via Flaminia from Rome

Losing count of the number of times Rome changed hands during the long Gothic War, I often found myself referring to a useful list compiled by Gibbon giving the various dates on which it was captured: 'In . . . 536 by Belisarius, in 546 by Totila, in 547 by Belisarius, in 549 by Totila, in 552 by Narses'. Determined to break the cycle of siege and capture, Totila was about to demolish the walls when he was dissuaded by Belisarius, who pointed out that such an act would make the Gothic king 'abhorred by all civilized men'. Such generous restraint on Totila's part (for which the modern tourist, who today is able to walk around the circuit of the walls in all their splendour, can be grateful) shows that civilized attitudes between enemies could still prevail – before the long campaign descended into 'total war', that is.

the nation of the Ostrogoths had ceased forever to exist

There is a terrible Wagnerian grandeur about the fate of the Ostrogoths – a heroic people who first emerge into the light of history, fighting (on the 'wrong' side) for Attila in the Battle of the Catalaunian Fields in 451, and vanish from it following the disaster of Busta Gallorum/Tadinae in 552. The 'Ostrogothic century' encompasses: first, *Völkerwanderung* on an epic scale – a search for a homeland throughout the Eastern Empire, followed by mass migration to Italy under their hero-king Theoderic (vice-gerent of the Eastern emperor); then a long and bloody war against Odovacar, king of another Germanic people, the Sciri, to secure their Italian homeland;

finally – following a long period of harmonious 'apartheid' with the Romans, under Theoderic's enlightened reign – their extinction as a people, resulting from Justinian's obsession with reconstructing the Western Empire. (See my *Theoderic*.)

Theoderic and Totila surely represent all that is best in the Teutonic character – courage and determination in the face of adversity, magnanimity, honour. Confronted by the overwhelming might of Narses' Roman army at Busta Gallorum, Totila must have known this was the end. Hence, I believe, his amazing war-dance before the battle; at least he and his warriors would go out in a blaze of glory. Surely this scene (which reflects a Teutonic strain of heroic resignation and defiance in the face of certain death) has echoes down the centuries: in *Beowulf*, in the great Anglo-Saxon war-poem *The Battle of Maldon* ('Heart shall be bolder, harder be purpose, more proud the spirit as our power lessens!'), in the last stand of King Harold's huscarls at Hastings, in the defence of the Alamo.

Chapter 29

the year that witnessed the destruction of the Ostrogoths
Some sources date the introduction of sericulture into the Roman Empire as 552, others as 554. A convenient discrepancy, as it enabled me to have the monks complete the round trip in two years (the usual time), after obtaining the commission from Justinian.

a description . . . of our Church of the Holy Wisdom
Paul the Silentiary's long and detailed work, which elaborates on the coloured marbles, precious stones and gold and silver objects in the building, was indeed recited to the emperor – not in fact in 552 as I've suggested, but in 562 at the second dedication of the church.

I would not have that on my conscience
Thus echoing (fictitiously) a sentiment of Vespasian. When it was suggested to that emperor that a special new machine (pulley-system? crane?) be used to convey heavy loads in the construction of the Colosseum, Vespasian declined, saying that its adoption would deprive many poor labourers of their living (which seems to confound the popular notion that the Flavian Amphitheatre was constructed mainly by slave labour).

Gibbon laments a lost opportunity in the failure of the monks to introduce printing to the West, nearly a millennium before Gutenberg: 'I reflect with some pain that if the importers of silk had introduced the art of printing, already practised by the Chinese, the comedies of Menander and the entire decads of Livy would have been perpetuated in the editions of the sixth century'.

the imposing gateway at the end of China's Great Wall
Jiayuguan today (a rebuilding of the Ming dynasty) is an imposing spectacle, carefully restored to something like its original splendour. In Justinian's time, it marked China's western limit. Since then, a vast new province, Xinjiang, has extended China's border many hundreds of miles further to the west, taking in the lands of the Uighurs and the Kazaks. These are Turkic people – very different from the Han Chinese in ethnicity, culture, and religion (many being Muslim). Chinese occupation has resulted in considerable friction with the indigenous population, leading to political protest, which the Chinese authorities (displaying their usual horror and intolerance of dissent) invariably put down with harsh severity.

Some sources have the monks smuggling out the silkworm eggs from China itself, others from 'Chinese-controlled Sogdiana'. Surely the first theory is the more likely. For such an important and jealously guarded state secret as sericulture, would the Chinese have permitted it to be carried on elsewhere than within the Celestial Kingdom itself? Somehow, I doubt it. Moreover, I remain to be convinced that Sogdiana/Bactria was actually 'controlled' by China in any meaningful sense; that it came within the Chinese sphere of influence is perhaps the most that can be argued.

a . . . species of enormous bear
This is *Ursus Torquatus*, larger even than the fearsome Kodiak. The sheep mentioned is the species now known as the Marco Polo Sheep.

Chapter 30
this latest theological dogma
'His [Justinian's] edict on the incorruptibility of Christ's body . . . is difficult to understand'. (Lucas Van Rompay, Chapter 10, *The Cambridge Companion to the Age of Justinian*.) The above quotation has to be the understatement to beat all understatements! Aphthartodocetism, in the words of Van Rompay, argued that 'Christ's body transcended human corruptibility and was *aphthartos* [incorruptible], even though Christ of his free will – not out of necessity – submitted himself to corruption and suffering'. Just how Justinian imagined that this impenetrable doctrine (which seems if anything to lean towards Monophysitism) was going to resolve the split between the Chalcedonians and the Monophysites, is hard to see. Robert Browning in his *Justinian and Theodora* affirms that

Justinian 'had again and again said exactly the opposite in the past', and goes on to admit that 'The matter is a mystery and will probably always remain one'. The decree containing the Aphthartodocetist dogma has not survived, but was probably promulgated in 565, a few months before the emperor's death. It seemed appropriate to introduce the doctrine into the story somewhat earlier than this, as Justinian must have thought about the matter long and hard, before issuing his decree.

bronze equestrian statue of the emperor
This occupied a prominent place in the Augusteum. Although melted down for cannon by the Turks after 1453, we know what it looked like from a drawing made before its disappearance. It is thought to have represented Achilles rather than the Roman general I've portrayed in the text.

yet another . . . tribe of steppe-nomads
Like the Huns before them and the followers of Genghis Khan after them, another fearsome Mongol horde – the Avars – swept across Europe in the sixth century, establishing a vast empire stretching from France to the Black Sea, while maintaining an uneasy alliance with the Romans. This precarious peace ended in the following century, when the Avars crossed the Danube, overran the Balkans, and nearly captured Constantinople. They introduced the use of stirrups into Europe, thus facilitating the eventual emergence of the heavily armoured mediaeval knight.

His victory against the Kotrigurs
While keeping essentially to the known facts of this bizarre and fascinating interlude, I have, for dramatic reasons, combined its two separate strands into a single event: Belisarius' tricking Zabergan into thinking his force many times larger than it really was, followed by his luring the Kotrigurs into an ambush and killing four hundred of them; Justinian's deal with Zabergan, which actually took place a little later, and his subsequent return in triumph to the capital. For a man of sedentary habits in his late seventies to become actively involved in such a *Boys' Own* adventure, is truly astonishing.

Chapter 31
a fresh conspiracy
Apart from invented embellishments concerning the roles of Procopius and the fictitious 'Horatius', my description of the plot to assassinate Justinian, and its consequences for Belisarius, closely follows Gibbon's account. (Chapter 43, *Decline and Fall*.)

Although the banquet took place in the autumn of 562, and the re-dedication of Hagia Sophia in December of the same year, it seemed appropriate, for dramatic reasons, to have these happen in the story on the same day.

We don't know if Procopius himself was directly responsible for un-masking the plot to assassinate Justinian; as prefect of the city it would certainly have been within his remit. So it would be surprising had he not been involved in some capacity, especially as we know that he interrogated the conspirators.

Chapter 32
this astonishing outpouring of hate and malice
It is doubtful if Justinian ever read *Secret History* (*Historia Arcana* or *Anek-dota*), but if he had, he may well have reacted in the way that I've described in the text. It is extraordinary how the author of *The Wars of Justinian* and *On Buildings*, in which he gives an objective (and generally favourable) as-sessment of Justinian's character, should also be capable of penning a vicious diatribe which, in portraying Justinian as a despicable moral degenerate, and Theodora as a shameless nymphomaniac with perverted tastes, reveals his bitter hatred of the imperial pair. (Belisarius too, comes in for some harsh denigration.) Written towards the end of Procopius' life, *Secret History* was probably intended for private circulation among friends, rather than for general publication.

our own Desert Fathers – Antony, Jerome et al.
Born c. 250 in Egypt to rich and pious parents, Antony ('the father of monachism') as a young man withdrew into the desert to practise a life of prayer, contemplation, and self-imposed austerities – which attracted the admiration of the many anchorites persuaded to follow his example. In 305 he founded a monastery in Egypt, returning to his desert cell (today inhabited by a venerable priest!) in 311, where he lived – a celebrated hermit – until his death, at over a hundred, in 356.

Jerome was born c. 340 probably in what is now Croatia. Educated in Rome, he travelled to the East where, in 374, he retired to the desert. Here, he spent four years in penitential exercises and study. Ordained priest at Antioch in 379, he became secretary to Pope Damasus, then went on to achieve fame as a polemicist and spiritual director to many pious persons. Best known for his translation of the Bible into Latin (the Vulgate), he also wrote many letters, treatises, and commentaries on Holy Scripture. He died in 420 at Bethlehem.

a pilgrimage . . . To the Church of Saint Michael, at Germia'
As he approached the end of his life, two important things happened
to Justinian. He undertook a pilgrimage to the remote Church of Saint
Michael at Germia in Galatia, a remarkable undertaking for a man of
eighty-one with sedentary habits. And he developed a profound interest
in a strange doctrine known as Aphthartodocetism (the belief that Christ's
body was incorruptible) to the extent of trying to impose it as dogma on
the Roman Empire in a decree of 565 – the year of his death. Intended
to resolve the rift between the Monophysites and the Chalcedonians, it
became a dead letter following Justinian's death.

In his *Justinian and Theodora*, Robert Browning suggests that the emperor was impelled to embark on the pilgrimage to Germia by some dream
or vision, or through the suggestion of some of the monks or theologians
whose opinions he was increasingly consulting in an attempt to resolve the
anxieties which clouded his final years. I have tried to bring these various
strands together in my account of the pilgrimage (of necessity resorting
to imagination to supplement the paucity of evidence), which I have also
linked to Justinian's obsession with Apthartodocetism.

Which raises the question: could a man as profoundly religious as
Justinian have interpreted the abovementioned doctrine in terms of a
materialist philosophy such as Lucretius' Atomic Theory? That would
certainly have called for a conversion of Damascene proportions. Still,
stranger things have happened. Paul himself, on the road to Damascus,
changed from being the arch-persecutor of Christians, to becoming probably Christianity's most successful proselytizer. Constantine, as a result of
a compelling vision, virtually overnight altered the status of Christianity
from that of a persecuted minority sect, to the official creed of the Roman
Empire. Darwinism, once equated with atheism, is today comfortably accepted by most leading churchmen, including the Archbishop of Can-
terbury; indeed the Church of England was among the first to embrace
the theories of Darwin. Two of anthropology's leading researchers were
priests – Père Teilhard de Chardin and the Abbé Breuil. Darwin himself,
before embarking on a scientific career, seriously considered the priesthood as a vocation! And it was a Catholic priest, Georges Lemaitre, who
first proposed the Big Bang theory of the origin of the universe.* Stephen

---

* In Dan Brown's cerebral thriller, *The Lost Symbol*, mind (according to Noetic Science),
not only can affect mattter, it can actually create it. By extension, this could suggest
that Mind (i.e. God) preceded and originated the laws of physics plus the Big Bang
– which is consistent with the Catholic Aquinian argument for a Prime Mover.

Hawking, one of the greatest scientific thinkers of our time, has spoken of 'the mind of God'; even the mighty Richard Dawkins, the high priest of atheism, has conceded the possible existence of superhuman intelligence within the universe. Perhaps, in support of my suggestion, the following could be argued. Viewed in a certain light, Lucretius could be seen to provide the sort of intellectual reinforcement for Aphthartodocetism that Justinian – desperate to find a formula to stave off schism in the Church – may not have found unwelcome.

Read De Rerum Natura'"
This great poem in six books, by Titus Carus Lucretius – a contemporary of Cicero and Julius Caesar – is astonishingly modern in feeling. In proposing that the universe and everything in it is composed of an infinite number of atoms, he is popularizing earlier theories of Democritus, Epicurus, and Leucippus – theories very much in accord with current physics. For Lucretius, life, mind and soul are simply functions of man's corporeal body, the atoms of which disperse at death. Thus anything like individual survival in an afterlife becomes impossible. He explains contagious diseases by the flying about in the air of minute particles – thus anticipating our knowledge of infection spread by germs. His account of the various types of animal life as they successively appeared on earth strikingly suggests 'the survival of the fittest', with parallels to Darwin's theory of evolution. And all this – developed through the sheer power of intellectual reasoning, rather than by scientific experiment!